Silent Subversion I

by Hyrum E. Jones

To Rebecca Patison

Thanks for entering the drawing!

Hyrum Jones

Silent Subversion I

Anxiety Publishing
Camas, Washington
anxietypub.com

First edition: January 2016
ISBN-13: 978-1523719051
ISBN-10: 1523719052

Acknowledgements

Not only has my Silent Subversion project cost several thousand personal hours, but also the great sacrifice of those who helped build my life. Thanks to the following for infecting me with their sublime virus, in chronological order. Thanks to my parents, A.A. Milne, Theodor Geisel, Stan Ridgway, Glen Cook, Peter Murphy, Ian Astbury, Bill Watterson, Jules Verne, CJ Cherryh, (Grant Naylor), Alexandre Dumas, Richard Knaak, David Eddings, Stephen Donaldson, Karen Orzolek, Win Butler, John Kennedy Toole, Svein Berge, Torbjorn Brundtland, Neal Gaiman, Edmund Shklyarskiy. Thanks also to my amazing wife and children, George Carlin, Howard Zinn, Fawn M. Brodie, Halton C. Arp, Laura Knight Jadzyk, G. Edward Griffin, Jason Sorens, Ron Paul and Bill Maher, to name just a few, for helping open my eyes to a larger and more mysterious world. A special thanks to Dr. Colin A. Ross for his historical research and advice and to Bernard Burchell for his assistance with the NMG concept and his personal efforts. To culminate my excessive appreciation, thanks Aaron, Randy, Shelly and Carrie for your invaluable feedback and encouragement. Everyone needs a group of friends who enjoy telling you what they don't like about your work.

Sections

I: MOMENTUM

After the fire created
You will see
The beast illuminated

1

Gerald

January 2009

The phone rang at 12:34 in the afternoon, magic time.

When Gerald Fuger heard his office phone ring that afternoon, he instinctively glanced at the computer screen on his desk, to the digital readout of the time and then to the incoming unlisted number. He never intentionally noticed that special time of day, but nonetheless he usually glanced at a digital clock during those unique sixty seconds.

"Law offices of Fuger and Fowler," he said tentatively. "Gerald speaking."

"Hi Gerald," said a familiar voice. Gerald paused to let his memory supply the corresponding name and face, but the female voice provided the information before his memory could. "This is Taylor. How are you doing Gerald? It's been a while, eh?"

"Taylor Ewell," he said with the relief of recognition and his mind quickly transitioned from the expected business conversation to a personal one. Her voice reminded him of when they met at the University of Oregon. He took a breath then answered her question. "I'm doing good. How about ...?"

"Great, just great," she said in a rush, as if she had not heard his answer. "Listen, I'd like to see you on your next visit to Portland. We can have dinner or something."

"Sure," he said. "That would be fun. It's been…"

"Cool, email me the time and place, and I'll be there. I have something I want to show you. Sorry for the short call, but I really don't have time to talk. So, you'll arrange the time and I'll see you then?"

"Sure," he said and smiled at the thought of another encounter with his friend, the anarchist.

Before his brain could supply the next question, Taylor gave a quick farewell and cut the connection. For a moment, Gerald just held the phone to his ear. Had he imagined the conversation? When he turned back to the computer screen, magic time ended.

2

Gerald

After the brief phone call, Gerald sat at his desk and let the pleasant memories of the intelligent and beautiful Taylor glide through his mind. She had first introduced herself to him at an anti-war rally at the University of Oregon. She had specifically wanted to meet him, the organizer. Through a brief interrogation, he learned how her younger brother became another casualty of the Iraq invasion, a young man dead at the age of nineteen.

Through subsequent encounters, he came to understand the full impact of her brother's death. The tragedy almost destroyed her family and intensified her pre-existing anger at the government for all the lies used to invade Iraq, the lies which enticed her brother into military service under the illusion of patriotism. She hated the political establishment for facilitating the conflict. She hated the media for pushing the agenda on the public and painting the possibility into an inevitability. She hated the education system for conditioning the human mind to validate and accept perceived authority.

Gerald had more intellectual reasons for hating their collectivistic environment, less personal than Taylor's, but just as potent. The journey to his present state of mind had started with a book. Whenever he reflected on his psychological transformation, he marveled at its tenuous set of circumstances, at its low probability of occurring. What if he had chosen to ignore the book on the table at his friend's house? What if his encounter with the book came when he still lacked any interest in history? The public education system had almost completely performed its function and removed all his curiosity about the past.

While reflecting on the event, he turned to his bookshelf and located the volume, "A People's History of the United States", by Howard Zinn. Gerald imagined the book as a living creature, asleep and asking him to wake it.

He walked to the bookshelf and slid the book out of its resting place. In his hands, the book seemed to open by itself to a bookmark, a simple index card with Taylor's email address written in her sloppy handwriting. The card contained only one other marking, a simple smiley face.

As he held the piece of paper once held by Taylor, memories of her and law school intensified. They mixed with his memories of relearning history and his transformation began by the book in his hands. During those hours, days and months of investigation, he remembered feeling like an explorer, discovering all the secrets of a new land, a place he had difficulty calling home anymore. After consuming the book by Howard Zinn, he read other books and other historical accounts.

Standard textbooks from school had oversimplified the details of history and interpreted historical events for him, resulting in a feeling that history had only one interpretation where good people worked together to fight against evil. His own investigation of history, however, produced a reaction similar to the one Taylor experienced after the death of her younger brother. In the end, he felt cheated. He acquired an entirely new perception of the world, a frightening and sinister place controlled by psychopaths.

While Gerald learned to view the world through a new pair of eyes, he had to endure a difficult period of psychological readjustment. He felt betrayal by society, his parents, the government, the media. He developed a personal guilt for living in an ignorant bliss his whole life. He finally understood the true sources of all the horror in the world and found his only escape to be part of the solution. He would no longer participate in apathy.

After becoming acquainted with Taylor, he quickly learned to appreciate her enthusiasm and energy. He even learned to enjoy her abrasive personality and impatience for people, the exact opposite traits of his own. He generally liked people and usually tried to be a peacemaker.

If not for their shared political interests, they never would have become friends. She loved science and engineering and he loved being part of society and helping people. They both, however, wanted to make a difference. They belonged to a very small part of the political spectrum and craved interaction with others of the same population. Gerald preferred to identify himself an individualist. He lost no clients with that non-threatening term.

Gerald's proclaimed political identity produced curiosity in others rather than any preconceived social stigma. Taylor, however, felt little concern about how others perceived her and even seemed to enjoy anything that might potentially cause a confrontation. She identified herself as an anarchist and proudly accepted the accompanying social stigma whenever anyone asked her political views.

To Gerald, both terms fundamentally meant the same thing.

Gerald arranged the meeting with Taylor for the next Friday, on the monthly visit to his clients in Portland Oregon where she lived. That next week, he mentally prepared himself for the encounter by imagining himself in her set of circumstances. The exercise made him shudder. She had graduated from college during the worst economic collapse in their lifetime. How did she manage to cope with the bleak job outlook?

Other than what Taylor wanted to show him, the collapse of the housing market of the previous year would definitely become a topic of conversation. Gerald prepared himself to encourage her rant about it. They could discuss how the big banks had orchestrated the event and then they could attempt to predict what might happen next. He hoped the discussion would be therapeutic for Taylor, but he could also imagine the anger it would generate.

On this trip from his home in Seattle to Portland Oregon, Gerald planned to visit Quantrial Children Services, a non-profit organization that provided mental health care for troubled children and youth. Gerald and his partner helped manage the organization's liability insurance, tax issues and government grant proposals. Gerald insisted on providing the service without compensation.

Soon after starting the law firm, when they had less paying clients and more free time, Gerald kept busy providing free services to those who had few resources to pay for them. He had quickly learned how the work earned more than just emotional satisfaction. Through their charitable efforts, both he and his partner had made valuable contacts with other individuals and businesses in need of legal assistance. At that point in their business, he could have made a lot more money by spending more time on paying jobs, but he genuinely enjoyed working pro bono. In a small way, he wished that Taylor would be in need of his services. That would give him an excuse to see her more.

A few minutes after ten that Friday morning, Gerald drove over the swollen Columbia river on interstate five from Vancouver, Washington and entered Portland. He planned to do as much as he could for their client until five pm and give himself an hour before meeting Taylor.

Thinking of her chosen rendezvous point caused him to smile. Gerald usually met with clients at nice, upscale restaurants where they dressed in suits. Taylor wanted to meet at Burgerville, a fast-food restaurant. Gerald remembered going there once or twice in his college days. Did he ever go with Taylor? He only remembered feeling unimpressed by fast food establishments.

When he arrived at the specified location, he saw no sign of Taylor. Without waiting for her, he ordered a burger from a feeling of obligation and fear of making a social blunder for failing to purchase a burger at Burgerville. The lady behind him in line noticed his hesitation and said he had to try their rosemary shoestring potato fries.

"Thanks for the suggestion." he said with a smile.

Gerald chose a table near the back of the eating area where he could watch the entrance. While waiting, the aroma of hamburgers and fries made his mouth begin to water and the oil in the air coated the lining of his nose.

Would Taylor look any different? Would she have a new hairstyle? Painted fingernails? That would be a sight! Taylor with painted fingernails! He laughed at the mental image. Taylor kept her fingernails cut short and they always looked scratched. For some strange reason, he remembered her fingernails.

In college, Taylor failed to fit the mold of the typical twenty-something female. She never wore makeup, or at least, Gerald noticed none. In his opinion, makeup would have detracted from her appearance. Her dark red hair and bright green eyes added enough color to her Irish-white skin to satisfy even the worst fashion critic. Although her physical appearance impressed Gerald and others, people became most intimidated by her confidence and intelligence. In addition to being smart and quick-witted, Taylor often exhibited impatience and a searing-hot temper. He enjoyed being around her, even when he became the target of her displeasure.

When Gerald first met her, he wondered if they might ever become romantically involved. He required only a few encounters to realize that Taylor would never have patience for him or probably any man. Romantic relationships seemed to interest her less than science, engineering, or politics. He indulged her when she wanted to talk about science and relished their conversations about society and politics. Being with her helped him endure life in the ultra-liberal atmosphere of the University of Oregon. She helped him transcend the bipolar political world.

Even without any possibility of romantic interest, Gerald felt content to simply share her company. She felt like a true work of art, complete and mysterious. In the short time of waiting at Burgerville, Gerald realized how much he had been enamored by the girl.

When he saw Taylor enter the restaurant, Gerald stood from the table and eagerly walked to the front to meet her. She looked the same as he remembered. She had her dark red hair in a ponytail and wore a forest green jacket, dark blue jeans and boots. She seemed a little more fashionable than in her college days when she only wore jeans and a t-shirt.

Her green eyes fixed on him instantly. She smiled and waved then continued walking to the counter to order her meal. With relief, Gerald realized that approaching her produced no discomfort or hesitation, as if they had seen one another recently. Before speaking, he let her finish ordering her meal.

"Taylor," he said, extending his hand. "It's good to see you."

She glanced at his hand and acted surprised at the formality then immediately smiled wider. When she grasped his hand, she pretended to meet him for the first time, shaking his hand vigorously.

"It's great to see you too Gerald. Three years just slipped by, eh?"

3

Gerald

"Is that the same backpack you had at the University of Oregon?" Gerald asked, remembering her simple canvas backpack.

"Yep, the same."

She turned to the counter as the man in front of her finished his order. While she ordered her food, Gerald glanced around at the people in the restaurant with them. The restaurant had between ten to fifteen people, filling several tables.

"Is that the table you chose in the back?" she asked with a sigh, failing to hide her disappointment in his choice. She looked at the table he chose where an employee delivered his food and removed his order number. "I suppose that will do, for what I want to show you."

Gerald instantly recognized the same get-down-to-business girl he knew in college. They had written enough to each other over the years, so he felt no need for idle chatter or to spend time becoming reacquainted. After sitting at the table, Gerald looked into her green eyes, searching for any sign of anxiety. He only saw his own reflection.

"You aren't in any trouble, are you?" he asked with concern.

"Not yet," she smiled, then pulled the backpack from over her shoulder and put it between her feet on the ground. "But it's a definite consequence if I screw it up. That's why I need your help, why I called you. Don't worry, I also wanted to see you. It's not just business."

Gerald ran his hand through his hair and shook his head.

"Thanks for the vote of confidence."

She smiled in response, then reached her hand across the table to rest reassuringly on his. Her smile faded quickly.

"Before you get all worried, let me explain, although it will take some background before I shoot you with the big bullet."

"Well, I'm intrigued," Gerald looked down at his own burger as if still deciding to eat it. "Interesting place for a secret meeting. And we can say this is where it all started, Burgerville."

"Yeah, don't make me wait for my food, or tip someone for bringing it."

As if on cue, Gerald noticed a female employee approaching from behind Taylor with a tray of food. He nodded and smiled at the girl and Taylor stopped talking. When the girl left, Taylor looked carnivorously at her burger and took a bite. Before continuing, she sighed with pleasure and spoke while chewing.

"Before I start," she said and swallowed. "Let me just say, that it's really good to see you. I've been surrounded by shitheads for too long, even mom, god bless her. You're just about the only one I can trust, at least from my pathetic social circle."

"I'm flattered to be in such an elite social group," he said with a smile.

She paused as if considering a response, but then changed her mind and took another bite. Her words raised his interest, more than the desire to eat. She seemed to have confidential matters to discuss with him and not just seeking free legal help. Not wanting to make her eat on her own, he hesitantly took his first bite, keeping his eyes fixed on hers.

"After I graduated last fall," she began. "I finally had a chance to work on this project of mine, one that's been in my head for a long, long time. I was so damn busy jumping through the stupid and pointless hoops they require in college that I didn't have time to work on it."

While talking and chewing, she seemed to be annoyed at the additional requirement to breathe. He took the opportunity to speak.

"Slow down. I'm in no hurry. We've got all night."

She shook her head and smiled, but continued.

"So, I finally had some time to work on this project. I never took it too seriously because it seemed so crazy. No, it didn't *seem* too crazy. It *was* too crazy. After graduation I came to live at home to use my dad's shop. It was such an insane idea, I never, ever seriously thought it would work, but I couldn't stop thinking about it. My mind must have been working on it when I wasn't aware because I even dreamed about this thing. If it did work, however, I'd be rich and famous, or so I thought. As you know, I'm not into anything because of fame, but the money would be nice. Selfishness makes the world go around, don't you know."

"It does indeed!" He smiled.

"So, since I didn't have any obligations, I quit my dead-end job, moved back home and became kind of a recluse, and a freeloader on my mom."

"Does your mother know what you're doing?"

"No. I couldn't talk to her about it anyway. She wouldn't understand what it was, what the implications would be and I wouldn't want her to freak out or do anything rash about it. For now, it is in her best interest to remain ignorant. That's why I didn't want to meet you at my house."

"Seems reasonable," he said, barely constraining his impatience. Even though he enjoyed listening to her, he wanted her to get to the point of the meeting.

"Well a few weeks ago, after months of failure after failure, I finally found success. When the reality of it all hit me, I seriously almost passed out. It felt like waking up in bed, looking out the window and finding yourself in space." She paused for a moment, perhaps to relive the memory. "I got really dizzy and had to lay down so I wouldn't blackout."

She paused again and took a deep breath, then looked at him with half-closed eyes. Was she reconsidering telling him her secret? In the uncomfortable silence, he widened his eyes and smiled uncomfortably.

"Go ahead Taylor. You can trust me."

She looked around again to assure that no one else paid them any attention, then she lowered her voice.

"A few days after I found out that it worked, I thought I had it all figured out, but now I don't know what to think. There are so many implications, so many little worries that are filling my head. I don't know if they're real or imagined. Is the government watching me? Do they know about it?"

"The government?" Gerald asked, but she interrupted him with a whisper.

"Am I just dreaming all this?" she asked while leaning toward him. "What if I'm going crazy?"

Her whisper made Gerald start to feel paranoid so he quickly checked for anyone else in the restaurant looking at them. When he turned back to Taylor, the look in her face seemed to plead for emotional relief, to be assured of her sanity. He leaned forward and put his hand on her upper arm. At his touch, she closed her eyes. Did he see tears of frustration in those beautiful green pearls?

"Believe me Taylor, I've seen you far crazier than this."

Gerald laughed, feeling instant relief when he noticed the smile return to her lips. She wiped her eyes, and then attempted to look offended.

"Hey, you haven't seen anything yet," she answered.

Despite her apparent relief, Gerald felt complete shock. Never in any of his experiences with her, had she appeared so disturbed. Before she could say anything else, he continued.

"You're not crazy Taylor. You should have asked me to come earlier. I would have driven down in an instant. Sorry you had to wait so long."

When she continued, no trace of emotional distress remained.

"I just need someone to see it, someone to help me plan. I know it's a stupid worry, but I'm afraid it won't work for you, that I just imagined it all. That would mean that I have lost my mind." She took a deep breath and positioned her backpack on the floor between her feet. "I can't believe I brought it here. I feel like I have a billion bucks in this bag and I'm about to be robbed."

Using her foot, Taylor pushed the backpack to him under the table.

Before reaching down to pluck her bag from the ground, Gerald hesitated. He had the feeling that some creature waited inside the bag, like a snake ready to bite. After securing the bag on the seat between him and the wall, he opened the main compartment.

"Ok, what do I do?"

4

Freddy

Freddy Carlson waited before answering the phone, especially when he saw the caller ID. Most likely, his sister or mother waited on the other end and he had a difficult time deciding which family member induced more anxiety. Considering the late hour, his sister Wanda most likely wanted to talk. His mother went to bed early, and she rarely called anyway.

Freddy hated answering phone calls, but his employer, Mr. Smith, had already gone to his room upstairs to read a book in an attempt to put himself to sleep. In his old age, he had trouble sleeping so some nights he would sit up there for hours, reading or typing on his computer, but mostly reading. If Mr. Smith heard the phone keep ringing, he would get out of bed and Freddy wanted to avoid that. His sister Wanda purposefully put him into the awkward position. She knew he would not answer her call at any other time.

"Yes, hello," Freddy said, after quickly lifting the receiver. While waiting for a response, he checked behind him, just in case Mr. Smith silently watched.

"Hey, Freddy," the voice said after a long sigh.

"Who is this?" he asked, before she could finish. "Wands?"

Freddy waited through a longer sigh on the other end of the line.

"Who else would it be Freddy? You know Mom's gone to bed."

"Say the word then," he replied in annoyance.

Only his sister or mother could give the correct code word to identify themselves. If they gave the wrong one, he would know another human attempted to deceive him. Usually his boss answered the phone, and like every other normal person, the old man would know the identification of the owner from their voice.

Freddy had a very unique and unfortunate problem. Voices made no emotional connection with him, not even the voices of close friends and family. In order to recall the owner of a voice, normal humans needed an emotional connection to the voice. Freddy's mind lacked the capacity to form that connection. Without the ability to connect a voice to a face, he had to confirm identification by another method.

People in his life had used this particular disability to ridicule and laugh at him, but unfortunately, he had a long list of other peculiarities to ridicule. Long ago, he had quit wanting to be normal. Freddy just wanted to be left alone. As an assistant to an old man who lived alone, only his sister ever caused anxiety.

Freddy waited for his sister to say the word. When she finally answered, she almost shouted.

"Spider, spider, spider," she said in frustration and he imagined smelling the alcohol on her breath.

The high volume of her shout made him drop the phone with a loud thud. He listened for any indication that Mr. Smith had heard the sound. Only silence answered. Although he heard her anger, he felt better after hearing their secret code word. He did not want to deal with an angry Wanda, so he changed to a softer tone.

"What is it that you want Wands?"

"I want to show you something," she said, her tone softening and becoming almost friendly.

"The time is late Wands and Mr. Smith is in his room. I do not want to disturb him. Can we do this tomorrow?"

Freddy could hear his sister's breathing between responses. She continued after a short pause.

"Don't worry. I'll be quiet. I want to show you something I bought today. Come on, just let me come over. I'm coming through your neighborhood anyway."

"Well," he said in his final attempt to dissuade her. "You know that Mr. Smith does not want any visitors after he goes to bed."

His boss specifically did not want Wanda to visit unless he could chaperone. When Wanda visited, Mr. Smith became Freddy's emotional advocate.

If his sister spoke the truth and really did have something to show him, did Freddy want to see it? Probably not. He could not remember his sister ever giving him a gift, unless as a cruel joke, but it had been several years since she tried anything like that. Since he started working for Mr. Smith, she pretended to like him. No matter how much she tried to be friendly, however, her true vindictive and selfish personality usually rose to the surface.

After Freddy turned eighteen years old, Mr. Smith rescued him from the Oregon foster care system and from his parasitic mother and sister. Now at twenty-two, he lived with Mr. Smith doing errands and keeping the house in order. He did almost everything, except answering the phones, and especially when his sister called.

"Freddy just let me in when I get there. It'll just be for a minute. Old Bill won't know I was there."

She cut the connection.

Before setting down the receiver, he held the phone for a few seconds and sighed. How many times did he have to play this game with her? He had some consolation. His sister visited much less frequently since he moved to his present location.

Her five-year-old son kept her busier lately too. Usually, Freddy liked children, but not pre-schoolers being groomed to be tyrants and dictators. In just a few years, the transformation into his mother would be complete. Freddy tried his best to hide his displeasure at seeing the boy whenever they came into contact. After the boy's last visit a year ago, Mr. Smith had forbidden him from entering the house again and he let Wanda know it.

Freddy walked to the first room near the main entrance of the mansion, the drawing room. He opened the curtains and peeked outside, but only saw the street light past the driveway gate. From that location, he would be unable to hear the sound of Mr. Smith's movement so he went to the main staircase and silently walked upstairs. He walked to the hallway and saw the closed door to Mr. Smith's room. After listening for a moment, he heard no movement or sound.

Freddy went back to the drawing room and stood at the closed curtains, watching for light at the main gate. After a few moments of silent watching, he became impatient and walked to the grand piano at the far end of the room where it faced the window. He spent the next ten minutes, walking from the piano to the window and back again. He counted twenty-seven trips before he saw the light from his sister's car through the curtains.

5

Freddy

After his sister stopped at the closed gate and waited, Freddy held his finger over the button which would open the gate and waited until he felt mentally prepared. After ten seconds, he finally pushed the button. Even though she had given him the code word over the phone and the car looked like hers, Freddy would feel better once he saw his sister's face.

Wanda soon came to stand silently outside the door. He looked through the peep-hole and breathed a small sigh of relief after seeing her face. Before opening the door, Freddy silently keyed the code to disable the security system he had installed.

"Hi brother dear," his sister said right before stepping into the house. He glanced behind her and breathed a larger sigh of relief when he failed to see her son.

After closing the door, he noticed his sister's hair. Her blonde roots had grown by about an inch. The light roots contrasted sharply with her dyed brown hair and red highlights. Her hair also seemed to be covered in about three days' worth of hairspray. Like Freddy, she had natural blonde hair, but she always wanted to be different and seemed to be fighting nature. She usually ridiculed him for his white and bushy hair.

"Shhhh," he said in warning and holding his index finger to his lips.

"Oh pfah," she said and walked past him. "Old Bill can't hear half of what we say when you're standing right next to him."

He did not like her saying anything disrespectful about his boss. Before following her, he took a deep breath and tried to keep the irritation out of his voice.

"What do you want to show me?"

Wanda ignored him and headed through the hallways to the kitchen like she would through her own home. Freddy felt a slight irritation that she knew her way in the house so well. He followed her like an obedient child, afraid of being spanked by an angry, loud response.

"I just gotta get a drink first. You're gonna love what I got for ya."

She opened the refrigerator and instantly looked disappointed, probably due to the lack of alcohol. A moment later her smile returned and she got some juice.

After taking the first gulp of some red juice, she spoke as if reading from a prepared statement.

"I know what you're thinking Freddy. I'm here to ask for some shit, but I'm not. I just couldn't wait for an old-Bill-approved time to give this thing to you."

Even though her statement sounded rehearsed, she seemed genuinely excited. After breaking eye contact with him, his sister placed her purse on the counter by the refrigerator and loudly rummaged through its contents. Finally, she retrieved her intended object and held it out to him in the palm of her hand. Freddy had to blink several times before he could see clearly.

Wanda held a flat rectangular crystal with rounded corners, about thirty percent smaller than a credit card. Freddy estimated the thickness to be around five millimeters. As he leaned forward for a closer view, he felt uncomfortable being so close to his sister, but he felt a strong attraction to the object.

After looking closely, he noticed a finely grooved crystal surface which refracted the light from the ceiling. No matter what angle of his view, the surface threw a rainbow in his eyes. After admiring the beautiful light for a moment, he noticed the shape encased inside the object. At first, he failed to recognize the familiar shape, but when he did, he could not stop his smile from stretching across his face.

A spider filled the inside of the crystal and appeared to be made of different kinds of stone and only two-dimensional so that when he looked at the object from the side, the spider nearly disappeared. From what he could see, several rows of red eyes lined its light gray head. The body looked like granite with silver streaks across it. Different colored bands encircled its beautiful long legs.

When he tried to look closer at the eyes, his vision became fuzzy at the attempt so he looked away and had to blink several times for his vision to return.

"It is amazing," Freddy said before taking the crystal from her hand. He turned the rectangular object over and noticed that the spider on both sides looked exactly the same. He carefully tossed it up and down in one hand to judge the weight. It felt good in his hand.

"It is dense."

"I know I shouldn't indulge your spider fetish, but this had your name on it."

"It does?" he asked and then began inspecting the surface for his name.

Wanda sighed, frowning in irritation.

"Just a figure of speech, Freddy. I bought it for you. Do you want it or not?"

The question struck warning bells in his mind. He closed his hand over the spider, afraid of her taking it back. If he accepted this present, he would be in her debt. Wanda's nature only involved gifts with strings attached. She would expect something in return, if not now, then in the future. He opened his hand and looked at the crystal spider again. The beautiful object seemed to trap his gaze and he had difficulty looking away. When he did manage to return his attention to his sister, she had a strange look in her eyes, some kind of pleasure.

"Yes, I do want it," he said quickly. "Thanks Wands."

After only a moment's hesitation, however, he realized that no matter what she thought or said, he owed her nothing. Even with this present, Wanda would be still in his debt. He failed to recall a time in her life when she had thought of him.

"You're welcome," she said with a genuine smile on her face.

"Where did you purchase it?" he asked and attempted to attenuate his excitement. He planned on going to wherever she made the purchase, to see what else they sold.

"A friend of mine had it," she said. "When I saw it, I had to get it for you, so I bought it from her. You don't know the best part."

"What best part?"

She put her index finger on the center of the crystal, covering part of the spider. "That rock, the head."

"Yeah."

"She says it's a piece of an asteroid."

He stared at the head, but stayed silent.

"Yep, that little piece of rock was flying through space for thousands of years probably."

"How did she know that?"

Freddy ignored the ridiculous estimation of its possible age.

Even if untrue, he still wanted the crystal. If the head did come from an asteroid, he would want the object even more, but the true identification of the rock did not seem as important as its origin. He already had a piece of an asteroid and even that seemed unimportant. Everything on the Earth had also been flying through space for a long time.

He held the crystal up closer to his eyes and examined it again. He never owned anything as beautiful and he could not recall ever wanting something more. How did her friend acquire the crystal object? He failed to imagine any of his sister's associates having something of similar quality. The closer he stared at the shiny rainbow surface, the more exquisite it looked.

Normally, some company in China, Taiwan, or Indonesia, made cheap and interesting baubles like it. They looked interesting from afar, but upon closer inspection, their true absence of quality or value became apparent. After inspecting the object from several angles, looking for any sign of make or model, he saw no inscription. He would use his instruments later for a more detailed inspection.

"The girl I got it from was certain about it being an asteroid. She would not lie to me."

"Do you know where she got it?" he asked casually, trying to conceal his real curiosity. He felt something strange about the affair, as if the trinket came from a secret government laboratory instead of a cheap labor factory.

"She wouldn't say, but what does it matter? Can't you just be happy for once and not follow up with a million questions?"

From the tone of her voice and the look in her eyes, he knew he had to stop the interrogation. If he persisted, she might demand for him to return it.

"Sorry Wands. This is awesome. How can I pay you back? Why don't you take some food back home to Charlie."

Freddy grabbed a plastic bag from a drawer and began filling it with food from the refrigerator. Whenever she visited, he gave her food, but this time he felt glad to return the favor. The faster she acquired it, the faster she would be gone.

"Thanks Bro. Bill won't notice?" she asked.

"Probably not. I'll just go to the store tomorrow or tonight and restock."

"You got a sweet set-up here, brother. Don't ruin it."

After he walked her to the front door, he failed to stop himself from asking one more question.

"Who is this friend you got it from?"

She opened the door and turned around with the two bags of food swinging.

"She's not really a friend, more of an acquaintance. I met her yesterday when she was moving out of the apartment down the hall. We got to talking and I noticed the crystal. She seemed glad to be rid of the thing. But, she's all moved out. I'll probably never see her again."

He smiled awkwardly then shut the door.

"Now I will never know where she got it," he said quietly to himself.

Freddy walked to the curtain and looked outside then watched as his sister carried the bags of groceries to her car and drove away. The entire time, he felt the weight of the crystal in his closed hand. A moment later, the sound of a soft voice paralyzed him. He squeezed his hand tightly over the crystal and then let the curtain fall back in place.

In the silence, he felt the presence of his boss standing behind him. Freddy did not want his boss to see what he held in his hand.

6

Freddy

"When are you gonna stand up to your sister?" said the shaking voice of his boss, Bill Smith. He leaned against the piano, holding his black cane in his withered hand. "You wouldn't have to see her if you followed the rule of letting me answer the phone."

"I do not know why I picked it up," he said automatically. When Mr. Smith spoke to him, he usually responded too quickly. The habit gave him little time to think. "I thought it might be an emergency."

"Everything's an emergency with your sister."

Freddy relaxed his grip on the crystal and discreetly slipped it into his pocket. He felt some anxiety about his boss noticing and making him show what he had. In the dim light, the old man would have a hard time to see it.

"If you knew she was here, why did you not stop her?"

Freddy instantly regretted asking the question. The words felt impertinent.

"Talking to your sister requires too much energy and it's late. I just didn't feel like going through the trouble since she was here already. She's gone I guess. That's all the matters."

"How long were you standing there?"

"Long enough to see that the refrigerator is probably empty again."

Freddy looked down, ashamed.

"I am sorry. Next time, I will let you answer the phone next time. I did not want to wake you."

"Thank you. I'm going to bed now, again. Goodnight." He turned to leave the room, then turned around again. Freddy remained motionless and waited. "By the way, did she have anything important to tell you?"

Freddy paused and Mr. Smith noticed. Nothing seemed to escape his notice.

"She just wanted some groceries, as usual."

Mr. Smith looked at him critically, but before the old man could say anything else, he began coughing.

"Goodnight, Freddy," he said when the coughing subsided.

He turned and let the dark of the hallway swallow him.

7

Gerald

"Put your hand in the main compartment," Taylor began with a seemingly normal glance around the room. "Don't take anything out of the bag. Just put your hand on the small box and slide your hand around the side until you feel the switch."

Gerald put his hand inside and felt a cool metal box with a smooth surface. Unexpectedly, his heart rate began to rise.

"Ok, I feel it."

"Before you flip the switch, make sure to put some pressure on the box, downward."

"It's not going to hurt me is it?" he asked, followed by a nervous laugh, a failed attempt to defuse the tension he felt. To any observer in the restaurant, Taylor probably appeared calm, but the visible pulse in her neck said otherwise.

"Putting pressure on it?" she asked.

"Yes."

"Ok, flip the switch."

He pulled the switch until he heard a small click. Nothing happened.

Gerald's heart seemed to stop for a moment, not because of the box, but from his fear of her reaction. Did he fail to notice something? His eyes widened in anticipation of a shriek from the girl across from him. He imagined her hand reaching across the table to strangle him.

After a moment, her features froze and a look of panic appeared on her face. Gerald prepared himself to reach out and catch her before she collapsed. After a horribly long a second, her eyes lit up.

"Oh my God," she said, putting her hand over her heart and laughing in relief. "I know what the problem is."

"That's good," Gerald said with a mixture of shock and relief. "I thought you were going to kill me."

"I almost forgot," she said, ignoring him. "Here, stick this next to the switch, then flip it."

She handed him a shiny piece of square metal, about two centimeters long. "This was just a precaution, in case someone stole my backpack and found this thing. They wouldn't think anything of it because it won't work without this magnet activating an internal circuit." She took a deep breath and smiled again.

Gerald put the magnet next to the switch and it loudly snapped to the metal, then he flipped the switch again. Instantly it seemed, the box began to hum with a fast-paced, vibration like his iPhone, only weaker.

When he felt the metal box push up against his hand, he jolted in shock and instinctively wanted to remove his hand from her backpack. To help relieve his anxiety, he looked up and met Taylor's eyes, the vibration feeling steady and powerful under his hand. Taylor seemed to be holding her breath and looking directly into his soul. For an eternal instant, he felt paralyzed.

"So?" she said, breaking the silence like a whip.

"I don't know," he began hesitantly. "It's pushing back. What do I do now?"

He felt a little stupid and almost wanted to laugh, but the fiery look in Taylor's eyes kept any hint of a smile from appearing. Apparently, he failed to see the importance of what he felt in her backpack.

She let out a sigh of relief and closed her eyes, then after a long pause she shook her head and laughed at him until he saw tears begin to form. Her laughter made a group of teenagers at another table look at them. Gerald felt relieved about her not being angry or upset.

"I'm kind of disappointed that you don't get it yet," she said and wiped the moisture from her eyes. "Lift up your hand a little bit."

He lifted his hand and the box followed him, as if it wanted to escape the backpack. The small metal box felt alive. Chills ran from his chest to his neck. Gerald flipped the switch and the metal box fell back down to the bottom of the bag.

"What the hell is this? Sorry, just tell me."

Gerald pulled his hand out of the bag and pushed it back to her under the table, as if her bag contained poisonous gas. He usually tried to act composed and speak in perfect English, so he felt stupid for losing control and swearing. She laughed at him even more, but more composed so people would stop looking at them.

In the closest populated booth, Gerald noticed the sound of two small children complaining conspicuously about not wanting to eat their food. The mother sitting with them made no attempt to stop the noise and just watched with apathy in her eyes. Gerald looked in their direction for a moment and the woman made brief eye contact with him. Had she noticed anything? He felt slightly paranoid again.

"So what do we do now, right." Taylor said, pulling his eyes back to her. Her words felt more like a statement, than a question.

He felt unprepared to answer her. Maybe he just needed time to decode the experience.

"Just give me a second here," he said. "I have to get my head wrapped around this. You invented anti-gravity?"

"Shhh," she said and her eyes opened wide in warning. Then she shook her head and smiled, almost as if repressing more laughter.

"I guess you might call it anti-gravity," she said, lowering her voice. "Just like you can call throwing a rock in the air, 'anti-gravity'. A more accurate and cleaner description is a Net Momentum Generator. I shortened it to the NMG, simple, sweet."

"NMG huh," he said and nodded his head in approval, feeling like a puppy trying to obediently please her. "At the moment, I don't know what to say. It's a lot to take in. No offense intended, but part of me doesn't believe it. I mean, why hasn't anyone else figured out how to do this or have they? Don't worry, I give you full credit for being a genius, but there's a million geniuses out there, right?

People have been trying to do something like this for thousands of years."

"Yes they have Gerald," she said with disappointment in her voice. "I've considered two possibilities. Either someone has invented it before, but the military or someone else has covered it up, or I'm just the super genius of them all." She smiled and gave a slight bow of her head. "You have to admit, there's no one else like me."

"True," he said and felt himself relax a bit. "Well, at least, this hasn't damaged your humility."

"I just feel so much better after showing you, telling someone I can trust." She threw a fry in her mouth, then continued almost impatiently while chewing. "Seriously though, I kind of doubt that anyone invented it yet. Anyone educated in science would have instantly dismissed the idea, my initial moment of inspiration. I would have dismissed it too, but I couldn't get the idea out of my head!"

"OK, I think I'm ready for you to continue with your scientific explanation, but give it to me gently. Remember, I'm not a science geek like you."

Her eyes narrowed in feigned outrage.

"Gerald," she said slowly. "I'll try to explain it so a lawyer such as yourself, can understand. To put it bluntly, I broke the law, one of the most fundamental laws of science and engineering. I broke a sacred conservation law, the conservation of momentum!"

She put both hands on the table between them and made quote marks.

"*They*, won't like what I did."

"By *they,* you mean other scientists? The institutional ones in charge, right?" Gerald began to feel less intimidated and more interested, like a child about to hear a bedtime story.

"Yeah those ones," she said with a sneer. "The gods of science."

Her reference to the word 'gods', cast the image of a huge statue in his mind, a college professor wearing glasses and a robe with a book held to his chest. "You broke a law huh? And the first person you told was a lawyer?"

"If I explained to you how it works, in detail," she said, ignoring his jest. "You probably wouldn't understand, so I'll try to explain in the most basic way I can. What this is, is related to the conservation of momentum which depends on forces being equal and opposite. That's what is seen macroscopically. Things average out and no net momentum is observed, but on an atomic level, the balance can be broken, but only slightly. A little, however, can add up to a lot and I designed a way to extract net momentum out of semi-isolated systems."

While she gave her explanation, Gerald's mind began considering the implications of her invention. Those implications interested him more than the scientific explanation. He understood what frightened her.

8

Gerald

"So, where do you go from here, right?"

"Yes," she answered. "Your initial thoughts?"

He looked down at the table between them which blocked the view of her backpack. He could see some straps on the ground. He spoke slowly, tentatively.

"My gut instinct tells me that the military would want it, cover it up even. An invention like this would revolutionize combat, especially if we were the only military to have it."

"When you say 'we', do you mean the United States Military?" she asked with derision in her voice. "Or do you mean, 'we' as in you and me?"

He shook his head in irritation when he remembered her feelings on the subject of the military and realized he had to speak more precisely. She'd caught him talking like a collectivist so he smiled apologetically.

"Sorry. If you aren't careful, you might find yourself working in a secret military base the rest of your life. Those are just my initial thoughts. You've had a lot more time to think about this than I have. What have you come up with?"

She looked at him imploringly and he felt an intense empathy for her. He could imagine how excited she must have been when she finally got her NMG device to work. And then imagining so many frightening roadblocks in her way. No wonder she felt paranoia. Not only would the US military want the NMG, but so would all the other nations' militaries. Being locked away in a military base would probably be the best option. He needed more time to think, but knew she needed to discuss the situation with him.

"Those were my first thoughts too," she agreed. "I've been trying to think of ways to avoid it, maybe start my own company? Flood the market with the device?"

"Hmm yes," he began. "You're in a very tricky and delicate situation. You would need to give very little time for your opponents to begin countermeasures. If you're not careful, you'd lose control and the corporate sharks will come and eat it up and that's if you successfully escaped military intervention."

As he spoke, more thoughts and possibilities kept crashing into his mind, possible ways to proceed and what to avoid. Speaking helped control the flow of thoughts.

"Perhaps the best possible outcome from that strategy is a Nobel prize, a good chunk of money and fame. But, that wouldn't be enough would it? Am I right?"

She smiled deviously.

No, he thought with a smile. Taylor would not be satisfied by just a chunk of money and fame. She wanted every last drop of juice from that fruit. The thought of someone else profiting from her hard work would be unacceptable.

"Nobel prize!" she scoffed. "Then there's the problem of filing for a patent and all that mess. I'm not sure how easy it is going to be for a patent, but I read that it takes forever. But, that's not going to work either. Something this big cannot be kept a secret when it passes through the hands of a hundred patent clerks."

"But," he began, but she ignored him and continued speaking.

"That seems like a dead end. One of the corporate sharks, as you call them, will make something similar, ship the production overseas and make it for half the price. We might be able to make it work, somehow, maybe make a high-quality, American-made novelty for a niche market but... blah, blah, blah."

"All that just seems so boring compared to what this is." She took a drink of her water. "God, I hate those arrogant corporate snakes, the bastards who sit in their fiftieth story board rooms and steal the sweat and labor of the scientists and engineers, those who do all the real work. They give us a hundred thousand dollars while they take a hundred million."

"Thanks for the help, we'll take it from here," she said mockingly. She picked up the backpack and put it in her lap. She patted it like a favorite kitten, like she dared them to take it from her. "Businessmen, bastards!" she sneered.

Gerald considered taking his half-eaten burger and taking a bite, but decided on a fry instead while she continued.

"I think the most likely outcome from taking it public would be a failure," she said finally.

Gerald thought she looked like a kid who just learned about how her parents faked the whole Santa story.

"You're right about the patent," Gerald said, laughing sarcastically.

He agreed that they could not keep her invention a secret for a long enough time to fully capitalize on the possibilities. The legal team from a company like Lockheed Martin would tie her up in court with fake patent infringement lawsuits and the government would make it impossible to defend by classifying the case as a national security matter. In reality, Gerald assumed the case would never be brought before a judge.

After that thought, a bigger question materialized into his mind and felt like a slap in the face. The question wiped the sarcastic smile away from his mouth. The new possibility scared him more than any other yet and he wondered how Taylor managed to sleep peacefully at night.

"Will the military even want something like this to be invented? I mean, something this big would alter the game for everyone on the planet. It might cause too much uncertainty. Western military dominance might be in jeopardy."

She sighed and nodded. Apparently, she had already considered that possibility. She looked defeated, but angry. Like many other people he knew, Taylor used anger as a self-defense mechanism.

"I think that no matter what we try, the government will squash us. That's why I brought the problem to you. If anyone can find a way, it's Gerald Fuger!"

Despite what he felt, her words resurrected his smile.

"Thanks for the confidence, but at the moment, I'm just going to be a disappointment. Don't worry. I will help you come up with a plan. I just want to consider the possibility of coming out in the open with this. So, they'll most likely first threaten your family so that you won't be able to fight back. At the same time, they'll discredit you and if that doesn't work, they'll kill you, and me, and everyone else who knows about it. There's always the possibility that they will pay us for our silence, but I wouldn't take that chance.

"The system will probably pay some establishment scientists to make your device, a flawed version, and show how it doesn't work. They'll call you a fraud and you won't be able to do anything about it. The media will paint a perfect picture of your incompetence. I don't have to remind you how many times they've done this."

"I know. I know," she said in a tone of acceptance rather than disappointment. She met his eyes and despite all the negativity he felt, he saw hope. "I did the hard part and now I'll just let you tell me when you've figured out the rest."

She laughed and the sight of her relaxation made him feel better. He decided to change the direction of the discussion.

"The NMG, how scalable is it? How much can it lift?"

"Whatever weight you want. If I gave it more power, this little box could lift you." She tapped her fingers on the table, as if counting. "For this design, not this prototype mind you, I don't think it would do such a good job over about twenty thousand kilograms, but I could make a configuration to lift much more. This is just my latest design. It would blow your mind seeing the energy balance equation I had to solve to get it to work! Well, I didn't actually get an exact solution, I more or less minimized the..."

He needed to put her words into terms he could understand, so he cut her off.

"So, could you fly a 747 with this thing?" Twenty thousand kilograms seemed like a lot, but the number made no connection to anything in reality.

She looked annoyed at the interruption, but quickly transformed her emotion into a smile and he smiled in response.

"Absolutely, I mean not this little prototype I made, but we could design one to do that job, for sure. Of course, you understand that aerodynamics is unnecessary for flight?"

She sounded doubtful of his mental competence, but he ignored the tone. Her use of the word 'we' gave him too much credit. He had no training in mechanical engineering, as she did, or in any engineering for that matter.

"OK, here's what I'm thinking. Hear me out. There is another alternative. We keep it secret, for now until we come up with a better plan." The rest of the idea unfolded as he spoke. "First, we get someone to help you, someone like us, and develop it on our own. Then maybe when the time is right, we'll be able to show this NMG technology to the world and in a way that cannot be squashed or repressed. If we're smart about it, no one will be able to stop it."

By the warning look in her eyes, he became conscious of his voice beginning to rise so he leaned forward and spoke in a whisper. He could feel his smile stretch the muscles in his face, all the way to his ears.

"First we need to develop an escape plan, should anything go wrong. We make a vehicle, a spaceship. With this technology, we can at least have something to escape their grasp. This NMG thing should be able to outmaneuver anything currently available."

From the look in her eyes, he could almost see the stars reflected back at him. His idea stuck. At least, he thought she failed to show any sign of rejection.

9

Gerald

After hearing Gerald's proposal, Taylor became silent. She seemed to be working through his idea, like chewing the last bite of her burger.

Gerald peered closely at her face, searching for signs of the same excitement he felt and she returned his look with a blank stare. His new idea and optimistic attitude helped replace fear of the possible negative consequences. After the silence had lengthened into an awkward region, he wondered if she would laugh at him, laugh at how stupid he sounded. He suddenly felt like a little child talking about dragons or magic. If he heard someone else talking like this, he would think they had lost their sense of reality. The idea sounded totally outlandish, but given Taylor's astonishing revelation, it made perfect sense to him.

After another moment, life returned to her eyes.

"I thought of space travel, but just as one use for this, not as a means of escape." She took a drink of her soda to wash a fry down her throat. "We wouldn't have the resources to live in space."

"I don't mean we live in space, but should we need to escape, we can just hop on our new spaceship."

She failed to return his smile so he continued.

"It's not perfect, I agree, but like we already agreed, they'll never let this get off the ground, so to speak." He did not intend for the pun, but for a second it interrupted his thoughts. "As soon as we go public, or even if they find out about it secretly, that's the end. We're finished. But, if we can escape into space, and let everyone know about it, there's no way they can hide it. Every amateur astronomer on the planet would be able to see it for themselves."

Taylor laughed.

"We can make a banner and drag it behind us." She dramatically waved her hand in the air. "Suck it! Assholes."

She spoke a little too loudly, and the mother sitting a few tables away scowled at them. Taylor ignored the woman and chuckled to herself. Gerald shook his head, but failed to suppress his own quiet snicker.

After her comic outburst, she quickly became serious again, pinching her lips together in thought, and looked down at the table. He imagined hearing gears grinding in her head. Finally, as if coming out of a trance, Taylor continued.

"It's definitely an idea to explore, of course not to live in space, but definitely having the possible escape route would be beneficial. Who can we trust to help us? We need someone else. No offense, but someone with more of a technical background."

"Let me think," he said as he reached for her backpack again. He wanted to hide how relieved he felt at her initial acceptance of his idea. "I want to try it again. I'm not afraid anymore."

She checked for any spying eyes then relinquished the prized backpack into his possession. This time, he opened the bag and looked inside before attempting to touch the NMG. Instead of a shiny metal object as he expected, he found the dull black surface of a metal box.

"A black box," he said with a quick smile. "Seems fitting."

"Hmm," she said seriously. "Didn't think you'd recognize that."

He put his hand inside the compartment, activated the device and suddenly felt like a child opening a present on Christmas. His already wide smile, expanded when he felt the box push up against his hand. Before deactivating the object, he let the backpack lift completely off his lap.

"Wow!"

Taylor smiled with pride.

"I hate to burst your bubble Gerald, but after thinking about it, I think *your* plan's got too many holes."

She always spoke with bluntness and in this case, he wished she had the ability to sugarcoat something. Gerald had thought they both agreed with the plan. Sure, a spaceship seemed like an impossible task, but after seeing her invention, the impossible was possible. Only a spaceship could escape the grasp of the government.

"What's the matter?"

"Don't get me wrong, I like where you're going with this whole escape Earth option, but I think you might be fantasizing again. You do have the tendency to avoid looking at the major obstacles."

Despite his disappointment, his lawyer instinct never left him speechless. He never quit without a fight and would tackle her obstacles one at a time.

"What specific obstacles are you talking about?"

"Oh, I think the most glaring one is about money? It's going to cost a lot of money to make something that can go into space."

"You're thinking about it too closely," he said with relief that she failed to use the word 'impossible'. "You've got to look at the big pic-"

"Oh don't get all worked up Gerald," she said holding her hand up to cut his retort short. "I still think your idea is worth pursuing. I just don't want to get your hopes up too much. We really need to be discreet with this, but more heads are better than one so we do need to find someone. Success is more likely achieved by a team effort."

Gerald sighed in deep relief and felt a little better. He already had several people in his mind to help, people who shared their same ideological views. Ideology felt more important than technical expertise. He had several libertarian friends to consider. After just a few seconds, a face materialized in his mind and made him smile. He spoke without first thinking about her reaction.

"I know the perfect person to recruit first. You'd like him. I helped him with his business start-up a few years ago, just after he came here, from Mexico."

He pulled his hand out of her backpack and returned the whole package into her possession. The look on her face indicated a concern. Did the designation of 'Mexicans' fail to inspire confidence? He stood and started gathering up the remnants of his dinner.

"Come on. Let's talk more in my car."

"OK."

10

Freddy

Freddy stood at the window for a long time and listened as Mr. Smith walked up the stairs. The memory of hearing even the slightest tone of disappointment from his employer made Freddy cringe. When the sound of the old man's movement faded into nothing, Freddy counted how many steps it would take for him to get to his room. After feeling certain that Mr. Smith made the journey to his room safely, Freddy closed his eyes and cursed himself for doing what his sister wanted, but at least, it had resulted in an amazing gift.

At five years of age, his father had abandoned them, leaving his mother to deal with Freddy and his sister on her own. Freddy never heard from his father again. For all he knew, his father had died. He'd even forgotten the man's name and failed to remember his face. His mother had burned any picture containing his father's image.

With all of his mother's emotional issues, she could only manage to take care of one child, the daughter without any special needs or abnormal emotional issues. Freddy, on the other hand, required more effort than she could emotionally provide.

His mother blamed Freddy for being the reason his father left them and she never let her children forget it. Thanks to her constant reminders, his sister Wanda shared the same resentment. As a young child, Freddy had believed her, but he ultimately decided to believe that both of his parents lacked the mental capacity to care for children and that he had just pulled the shortest stick from the hand of a malevolent god. After spending time in a more emotionally stable environment with Mr. Smith, Freddy began to see his mother and sister as the psychologically troubled ones. Years of bitterness would probably never completely dissipate, but he could look to the future with some optimism.

Officials from the state eventually helped to convince his mother that other families were much more capable of fulfilling her son's special needs. Other families showed more eagerness to accommodate Freddy's problems, for an extra thousand dollars a month.

His first foster family, the Coopers, had one boy two years younger than Freddy and one boy a few years older. When he came into the family, they enjoyed watching their father hit Freddy which meant the man stopped hitting them. The older boy would always divert their father's anger toward Freddy and sometimes if Freddy displeased them, he would lie just to get their father angry. Freddy learned to stay out of their way, as much as possible.

Freddy would always remember his first punishment at the Cooper's house even though he'd forgotten the reason. Mr. Cooper took a ruler and hit Freddy's knuckles so hard they bled. Freddy remembered the reason, however, for the next time he got in trouble. While Mrs. Cooper explained his chores for the first time, Freddy closed his eyes in fear and began humming. Mrs. Cooper did not like the reaction so she called her husband to deal with the boy and the man used the only method he knew, inflicting pain.

When Freddy felt stress or if situations caused him any form of anxiety, he would attempt to remove himself from the world. With the Coopers, he soon learned to delay his instincts to when he could be alone. He always went to bed early and spent many hours in his room cuddled up in a ball, humming as silently as possible. Retreating into his mind became his only refuge.

During most of his younger years in foster care, Freddy had no friends and learned to stay away from other people his age. He occasionally visited his mother and sister and for the only time in his life, they treated him better than anyone else he knew. At first, he tried complaining about his abuse, but they both ignored him. After several years, he learned to stop crying when leaving his home and just accept his fate without outward emotion.

Overall, he spent his youth in five foster families. In his final foster family he had a small reprieve from most emotional distress. The older couple had children who lived away with families of their own. Fortunately for Freddy, they seemed to want the least interaction with him as possible. Raising their own children seemed to exhaust all their patience for children and with all their grandchildren, they had no time or energy left for him. They used the state money to help them retire and Freddy had to take care of himself. Despite all the neglect, he liked living with them the best.

The blissful neglect of his last family helped Freddy cope with the next phase of his life, namely friends! He made friends with Sadi and Brian Jacobsen, the first reciprocal friendships of his life. He instantly fell in love with Sadi and came to view her as the model female. He failed to hide his affection. Although she never encouraged his feelings, Sadi always treated him kindly and even seemed to enjoy visiting with him.

Her younger brother, Brian, also seemed to enjoy Freddy's company. Everyone who knew Brian wanted to be his friend. Among all of his many attractive characteristics, his confidence drew people to him like the warmth of a fire.

Brian only wanted one thing in life, to have fun. If Brian found someone who interested him, he wanted to be friends, no matter their lack of popularity or normality. He and his sister spent a lot of their time together and made a project out of Freddy.

When Freddy came into their lives, Sadi had just started experimenting with drugs, and Brian followed her example. As a musician in a high school band, Brian found easy access to drugs. Although Sadi never let Freddy join their drug experiences, sometimes he visited them when they were high.

"If I tried it, will it have the same effect on me?" he remembered asking.

"I'm a nobody," she answered him with a sardonic smile. "But, you're special. We shouldn't mess with that."

During his time with the Jacobsens, his visits home became more frequent, but they felt bittersweet. His sister taunted him mercilessly about his new friends, especially Sadi. Wanda used the situation to turn Freddy into her slave.

If he ever felt tempted to refuse Wanda's bidding, she would threaten to tell Sadi all his horrible and embarrassing secrets, especially Freddy's feelings toward her.

He especially hated when his sister wanted him to go shopping with her. During that time, she invented a new nickname for him, 'The Gifter Lifter'. Due to his timidity, almost no one ever suspected him of shoplifting which made him a valuable asset to his sister. He got caught only a couple of times and for his final punishment, he went to juvenile detention. He still had nightmares of that experience. After returning, he refused to talk to anyone for several weeks and when Wanda threatened to tell Sadi about him, he pretended not to care. Wanda never talked to Sadi and Freddy swore never to fear her threats again.

Freddy visited with Sadi and her brother whenever he could. They tried to stay off drugs when he visited, but he often found them in an altered state. Although he preferred them under the influence of natural human chemicals, Freddy just wanted to be around people who enjoyed his company and who treated him like a normal human being. Freddy always remembered Brian's response when he asked what made some drugs illegal and some legal.

"Some rich white guy had a board with all the drugs on it," he began with a melodramatic wave of his hands. "He threw darts at the board and whatever drugs he hit, they would be illegal. He missed alcohol, nicotine and caffeine, thank God!"

His experiences with Sadi and her brother became the first to give him hope for the future, a future with more positive influences in his life. His special problem of being unable to recognize voices and only recognizing faces, never became a problem for his new friends. When Sadi called him the first time on the phone, she pretended to be his mother and then laughed until she realized the effect on him. Freddy thought his mother learned about his friends and planned to forbid any further communication with them. Sadi came up with the idea to use a secret code word and chose 'spider'.

"You're quiet and calculating," she explained one day. "Like a spider."

From that day on, Freddy loved spiders. Even after Sadi moved away to college and he lost contact with her, seeing a spider always reminded him of her. Her younger brother kept in touch with him, but not as much after she left.

11

Freddy

Before his eighteenth birthday, he had to make a choice. As a young child, the doctors had diagnosed him with autism. His mother wanted to send him to a home for autistic kids, with many unable even to take care of themselves. The thought of living in that situation stole all his hope for a happy future.

Freddy felt sorry for other children who had abnormal social and psychological behavior like himself, but he thought the doctors incorrectly diagnosed him with autism. Like autistic children, he required more time to read and speak. He specifically had difficulty connecting words to the objects or actions they represented. Unlike children with autism, Freddy felt comfortable making eye contact with people and sensed humor, but chose not to show it. His own peculiar symptom of being unable to associate a voice with a face made his true diagnosis even more complicated. In the end, he chose to live on his own and not categorize himself with any official psychological condition.

Although thoughts about getting a job or going to college filled him with anxiety, he felt confident in his ability to achieve success if he tried. He considered asking for Sadi's advice, but she'd gone to college and calling her caused him to feel too much embarrassment. Did she not want him to contact her anymore? If true, he could not bear to know it. He could not ask her brother. Brian loved music and being in his band more than an education.

The hope of a life without abusive foster parents or the humiliation of school gave him the courage to ask others for help. For the second time in his life, he intentionally turned to his foster care case manager for help. His first attempt failed to result in any help, but he had hope with his new case manager, a friendly Hungarian woman named Malika. At first, she seemed as useless as his first case manager, although not due to apathy. Instead, she just seemed overwhelmed by the high number of cases to manage. Due to his persistence, he managed to become her priority.

Malika had a sister who worked as a housemaid for an old man named Bill Smith. One day her sister needed a quick favor and Malika called Freddy to help. She needed him to help clean the mansion before her boss returned from a trip to visit his son. In the owner's absence, Malika's sister's friends had held a party there and had trashed the place. She needed help cleaning before he returned. She would pay him to help.

Before they finished, however, Bill Smith had returned and enraged, fired Malika's sister, offering the job to Freddy on a temporary basis. After only a single day on the job, however, Bill asked Freddy if he wanted to live there and take care of things for him. Freddy never talked with his foster care parents again.

Even though Bill Smith never gave Freddy any reason to distrust him, Freddy required a long time to feel comfortable with their relationship. Did Mr. Smith genuinely like Freddy, as it seemed? Would repressed anger eventually result in an emotional outrage at Freddy? Over time, his doubts dissipated. At first, his boss always insisted on being addressed as Bill, but after the first six months he quit trying. Freddy would only call him Mr. Smith.

For fear of getting fired, Freddy delayed telling his new boss about his problems. Mr. Smith knew some of Freddy's peculiarities, but not his inability to recognize voices. The first few times Mr. Smith called him from somewhere out of sight, Freddy would never immediately answer. Instead, he would come within eye contact before responding. Mr. Smith refrained from saying anything about the incidents until one day when he called the home and Freddy failed to answer.

When Mr. Smith finally asked for an explanation of the strange behavior, Freddy confessed everything. Instead of the expected angry reaction, Mr. Smith called Freddy's case manager for more information. When she failed to have any knowledge of the issue, Mr. Smith paid for a psychiatrist to come and evaluate Freddy. The psychiatrist determined that Freddy had some extremely rare psychological traits.

"He seems to have a condition similar to what is commonly known as Asperger syndrome," the doctor said in Freddy's presence. "But I hesitate to put him in the same category. Every case is unique. His most interesting symptoms are related to what is known as phonagnosia which is exhibited as an inability to recognize voices that should be familiar. Freddy requires vision to confirm the identity of people he knows."

The psychiatrist also explained how Freddy failed to fit the classic model. In every case the doctor could recall, phonagnosia could be traced to a physical trauma to the head. Freddy, however, showed no signs of such trauma and had no history of it. The psychiatrist wanted to enroll Freddy in a psychiatric research program, but even though Freddy found no reason to refuse, Mr. Smith did.

"He is who he is and he's not going to be a lab rat."

12

Freddy

After his sister went home, Freddy entered his room and took the crystal out of his pocket and placed it on the dresser. He had to push the science fiction novels and a textbook out of the way to make room for the beautiful spider in the crystal. While he dressed in his normal sleeping attire, shorts and a t-shirt, he glanced at himself in the mirror at the head of his bed. His short and almost white hair needed just one good brushing to be tamed and more presentable, but he never had the patience for comprehensive grooming.

Near his door, a spider hung from the ceiling by a linked silver chain. If an intruder ever entered his room, they would first see the hanging arachnid and probably have a heart attack. At least, he hoped they would. He made sure to inform Mr. Smith when he first hung it there.

After looking at the motionless spider pendulum for a moment, he decided to remove it. The new treasure on his dresser made the hanging one seem a bit pathetic in comparison. He slowly untied it and put it in his top drawer with all his other trinkets. When ready for bed, he picked up the crystal and carefully laid down on top of his bed, on the covers without a single wrinkle.

He glanced at the digital clock on the wall and noticed the time, ten twenty-seven. He held the spider up to the light and while twisting it, he watched the light refract through the glass, spilling rainbows onto his shirt and bed.

Upon closer inspection, he noticed numerous eyes on the head and thought they were made of different colors. When he attempted to see them more clearly, however, Freddy experienced a strong sensation similar to vertigo, nearly making him lose consciousness. He only attempted to focus for a few seconds before the intensity forced him to look away. After the feeling passed, he felt different. Something had changed. Something in his environment.

Freddy looked around the room, searching for evidence to validate his suspicion and noticed something strange about the digital clock. He stared at the time for several seconds until he realized the problem. The clock now showed ten forty-five. Freddy had been staring at the spider for eighteen minutes, but he knew the time could not have been longer than a minute. He remembered no thoughts during that time. If anything had happened, his memory of the events had vanished.

"Must be tired", he said to himself.

For the next five minutes, he tried to convince himself of being mistaken. He went to the light switch, turned off the lights and crawled on top of his covers again, holding the spider in his hand.

"You are a strange little thing," he said to his new lifeless pet. He carefully set the crystal on his chest and closed his eyes.

As usual, he fell asleep on top of his covers, on his back. He always woke on his side, but never under the sheets. They needed to be smooth and free of any wrinkles. To him, beds were meant to look undisturbed. He could not fall asleep under wrinkled covers.

While slowly losing consciousness, his mind attempted to rationalize the reason for his sister being so considerate. Never in his life had she ever shown him such generosity. Why did she give the crystal to him? He would have paid a lot of money for the crystal and his sister would have known that. Soon after that thought, he fell asleep. In the darkness of his room, he failed to notice the small light emanating from the eyes of the spider.

13

Freddy

As usual, Freddy woke at least an hour before the sunrise. Light from the street lights filtered through his window, enough for him to see. Almost in a panic, he grabbed the crystal on his chest and slid his fingers over the grooved surface. The glass felt good in his hands and the excitement from its touch helped to wipe sleep from his tired eyes.

Thoughts of running and trying to catch something filled his memory, but the harder he tried to remember, the further away the memory drifted. His awareness of the dream began to evaporate like a thin film of water on a hot surface.

Freddy had an easy job. His official job function of keeping the place clean required the least amount of his time. His employer always cleaned up after himself and hardly ever disturbed anything. Freddy had free reign over the entire house, even Mr. Smith's room. His other responsibilities included cooking, shopping, reading mail and whatever else Mr. Smith wanted of him.

At the start of every day, he made breakfast for them both and they ate together. Mr. Smith liked to have something different every day and had a list of things he liked. Freddy just had to prepare what he wanted from the list.

Mr. Smith came from a long line of rich and influential people. Freddy accepted that fact and never investigated where they acquired their money. He only cared about one thing, his security. As long as he worked for Mr. Smith, money would never be in short supply again. After only a few months of employment, Mr. Smith gave Freddy his own bank account, always to be kept at a balance of one hundred thousand dollars. Freddy never became fully accustomed to the idea, and never had the temptation to take advantage of all the wealth at his disposal. Money seemed to be in endless supply so behaving greedily felt pointless.

"I trust you Freddy," Mr. Smith had said. "This will make it easy for you to take care of things, and you can use it for your own expenses as long as you live with me. I know you won't abuse it."

He never did abuse the trust given to him. He felt too afraid that he might. The possibility always waited in the back of his mind, a fear that Mr. Smith would find something abnormal in the account and he would be fired. Whenever he considered something he wanted or needed, he nearly always consulted Mr. Smith.

Freddy remembered the first time he had felt a desire to buy something.

"Freddy, why don't you go get that telescope you were looking at the other day. It is a fine idea to study the sky. Astronomy is a worthy pursuit."

Freddy had found the logic to be sound and did not dare disagree.

His boss even seemed to enjoy indulging Freddy's interests. Over the three years in his employ, Freddy had accumulated three different telescopes, several computers, and a well-equipped laboratory with microscopes and many other analyzers. If he wanted, he could have even bought himself a car, but he already had access to any of the three cars at the mansion.

So far, college remained Freddy's largest expense. He felt guilty about the drain on his account, but Mr. Smith insisted they were just part of his wages. With Mr. Smith's recommendation, Freddy had no trouble getting into college. As a former Cabinet member to President Lyndon B. Johnson, Mr. Smith's recommendation helped guarantee a spot into almost any college. In order to stay in Mr. Smith's employ, however, he needed to choose a college in the city so he chose Portland State University.

"An education is more about the effort you put into it," Mr. Smith explained. "And less about where you go. If you work hard, you can get a fine education at just about any university."

Motivated partly by his interest in spiders and partly by Sadi Jacobsen, Freddy chose to major in biology. He had a great interest in biological organisms like animals, plants and insects, but he found the cellular level and beyond to be of more interest. In his free time, he liked exploring through his microscopes and telescopes. In both activities, he wished more than anything to find something, a secret of life which might help him understand the purpose of his being. Maybe the secrets lay hidden inside living cells, the basic structure of life, or in deep space and they could only be detected by enhancing normal human senses through the use of instruments. He loved exploring so much, it became an obsession.

As a side effect, he found friends on the internet, friends who only existed in cyberspace and from all over the world. He felt no particular connection to any of them and considered most of them as too immature. He enjoyed talking to them about science and technology, but never social topics.

He secretly played games online with his friends, games like chess, go, and a few role-playing video games, but he kept those activities from Mr. Smith who might think the time was wasted. He might lower his opinion of Freddy. Now that he had the crystal, he had two secrets from his employer.

He continued rubbing his fingers over the grooved crystal surface for a few more moments, then put the crystal in his clothes drawer under his socks. Although he felt no real concern that Mr. Smith would find it, he hated the thought of leaving the object exposed. Sometimes Mr. Smith had visitors and maybe one of them would take a tour of his domain, the entire lower level. Freddy did not trust some of Mr. Smith's guests.

After breakfast, Mr. Smith gave him an update about all the tasks he needed to be accomplished that day, then Freddy went to his classes. Neither of them mentioned anything about the previous evening.

For the two hours between his morning class and afternoon laboratory, Freddy studied in the college library. He had two tasks to perform in the library that day, his homework for biochemistry and to find some astronomy books for Mr. Smith. Freddy's interest in the subject inspired Mr. Smith to study astronomy himself.

Before Freddy bought his telescopes and special cameras, he used to show his boss images from the Hubble Telescope on the internet. The images impressed the old man, but, when he first saw Orion's belt with his own eyes through a telescope, he became an addict like Freddy.

14

Gerald

"Don't worry," Gerald said reassuringly once she closed the door to his car. "The man from Mexico I want to include in our plan is not an illegal."

He hoped to relieve Taylor's anxiety about the Mexican. She sat in the passenger seat and they talked while waiting for the car to get warm. A light rain pelted the window and scattered the lights of the restaurant signs on Taylor's face. He paused to admire the view.

"Actually," he continued. "He's more of a political refugee. He used to be the governor of a large Mexican city. You should hear his story. It should be a feature film."

"A political refugee?"

"I'll let him tell the story, but it has something to do with a drug cartel and their candidate who ran against him."

She looked concerned. "Is he in, any danger? I mean, are people still after him?"

"I don't know, but he doesn't seem to be worried about it. I think you'll like him, personally and professionally."

"What do you mean?"

"Well, he runs his own machine shop. You like making things. He likes making things. He has a lot of customers from the local Mexican population as well as several large manufacturers. He's doing really well."

She leaned forward, interested.

"So what makes you trust him."

"He shares our views, and he's very passionate about it. If I remember right, his son and wife were killed by the drug cartels. It's very sad. He hates the 'War on Drugs', I mean the war to keep drugs extremely profitable. He has direct experience with the real drug war, not the story they tell on the news."

"Oh my God! Poor guy! What's his name?"

"Cesar Sanchez. He's an older gentleman and lives in Seattle with some friends, only about thirty minutes away from me."

"Before we tell him anything, I need to meet him first." Her eyes widened, challenging him to argue. "You say we can trust him, but I just need to see for myself. It's my baby and I call the shots."

He had no intention of arguing with her. On the contrary, he felt honored to be part of her discovery. Even more, her lack of arguments gave him hope for including Cesar in their plans.

"I promise," he said, "that I won't reveal anything to anyone without your prior approval."

Since she wanted to meet with Cesar personally, Gerald said he would arrange the meeting as soon as possible. He had to stay in Portland that night, but would call in the morning.

They talked for another hour, mostly about all that would be needed for a temporary visit into space. At Gerald's request, they took money constraints out of the picture. Taylor never had much money in her life, so she worried more about money than Gerald. To him, acquiring the money became just another task, another easy hill to climb.

As he explained, they merely needed to recruit the right people and then, there would be plenty of access to money. Keeping her invention a secret while they prepared seemed to be the real problem. Even if they only recruited people whom they could completely trust, it would still be a major danger. The probability of exposure increased exponentially with more people aware of the secret.

Without any conscious effort, Gerald started planning ahead. With more people, they would need a way to communicate. They both considered communication by telephone and normal email as too insecure. Their project needed a secure website and Gerald had a friend who could build one for them. He planned to ask for Taylor's permission after meeting with his friend from Mexico.

Their conversation ended for the evening and she agreed to meet his friend. Gerald would contact her again in the morning. After she drove home, Gerald checked into a hotel. For almost two hours that night, he laid on the bed in a futile attempt to sleep. How could he sleep after being part of possibly the most important development of the millennium? Even with his limited and incomplete understanding of the implications, he knew his life would never be the same again. He liked the feeling.

The more he thought about her inventions, the more his excitement grew. After a long time, sleep finally overpowered him. He dreamed of leaving the Earth, traveling into the cosmos and finding the freedom he so much wanted. No more being forced to pay for war, massacre, or some dictator of the third-world. No more force-fed democracy. No more IRS. In space, he would be completely free.

15

Gerald

When Gerald awoke the next morning, he called his friend Cesar Sanchez and asked if he could visit with a friend. Then he drove to Taylor's house.

"So, our story is that I have a shop project for Cesar," Taylor said after they pulled onto interstate five, heading north towards Seattle. Taylor repeated Gerald's plan about how they would approach Cesar, without letting him know of their true intentions. "And I want to go over the plans with him."

Just in case she felt uncomfortable letting Cesar know of their secret, Taylor brought some drawings for another project she planned to do one day. Gerald said he would pay for the decoy project if that happened. It worked either way for Taylor.

On their drive, they talked more about the idea of traveling into orbit than they did about her invention. She seemed excited about the possibility, but Gerald thought she might just be humoring him. She had a lot of concerns about traveling in space and knew more about the requirements of surviving in an environment of total vacuum, conditions where the only thing standing between the passenger and death is a leak-tight design, a very expensive design. While listening to her, he also began to have doubts.

He loved that aspect about her. While his head floated in the clouds, she kept her feet on the ground. Yet, she also needed him, someone to disregard seemingly debilitating obstacles. To Gerald, the specifics of a project or the costs were of little concern. He had his own philosophy. 'Where there's a will, there's a way!' He could always find someone intelligent enough to fine-tune the details and they could always find someone with money.

"If we were actually forced to escape into space," he said.

"And we survived," Taylor interjected.

"NASA and all the other government agencies would probably have a nasty panic attack," he said with a sarcastic sneer. "We would be viewed as a security risk. Bureaucrats and government officials would not want potentially dangerous people in orbit above them, people with a chip on their shoulder from the damage inflicted by their corrupt government."

"How would they get the IRS to collect their precious taxes?" Taylor asked with thick sarcasm.

"True."

The idea of requiring permission to leave the planet infuriated him. Who were they to require permission? Thoughts of all the permits, taxes and special permissions required by government always caused him intense anger.

Even if they had to change their plan, Gerald had faith in their combined talents. *You'll find a way*, his mother always said and then one of her other sayings materialized in his memory. *The future is dark, but just until it arrives.*

"Too bad we can't just go live on the moon or Mars or find another solar system to live in somewhere," Taylor said and sighed. "Now the cost of that would be out of our reach, no matter how much of your fluffy optimism you threw at it. Even if we were able to carry enough fuel to visit another solar system, the probability of finding an inhabitable planet is practically zero."

During the subsequent pause in their conversation, Gerald's thoughts filled with the possibility of other inhabitable planets. As they entered Seattle, Gerald turned to Taylor and saw her watching the Space Needle coming into view.

"So, if you believe there are more planets like Earth out there, does that imply that you believe in aliens?" Never in his entire life, had Gerald seriously considered aliens, until that moment.

"In my opinion," she said without looking in his direction. "The existence of other inhabitable planets is nearly certain, but reaching one? The nearest star is something like five light-years away. The probability of alien existence seems pretty certain to me, considering how many galaxies exist and how we happen to live on a life-containing planet out of only a handful in the solar system."

"Do you think aliens are in contact with anyone on the Earth?" he asked.

She laughed. "Who's the conspiracy theorist now?"

"I'm serious."

"Gerald, aliens aren't going to help us. We have to figure this out on our own."

He decided to stop talking about aliens and keep his thoughts on the subject to himself. Later, he would try to discover if some credible evidence existed, on his own. He had always just assumed the many alleged cover-ups about aliens to be either an unfounded theory or a government disinformation, a diversion from other issues.

On the phone with Cesar that morning, they agreed to meet at his machine shop. He usually only worked Monday through Friday, but had projects to prepare for the next week and would be working that Saturday morning. Gerald had never visited Cesar at his work. If Cesar needed anything, he usually visited Gerald's law office in downtown Seattle.

As they approached the machine shop in one of the industrial districts, near a waterfront, Gerald's anxiety developed into an intense urge to get out of the vehicle and start using his leg muscles. Did Taylor feel the same before meeting him the previous night? Probably worse.

The GPS unit in his car used a female voice that made Gerald feel on edge, but he felt relieved when 'she' said they reached their destination. He recognized the red brick shop from Cesar's description, a two-story building across the street from an old diner. An ornate tin sign hung over the main double-doors. 'The Stainless Forest'. They drove around to the back parking lot next to the only other vehicle, an old Ford truck.

After walking through the entrance a small crystal bell rang. They stopped at a large front counter with the large stainless steel top littered with papers, blueprints and a scattering of pens and rulers. Gerald noticed the displeased look on Taylor's face, probably from all the messiness. Vaguely, he remembered her complaining of people she felt were unclean and disorganized. Gerald knew his friend would repair any negative impression Taylor had that moment.

A door behind the counter opened and an older man walked into the room. Beyond the door, Gerald saw into an immense shop.

16

Gerald

"Good to see you Cesar," Gerald said in a happy tone. "Como Estas?"

Gerald extended his hand in greeting. The old man squeezed hard.

Taylor smiled at Gerald's attempt at Spanish. Even Gerald knew he sounded horrible, almost like he intentionally tried to speak with an exaggerated Northwestern accent.

"Bien, Bien," Cesar replied, the tone of his words contrasting strongly with Gerald's forced accent. He turned to Taylor. "And you must be Miss Ewell."

Gray strands streaked through Cesar's coarse black hair and the lighter hair made his black eyes appear even darker. He stood slightly taller than Taylor, but much shorter than Gerald who stood about six feet two inches.

Although Cesar had always been kind and hospitable, his eyes reminded Gerald of a mafia king on a Godfather movie. He had the eyes of a man who demanded respect from those around him, even if the man held a gun to his head.

Gerald turned to Taylor, to see her response at meeting Cesar. She extended her hand confidently in response to his gesture and Cesar completely enveloped her hand in his. When Cesar shook Taylor's hand, her whole body quivered slightly. Gerald felt pleased to see the genuine smile on her face.

"Strong grip, for a girl," he said and smiled. He turned her hand over to see her palm. "Not too soft either."

"Thank you, sir," she said. "I always try to return what's given."

"So, you say you have some kind of job for me," the man said as he turned and motioned for them to follow him. "Come in the back and we'll talk about it. You can show me your plans."

They went into the back shop area. Unlike the counter in the front area, Cesar kept the shop clean and uncluttered. The whole time, Gerald kept one eye on Taylor and one on Cesar. He paid little attention to the machines in the shop, or their condition, although he had difficulty ignoring the pungent odor of burning metal which reminded him of fireworks.

As they walked past all the machines, Taylor reminded Gerald of a cat in a mouse factory, on an invisible leash. Her eyes were almost as wide as her smile. She seemed to have difficulty walking past each item without stopping for an inspection.

After winding through the shop, they entered an office in the back. The walls of the room were lined with shelves and covered with books and rolls of blueprints. To Gerald, the office looked cozy and relaxed, like a refuge away from home.

A large painting hung on the wall directly opposite his desk, intended to view while sitting. The portrait showed Cesar with a lady at his side, two boys who looked like twins about fourteen years old and a teenage girl. All the children had their father's blunt nose, but no other similar feature. Gerald saw a resemblance to the mother in the high cheek bone of each child. He had no doubt as to who gave birth to each child. Gerald considered her more regal than beautiful, like an ancient Greek statue. He found beauty in delicacy and she looked tough like Cesar.

Cesar sat down at the desk behind a seventeen inch laptop.

“Before we go over what you want of me, I just have a few questions for you,” he said and his smile disappeared.

Gerald felt a tinge of dread. Cesar turned the laptop around and displayed the results of a Google search with 'Taylor Ewell', 'Washington State', and 'mechanical' typed in the search field. There were several results.

Taylor looked only briefly at the screen, then back to Cesar.

“There I am,” she said in the mocking tone of someone proud of their popularity. “So, what did you discover?”

She asked her question with calm curiosity. When Gerald had first met Cesar, he'd felt slightly intimidated. Something about Cesar kept him and everyone at full alert, but Taylor seemed impervious to intimidation.

“Well, the first thing I discovered, was that your team won the best alternative fuel car contest in 2007 and you were the team leader.” He stumbled over the word ‘discovered’, and his accent gave special emphasis to it. “The announcement said that you showed amazing promise.”

A slight smile swept across Taylor’s face, but disappeared almost as fast.

“Yeah,” she said. “That was fun.”

Cesar still did not smile. Gerald wondered if he acted impressed or angry.

“After digging a little more, I found that when your father was alive, he used to have his own machine shop, and it’s still in operation, but under different ownership. For what you want to do, could you just use that?”

“I could have but we need something especially complicated and Gerald said he knew the perfect man for the job, you.”

Cesar smiled again at the compliment.

“So do you often consult with Gerald for technical matters?” he asked.

Gerald could see where Cesar intended to turn the conversation. He wanted to interject, but the look from Taylor stopped him. In a small way, he started to enjoy the show and wondered how long Taylor would perform her act. At the moment, she looked sincerely amused.

"Gerald and I talk all the time and we happened to talk about this project of mine."

Cesar turned to Gerald.

"So what is this project she wants me to do?"

An embarrassed smile involuntarily and slowly spread across his face. While attempting to remember what Taylor said, she laughed.

“Damn Google!” She slowly shook her head and looked at Gerald accusingly. "It was Gerald's idea. Not mine."

“Cesar, let me explain,” Gerald started to say, but Taylor held up her hand to stop him.

"Not yet," Taylor said, turning to Gerald then back to Cesar. He swiveled the laptop so that only he could see the screen again. He sat back in his chair and waited, eyebrows raised.

"Mr. Sanchez, I apologize for the subterfuge. Normally, I would come out in the open at the very start, but our friend here has his own way of doing things. Maybe it's just how lawyers think? Anyhow, I wanted to get to know you, to determine if I wanted to share something with you. We do have a job for you, but I'm not sure you'd be willing to do it, or if we can trust you."

As Cesar sat forward, his smile finally returned. His demeanor changed from accusatory to sincerely curious.

"Miss Ewell. Do you want to know what I thought when Gerald called me?"

"Of course."

"My good friend Gerald Fuger, the man who helped me set my business and new home in this country, a man who has a true understanding of the world, wants to introduce me to a brilliant, young engineer who wants me to help her make a machine, one that could most likely be made by herself. Just from the tone of your voice Gerald, I knew you were hiding something. I've actually looked forward to this all morning. Frankly, I was disappointed you thought it would be that easy to fool me."

In anticipation of her reply, both Cesar and Gerald looked at Taylor. Under the scrutiny from those intimidating personalities, most other girls of her age would have folded, but not Taylor. She hesitated only a few moments before responding.

"So what do we do now?" she asked. "Our true purpose cannot be shared with just anyone."

"Of course Miss Ewell. This is obviously very important to you and I don't want to rush you, although you have my curiosity caught on a hook." He turned his gaze from her to his laptop screen and seemed to be lost in thought for a moment. After closing the computer, he continued. "Let's do this. Come to my house, we'll relax, have lunch and talk. You can meet my friends and we can go from there."

"Sounds like a great plan," Gerald said without any hesitation.

He'd hoped the initial meeting at the shop would end like it did. In reality, he'd put only minimal effort into fooling Cesar. He knew they would eventually get to their true intentions. Normally, Taylor would have instantly rejected his plan, but anxiety had probably corrupted her judgment. He wanted to emphasize the importance of what they wanted to share. Besides, he'd wanted to see how Taylor reacted when backed into a corner.

Again, they both turned to Taylor. She smiled and agreed.

17

Freddy

That evening Freddy walked in the front door to find Mr. Smith sitting in the drawing room, in a chair by the piano. After shutting the door, Mr. Smith looked up from his magazine.

"How was school? Come sit down."

He motioned for Freddy to sit opposite him, on the couch.

"Class was good. We finished up a laboratory project that we have been working on." Freddy put his backpack down on the floor next to him and the pile of books he had picked up at the library. "My partner was absent so I had to do everything myself. Very rude. Very rude."

"Thanks for the books," Mr. Smith said with a quick glance at them.

"You are welcome."

"I wanted to give you some warning about tomorrow," Mr. Smith said and looked directly into Freddy's eyes. "We will have a visitor. My son is coming."

"When will he be leaving?" Freddy asked, trying to hide his anxiety.

"Oh, he'll be leaving tomorrow night. I'm just telling you so that you might want to stay out of sight." He shook his head in irritation. "I don't like having to suggest something like that, but just like last time, I don't think he'll be too friendly. I apologize again for his behavior."

During his last visit, Mr. Smith's son had yelled at both of them when he discovered that his father paid for the boy's schooling. He spent some time attempting to accentuate the difference between Mr. Smith and his support staff. His father needed to emotionally separate himself from Freddy and other people socially below him. He even suggested that Freddy would attempt to manipulate his employer in his old age.

Freddy remembered the incident with pain and shame. After being away from traumatic social experiences for so long, he'd felt totally unprepared for the contentious encounter. He'd just stood as if in a trance and listened to father and son argue over him, among other topics. He had never seen Mr. Smith so angry and it scared Freddy. After the incident, Freddy thought his time with Mr. Smith had come to an end, but after his son departed all had returned to normal.

Mr. Smith's relationship with his son stood on unstable ground already and Freddy merely added fuel to that fire. Mr. Smith explained how his son always looked for reasons to argue with him and encouraged Freddy not to take the negative sentiments toward him personally. Had Freddy been absent from the scene, Mr. Smith's son would have argued about something else. Freddy required almost three days to forget the pain of the encounter and feel normal again.

"It's my fault really," Mr. Smith said, shaking his head in disappointment and sorrow. "He's grown up just like I raised him. I cannot blame him for who he is."

Mr. Smith spent a lot of time explaining the situation to Freddy. He seemed to give the impression that he regretted almost his entire life and wished to recompense the world for his mistakes. Several times in the past, Mr. Smith had attempted to convince his son where his pathway would lead, but those efforts resulted only in more resentment and anger towards his father. There seemed to be no love between them. Freddy understood that situation very well.

In Mr. Smith's opinion, most of the contention originated from one motivation. His son wanted Mr. Smith to sell him the remainder of his shares in their company and relinquish control. Freddy lacked the background in business to understand the specifics. The situation sounded like something he might see in a movie or television drama.

"You've lived your life, father," Freddy remembered his son saying before leaving. "Now step out of the way and let me live mine."

That night around 18:30, Freddy's smartphone started vibrating, a notification from the front gate of someone pushing the call button. Receiving a phone call from the inanimate object would normally cause Freddy to smile, but the potential identity of the man at the gate only caused anxiety. After peeking out the second story window, he recognized the black sedan which contained the unwelcome visitor. A heavy rain sliced through the lights from the street and reflected off the shiny black surface. Freddy silently signaled for the gate to open and then hurried to Mr. Smith's room to tell him of his son's arrival. Then he ran to the basement, shut the door at the bottom of the stairs and held his ear close to it.

The son reached the front door before his father and Freddy heard the doorbell ring. Normally, Freddy would welcome visitors, but Mr. Smith had said that he would open the door for his son. He listened for a few moments through the door, and then walked to his room after failing to understand the muffled speech.

If they went to the drawing room or dining room, Freddy had the option of listening to their entire conversation with clarity. After his first few months at the house, Mr. Smith had given amused permission for Freddy to install hidden microphones in different spots throughout the house. He had motivations other than spying. He loved working with electronic devices and connecting them to computers. On that night, however, he wanted to avoid hearing negative comments about himself.

Freddy shut his door and decided to postpone energizing the ceiling lights. Due to the heavy blinds and curtains covering the windows, his room darkened much earlier than outside. Freddy liked the feel of the dark. The dark provided cover, protection from harm. The only light came from all the electronic equipment that he had accumulated during his time there. The LED lights made his room feel like a mixture of scenes from a science fiction novel and Christmas.

He owned two desktop computers, one for gaming and one for his school work. They both sat on his large wooden desk and close enough to use simultaneously. More LED light came from a thirty-two-inch flat screen, with accompanying DVD player. He had contemplated getting the Xbox game system from Microsoft, but his classes, job and other interests like astronomy and cell biology consumed most of his time. He decided to limit his gaming excursions exclusively to personal computers with sufficient graphics capabilities.

After convincing himself that no one would be visiting his room, he released the door handle and went to his dresser, the one containing the crystal. He had been wanting to hold it again, but did not have the chance until then. When he saw the two-dimensional spider within the glass, he felt the excitement of the previous night return. Holding the crystal in his hand felt like satisfying a secret addiction.

The surface felt cool to the touch and Freddy tossed it carefully from one hand to the other, enjoying the feel of its weight. A feeling of paranoia slowly began to creep into his thoughts and he felt like Frodo Baggins from *The Lord of the Rings* novels. No one else should see his new possession.

Suddenly, and for the first time that day, he remembered the suspicious event from the previous evening, his loss of memory before going to sleep. How could he have forgotten about that? He decided to try to repeat the phenomenon, to convince himself that the event had actually happened, or if he had fallen asleep.

He failed to see the need for extreme magnification, so he grabbed a simple magnifying glass. After securing the object with two small laboratory vices, he positioned one of his digital cameras so that light from the crystal surface would travel through the magnifying glass into the camera lens. He then connected the camera to his computer which showed the image on the screen. After focusing the image, he could begin examining the head. No matter what technique he tried, Freddy failed to get a sharp image of the spider eyes. He only managed to get a rainbow blur.

"Impossible," he said and then moved the crystal so that the focus shifted to the spider's abdomen. He had no problem focusing on any other part of the spider. "It is all in the same plane, so why can I not get it to focus?"

In frustration, he took the magnifying glass in his hand and put the crystal under it on the table. Under the light of the lamp, he examined the rock which claimed to be from space, and then the eyes of the spider. For the third time since acquiring the object, his vision became blurry while attempting to focus on the eyes. In sudden surprise, he found himself staring at a black computer screen. His room had become dark again, with LED lights as the only light source again.

"What was that," he said quietly, shaking his head and looking at the time. It was ten minutes after seven. Apparently, he'd just blacked out again and this time for at least twenty minutes, long enough for his computer screen to go to sleep.

He left the crystal on the desk and sat down in his leather office chair. After concentrating as hard as possible, he failed to remember one moment from the blackout episode, no dream, no image in his mind or impression, nothing. He had to be scientific about the investigation in order to eliminate the possibility of the root cause being merely his imagination.

"There has to be a test I can do," he said to himself as he swiveled back and forth on the chair. Before devising a more detailed plan, he decided to ask his sister about the crystal origin just one more time. In calling her, he risked the possibility of giving her an excuse for another visit, but he would take that risk. Other than his sister, Freddy had no other physical link to the crystal.

With considerable anxiety, he dialed his sister's phone number and then waited for three unanswered rings.

"Spider?" A female voice answered in an uncertain and impatient tone. "What do you want?"

"Hey Wands," said Freddy. "I wanted to thank you for the crystal."

"What crystal?" she asked with more impatience. "What are you talking about?"

"The crystal you gave me?"

"I don't have any crystals, and if I did, I wouldn't give them to you." The tone reminded him of her normal abrasive personality, unlike the previous night when she acted almost nice. "You've got everything you could ever dream of so why would I give you anything? Is this all you called me about? I'm busy."

Freddy felt another wave of irrational paranoia. Perhaps a friend of his sister's friends had answered the phone again, making fun of him and now she knew the secret word? No, Wanda would not do that to him again, not after so many years. He needed to think rationally and trust his judgment. The girl spoke with his sister's tone and attitude and she used the code word. She had to be his sister.

In order to prevent more anger or frustration from his sister, Freddy decided to stop the conversation. After the phone call, he would consider its meaning.

"Sorry Wands." he said, attempting to sound sincerely apologetic. "I must have been thinking of something else."

Wanda spared him the need for any more groveling by wordlessly cutting the connection.

18

Freddy

Freddy energized his computer again and followed his habit of recording all his observations and thoughts so he could see how they looked in the real world. He used the Notepad program on his computer and made a simple numbered list of everything he could recall. Since his mind had the tendency to race faster than he could remember, typing his thoughts helped to keep all the major pieces of the puzzle, right in front of him.

"Yes," he said triumphantly as an idea came to him.

He would record his blackout episodes on video, if he had any more. Deep down, he wanted the video to show nothing happening. He went to another room in his basement level and retrieved his digital camcorder. He silently opened the doors so Mr. Smith and his son upstairs could not hear him. He heard a faint murmur of human voices, but ignored them.

Freddy placed the camera on the desk in the optimal position to record video and then tested it on the computer. The image showed just as expected. He remembered to change the screensaver settings on his computer to an hour so it would not interrupt the experiment.

"This is ridiculous," he said to himself, almost loud enough to be heard through the closed door. "Nothing is going to happen. It is just a trinket, an inanimate object."

Lower in his conscious thoughts, Freddy wished to be mistaken, and yet feared the implications of being right.

He started the recording at thirty-three minutes after seven and looked at himself in the computer screen, at his profile in the camera. His pupils seemed larger than normal. For a brief moment, he felt as though someone else looked back at him. He took a deep breath and then looked down to the crystal, at the spider just a few inches away from his face. Like his previous experiences, the more he tried to focus, the fuzzier the eyes became. This time he tried harder and the effort actually hurt his eyes.

While concentrating, Freddy felt something like a blip in his mind, as if the scene changed slightly. He tore his gaze away from the crystal and looked to his watch which showed seven fifty-seven. He slowly reached over and picked up the camcorder and turned it off. Time seemed to be moving slowly as he moved and clicked on the video player, to the beginning. Instead of pushing play, however, he spent a moment staring at the still photo of his green eyes staring away from the camera.

Before pushing play, a new fear washed over him. What if he saw something disturbing in the video? The possibility seemed highly likely. After a moment, however, his hesitation passed and he decided to stop thinking and just push play. Sometimes, thinking hindered progress. Sometimes, he just had to move forward. After holding his finger over the left mouse button, he clicked play and learned how he spent the last twenty minutes.

His last memory involved trying to focus on the spider eyes. What happened next caused more surprise than fear. His eyes became very wide, as if he saw something unbelievable. Freddy watched as his eyes stayed open the entire time, only blinking in very long intervals. He felt strange watching a close-up of his face staring at the crystal.

For the first thirty seconds or so, nothing happened. Slowly, however, from inside the crystal, blue-orange lights began to shine onto his face. Despite the intensifying blue and orange lights, his face remained expressionless, unnaturally still. Chills raced through his body and he started to feel paranoid, afraid that some ghost would shoot out of the computer screen.

He turned his attention from his face to the source of the light inside the crystal. Instead of the light shining out homogeneously like a flashlight, the orange light seemed to focus on his eyes like several thin laser beams, and diffuse blue light mostly spread evenly over his face. In another situation, perhaps he would have considered the light to be beautiful, but the entire scene felt disturbing. The majority of the light seemed to emanate from the eyes of the spider, as if millions of multicolored LED's shone from that one spot.

He pushed pause on the video and stared at the still picture. Why did he have no memory of the events? The unknown scared him the most. His imagination could create more nightmares than reality could possibly generate. He thought of all the crazy alien abduction stories of when they wipe your memory clean after finishing with their horrible experiments. He had always depended on his memory, but now he had to depend on this video.

Where did his sister get the crystal and why did she have no memory of giving it to him? Did she have a similar experience of losing her memory? What if the memory of how she acquired the crystal only happened in her head? Too many other questions fought for his consideration. In the end, he only made one conclusion.

Someone wanted him to have the crystal.

Freddy pushed play and sat forward to watch the remainder of the video. For several minutes, the lights flashed and swirled, and for the entire time he remained perfectly still. He disliked seeing himself in a trance. Any second, he imagined his head turning to the camera and smiling strangely, but it never happened. Would watching the lights on the recorded video, cause him to fall into another trance? Fortunately, the lights on the computer screen failed to have the same effect as the spider eyes. The rest of the video showed him in the same trance-like state. At the very end, the lights just turned off and his consciousness resumed.

When done watching the video, Freddy noticed the darkness of his room again. He felt as if he had just watched a horror movie. Suddenly, he felt a strong urge to turn on the lights, to extinguish his eerie feelings, but before he could move, another light came to life. The crystal began to shine orange and blue.

Without thinking, he looked to the source of the light and the room disappeared. The light immersed Freddy in nothingness.

Freddy opened his eyes and found himself standing in darkness. Without being able to see, however, he felt the emptiness, the freedom. He stood in a plane stretching to eternity in every direction. The hard, flat surface became the only concrete sensation. He felt no air and saw no source of light.

Fortunately, his memory seemed to be intact. Memory helped provide orientation, like gravity connected his feet to the ground. He remembered his room and the video, but the events of the day seemed to have occurred a long time in the past, as if his life felt like a dream and he just reawakened to reality.

While standing in the darkness, Freddy turned his head in a vain attempt to see something. As he expected, he saw nothing and then wondered if he should be afraid. He spent a moment reflecting on his emotional state and found himself to be free of all fear and anxiety. Should he be afraid? Probably, but why force himself to feel something that failed to come naturally? He stood in the room without walls and felt as though patiently waiting for a movie or play to begin. Did the spider eyes transport him to this plane when attempting to focus on them?

After a long time of standing silently, the floor slowly began to be illuminated. At first, he failed to notice the transformation. It happened so slowly, like when the sun rose in the morning. When the light became bright enough, he found himself standing on what looked like beautiful black marble.

When he noticed his shadow extending several meters in front of him, he turned and saw a single star rising in the black sky. A bright orange and blue star rose from the horizon, becoming larger the higher it went. The intensity of the light grew and grew until the radiation would have vaporized the retina in his natural eyes. He watched in amazement and wanted to look at the beautiful object forever.

After a long time, he turned to survey his surroundings to see if anything existed in the distance. As he guessed, the horizon stretched to infinity and only his shadow, the ground and the star existed with him.

When the voice spoke in his head, he almost expected it.

"There's nowhere to run," the voice said in a sarcastic tone. "And there's everywhere to run."

When he returned his gaze to the sky, to the orange and blue star, he noticed a group of lights. Thousands of colored points of light hovered in the horizon. As they moved towards him, they remained dimensionless, just points of colored light. After a while, they stopped and hovered several meters above his head. He could not see them distinctly and when he tried to focus on a single point, it became a blurry rainbow haze with its neighbors.

An instant later, the lights extended into two dimensions and became familiar shapes, two eyes, a nose and lips painted against the black sky. Instead of round eyes, they were oval with the pupil shaped like the cross between a human and a cat. The colorful face floated above him and continually transformed into the faces of different people he knew. The face appeared to be alive and stared at Freddy with blinking eyes.

"Hello," Freddy said tentatively, but instantly regretted speaking. Sound felt like an intruder in the silent world and seemed to cause shock waves in his mind. He had to wait a few moments for the reverberations to stop. When he spoke again, he whispered very quietly. "What are you? Where am I?"

As if mocking him, the mouth in the sky silently repeated Freddy's words. When finished with the parody, the facial features exploded into the colorful swarm of lights and instantly began another transformation. The lights coalesced into a recognizable three-dimensional image. A massive glowing ball of fire formed first and became the center of the image. Then other objects materialized, the planets.

Freddy could see each heavenly body distinctly. Mercury appeared. Venus appeared. Then the Earth appeared with the gray moon circling it. Next came Mars, then the gas giants of Jupiter, Saturn, Uranus and Neptune. For a long time, he watched as they all orbited the brilliant sun. He could even feel the sun's radiation on his face and exposed skin.

Watching the solar system put him into a semi-conscious trance. He could have spent the rest of his life watching the scene of lights. He marveled at the complex cloud formations above the Earth and repeating cycles of the polar ice caps melting and reforming. He watched the hostility of Venus, the desolation of Mars, the beautiful rings of the gas giants and the great storms on Jupiter.

The events he witnessed would have taken thousands of years in real time. He watched until the voice broke the silence.

"Freddy," a voice said behind him.

The voice sounded small like the whisper of a distant wind, but felt like an explosion to his other senses. Freddy turned from the solar system above him to see a bright point of light flying away from him into the distance. The light grew dimmer until it dipped into the horizon and disappeared. Then Freddy heard the sound of footsteps from the same direction.

After a long while of listening to the movement, the noise materialized into the form of a woman walking toward him from very far away. He first noticed the long dark hair falling over a white shirt. She wore what looked like simple blue jeans. When he recognized the woman, his heart stopped. His friend from late childhood moved gracefully towards him, a woman named Sadi Jacobsen, the woman who occupied so many of his dreams and fantasies.

She seemed to walk forever in his direction and Freddy began to consider her movement even more intoxicating than watching the solar system. She eventually stopped in front of him. Her dark hair swayed as if from an underwater current he could not feel. When she stopped, he became aware of his beating heart. It pounded too hard for him to say anything so he just watched and waited for her to speak.

She smiled and appeared to be studying him.

"Who are you?" he asked after taking a deep breath.

"That's a funny way to greet someone you know so well, Spider." She smiled and turned her head slightly. "I know you remember me."

19

Freddy

"You are not Sadi Jacobsen," he said.

She walked slowly around him, and looked up to the suspended inner solar system. "It's beautiful. Isn't it?"

"Yes. It is."

Although Freddy wanted to turn back to the beautiful scene, he had difficulty looking away from the woman. She was just as he remembered when they first met.

"It can show you whatever you want," she said while keeping her gaze on the sky. Her words felt like an invitation to make a wish. Did she mean the swarm of lights above them or the crystal he faced in the real world?

"What is in the eyes of the spider?" he asked. "Why does it make me lose my memory?"

She turned from the hovering solar system and stepped very close to him, stopping with her face inches away from his. Instead of meeting his eyes, she inspected his face from different angles, moving slowly from left to right. He could feel her warm breath on his face. It smelled of cinnamon. His heartbeat began rising again.

"Am I upsetting you?" she asked, her lips inches from his chin.

Although she appeared to be an exact replica of Sadi Jacobsen, her eyes were not human. He had the impression of looking into the eyes of a dangerous predator like an owl or a hawk, as if a sinister and unpredictable presence stood before him. At any moment, her intoxicating smile might disappear and be replaced by fangs.

"You do not upset me," he said, while fighting the urge to retreat. "What do you want with me?"

She backed away as if conscious of her effect on him. "I've been searching for something like you."

"Why me?"

"You're different," she said and her smile disappeared.

People usually called him "creep", "retard", or "freak", but the way she said *different* felt like a compliment. She walked slowly around him again, like someone would inspect a statue at a museum.

"You are accessible," she said after orbiting him completely and arriving back at his face. "And uncorrupted."

Her answer meant nothing to him. More than anything, he wanted to know her identity, but he feared the answer.

"That does not make any sense," he said with as much confidence as possible, hoping to cover his anxiety. "You do not want me."

She stopped walking around him and stood just behind his head. He heard the mocking tone in her voice and her warm breath on his neck. "Yes I do," she whispered.

"Will you answer my questions please?" he asked after the hot and cold sensation passed. He used all his frustration and fear to energize the demand. "What is the crystal?"

"That was very clever of you, to use, the computer," she said, walking around to the front of him again. "You earned intervention."

He waited.

"The crystal is a beautiful gift. Is it not?"

"Yes, but what is it?"

"Think of it as a mirror," she answered bluntly. "And a lens."

He thought for a moment. A lens focused light. A mirror reflected light. What did the crystal bring into focus? What kind of light did it reflect? The opportunity to search his mind for answers helped alleviate his anxiety at being in her presence.

"Am I the only one able to use the crystal?" he asked.

Being chosen brought a sense of pride, and also fear that the crystal might be taken away if he failed to satisfy the creature in front of him. As Freddy thought about his feelings, he became suspicious. Did she put the thought in his head or did he think of it himself?

She continued looking in his eyes and seemed to be in no hurry to respond.

"You don't really want me to answer all your questions do you?" she asked. "What's the fun of that?"

"You want me to have fun?" he asked, feeling sudden disappointment. His question seemed to float in the space between them and he realized that she would not be answering his questions. She would be asking him the questions.

Her next actions threw an ice-cold knife into his chest.

"You desire this woman?" she asked and put her right hand over her collarbone. He gulped at the sight of her cleavage, showing just above the gap in her v-neck, white t-shirt. While sounding like a simple question, her words also felt like a statement or accusation. She seemed to want his verbal confirmation.

'That is none of your business', he wanted to say, but the response seemed trite, something said in a normal conversation, not in a dream.

"What does Sadi have to do with this?" With considerable effort, he pulled his eyes away from the top of her breasts and back to her eyes. Embarrassment made his skin almost tingle. "You are not Sadi!"

She reached and took hold of his shoulder and his embarrassment instantly vanished. Her hand felt like an electrified stove heating element. He imagined smoke rising from his shirt, but the sensation brought no pain. The heat felt amazingly good. For a moment, he wished she would do the same thing with her other hand.

"Go to her," she said then released his shoulder. The scene instantly froze in time, as if someone just pushed the pause button on a movie.

He waited for movement, something to happen, but then light slowly began to fade as well. With wide and motionless eyes, she stared at him as life seemed to drain from her face. After a long while of staring at her lifeless form, Freddy realized that the creature had vanished, leaving a mannequin disappearing into a bog of darkness. When the darkness completely enveloped everything, the silence returned, leaving the stone floor as the only physical sensation.

Freddy found himself back at the beginning of the dream, where time flowed by him like a silent wind. He could almost hear it.

Freddy regained his consciousness in the last position he remembered, staring at the eyes of the spider. The only light in the room came from the blinking LED's of all his electronic equipment. Unlike the other episodes with the crystal, this time he remembered time elapsing and it felt much longer than a moment or a lifetime. He knew the whole experience happened inside his head, but it felt too real to be a mere dream. The creature who spoke to him did not originate from his mind. Freddy could still hear her voice distinctly from his own.

What did the creature want from him? What was she or it? How did she know about his interest in Sadi? The last question frightened him the most. What had happened during the previous episodes of lost time? Too many questions without answers.

He wiped his finger over the laptop touchpad and the monitor came to life. His still image from the video stared back at him and reminded him of staring at the lifeless face of Sadi in his vision. After a moment of staring into his own eyes, Freddy quickly closed the screen.

When the computer screen turned black, he glanced down at the crystal again, making sure to avoid the eyes. Freddy feared going back into another trance. After enclosing the mysterious object in his hand, he carried it to his dresser then inserted the object under his white tube socks.

Exhaustion swept over him so he laid down on his bed. Interaction with the crystal exhausted his energy and left him feeling hollow. Fresh images of Sadi flowed through his thought stream, as well as the vision of the solar system. In less than ten minutes he fell asleep.

Contacting Sadi Jacobsen became his last conscious thought. He spent the rest of the night dreaming about the encounter and what he planned to say.

20

Gerald

Cesar did not live in a house. He lived in a mansion. Gerald felt like entering an ancient and royal Mexican palace. The front drive had four white arches three meters high leading to a large patio walkway in front of the huge double doors. Large rose bushes in pots filled the empty spaces with life. If they only had sunshine and heat, Gerald would have thought they were actually in Mexico. The gloomy Seattle weather provided them with the normal drizzle.

A beautiful woman named Dominga Florez greeted them at the door. She had short black hair pulled back with an ornate gold and silver pin. When she focused her dark oval eyes on Gerald, they seemed to pull his attention away from everything else. She wore no ring and Cesar introduced her as one would introduce a foreign dignitary. She seemed to share the same age as Cesar, but still retained the beauty of her youth. Cesar excused himself to go and make them something to eat and she led them to a large sitting room.

Dominga sat on an ornate, single-cushion backed chair with elegant and simple Queen Anne style legs. All the furniture appeared to have the same theme, a style Gerald might have chosen, if he had the patience to spend the required time and money. At his first and only other time visiting the home, Dominga had not yet arrived and the arrangements were not as nice as the present. The woman definitely brought her own style. In the chair she looked relaxed, like a cat lying in the sunshine.

"So," she began with a much thicker accent than Cesar. She sounded unaccustomed to speaking in English. Both Gerald and Taylor sat forward in order to focus all their energy on listening. "I was unaware that we were having guests this early on the weekend." She laughed quietly. "You are lucky I was presentable."

Gerald could not imagine the woman in front of them looking anything less than pristine. The thought of her walking around in sweats and tousled hair seemed ridiculous.

"Yes, this was unexpected. I hope we haven't intruded."

"Of course not," she said as her face burst into a pleasant smile. "I love company. We get so few," she hesitated as if searching for the right word, "friendly visitors."

She turned to Taylor.

"Miss Taylor, Cesar called me on the phone and gave me some forewarning to your visit. He says you are the reason. How does your purpose relate to him? What could such a beautiful young girl want with my Cesar?"

She smiled affectionately without the smallest hint of jealousy.

"Does it have to do with business?"

Taylor required a second to process the woman's words.

"Yes, it's related to business. Cesar thought we could talk more comfortably at his house."

"Yes," Dominga agreed. "It is much more comfortable than that old shop of his. You will find Cesar to be the perfect host."

She turned back to Gerald.

"My dear Mr. Fuger, Cesar spoke of you before. He owes you a lot for helping him when he...arrived here. Sorry, my English can be poorly sometimes."

"No your English is perfect," Gerald said with a smile. "Did you know Cesar from Mexico, or did you meet him here?"

"In Mexico," she answered. "I am a friend of the family and arrived about six months ago. He was lonely and needed some company, more than just his infamous friend Doroteo."

"I was looking forward to hearing about Cesar's history," Taylor said, smiling patiently. "He was going to tell me his story. What can you tell me about him?"

Dominga's eyes widened a bit at Taylor's abruptness, but she also smiled wider.

"Cesar has had an interesting life, unfortunately, in his later years, it has become a tragic one."

"That's true," Gerald agreed.

"Before he gets back, let me tell you what I know," she said and her lips became tenser. "If you find yourself with Cesar's respect, he is a valuable asset. If not, then I would suggest you stay away from him. Many have made the mistake of taking his generosity for granted. If you are concerned about his, oh, what's the English word, "trustworthiness", just know that Cesar will never betray his own sense of morality. If you come to understand that, then you will have nothing to fear. You will want him as a friend."

Gerald loved the way she said, 'trustworthiness'. He fought the temptation to ask her to say the word again.

Cesar entered the room again before Dominga could continue, and brought a large tray of fruit which included green grapes, sliced apples and fresh cut pineapple. Cesar smiled and placed the fruit on a coffee table in the middle of the room. In his other hand he had a white bowl full of what looked like white fruit dip.

Another man followed behind Cesar. He made Gerald catch his breath and stare. While entering, he looked briefly to Taylor, then Gerald. He seemed unconcerned about making eye contact. He carried a tray with several little sandwiches and paper cups with a pitcher of water.

In another situation, Gerald might have laughed to see a man like him carry a tray of food. The man had scars all over his arms and his skin stretched tightly over bulging muscles. He stood a bit taller than Cesar, but still much shorter than Gerald. He reminded Gerald of a bouncer at a dirty bar. Gerald felt like he was having a Hell's Angel biker as his waiter.

The man silently nodded to them all without expression, as if he felt no social requirement to introduce himself or be introduced. He wore blue jeans and a silk button shirt that made him seem unaware of the freezing cold wetness outside.

Maybe his thick and bushy hair kept him warm.

Gerald feared the man's presence would negatively influence Taylor's decision.

"Sorry it took so long, Gerald and Miss Taylor, but good thing I had Doroteo here to help me, otherwise it would have been longer." Cesar smiled and nodded to Dominga. "Thank you for keeping them company."

"No problem. We were just talking about you."

The second man, Doroteo stood as if waiting for a command. Cesar turned to him and said, "Gracias, Doroteo."

"De nada," the man replied then vanished out the room without looking at everyone. After he left, the tension seemed to dissipate.

As he sat down, Cesar noticed Taylor watching Doroteo leave the room.

"Don't let his looks deceive you Miss Taylor. Let me assure you. He's meaner than he appears."

Dominga looked to Cesar with raised eyebrows of feigned shock and then they both laughed. Surprisingly, Taylor began to laugh also. Gerald smiled in relief.

"I wasn't thinking he looked mean, just a little rough around the edges," Taylor said.

For the next several minutes they ate and talked about Dominga's relationship to Cesar and how they met. Taylor took an immediate liking to Dominga who seemed to return the same assessment. Gerald thought the older woman's demeanor looked genuine, not just an attempt to make Taylor feel comfortable. She also seemed to crave the feminine company.

After spending a little more time getting better acquainted, Cesar took control of the conversation and changed from jovial to more serious. He directed his speech to Taylor, keeping almost exclusive eye contact with her. He did, however, glance from time to time at Dominga and Gerald.

"When I came to this country, I searched for a lawyer that I could trust. That's when I found Gerald. I don't know if he remembers, but when we first met, my English was very rusty, much worse than even now, if you can believe that. Anyway, he was very patient, helped me with my Visa problems and also helped me get set up with my little shop."

Cesar cleared his throat and seemed to be enjoying the memory.

"I will attempt to alleviate your concerns about me. At least, I will tell you everything you might want to know. I must admit, Miss Ewell, you have my curiosity. For someone like Gerald and you to try to trick me before you reveal your true purpose! I believe that is worth my time."

Dominga looked from Cesar to Taylor and failed to hide the confusion in her eyes. She waited patiently for Cesar to continue.

"Miss Ewell, you show strength of character to not base complete trust in others with something that must be very dear to you. You trust your own judgment more so than your most trustworthy friend. You probably won't believe everything I'm about to tell you, but Dominga can confirm it all. You've probably never experienced anger and grief to the extent I have. Consider yourself fortunate. I wish no one had to experience what I did."

Gerald sat back in his chair and tried to get comfortable. Dominga crossed her legs and rested her head on her hand. Her dark eyes focused on Cesar and her face expressed some sort of admiration, deeper than simple affection.

21

Cesar

First, let me tell you that up until recently, I had a good life, an extremely blessed life. I grew up in wealth, and with it, privilege. My younger brother and I went to the best private schools and had everything needed for a fine education and a perfect future. With my parents, we toured all over the world, vacationed in the Caribbean, traveled all through Europe and Asia.

Believe it or not, even though I had everything a person could possibly want, I was always the good kid. My brother, on the other hand, was exactly what you'd expect a life of privilege can produce in a child. You'll hear more about him later. I don't give myself credit for how I turned out, it just happened. Maybe it is all genetics. I don't know, but either way, I was always a good kid.

My father was a wealthy man. He was a great man, intelligent and shrewd where money was concerned. But he didn't start out that way. He started out in the slums of Ciudad Juarez, not very nice place to be. It's filled with violence, where the gangs and drug lords battle with each other and with the police. Fortunately, my grandmother was an amazing woman who knew how to keep her sons out of all that mess. Eventually, she earned enough money to move out and my father got a good job with a car parts manufacturer. Eventually, he moved up the ladder and became the CEO. It was the perfect fairy tale story.

As CEO he doubled the company's revenue and profits in two years then he expanded the business. I wish I could say my father accomplished all this ethically, but sadly, I learned later that one factor in his success and the success of the company was due to their involvement in the drug war, or I should say, with the CIA.

I didn't learn of this until after I completed my formal education. My younger brother knew about it before I did. I'll get to that later.

My father wanted my brother and me to have a college experience in America, so he sent us to Stanford. My brother chose the school because he wanted to go to California. Like I said, I was a good kid and usually did what my father asked of us. Besides, it was Stanford and I was not about to complain. Following my father's advice, my younger brother and I majored in business. I soon became bored with the subject, although I did stick with it.

Business classes did not require much of my time so I started taking classes in mechanical engineering and focused on automotive engineering. This was partly due to my father's business where I planned to work. It just made sense to know more about that subject. Fortunately, I found it very interesting and I spent more of my time on those classes than my business classes.

My brother, on the other hand, spent all his time with girls and his fraternity brothers. We've always been friends, but our relationship was usually strained. At home we were forced to spend our time together, but at school our lives went in different directions. For him, every weekend was filled with alcohol and women. I wasn't opposed to extracurricular activities, but I was always blessed, you can say, with an intense curiosity about this world and could not be kept from trying to learn all I could. You can imagine that at Stanford, it was easy to get lost in my studies. It was just another step in my charmed life.

It took me six years to get both my business and engineering degrees. I have to admit, more energy was put into automotive engineering than business. It's funny because my brother and I graduated together. He got his MBA and I got 2 Bachelor's degrees. One of his frat brothers was the son of a senator who was also a friend of the Mexican ambassador. My brother went to work with him as an aide.

My father was excited about this, to have a connection with a US government official. After working for a couple of years, my brother went to work for my father.

I finished my M.S. engineering degree and wanted to continue on to get a doctorate, but my father talked me into coming back to Mexico to work for him. It wasn't that big of a disappointment because I figured I didn't need school to learn when I had all the resources for research back at home in my father's company. Maybe I just wanted the title of doctor? I was young and things like that seemed to matter.

After working for my father for a couple of years, I talked him into branching out into motors, one of the only products he did not manufacture. We had the capital for it and I knew there was some market share we could capture. As you can guess, it was partly because I wanted to do some design work. We hired a friend of mine from school and some other local folks and got our first few engines out in about a year. After three years the new engine division I started was contributing ten percent of our total revenue. A couple of years later, I offered to buy out the division as a separate entity. It was a good deal for both of us.

A year after I arrived back in Mexico, at one of my mother's frequent parties, I met the daughter of the governor of Chihuahua, the Mexican state where Juarez is located.

This girl was the most beautiful creature I'd ever seen. I had to see her again, and then again and again. Six months later we were married and then a year later our first daughter Sophia was born. Those years flew by, then four years later, my twins Max and Geraldo were born.

The business was going amazingly well, and still I was oblivious to the connection between my father's business and the CIA. I became suspicious when one of our pilots mysteriously died. So far, my father's and my business were sharing some planes for shipping our goods to America and other places. When the pilot died, I became involved with hiring a new one. After looking into that side of the business, which I had previously let my father handle, I decided that it made more sense to buy my own plane and hire my own pilots.

Unexpectedly, I ran into a load of trouble when I tried to do this. Doroteo, who you just met, was in charge of security and found out that a couple of the people causing us trouble were actually on the CIA's payroll. They coordinated the movement of some illegal material and suddenly I was messing with that operation. They wanted to be the ones to choose the pilots as my father had always let them do. They needed special training and instruction.

You would probably be surprised to learn that Doroteo was a very close friend from my childhood. He was the type of friend anyone wanted. He wasn't the strongest kid on the block, but he was the toughest. Our lives separated for a few years when I went to college. He got a job with the police and spent much of his time undercover, fighting the drug supply chain which also included some very corrupt government officials. Whenever that much money is involved, a lot of people want a piece of the pie.

When my business began to get going, I hired him as head of security. He would have figured out about our drug involvement earlier, but my father's company managed the shipping aspect. I always avoid this topic with him because he still blames himself for it.

We finally realized what was happening. Our products shipped by air to close cities in America, like Albuquerque, then they would head to either Seattle or Salt Lake City or Buffalo. Instead of a straight flight, they would stop in small airports where CIA agents would coordinate the transfer of their hidden stock of drugs. All of this had been coordinated for years, with the approval of my father, although he never did admit it.

I confronted my father with what I knew and he said they were merely cooperating with the law. I was very angry with the situation, but also scared out of my mind. Doroteo said it would be better to leave it alone for a while which we did. However, I was determined to eliminate our participation. Doroteo felt the same, but knew that we were in a sticky situation and it would require delicate handling. The final decision was to buy a plane of our own and start by switching just some of our shipping to our own management. We would transfer a little at a time until all of our merchandise was being shipped in our own planes and by our own pilots.

Doroteo said he would cut all ties to the drug trade and gratefully, I put a blind eye to his methods because they tended to supersede the law. In my mind, this was justified because the government officials from Mexico and the U.S. were working against us. My whole life, it never crossed my mind that the CIA would be involved with the drug war in this way. Doroteo can tell you more about it, but they fund much of their covert activities in this manner. That is the reason why nothing has been done to end the drug war. All that matters is that the money keeps flowing. If anything gets in the way, it is soon eliminated.

After a year or so, we were shipping all of our own goods and I thought the problem was solved. All would have been if my wife hadn't succeeded in persuading me into politics. When I turned forty-nine I decided to run for mayor of Ciudad Juarez. Part of me thought that I could do more good in government than I could as a business leader. In my mind, I owed it to the city that had given me so much. I decided to retire from the business and enter the political game. I stayed with the company as a board member, but left the management to others.

My wife's father, who was no longer the governor of Chihuahua, had become a cabinet member in Ernesto Zedillo's administration. He guided me on how to win the election. Little did I know that the establishment already had their pick for mayor and it wasn't me. From the very onset of my public campaign, I got death threat after death threat. Doroteo became my security manager. He's the reason for my current heartbeat.

Cesar laughed silently. During the break in the story, his audience took a collective breath.

Yes, I owe my life to him. Many times over. Anyway...

So, not only was my life threatened, but the media tried to ignore me. If it hadn't been for my friends in the media, they wouldn't have given me the time of day. Yes, I had connections, and I owe them my victory. The media is key to getting elected and don't let anyone tell you otherwise.

It's funny and tragic, but before you become a political leader, you have this fantasy that you're going to change the system. What I found was that things were already well-established and politicians only have the power to keep the money flowing, not stopping or diverting it. You would not believe the number of bureaucrats that work independently from any elected official.

When I decided to run for a second term, that's when things started to heat up. During my time as mayor, there were the usual death threats, but nothing out of the ordinary. Of course, many of them were serious, but my security, as led by Doroteo, was flawless. Now that I look back on it, I think those that I thwarted the most as mayor, were just biding their time until my term was over. Then they could go on as they were, making the people pay for all their programs, continuing to fatten their bank accounts. Up until that point, my family was relatively safe. Their lives were never really in much danger.

Now that I look back at it, I was naïve, and stupid. Somehow, I felt that we were invincible. Like I said, I had a charmed life. Nothing bad had ever happened to me, every obstacle had been overcome so why not this one? Now I don't blame anyone but myself, but at that time, I was angry and blamed everyone else.

22

Cesar

At the very beginning of my second campaign, my boys were kidnapped. I cannot describe the horror. It was like they always say, a waking nightmare from which there was no awakening. My wife actually collapsed with grief and worry. That was how bad it was. When that happened, I was actually jealous that she could escape the reality for a while. The kidnappers did not want money. Instead, they wanted me to promise not to run for mayor and not say anything about the kidnapping, or else the boys would die. They even threatened to kill one of the boys to show that they were serious.

At that point, I was willing to promise anything. That one act was all it took to break me. I lost the confidence that this would be overcome. My wife and I were a wreck, as I'm sure you can imagine. Every night during the ordeal, we slept with Sophia in the same room. It was the first time in my life when I felt that I could not rely on myself. I tried turning to religion, but that didn't help. Nothing did.

After a few days, there was a breakthrough. Doroteo found out where they were keeping the boys. I'll never forget the excitement and hope that information can bring. It was almost as good as if they were back at home. I imagined charging into their compound with Doroteo and the police, guns smoking, and saving the boys. It was the same invincible confidence I had before, scarred only by fear. I was confident that even if I died in the attempt, so would the kidnappers, and my boys would be safe.

Doroteo was the one who made the rescue. He tried to forbid me from participating, but I could not be kept away. I was expecting the rescue to be like what you see in the movies, but instead, it was almost anti-climactic. The boys were being held by only two men in a small house in a bad part of town.

I imagined killing the kidnappers a million ways, but when we actually retrieved the boys, all I could think of was getting them back to their mother, back to safety. I almost forgot about the men who held them. The two men happened to be just a couple hired thugs who were playing video games with my boys. Doroteo put the fear of God in them and we let them go.

Even though I had promised not to run again, I figured that since we got the boys back, I could go back to my preparations for the campaign. A promise to someone threatening your family can be dropped. I would just be extra careful and have to worry about my family in addition to myself. Even Doroteo, who was normally more cautious than I am, was OK with our campaign preparations.

For a few weeks after getting the boys back, we didn't hear a thing about the kidnapping. It was as if the whole thing had never happened. It took two weeks before we were comfortable with the boys sleeping in their own rooms again. It seemed quiet until a week after I had made the official announcement of my campaign plans.

I'm sorry, but what happened next I cannot talk about in much detail.

Cesar took a deep breath, as if preparing for a physically exhausting experience like preparing to climb a mountain. After a brief, but intense look in Dominga's eyes, he sat forward in his seat and clasped his hands.

It started when my wife and boys were in a car accident. My twin boys who were fifteen at the time, died instantly. My wife was taken to the hospital in critical condition, but she died within an hour. Before she died, she was able to tell me what happened. I would have thought it was just an accident. Apparently, she was being chased by a car with armed men. Her driver lost control of the car. It had happened so fast that she didn't have time to call anyone. My grief, anger, and shock were too great to think clearly. In one day, most of my family was taken away.

My daughter was not with them when it happened, but was with her boyfriend. He was a great boy and I had always trusted him to keep her safe. Frantically, we searched for her. She was all I had left. I could not accept the possibility that she could be gone too. That would have been too much and I would have killed myself right there. When I tried to call her to see if she was safe, I could not get a hold of her, or her boyfriend. We searched for her for a few hours and eventually found her boyfriend. He had been beaten unconscious.

When we got him conscious again, he told us what happened. Some men had found them and took her. Naturally, he struggled to keep it from happening, but they overpowered him and he was lucky that they didn't kill him. They only let him live to deliver the news to me. I was still in shock from what had happened to my boys and wife. Now that my daughter was missing, I actually felt like I was going to have a heart attack.

The only thing left was my daughter and getting her back kept me among the living. My daughter's boyfriend seemed as distressed as I was. That experience bonded us. Despite my grief, what we shared gave me strength. I cannot describe it. To this day, I regard him as my son.

When the kidnappers contacted us, they told me it was my fault that my wife and boys had died. In a way, they were right, although at the time, I could not accept it.

The instructions were similar to the previous time when my boys were kidnapped. If we told the media, my Sophia would die, so we had a quiet funeral while Doroteo went to work finding her.

So, Doroteo came to the rescue again. That man is more connected in the underworld than any CIA or FBI agent. He was able to find where they were keeping my daughter. For the second time in a month, I found myself in the role of rescuer. This time, Doroteo did not even try to keep me from coming, or my daughter's boyfriend. At the time, my thoughts were that I was either going to die in the attempt to rescue her, or if she was dead, take my revenge out on as many of her kidnappers as possible.

This time, it wasn't nearly as easy. She was not being held in some faraway place by a couple of nobodies. They were holding her at the compound belonging to one of the worst drug cartel's leader. Even Doroteo had doubts about success. It was no secret about this man's involvement in the drug trade, but most people did not know he was one of the most influential men in all of Chihuahua. Once we found out where they were holding her, we knew that they did not intend to let her go alive. She knew the place and the people. I personally knew the man and had been at political functions with him. We were never friends because of what I knew of him.

We left one night after midnight. Doroteo had a friend who had been in the military Special Forces. He was the one who planned the rescue and told us what to do. The man's house was well guarded, but the guards were lazy and not expecting anything. That night, they were not ready for an assault. Fortunately, plenty of firepower helps with a feeling of overconfidence.

The details after we got past the guards are a little fuzzy. I was too worried about my daughter to think about what we were doing. After a horrible time trying to locate her, we finally found her, but everyone had woken up and we were surrounded by his men. There was no way we could have gotten out of there alive. I thought all was lost, but luck was with us.

One of our captors was an undercover CIA agent. By some miracle which I'll never understand, he decided to help us. It wasn't entirely because of any desire on his part to do what was right, but because they, the CIA, were planning to dispose of the cartel leader anyway. We just provided the perfect opportunity to do so. They could blame the incident on a local political leader in his campaign.

So, this agent turned on his compadres and killed them. We thought he was going to kill us next, but to my surprise, he turned to us and said we could take my daughter and leave. He told us several things, which I won't go into now. Let me just say that he gave us some warning that there was going to be a major upheaval in the country and it wasn't going to be safe for us. He told me that I had to leave the country, keep my mouth shut about what happened and stay away from the media.

You can see the reality of it in the news even now, with the war between the government and the drug cartels and all the increased violence. The CIA decided that they didn't like the current drug trade administration. With the help of the US military, they are accomplishing their goals, but I better stop talking about it. I get too angry, to see what is happening to my home. I cannot do one damn thing about it.

In the end, I could not persuade my Sophia to leave Mexico. She and her boyfriend fled to his relatives' home, far away in Jalisco. They plan to marry later this year sometime. I am hoping to convince them to come and live with me someday. Eventually, they probably will.

23

Gerald

When Cesar finished telling his story, Gerald looked to Taylor. Her head shook slightly from side to side, as if in disbelief and amazement. After such a detailed explanation of horrible events, Gerald had difficulty keeping his good mood, but he knew the story already. Dominga had sat quietly during the entire discourse and acted as though watching a television program. She let the two guests ask all the questions. Gerald wondered how she fit into Cesar's emotions. She had an obvious affection for the man.

Unexpectedly, Dominga rose from her seat. She looked to both of her guests before speaking.

"Well, it appears that you have business to discuss with Cesar. I'll leave you to discuss, but you must not leave without saying good-bye!"

Gerald also rose from his chair, but Cesar and Taylor remained seated. When Gerald looked in his friend's direction, he noticed Cesar staring into Taylor's eyes, as if studying a painting. As Dominga silently left the room, he sat back in his chair.

"Mr. Sanchez," said Taylor once Dominga disappeared from their view. She kept her gaze on Cesar. "I appreciate you sharing your personal history, more than you can know. I appreciate it and want to ask for your trust. I feel that I can trust you."

Gerald thought he understood Cesar's motivation for sharing so much personal information. The action was a classic psychological manipulation. After such an emotional display, Taylor would feel obligated to return the emotional trust.

Cesar broke their eye contact finally.

"Before you tell me anything, should I be worried? To keep your trust, will you ever require me to lie for you?"

"Honestly," Taylor began, trying to sound sincere. "I don't know for sure, but such a possibility would be required only for your personal safety."

"Is it illegal?" Cesar asked, turning to Gerald.

Gerald acted offended, but with a smile.

"Me, illegal? Come on Cesar. You know me better than that. Even if our purpose was illegal, which it isn't of course, would I ever admit to it?"

Cesar laughed. He sat back and exhaled slowly.

"No, you wouldn't."

"Mr. Sanchez," Taylor said. "I trust Gerald completely and I know that he trusts you so I'm just going to tell you, bluntly, how you can help us and ask for your participation. If you want no part of it, it won't be mentioned again. Just give me your word that this will be kept confidential."

Cesar leaned forward.

"Go ahead."

"I've made a discovery," she said bluntly. "If we're successful in bringing it out in the open, it can change the world. Some people will not want that to happen."

She leaned forward, unzipped her backpack and pulled out the black box. So far during their visit, she kept the backpack between her feet and Gerald noticed that she did not look once in its direction. Both Gerald and Cesar stared at the box as if a rattlesnake just appeared. She let the magnet snap to the surface with a loud snap and then handed the box to Cesar.

He turned the box over in his hand, examining its size and weight.

"Do I open it?"

"Flip the switch on the side," said Gerald, failing to control his excitement.

Taylor glanced at him in irritation, but said nothing.

Cesar put the box on his lap, clicked the switch and the box slowly floated towards the ceiling like a balloon full of helium. He jumped back in his seat and put his hands to his side.

"¡Cáspita!" he said in surprise and sudden paralysis.

Taylor laughed sharply and clapped her hands once together. She and Gerald watched the box float at a constant speed towards the ceiling. Gerald jumped to his feet and grabbed the box out of the air, pushing the object back on Cesar's lap. The force against his hand felt quite unnatural.

"This is impossible," he said quietly, more to himself than anyone else.

After a moment, Cesar seemed to regain his composure. His lips slowly transformed from tension to a relaxed smile. Silently, he put his hand on the box and Gerald went back to his seat. Cesar let the box rise a few times and then pulled it back again to his lap. For a few moments after flipping the switch to off, he kept his hand on the box and silently stared at it.

Gerald and Taylor waited for Cesar to speak. His mouth moved slightly, as if chewing on a million thoughts. Finally, he turned to Taylor.

"You must tell me how this works."

"Would you have believed me if I would have just told you about it?" Taylor's smile disappeared and her normal inquisitive look returned.

"No," he said, laughing slightly. "I would have thought you were crazy. It appears to violate the conservation of momentum, but that cannot be possible!"

Gerald also felt curious about how the device worked, but hoped they would not spend the entire afternoon talking about that. He glanced at Taylor and imagined seeing her mind preparing to explain the technical details. He spoke before she could.

"We can go over the details another time," he said quickly. "We came here to ask for your help with what we want to do with it."

"You definitely do not want to go public with this," Cesar said while staring at the box. "Agents from the government would be at your doors faster than the wind."

To Gerald's relief, they spent the next two hours discussing the plan he and Taylor agreed to pursue the previous night. Cesar listened to their plan and the reasoning and seemed to be unsure about the idea of using the device to travel into space, but he did not immediately reject the idea. He claimed to be more interested in working with Taylor to develop the technology. They could use her invention however they wanted.

During the conversation, his tone of address toward Taylor changed. He acted impressed and almost afraid to argue with her, as if he occupied the same room as Nicola Tesla or Albert Einstein.

Cesar shared the same goal as Gerald and Taylor of establishing a free society and they spent a significant amount of their time discussing how her invention could help set humanity free. Releasing her invention to the world had the possibility to shift the military dynamics in the world and ultimately decentralize the current power structure.

In his opinion, however, using the technology for space travel had too many obstacles. He thought there might be a better way although he agreed that they would need a way to escape the government's grasp should the need arise. Like Gerald, he just needed more time to consider the idea.

"There is another option that you have not considered," Cesar said, sitting forward on the couch.

"What is that?" asked Gerald and Taylor together.

"It involves doing what we already agreed to first do, develop it. I'm sure we will think of a way to use this to make some money and eventually challenge the puppet masters. For example, asteroid mining has vast potential. What you've created may be able to economically accomplish that."

At the end of the discussion, they all agreed to start the project of perfecting the NMG design. Gerald felt excitement begin to grow inside him. He could now let them take control of the project. How to start?

"Miss Taylor," Cesar said in a tone of cheerful insistence. "While we are working, you must stay here with us. We will use my shop."

While he explained his reasoning, Gerald found no reason for argument. Simply for security reasons, living with him would be the most secure and he had plenty of room for her. As soon as she could make the move, they would start working. Gerald had expected this, but he did not know if Taylor would be comfortable with the arrangement.

At his request to live with them, Taylor sat back in her seat, rubbed her chin and stared at the ground. After just a few seconds, she agreed and looked at him straight in the eyes.

"You seem to already know what you want to do first."

"I do," he said with a devious smile. "You came to the right person."

Taylor looked to Gerald. They both smiled.

24

Taylor

"When can you move in?" Cesar asked without trying to hide his excitement.

He acted like a child looking at a present, wondering about the contents. Taylor thought he looked adorable.

"I hope you don't find me too forward, Miss Taylor, but if you're going to live here, I would like to talk to Dominga and Doroteo about this. They will need to know what is going on. You have my assurance that they can keep this confidential. I trust them with my life."

"I believe you," Taylor said then turned to Gerald. He looked like a spectator, rather than the driver. He seemed to be enjoying his position, as comfortable as her mother's cat on the sofa. Without understanding why, Taylor felt comfortable with the situation. After listening to the tragic story of Cesar's life, the man seemed like a relative.

"I suppose we should show them the NMG as well."

Did having a baby feel the same as inventing something? Parents seemed to always want to show off their creation and she had difficulty hiding the pride and excitement in her voice. After showing Gerald and Cesar, she felt less hesitation to show others. When she showed Gerald the previous evening, an overwhelming relief replaced her fear of having it fail to work, almost as if the NMG finally came into existence. She had definitely made the right choice of going to Gerald. She had doubts about his plan, but he knew how to get things done. With a development as big as the NMG, Taylor needed someone like Gerald.

Before hearing Cesar's story, Taylor had a good feeling about them all, even the dangerous-looking one, Doroteo. She wondered how the man would react if she called him the name she wanted to call him, Dorito. Imagining his possible reactions caused her lips to stretch into a smile.

"I'll go get them," Cesar said.

He seemed to share her excitement at showing the NMG. While waiting for Cesar to fetch his friends, Gerald and Taylor sat alone in the room in anxious anticipation.

"It's like we've jumped into a raging river," Gerald said. "The current has taken us and we're not getting out."

After a few minutes, Dominga followed Cesar back into the room and then Doroteo appeared. The dark stubble on his face and disheveled hair made him appear much darker than the other two Mexicans. The man gave Taylor the impression of being pulled away from an enjoyable activity, to a tedious one. Despite his intimidating presence, Taylor did not fear him, but thought of him as a mystery, in need of discovery. If she ever needed help in a physical fight, she would want to have Doroteo on her side. She would have to put some extra effort into developing a relationship with him. Making friends with a lion required special effort.

The man ignored both Taylor and Gerald until he sat in the chair, then he turned and shot a brief, but threatening look toward them. Taylor met his gaze then casually turned to the beautiful Mexican goddess. She rushed to Taylor's side, sat down and put her hand on Taylor's knee.

"Is it true you will come live with us? This is so exciting! Another woman in this house to keep me company. Tell me it is no jest."

Dominga's excitement caused the last of Taylor's minor reservations to evaporate, including the one about her being jealous of another female in the house.

"It is no joke," said Taylor, failing to suppress a smile.

"This is better in more ways than one," said Gerald in a more serious tone, then he smiled. "Taylor could use some female mentoring."

Both Taylor and Dominga glared at him.

"She needs nothing of the sort, Mister Fuger." Dominga attempted to say Gerald's name with a country twang. The barely-passable English accent made Taylor laugh. "But yes, the first thing we're going to do is some shopping. You've brought me a beautiful mannequin. I must dress her up."

Doroteo spoke for the first time since entering the room. Unfortunately for Taylor and Gerald, he spoke in Spanish and directed his words to Cesar who responded in Spanish. Taylor waited patiently for Cesar to finish his response then she spoke directly to Doroteo.

"You do speak English don't you?" Taylor looked first to Doroteo then to Cesar and finally to Gerald who seemed to sink into his chair.

"Of course," Doroteo quickly answered with a thick accent like Cesar and just as clearly.

"I think you might be interested in what Taylor has to show you," interjected Gerald in an attempt to diffuse the tension he felt.

Taylor cared little for the social tension in the room. She just wanted to see Doroteo's response. In her opinion, the man needed someone to challenge him.

"Do you want to see?" Taylor asked, directing her gaze to Doroteo and then Dominga.

"Yes," Doroteo answered blandly.

Did she detect a hint of a smile on his lips? She removed the black box.

"Who wants to be the first one to try it?"

Both Dominga and Doroteo looked at each other hesitantly. Dominga motioned for him to go ahead. Taylor stood and held out the box. When Doroteo stepped forward to grab it, she smelled a hint of pipe tobacco on him. Unexpectedly, the strangely pleasant smell made her momentarily pause.

After explaining what to do, she stepped back to her seat and watched. He activated the box faster than Gerald did. When he activated the box, Taylor noticed with delight, his jolt of surprise. He muttered something under his breath in Spanish then he looked to his friends in the room with an obvious question on his face.

Slowly he let go of the box and watched it rise into the air. When the box reached about two feet above his head, he realized that it would not be stopping. He put his left hand on top of the box before pulling it back.

Dominga put her hand on Taylor's shoulder, but kept her gaze on Doroteo.

"Ay dios mio!" she exclaimed with her eyes fixed on the NMG. "Where did you get this thing?"

"I invented it," she said.

For the next few moments, they all watched Doroteo play with her invention. For his final trick, he pushed it to the floor and then let go again, watching it move silently upward. He seemed oblivious to those around him and looked like a child playing with his first yo-yo.

Reluctantly, Doroteo relinquished the black box and let Dominga play with it. She held the object like one might hold a twenty million dollar vase. Taylor waited long enough for the excitement to diminish so they could have a normal conversation again.

As Taylor and Gerald explained their thoughts and plans, their captivated audience listened intently. She expected them to have a lot of questions or objections about their motives, but when explaining the topic of promoting freedom they sat quietly and showed no signs of disagreement. When they talked about the possibility of flying to space, Taylor felt some anxiety, prepared for Doroteo to scoff at the idea. Surprisingly, she almost cared more for his opinion than the others.

"Of course," interrupted Taylor after Gerald explained his desire to gather more people. "All this might not work out, so we'll have to take it slowly, but I believe it's definitely something to pursue."

"I don't think going into orbit is as easy to accomplish as you think," Doroteo said politely. When he spoke, Doroteo hid his emotion well.

"Why do you say that?" Gerald asked. "They shouldn't have enough time to stop us."

"As soon as you are detected on their radar or infrared detectors," he began as if explaining to a bunch of children. "You will be considered hostile. Before you even see them coming, you will be destroyed by a missile or a fighter jet. You are fooling yourselves if you think you can outrun them."

"I think you're being a bit paranoid Doroteo," said Taylor. "Not every inch of sky is monitored by radar. I bet there's plenty of unmonitored places to quietly escape. Besides, we can make something more maneuverable than anything they can make, in space at least. Once we make it to space, we'll be out of their reach."

"Overconfidence, Miss Ewell, will get you killed."

"I'll keep that in mind." Taylor smiled, intending to challenge him.

She would enjoy their future conversations. Dominga sat back in the chair next to Taylor, preparing to speak.

"I'm sure they've thought of this Doroteo. We've got time to work things out."

"How do you plan to not bring any attention to yourselves?" Doroteo asked, ignoring Dominga's comment.

His use of the word 'you' instead of 'we', gave Taylor the impression that he considered himself outside their group, not a part of it. He seemed to disagree with that part of the plan, but she thought he might be testing them, to see if they had thoroughly considered all the issues. Despite his antagonism, she felt comfortable with him knowing their secret.

"Right now, I'm more concerned about the fuel issue," she said.

"What do you mean?" asked Gerald. "I thought your invention made it much easier to do?"

Before she could respond, Cesar spoke.

"Yes Gerald, her device is a monumental achievement, but it still will take a lot of energy to escape Earth's pull. Acquiring enough fuel discreetly is going to be one of our biggest obstacles."

Even with his thick accent, Cesar's vocabulary impressed Taylor.

"Gerald, we didn't talk about it last night because it's just one of many things that need to be worked out before we can accomplish what we want."

"Well, I'm glad that you and Cesar can figure it all out." Gerald put his hands behind his head and looked out the window. "Like I always say..."

"Where there's a will, there's a way," Taylor said, finishing his sentence. She followed his gaze and noticed the gray winter light beginning to fade. "Yes Gerald, we know, but you get the easy part. We've got to figure out 'the way' part."

"That's what I love about this whole thing," Gerald said, smiling.

"This is an engineer's dream Gerald," said Cesar. "I feel fortunate that you recommended me to Miss Taylor. I cannot wait to get working on this. The energy requirement, however, is going to be a huge obstacle, but there might be a possible solution."

"And what is that?" asked Taylor staring intently at him.

"Well," he said, returning her question with a smile. "You provided one solution to the age-old dilemma: *acceleration*. I think I might know of the required power source, but it might not be easy to find, if it exists at all."

25

Taylor

Only three days after their first meeting, Taylor transported most of her possessions to Cesar's home, to live with him, Dominga, and Doroteo. Her mother vainly tried to dissuade Taylor from the action, but soon capitulated when she saw the futility of arguing. Taylor put more effort than usual in convincing her mother that she had nothing to worry about. An older woman would be living with them and they would be working long hours on a time-sensitive project. Living somewhere else made no sense.

She neglected to tell her mother the specifics of the project, and her mother neglected to ask. Her mother rarely asked for technical details and hardly ever understood when Taylor tried to explain anyway. Usually, her mother felt satisfied knowing that her daughter would be working on a project that might become profitable.

"This could be big Mom," Taylor said in the hopes of instilling additional reassurance. "But I don't want too many people to know about what we're doing. You can't spill any milk if your glass is empty right?"

Cesar gave Taylor a very large room next to where Dominga slept. She felt extremely satisfied with the size of the room, but it felt too feminine for her taste. The window curtains and bed had too much lace and too many of the blankets and pillows contained too much pink. However, she never considered complaining over such a trivial matter and might eventually change some things, but for the moment, she chose to keep Dominga happy. The woman had taken too much pleasure furnishing the room for Taylor to say anything negative. Seeing Dominga's delight also helped curb the guilt she might have felt for receiving so much attention.

When Taylor finally felt settled, she immediately wanted to start working. Dominga, on the other hand, had alluded to other plans when she first learned about Taylor's future living arrangements. Taylor lacked the social energy to refuse Dominga when she demanded that they spend the first two days shopping.

Despite Taylor's feeble protests, Dominga managed to accomplish her overall mission and treat Taylor like the daughter she'd never had. Coming from her less-than-fortunate financial situation, as Dominga liked to say, Taylor felt uncomfortable receiving so much attention and gifts of monetary value from the woman. As she quickly learned, however, Dominga had little concern about money or price. She hardly ever looked at the price tag, and only haggled over price for amusement.

Taylor required only a few hours with Dominga, to appreciate the woman's skill at manipulation and keeping her victim ignorant of the process. The woman seemed to instantly and effortlessly assess the mental and emotional state of her target, even difficult cases like Taylor who projected a warning message, that conversation with her would likely result in conflict. Dominga seemed to effortlessly maneuver through difficult conversations, acting oblivious to tension and social barriers. Taylor never realized until afterward, that she had revealed information she normally kept hidden, by simply and reluctantly spending the day shopping.

When Taylor learned of Dominga's father and his various political appointments, the information failed to cause surprise. After the first day with Dominga, Taylor could easily envision the woman at elite social functions, adeptly engaging the narcissistic crowds like the conductor of a symphony.

"When I discovered that Cesar was driven away to the USA," Dominga said on their second day of shopping. "I told myself that I must visit him and help in the transition."

Taylor followed Dominga like a puppy through several clothing stores. Taylor would never willingly patronize many of the stores they visited. Expensive clothing went against her moral code. That much money could be better spent on parts for her projects.

"Of course," she continued. "He tried convincing me it was unnecessary, but that was only the polite way a gentleman would answer. I could tell from his tone of voice, however, that he had no objections and suffered for more refined company. Can you blame him? Imagine what it would be like to have Doroteo as your only companion. Yes, their friendship goes all the way back to childhood, but can you imagine that man's effect on your spirit? Oh, I could not abandon him to that fate."

"Of course," she said conspiratorially. "I have nothing personal against the man, you understand. It's just that he's a fish from a different pond, you might say. I have not had much luck engaging him in conversation. What little I do manage to squeeze out of him leads nowhere."

"I can understand that," said Taylor, smiling.

Dominga had several blouses slung over one arm and with the other arm, she held a blouse to Taylor's neck to see how it looked. She did not bother to ask for Taylor's opinion. After gathering a few more items, Taylor followed Dominga to a dressing room. She put on the first pair of pants, looked at herself in the mirror, then took a deep breath and sighed before going out to show Dominga. She lost count that day how many times she had to dress then undress.

When she exited the dressing room, Dominga clapped her hands together in delight.

"Those pants fit you very well, but I must say, the top is not as flattering as I imagined it. Here, try this one instead. Are you sure you won't try the skirt?"

Taylor politely refused to wear any skirts and Dominga made no attempt to convince her. Pants felt more comfortable. Usually when purchasing clothes, if she could not see herself cutting or polishing metal or welding with them, she would put them back on the hanger.

During lunch on the second day of shopping, they ate in the mall food court.

"You must forgive me," began Dominga, "For stealing you away from what you came here to do. I understand that this is not exactly what you would do of your own choice."

"Not normally," Taylor agreed. She failed to think of a good reason to paint a false picture of herself. "Although, I am enjoying your company."

"That's good of you to say. I cannot say how enjoyable this has been for me. You are a gift from the gods, Taylor Ewell. Now, it's overdue for me to shut up and let you talk. There are many things I must learn about you."

"Like what?"

"For one, I see you possess the same hatred of government as Cesar and Gerald. For what they did to Cesar and his poor family, there is no forgiveness or reason. But the one thing I want to understand, is the reason for *your* feelings. You are young and I cannot imagine what could possibly have happened to make you feel the same way. Something must have happened! I am right, am I not? One of your main purposes, is to escape our oppressive systems. But why? Cesar has told me of Gerald's reasons, but you are a mystery, Taylor. I must know."

Taylor paused for a few seconds and looked down at her food. At first, she could not meet Dominga's eyes. The woman seemed to have some magic, a spell to strip Taylor's reservations away. She also felt like Dominga deserved to know her story. The older woman genuinely cared for Taylor and had devoted all her time to making her feel welcome. Taylor decided to just start talking and ignore her usual reserve.

"When my older brother joined the army, I told him he was crazy. I knew the military works for big business and not for any ideology like freedom or the American way, whatever that is. He went anyway and after a year, he returned a broken man. They sent him home for PTSD or some other bullshit excuse. He refused to talk about his experiences and then one day-"

She paused and looked up into Dominga's big brown eyes and realized her own had filled with tears, almost ready to fall. She'd never told the whole story to anyone, not even Gerald. He thought her brother died in the war. She'd hardly even discussed the matter with her mother. Before any tear fell, however, anger returned and stopped the flood.

"I'm OK," Taylor said before continuing. "A few weeks after coming home, he committed suicide."

"Such a waste," said Dominga with a mixture of anger and sadness. She extended her hand and grasped Taylor's hand. "It takes courage to accept the truth of it, that they are unnecessary deaths, that they are the result of hidden agendas of evil men. Most people try to console themselves by making the tragedy sound either patriotic or to fulfill some higher purpose."

Taylor felt no need to pause now that she started talking. She actually felt good talking about the tragedy which affected her so much. Dominga had a way of making Taylor want to continue.

"I think of his death as a murder. I didn't start functioning until about two weeks after the funeral. My father never got over it. He was depressed and angry for two years, then he got sick."

"And then he died too," said Dominga figuring out the connection. Dominga's boldness surprised Taylor. She spoke as if completely unafraid of saying something offensive or even anything which might trigger a negative emotional response. “Oh my poor girl. Some people have too much sorrow in their lives don’t they? What has gotten you through it?”

“Can’t let it control you,” Taylor answered. “Besides, I’m the only thing my mother has left.”

“I must meet her one day.”

“Yes. You should, someday.” Taylor smiled.

“It must make you angry to think about it,” continued Dominga. “Do you ever desire vengeance?”

Taylor paused to think about the question. “Sometimes I daydream of an asteroid destroying the White House or the mansion of an infamous banking family.” She smiled and took a deep breath. “If there’s no justice at the end of this life, I’m gonna really be pissed.”

Dominga’s smile vanished and she became serious.

“I hope so too Taylor.”

II: DISCOVERY

A ring of fire gold
In a wet bed of cold
Waiting for a hand to hold

26

Taylor

Jan 18, 2009

While Dominga monopolized all of Taylor's time, Cesar tentatively suggested on several occasions that Taylor begin working at the shop, but his friend dismissed him with a wave of her hand and a smile. Eventually, Cesar seemed to lose hope of changing Dominga's mind and silently waited for his friend to finish with his future shop partner. Taylor noticed the impatience in his polite smile whenever Dominga told him about their plans for the day.

Despite her anxiety at postponing her project, Taylor enjoyed their time together and became well acquainted with Dominga. She pretended to ignore the private exchanges between Cesar and Dominga. Although Dominga refused to admit it, Taylor suspected she had been in love with Cesar for a long time and spent her time there in the hopes that Cesar would someday reciprocate her affection. From what she could see, however, nothing romantic had happened between them. Taylor suspected the death of Cesar's wife and sons prevented his action. Even though Taylor had the experience of losing her brother, she imagined it even more difficult to lose a wife and children. After a few days of shopping and preening, the excitement of her arrival subsided enough for Taylor to feel comfortable separating herself from Dominga and devoting her time to the purpose of her stay.

Since the day they showed the NMG to Cesar and his friends, all contact with Gerald had stopped. After Cesar explained the possible other energy source, he'd sent Gerald on a quest to find it and Gerald had departed excitedly on his mission. Taylor had serious doubts he would find anything, but for his sake she remained hopeful. She remembered how excitedly Cesar had spoken about the matter.

"As soon as I heard news reports about the electrochemists at the University of Utah," Cesar began, "and they claimed to have discovered cold fusion. I followed the story like you Americans follow your football teams. I knew the department of energy would fight to stop it."

"But wasn't it disproven?" asked Gerald. "That's all I heard."

"There's a lot more to the story, Gerald," explained Cesar calmly. "Dr. Pons was the head of the chemistry department. Don't you think it a little bit suspicious that the head of a chemistry department at a major university would make such an announcement to the press, if he hadn't verified it beforehand? That's something you don't take lightly. These were very intelligent people."

Gerald sat forward in his seat.

"I guess I didn't follow it all that closely. It happened in my ignorant, bleeding-heart liberal years."

While listening to them talk, Taylor wished she had her computer available so she could use Wikipedia to resuscitate her memory of the story highlights. Both Cesar and Gerald remembered the events in the news and had more direct experience. For Taylor, the story existed with countless other historical curiosities and she'd never spent any time investigating them.

If the immense power of the energy and finance industry *had* successfully duped the public, cold fusion could be the solution to their dilemma. She listened with interest, but did not want to get her hopes up too high. Even though Cesar's explanation made sense and Gerald could probably reveal more of the true story, the solution seemed too easy and convenient.

Cesar looked to Taylor and Gerald and shook his head. He spoke slowly as if explaining to children.

"Right after the announcement was made, the department of energy, which everyone knows is controlled by the oil and finance industry, met with the president. They claimed to be interested in investigating the matter to see if it was true. All the evidence, however, shows that they were only planning how to disprove the concept and discredit the men who made the announcement."

"Sorry to interrupt you, Cesar," interjected Dominga. "But why would they want to disprove it?"

"For years," he said, turning to her, "governments all over the world have been pouring billions of dollars into high-temperature fusion. Billions and billions of dollars, and can you guess where all that money goes? To very powerful corporations. The recipients of that immense treasure don't want the money to stop flowing, but I believe the deeper reason is because that solution requires big government. Since all that money goes to huge existing companies it is a self-sustaining strategy. If that energy source ever becomes viable, it will keep the current power structure in place. Only the big companies will be able to control the energy production process, and those are the same companies profiting from all the public spending."

The more Cesar talked, the more Taylor felt her excitement rising.

"So, if something simple and easy to produce, like cold fusion seemed to be, was developed and viable, smaller companies could afford to utilize it. Local communities could provide their own energy needs."

Cesar finished for her.

"Which would result in more local independence. And that's exactly what the big financial institutions don't want. They love big government spending. It keeps their accounts full. Those who have the power don't want to lose any of the market share."

"OK," Gerald said, trying to make sense of the new viewpoint. "If cold fusion was real, how did they keep it from being developed? Some company was bound to see the possibility and work on it."

"How familiar are you with how scientific research works?" Cesar asked.

"I've had no direct experience, so I probably don't know that much about it."

"The first thing you should know, it's like everything else in life. Funding is everything. Whoever controls the money, determines what research gets funded and what gets discarded. The same people who control research funding are the same people who control our politicians. All they had to do was to use the media to stigmatize those who believed Pons and Fleishmann. Those with a vested interest in hot fusion had a strong motivation to stop that research from going forward, and they have a limitless amount of money for the fight. Stop the funding of a thing and you stop that thing from development. It's like keeping sunlight away from the crops in your field."

"The government does control the majority of research," admitted Taylor, remembering many of her professors focusing on their next government research grant.

"I've got something for you, Gerald, that may help you start your investigation. It's a book by a science reporter from MIT. He did a lot of research on cold fusion and was involved with how they tried to discredit it."

Cesar stood and walked from the room. When he returned, he handed Gerald a book entitled *Fire from Ice* by Eugene Mallove.

"So, I'm the one to look into this?"

Gerald inspected the cover without opening the book.

"Taylor and I have to optimize the NMG. If anyone can get to the bottom of something, it's you. Remember that if there's something to be found, it's going to be a secret. I believe that's what you love uncovering, right? I've been wanting to make my own investigation for a long time."

As Gerald opened the book and flipped through the pages, he smiled.

"Thanks for the vote of confidence. After reading the book, I might just make a visit to the author."

"That would be a good place to start," said Cesar, shaking his head, "but it might be difficult."

"Why is that?"

"Eugene Mallove was murdered after publishing the book," he said sadly. "And just last year, the prime suspects in the case were acquitted."

27

Taylor

Gerald began his quest for fusion energy at the same time that Dominga and Taylor began their shopping extravaganza. They all waited anxiously for Gerald to make his first progress update, Taylor probably more than the others. She considered the lack of updates to be either a good or bad sign.

When Taylor and Cesar finally went to work in his shop, they were too busy to think much about Gerald and the status of his investigation. They only talked about the matter when Dominga or Doroteo asked about him at dinner. Even if Gerald had no chance of success, at least the excitement of the chase would prevent him from getting in their way. Cesar spoke with such excitement that Taylor felt like he had a chance of success. Cesar had always wanted to investigate on his own and Taylor had given him the perfect opportunity and tool, Gerald. Like he said, if anyone could find the truth, it was Gerald.

Cesar canceled all his appointments, extended all his project's due-dates and gave severance pay to his shop assistant and several referrals for another job.

"You have my undivided attention, Miss Taylor," he said when they went to the shop for the first time.

Taylor spent the first couple of days teaching Cesar the technical aspects of how the NMG worked and the theory of operation. For a man of his age, Cesar surprised Taylor. He learned quickly and possessed a large capacity to accept and understand new concepts. She had expected him to fight the concept of the device's apparent violation of conservation of momentum.

Once they both felt satisfied with his understanding of the NMG, Cesar wanted to focus on making a bigger prototype and had some ideas on new power couplings. In his shop, they had every machine they needed to build whatever they wanted. She had a quarter of the size in her father's machine shop with a third of the tools. In just a few days, they made a stationary, test NMG device which they bolted to the floor and connected a force gauge to measure the output. No matter how many times they tested their creation, Cesar would shake his head in disbelief.

"If I had not seen it for myself, I would not have believed."

"Typical human response," laughed Taylor.

She enjoyed watching his reaction. Taylor had never had as much fun, even with her father, and she adored her father. The excitement of their work helped keep the sadness away.

They spent long days together and both agreed that the days ended too abruptly. Neither of them took more than fifteen minutes for lunch, or any significant break. Usually, they only went home for dinner after Dominga called and complained about their dinners becoming cold.

Although she greatly wanted to learn about his personal life, she avoided questions about his relationship to Dominga. She would let him instigate that topic of discussion. She felt very close to both of them and wanted to know how he felt. In the house, they treated each other as brother and sister, but Taylor, and she suspected Dominga as well, secretly hoped for more.

She only had a few very brief encounters with Doroteo. Did he intentionally avoid confrontations with her, or did he just possess a naturally elusive personality, like a bat? If she ever had sufficient opportunity, Taylor planned to corner him for a conversation, but they spent so much of their time and emotional energy at the shop that after returning, she only wanted to sleep in preparation for the next day.

Once Taylor went to work with Cesar, Dominga knew she would have difficulty spending time together and would have to commandeer Taylor before Cesar did, if she wanted to spend any quality time with her. She even admitted directly of wanting to treat her as the granddaughter that circumstance had never provided. In the evening, however, Taylor felt too physically and emotionally exhausted to be of any use to anyone. She felt torn. Personally, she wanted to make Dominga happy. She seemed to miss Taylor more than Cesar.

They first heard from Gerald over a week later through a single email containing very little information. The email only gave his location, the Eastern United States, and his current objective, to obtain all the information about Eugene Mallove's affairs before the man died. Gerald had no other concrete information to share, but claimed to be following some suspicious leads before he would give them any useful progress update.

At the shop, time seemed to move too quickly for them to worry about Gerald. Although she felt extreme curiosity about his progress, Taylor focused on their work. Even Cesar failed to initiate any conversations about Gerald. Five more days passed before they had any other contact with Gerald. On that day, the phone rang just after noon and Taylor hesitated before answering it. Whenever Dominga called at that time, she usually wanted to complain of their absence, or ask if they would be late for dinner. Before answering, Taylor used a cloth towel to wipe the high-temperature grease from her hands.

"Hello?"

"Taylor," a woman said in a fake tone of exasperation. "What are you and Cesar doing over there? Watching movies or some other sort of foolishness?"

"Of course not," Taylor replied, laughing loudly. "We're working."

"Well, you should check your email, pronto. Gerald just called and said you need to answer his email."

"Why doesn't he just call the shop?"

"Do I look like Gerald's personal secretary?"

"Yes," Taylor teased then changed to a more serious tone. "I mean, of course not."

"Apparently, he doesn't want to talk about it over the phone. Maybe he's got sensitive information."

28

Taylor

"Ok, thanks for calling Dominga," Taylor said. "I'll check my email."

Over the fake exasperation, Taylor could hear a tone of curiosity from Dominga. After cutting the connection, she yelled over the noise of their testing to Cesar, telling him of the news.

She opened her email and saw the message from Gerald. He sent a simple and blunt message. From across the shop, Cesar asked what it said.

"He says one of us needs to go to Salt Lake City to meet with him." Taylor spoke while staring at the email in disbelief. "He says he's not technically qualified to determine what he found."

Later that afternoon, they left the shop early for dinner. When Dominga saw them enter through the door so early she seemed to go into shock. Normally, she would have been excited and probably asked Taylor to go somewhere with her, but she seemed impatient to hear the news. At the dining table, Cesar conveyed the news to her and Doroteo.

"Gerald wants you to drive to Salt Lake City?" asked Dominga incredulously. "Why on earth won't you fly?"

"Dominga," Cesar replied softly. "If things work out, we might be returning with something highly confidential. We cannot take such a thing on an airplane or have it shipped. It is too dangerous. Someone must drive down there and pick it up, and only Taylor and I are qualified to verify what it might be."

"If it is too dangerous to fly, then you should not go. Cannot you learn how to make this thing and just do it here? You are Cesar Sanchez! You can make anything."

"We'll be OK," he assured her and laughed. "We should only be gone for two to three days and we'll come straight back here. Everything will be fine."

"So Gerald will be driving back with you?"

"No," Doroteo said. "That won't work. Since Gerald flew to SLC, he has to fly out. Otherwise, it will look suspicious if anyone investigates this matter in the future. There can be no link to Gerald and Cesar and Utah. You should only use cash and Gerald leaves the same way he got there."

Dominga scowled at each of them. Taylor kept her attention on her food.

29

Gerald

Since departing from Seattle, Gerald attempted to follow the last few months of Eugene Mallove's life. He read the book Cesar gave him along with all other information he could find about the man. While reading the police reports, court records and media material, he knew key information had been either missed or deliberately omitted. The lawyer who defended the murder suspects had either been a fool or paid by the prosecutors. He would visit that attorney only as a last resort. After going through all the evidence, he came to the same conclusion as Cesar. The man's death had been much more than just a random act of violence.

Most of Mallove's relatives and friends refused to discuss the subject with Gerald, saying they already told the police everything they knew. He only had one useful interview, an old woman who claimed to have known Eugene Mallove since his childhood, one of the few people willing to talk with him. Old age had definitely inflicted damage to her coherency, but Gerald managed to extract useful information. He learned that just before the murder, Mallove returned from a trip to Utah. Gerald knew the twenty-two hundred mile trip to Salt Lake City would be required to complete the investigation. Maybe the story would even end there.

Before finishing the conversation with her, the ninety-three-year-old woman leaned forward, her eyes filling with sudden lucidity and life. With her cold fingers, she grabbed Gerald's arm. "They killed him, you know, murdered him for what he knew and what he was trying to do. I told him to be careful, but he never listened to me. He thought that being a famous hotshot reporter would protect him. He was so naive."

After a few moments, her grip relaxed and her hand reverted to cold bones covered by loose skin. She smiled sweetly, but the gesture failed to erase his sense of foreboding. He remembered her last words with extra clarity. She whispered and her trembling voice added extra emphasis.

"Don't let them know where you've been. Cover your tracks!"

"I'll be careful," he told her.

Gerald thanked her and then quickly left her house.

He next traveled to the place of Mallove's murder in Connecticut, at the apartment complex. While standing at the place where they found the dead body, Gerald wondered how other lawyers felt, the ones who defended or prosecuted people accused of murder. When they went to the place of the crime, did they have to imagine being the murderer? Probably. Gerald hated being so close to violence. He felt glad to have chosen a different legal specialty, one where he mostly helped small business owners maneuver through the legal minefields that the large corporations lobbied the congressmen to enact.

One of the older neighborhood residents also knew about Mallove's final trip to Utah and even remembered a name of someone Mallove visited, a man named Ammon. Even after the many years, the unique name stuck in his memory.

Gerald went back to his hotel room and spent over an hour investigating the name before he found an interesting connection to a Utah company named Cerametrics, located in the Salt Lake Valley. One of the company executives had the first name of Ammon and had been a lab assistant to Dr. Pons at the University of Utah, one of the professors who announced to the world that they had discovered cold fusion.

After discovering the connection between the name and cold fusion, Gerald had difficulty keeping his excitement under control. That same day, he booked a flight to Salt Lake City. The next day, he went to the airport and started his journey back to the West. On the flight, he wondered what he would find, either the final piece in the puzzle or a dead end. He had a feeling that Salt Lake City might be his final destination.

Gerald parked in the visitor parking of the Cerametrics Corporation in Salt Lake City. The cold of the dry winter desert seemed to extract all the heat from his bones. Remains from the recent snow storm had just been cleared from the parking lot. Dirty gray sand and salt dusted the pavement. Huge piles of the snow were deposited in the corners of the lot like some hastily erected fortress. The white snow would have been pretty, if not for the brown slush that stuck to everything. Just looking at all the frozen material made Gerald cold. He missed the warmer rains of Seattle.

He walked through the entrance and found a receptionist sitting at the front desk, staring at a computer screen. Gerald could see her browsing the internet from the reflection in her thick glasses. When she noticed the stranger standing in front of her, she quickly clicked the screen, erasing evidence of her indolence.

"Hello sir," she said, her nasal passage blocked by a slight cold. Her forced smile felt as warm as the slush outside. She squinted her eyes to get a better look at him and sat up straighter when she noticed the suit and tie. "Who are you here to see?"

"I'm here to see Ammon Brown. He won't be expecting me today." Gerald walked closer to the desk and put his hand on the counter between them. "Just tell him that Mr. Jones is here to see him."

Before arriving, he remembered his visit with the old woman back East. She had warned him to be careful with his name. Gerald hoped Ammon knew someone with the last name of Jones.

The receptionist sat back in response to his proximity.

"Is this a personal visit?"

"No." Gerald said, but did not elaborate.

The receptionist picked up the phone and dialed a number sequence. She talked so quietly that Gerald only heard a slight mumble and failed to distinguish any recognizable words. He attempted to act disinterested, but kept his eyes on her lips. When she put the phone down, she looked at him curiously before responding.

"He'll be down in a few minutes. Please have a seat."

A few minutes later, a man came around the corner of the main entrance area. He stood shorter than Gerald by several inches and several inches thicker. He wore a button shirt with horizontal stripes and no tie. When he saw Gerald sitting alone in the lobby with only the receptionist, he slowed his pace and squinted his eyes in an obvious attempt to determine if he knew Gerald.

"Excuse me, Mr. Jones," he said after stopping in front of Gerald. "Have we met previously? Am I expecting you?"

Gerald extended his hand with as warm a smile as he could fabricate.

"I apologize for coming to your place of employment, unannounced. I just wanted to know if I could arrange a time to meet with you, possibly for lunch this afternoon?"

Out of the corner of his eye, Gerald saw the receptionist look up from her computer at him. Gerald wondered if she would pick up the phone and call security, but she turned back to her computer screen, probably enticed by a message on some social networking site.

The man's smile faded almost to a straight line.

"What is this concerning?"

"I'd rather not go into detail here," Gerald leaned closer and lowered his volume so that only Ammon could hear him. "I want to talk to you about Eugene Mallove."

At the name of Mallove, the man's body stiffened and the remaining hint of a smile vanished completely. He looked like a man attempting to make a difficult decision, whether to flee, melt on the spot, or start crying. After a moment, Ammon seemed to slightly recover from shock.

"Whom, may I ask, do you represent?"

"Maybe I can take you to lunch or we can just talk in your office?" Gerald spoke as politely as he could, in an attempt to calm the man. If Ammon felt too much anxiety, he would be more difficult to handle. "Just me and no one else, at whatever place of your choosing. Today or tomorrow would suit my schedule the best. I hope you can spare some time."

"I'm very sorry, Mr. Jones." he said. "I have no idea what you're talking about. I know nothing about the man."

Gerald hoped to sound non-threatening, but he felt that Ammon needed just a little additional motivation.

"Are you sure you want that to be your official statement, Mr. Brown?"

"Where are you from?" Ammon's voice seemed to contain some courage, but his body language contradicted his confidence. "I could call security."

"What's the harm in talking with me and me alone? If you want, we could go to your office and talk there, if it's secure. I am not from the government, or the energy industry, if that's what you're afraid of."

Gerald took one step back to give the man some more room. Ammon ran his hand through his hair and looked back at the way he had come, as if he still wanted to run away. He looked at his watch before answering and when he spoke, Gerald could barely hear him.

"Listen, I really don't know what this is about," he said softly. "I will meet with you today, but I cannot do it at lunch. I can meet you later this afternoon, around four pm, but not here. I'd prefer to meet at the Christus statue at Temple Square, downtown. Just go to the North Temple Square entrance and I'll meet you at the top of the visitor's center. You can't miss it."

Gerald looked up in thought.

"The Christus? What's that?"

"It's the statue of Jesus in the north LDS visitors center," Ammon said curtly. "It's a very prominent landmark. If you want to meet with me, that's where it's going to be. If you'll excuse me, I have to get back to work."

"Thank you," Gerald said as Ammon turned to walk away.

"I'll see you at four."

Gerald watched Ammon until he disappeared in the hallway. After opening the door to leave, he glanced back and noticed the secretary looking at him. She did not look away after their eyes met. As he exited, she refused to return his smile.

30

Gerald

When back in the warmth of his car, Gerald sat and tried to remember if he knew the location of the Mormon visitor's center. He had never visited Salt Lake City before, but he knew Mormons first established the city and had their headquarters located there. Since Ammon wanted to meet at their visitor's center, Gerald would assume that Ammon identified himself as a Mormon. Did the man expect to feel some sort of spiritual safety at that location or did he just want to meet somewhere crowded?

Whether or not he could extract any information from Ammon, Gerald knew the meeting would be interesting. At least, his trip would be a sightseeing experience.

Since Gerald had several hours before the meeting, he decided to find the location of the Mormon visitor's center, Temple Square. He parked downtown, a few streets away from the Mormon Temple and used his iPhone to read about the city on Wikipedia. He learned about the founder of the city, Brigham Young, and how he wanted the temple to be the center of the city, both psychologically and geographically. The early Mormons based the coordinates of the whole valley in relation to the temple and then built the Temple Square visitor's center adjacent to it.

The immense granite building towered over the streets, cold and gray and solid. While not being the largest building in the city, it seemed to be the most substantial and impenetrable, like an ancient German castle. A golden statue sat atop one of its six spires, shining in the cold gray sky. When Gerald eventually got close enough to the building, he noticed strange symbols carved on the wall's surface. They looked like strange, astronomical symbols. The symbolism gave Gerald the impression that the Mormons believed additional ideas than the traditional Christians he knew.

While thinking about the city as founded by a persecuted religious group, Gerald began to reflect on Christianity and religion in general. The topic rarely intruded into his conscious thoughts. Even though some of his associates claimed to believe in a religion, it had never been a part of his life. After thinking about the people he knew, he realized that none of his close friends were religious. Was that by chance or did he unconsciously choose people more like him?

Neither his parents nor extended family had any association with religion, Christian or otherwise. His grandparents had been Presbyterians, but in name only. As far as he remembered, they had never talked about their religious beliefs or encouraged their children to participate in any religious tradition.

Gerald never felt any regret about the lack of religious indoctrination.

In his opinion, all traditional religions were nonsense. He considered himself extremely fortunate to have experienced a childhood free from a belief in mythical beings who mysteriously and arbitrarily helped him throughout his life. The thought always brought a silent, sarcastic laugh. Invisible beings helped humans, but the humans did not know about it and the creatures mysteriously left no evidence of that help.

After walking around downtown and getting some lunch, he decided to go to the place where he would later meet Ammon Brown. Instead of entering the north entrance, however, he entered by the west gate to Temple Square. He had almost an hour before the meeting, so he began walking and exploring the surroundings.

Despite his negative impression of religion, the place impressed him. The Mormon church kept the grounds very clean and even though a lot of people walked around him, he had plenty of space. Little islands supported by cement were filled with many different plants, flowers and trees. Remnants of snow could be seen in the corners. The air felt crisp and clean with the cold air of winter.

A few minutes after he passed through the gate, a pair of pretty young women stopped him. If not for the information on their name tags, Gerald would have thought they were women on a lunch break from some international conference. The shorter, dark-haired one looked like she came from somewhere in Southeast Asia, and the taller one came from somewhere in Latin America. Gerald had talked with a few Mormon missionaries in his life, but never with female missionaries.

In two separate incidents in Seattle, male emissaries from the Mormon church had stopped to talk with him. During his first encounter, he had asked them a few questions out of politeness, but with no real interest. When they told him about their motivation for leaving home to serve their church and God, Gerald found their rehearsed response amusing. He almost asked if they wanted to try again or he could refer them to a good acting coach.

After that first experience, he read some material about the church's history, about Joseph Smith, gold plates, and angels. Gerald found their history very interesting, especially as it related to the early American revivalist culture, but he wondered how it survived in the modern era. When another pair of missionaries contacted him, he'd said he knew everything he needed to know about their church.

Unlike his previous encounters with young male missionaries, Gerald had no reservation at meeting the two beautiful girls. They politely asked about his visit and seemed genuinely interested in him. The female missionaries told him about some of the buildings and how Brigham Young had founded the city, including the temple. When they started talking solemnly about the founder of the church, Joseph Smith, Gerald had to force the polite smile to remain on his face. He felt sorry for the two beautiful young women. Most likely, they only knew about the respectable aspects of Joseph Smith's life. They seemed happy to be missionaries, so Gerald would not attempt to challenge their view of reality.

No matter what he felt about religion, Gerald had to admit that the Mormon church understood marketing. If the church chose to use their male missionaries in their visitor's center, it might drive people away rather than towards it. He sincerely wanted to talk with the girls more, but needed to arrive at the meeting place before Ammon. After a few minutes, he asked them where he could find a statue of Jesus and they seemed excited to tell him.

"Enjoy your visit Gerald," the taller girl said.

Gerald thanked them and walked away in the direction they instructed. Since he wanted to minimize any evidence of his visit, he probably should have kept his real name a secret. He actually laughed out loud after realizing that two young women had caused him to forget the hazards of his visit.

On his way to the north entrance, Gerald began to understand the reason why Ammon wanted to meet him there. The trees, flowers, pensive statues of pioneers and protective walls seemed to transport him into a different world, an oasis from the commotion of the inner-city. Did Ammon think that the Mormon sanctuary would offer some form of religious protection? Gerald hoped so. If the man thought an omniscient being protected him, maybe he would be less cautious and reveal more information. The desire to meet in a safe place, protected by some deity, might be an indication that Ammon possessed dangerous information, the same information that had led to the death of Eugene Mallove.

When he came within fifty yards of the building, Gerald noticed the giant statue of Jesus where he would meet Ammon. "This is the right place," he said quietly to himself while looking up at the two-story building. Through the second story window, the statue of Jesus stood with his arms outstretched, reminding Gerald of an ancient Greek God. Gerald removed his camera from his pocket and snapped a few pictures of the building. Taking pictures would also make him look like a tourist.

Gerald consciously watched for Ammon or anyone else suspicious. When he looked at his watch, it showed three twenty-five, just a little while before he expected Ammon to arrive. The man would probably arrive early to stake out the place, but probably not earlier than Gerald. He unexpectedly felt a little excitement to play the game. Gerald played the part of covert agent and Ammon played the secret government scientist. He only needed a gun to complete the game.

After entering the building, Gerald became conscious of the temperature again and enjoyed the transition from the cold outside. Many more tourists walked inside the building than outside, including several other young female missionaries. Many of the people dressed nicely, as if waiting to take part in some formal event.

Gerald noticed some escalators going to a lower level. When he came close to them, he saw huge paintings on the lower level and felt tempted to visit them. After a moment's thought, however, he decided against the diversion and reminded himself of his reasons for being there. He hoped to arrive at the meeting place before Ammon.

He followed a large winding walkway up to the second level, to the statue of Jesus. Huge images of planets, galaxies, and large swirling cloud formations covered the ceiling and walls. He almost felt like walking through a planetarium dedicated to an interesting combination of astronomy and Christian mythology. At the top stood Jesus, frozen arms outstretched in welcome.

Several people sat in the rows of benches between the statue and the huge window. Gerald chose a seat in the back, where he could look from the statue to the people outside. After sitting on the soft cushion, he took a deep breath and felt his body instantly begin to relax.

While looking at the statue of Jesus, Gerald tried imagining how people felt centuries in the past, before Christianity. How did they feel when visiting the temples of their gods, bowing down to their beloved marble icons? The common person probably had little experience with art and elaborate dwellings. The experience must have filled them with amazement and probably a good dose of fear and intimidation.

After a moment, Gerald realized that the situation remained the same. Despite all the information available to the common person, the majority still believed in what these monuments represented. People lived with so much scientific advancement and knowledge, none of it achieved with the help of the gods. Did people like the idea of being led by someone or something more intelligent than they? It would be comforting, he admitted, to be given orders from an omniscient being. All accountability would be removed from the individual. It would also eliminate the necessary burden of critical thinking. For a very small moment, Gerald wished he could have that luxury.

Every few minutes, female missionaries would arrive to give a presentation to the people gathered in front of the statue. The presentation began with the recording of a deep male voice quoting biblical passages. While waiting, he watched all those who attended the presentations. Mostly, the people appeared to be a mixture of Mormon tourists and local church members who had nothing better to do. Many families came with their children. He stopped counting how many times he noticed the parents shushing their children for the slightest noise or interruption.

Finally, he saw Ammon ascend the walkway and enter the large upper room. He looked around and did not see Gerald at first, due to a small group of young adults standing in his way. When their eyes finally locked in recognition, Gerald stood and smiled. Ammon seemed as uncomfortable as when Gerald first met him. They shook hands again.

31

Gerald

Ammon led Gerald to the back where he had already been sitting.

"Let's talk here," Ammon said. After they both took a seat, Ammon swept his eyes suspiciously around the room, as if searching for someone watching them. Gerald also felt some paranoia, but he pretended to be calm.

"Excuse me for asking," Gerald began. "But why did you want to meet here, in this place?"

"This is as good a public place as any. I did not want to meet at a restaurant." Ammon took a deep breath and sighed as if emotionally exhausted. "Before we talk about anything, can I see some form of identification?"

"Of course," Gerald said and opened his wallet. He handed his driver's license and a business card to Ammon."You will notice that my name's not Jones', as I said at your work. I didn't want your receptionist to remember my correct name, but I don't care if you know my name. Just as you expect confidentiality from me, I also expect it from you. I work at a small law firm. You can look it up if you want. Are you worried that I might not be who I say I am?"

Ammon looked at both pieces of paper, studying them for anything out of the ordinary.

"One cannot be too cautious."

While Ammon inspected the license and business card, Gerald glanced over to the statue, and then to a man facing them. He was not looking at Gerald or Ammon, but appeared to be looking out the window. While everyone else took pictures of the statue, this gentleman seemed to be aiming his camera at them, or towards the window. Gerald had the distinct feeling of being watched, but then the man turned around and took a couple of snapshots of the marble Jesus. Ammon cleared his throat and handed the license back to Gerald and then put the business card in his jacket pocket.

Before beginning his prepared statement, Gerald rehearsed it in his mind. Like most things in the real world, his story would contain elements of truth and fabrication and he expected Ammon's story to be similarly composed. Gerald might be required to do extensive interrogation to gain an accurate understanding of the situation, but Gerald did that for a living and usually got what he wanted.

"Let me start at the beginning," Gerald began, changing to a business tone. "Our client contacted us two months ago because he was being questioned concerning the death of Eugene Mallove. There have been no arrests made yet, neither has he been named as a suspect, but they're showing signs of getting ready to do so. We're preparing a defense against the district court's possible allegations of his involvement in the murder. You are aware of the case, I take it?"

"Why do you say that?"

"Prior to the cold fusion announcement at the University of Utah, you worked as a laboratory assistant to Dr. Pons. Dr. Mallove was one of the few defenders of cold fusion. He must have been around the lab where you worked. Did you ever meet him? What do you know about the murder?"

"I read about the murder of course, but what makes you think I have any special information about it?"

"Do you know what I think of it all?" Gerald changed his angle of attack slightly.

Ammon's brown eyes widened.

"I have no idea."

"The original arrests they made in connection with the murder, smelled of federal interference. Someone higher up wanted that case closed and they didn't care if they got the right guys or not."

Ammon looked interested for the first time.

"What makes you think that?"

"After looking into the case, there was nothing to tie those guys with the murder. It was one of the flimsiest cases I've seen yet. Did you know the two charged with the murder were exonerated just last year? Seems convenient doesn't it? Right after the public forgets about the case."

"No," Ammon said. "I didn't know they were exonerated."

Gerald thought Ammon seemed to be more familiar with the case than he intimated. He continued speaking before Ammon said anything else.

"I read the book by Mallove too. He was quite the defender of cold fusion."

"I knew about the book," admitted Ammon. "He might have made some of the wrong people angry, for exposing what he did."

"I know about the conspiracy theories," Gerald said as if uninterrupted. He wondered if Ammon was starting to lower his defenses. "About how the oil industry doesn't want something like cold fusion being developed. I don't know if I completely agree. I think it goes to a higher level than that. Tell me, since you worked with Dr. Pons, what do you think about how the scientific establishment seemed to work with the media to discredit the claims? Were they really frauds?"

Ammon looked both offended and worried. He spoke quieter.

"Do you really think we would take that to the press without being absolutely certain of what we had found? Pons and Fleishmann spent years verifying the data!"

"If Mallove was killed for exposing a cover-up, why did they wait for him to finish the book?" Gerald asked the question, but gave no time for Ammon to reply. "I don't think they care as much about revenge as they care about letting the technology get developed. Mallove must have done something between his death and after his book was published. This is what I'm working on now, tracking what he was doing before he died. If things go the same way they did before, concerning the murder suspects, I'm going to need hard evidence as to the motive for the murder. We need the correct motive and that will keep my client in the clear."

"Seeking the truth, huh?" asked Ammon sarcastically. "And a lawyer too." He laughed for the first time then glanced up to Jesus. "Lawyers were always fighting with him."

Gerald knew religion would be broached sometime in the conversation. He laughed too, accustomed as he was to all the jokes about lawyers, but felt unsure if Ammon was joking or being serious.

"The truth of cold fusion will get out, eventually," he said quietly. "God won't allow it to be suppressed forever."

"How do you think God will do that and when?" Gerald decided to conceal his atheist views from the man.

"Seek and ye shall find," Ammon said gravely. "Someday, enough people will seek, and he will lead them to it."

Why did God need 'enough' people to seek, in order to reveal the truth? What was the magic number of people? Ammon looked up to the statue and Gerald followed his gaze. Jesus appeared to be looking at them, nodding gravely.

Was Gerald ready to accuse Ammon about his suspicion that Eugene Mallove visited Cerametrics before he died, or did the man need more probing? Gerald required only a moment to realize that he needed to divert the conversation away from religion, to more concrete matters.

"What exactly is the truth of cold fusion?" asked Gerald with reserved curiosity. "Is there more to it than what was presented in 1989?"

For the next few minutes, Ammon explained to Gerald what he thought about cold fusion research. Ammon thought the reason for the lack of progress could be attributed to the absence of capital investment in research. Even though several scientists and institutions experimented with cold fusion, they did not have access to the funds necessary for sufficient development. The media had effectively associated cold-fusion with lunacy and ineptitude and cut its umbilical cord.

If any scientist or researcher ever showed too much interest in cold fusion, they would be in danger of losing their jobs and reputations. All public funds were currently focused on hot plasma fusion. Ammon laughed bitterly about how hot fusion had failed to reach the break-even point yet, where the energy output equaled the energy input. In some of his experiments at the University of Utah, they had achieved several times the output.

"Wait a minute," interrupted Gerald, as if genuinely curious. "If that was the case, wouldn't they be using it to generate power commercially?"

Ammon stopped talking and looked at Gerald as if he just crawled out of a black abyss. For a moment, Ammon became speechless and Gerald frantically attempted to discover the reason. From the look on his face, Gerald wondered if Ammon had said something unintended. When he resumed speaking, he acted as if nothing had interrupted him.

"As with every new technology in its initial stages, the process was unstable and at times, unpredictable. At the time, we still hadn't understood the process. It's going to take a lot of money for the necessary research and development before they figure it out. I'm sorry I don't have anything to help you about the murder."

He turned to look out the window, to avoid eye contact with Gerald.

“Is it possible that Mallove was about to expose something new? Or perhaps he had something new?”

“Like I said. I don’t know.”

Gerald frowned.

“You may be telling the truth, but I think you’re holding something back. Do you want to know what I’m holding back?”

Gerald wondered what to tell him next, the truth about his real motives or what he knew about Mallove’s visit to Cerametrics? Eventually, he might have to reveal both. Ammon turned to look directly into Gerald's eyes, silently waiting for him to answer his own question.

“I know about Eugene Mallove’s visit to Cerametrics.”

Before continuing, Gerald wondered if his accusation had frightened Ammon too much. Hopefully, Ammon would think Gerald also knew the reason for Mallove’s visit, when he only had a guess, a hope.

“If I found out about it," Gerald continued. "Then there’s a chance that government investigators will also stumble upon it, but there’s also a good chance that they won’t. If they do find out, however, they might put two and two together.”

“Are you threatening us?” Ammon said and began to shift uncomfortably in his seat. His demeanor returned to one of suspicion.

“No, I'm not threatening you,” Gerald said, trying to suppress a smile. Ammon chose not to deny the accusation, implying the truth of it. “I'm just trying to find the motive for the murder.”

“Yes, but your client is your top priority,” Ammon said. He glanced up at the statue, as if he expected Jesus to give him hand signals about what to do. “I know how you lawyers work, *save the client at all costs*. How do I know that you’re not going to divert the investigation to Cerametrics? How do we know you are not working for the government?”

Gerald laughed out loud at this comment. A missionary at the base of the statue was talking on a microphone to the few people listening to her. At the outburst, all ten people in the seats turned to look at him. He whispered a silent “Sorry!”

“When you go home tonight, look up my name on Google and look up my law firm. You'll see that the government and I are not exactly friendly with each other.”

A simple search on Google would show his unsavory history with the government. Of course, his story could always be interpreted as an elaborate cover. Gerald began to wonder if he should have fabricated the story of the client in the first place. Lying to Ammon in front of his God seemed the ultimate desecration. Did Ammon think that meeting in front of Jesus would prevent Gerald from saying anything dishonest? He smiled at that thought.

“It's getting late,” said Ammon. “Can we finish this discussion tomorrow?”

Gerald wondered if the time had come for him to use his bluff. He needed Ammon to tell him the reason for Mallove's visit to Cerametrics, but the man would probably keep that information secret. Gerald had to make a guess about the visit and the reason might as well be what he hoped.

“Tomorrow, I need you to tell me what Mallove was planning to do with what you gave him.”

Ammon gulped, and to Gerald's surprise, he again refused to deny the accusation.

"I'll need a day to think about it."

32

Gerald

Ammon walked away without looking back, but he did pause to look up at the statue of Jesus. "Probably gives him comfort," Gerald said to himself.

When Ammon disappeared from his view, Gerald turned to look out the window one last time before leaving. The sun had taken its light away and the scene looked cold. He would rather stay inside, in the warmth. After a few minutes of sitting and watching the people outside, he reluctantly left the building.

On the return walk to his car, a tall, thin woman walking in his direction caught his attention. She gave him a friendly smile as she passed. Instinctively, he turned for a quick look at her walk away. After turning, however, he noticed a man walking behind him. He wore a long black coat, over a suit and tie. They made brief eye contact and then Gerald faced forward again and continued walking. The situation could have been coincidence, but Gerald felt uneasy about it.

He heard the footsteps behind him for at least, the next two turns, and kept his eyes ahead of him trying to act casually. After the third turn, he could no longer hear his follower so he quickly turned. Gerald could no longer see the man.

He had been followed before in his life, in Seattle and in Kivu, a province in the Democratic Republic of the Congo when he had volunteered there with an aid group. During the most recent incident, undercover cops followed him while investigating the Federal Reserve Bank break-in. At first, he tried confronting them, but they only denied his accusations, calling him crazy and paranoid. He felt foolish and frustrated. In the end, he decided to just ignore them and keep doing his business. Since he had nothing to hide, he let them waste their time. He would deal with the situation as it progressed. As an aide worker in Kivu, soldiers sometimes followed his group, but during those incidents, the soldiers made absolutely no attempt to hide their identity.

In this case, his anxiety levels rose to new levels. He tried to remain calm, but could only think about the death of Mallove. To make the situation more complicated and dangerous, his current worries involved more than just himself. The lives of his friends depended on what happened. If Gerald noticed anything too suspicious before his meeting the next day, he might have to delay the meeting until he felt safer.

After shutting the door to his hotel room, he finally felt able to relax a bit and once in bed, he had time to think. Since reality usually existed between extremes, Gerald decided to start at the best possible case, baseless paranoia.

Unfortunately, the best case scenario rarely existed so he had to consider the worst situation, clandestine government agents. If they existed and kept Ammon under surveillance, then Gerald would be under the same surveillance. In that case, he would need to find a way to make his visit to Cerametrics appear benign and then disappear to seek advice from Cesar and Doroteo.

After his paranoia dropped back to baseline, Gerald considered an alternate situation, a much better possibility than the worst case scenario. Perhaps one of Ammon's associates had followed him. Ammon was unlikely to have been working alone for this long of a time. Besides, he'd had plenty of time to discuss the situation with his friends. If the positions had been reversed, Gerald probably would have had the man followed.

The next day, Gerald stayed in his hotel room until ten, then took a short walk outside. He wanted to see if anyone would follow him again, but he saw no one. Light from another cold gray day helped him forget the paranoia of the previous evening. When he safely got in his car, he felt better.

Almost exactly twenty-four hours after his first visit, Gerald returned to the lobby of Cerametrics. He encountered the same receptionist doing the same activity, pretending to work and shopping on ubid.com. He saw the website distinctly reflected on her glasses. After a few seconds of standing in front of her, she looked up.

"Hi, Mr. Jones," she began hesitantly. To his surprise, she remembered his name. "Here to see Ammon?"

"Yes, I am. I'll wait for him here, in the lobby."

"OK, have a seat. I'll call him."

After a few minutes, Ammon entered the lobby, wearing another forced smile. He seemed less stressed that the previous evening. Perhaps the meeting at his religious sanctuary helped him feel safer, more secure. They shook hands and Gerald expected to be escorted to his office. Instead, Ammon said they were going on a drive.

"Where are we going?"

Instead of answering Gerald in the lobby, Ammon led him outside to the parking lot. As they walked to Ammon's car, he spoke.

"I discussed the situation last night with my friends and decided to give you the benefit of the doubt. I don't trust you completely, but after today, I should know whether or not I can. Of course, it all depends on your level of cooperation."

Ammon opened the drivers side, back door of his light blue Ford Escort, and indicated for Gerald to sit. Instead of entering, Gerald remained standing and held onto the top of the door.

"I need to know where we're going."

"Do you want to know why Eugene Mallove was murdered?"

"Yes," Gerald said, his excitement beginning to rise.

"Then get in the back and lay down. You cannot see where we are going. Understand?"

"You want me to lay down in the back?" Gerald felt an irrational fear of wrinkling his suit.

"Yes, or our meeting ends now. If you prefer, you can wear a mask, but that might look a little suspicious."

Gerald hesitated before getting in the back seat.

"Can't I just sign a non-disclosure agreement?"

"Not good enough," Ammon said, failing to show any amusement at the joke. "Nothing bad will happen to you, unless you're lying to me."

Gerald got in the back seat, but sat in the seat like normal.

"And what if I'm telling the truth, but you still think I'm lying?"

Ammon sat in the driver seat, shut the door, then looked back.

"We'll know. Don't worry."

Ammon locked eye contact with Gerald for a moment until he relented and laid down. Gerald could either follow their instructions, or he would not get any further. Even though the experience felt awkward, Gerald thought of the car ride as the final sprint to the finish line. How did they downgrade the risk he represented? Did they do an internet search to verify his identity? That might not have helped.

At the beginning of the ride, Gerald decided to keep quiet, and just relax. After about ten minutes of driving, however, he tried asking Ammon about his family and personal life. The man kept his answers short, with no informative details so Gerald quit trying to make conversation. He also quit trying to keep track of all the turns. The whole ride took about forty minutes.

As the car slowed to a stop, Ammon turned around and held up a black stretchy hat.

"Here, put this over your head. We're going to get out."

Before sitting erect, Gerald stretched the hat over his head, all the way over his eyes. The fabric appeared very dense so that Gerald saw nothing but blackness. The experience reminded Gerald of Christmas morning as a kid, when his father would lead them to the dining room, past the room with their presents.

When Gerald exited the car, the silence almost overpowered him. Even with the light wind in the distance, the silence still felt palpable. The amazing sensation helped wash away some of his anxiety. He had only felt that kind of silence in the Congo. The cold, however, made it an entirely different experience. Gerald felt every ice crystal falling on his bare neck and hands.

As Ammon led Gerald inside a building, he had the distinct feeling of being watched by more than one pair of eyes. Instantly, he noticed the familiar smells of mold and stagnant water. Having lost his sense of sight made the scent much stronger. Ammon led him into a room and sat him on a chair. Surprisingly, he felt no fear. If Ammon worked for the government, Gerald would probably be feeling much less excitement.

"Can I take this thing off yet?" he said after hearing the door handle quietly click.

Instead of answering, Ammon pulled the hat off Gerald's head. Ammon stood before him in an empty room with a single lightbulb hanging from the ceiling. Gerald quickly put his hand up to shield the light from his eyes, then turned to see his surroundings. They placed his chair in the middle of a large, empty room. He could see a window high up on the wall. No light came through the glass.

"Gerald," Ammon began.

"I don't suppose you're going to tell me where I am?"

"Not yet," Ammon answered while pulling a backpack over one shoulder. "This is where we find out if you're being honest with us." He tried to speak confidently, but Gerald thought he acted like a man about to pull a bloody piece of meat from the mouth of a lion.

When Ammon pulled a syringe out of his backpack, Gerald sat back in his cold metal seat.

"Wait a minute, Ammon!" he said, his eyes opening wide. "I have no idea where I am, and now you expect to give me some drug? What's in the syringe?"

"Sodium thiopental," he said as calmly as possible. "It can be used as a truth serum and it's completely safe."

Gerald turned around in a momentary confusion, as if looking for a hidden camera crew. Was a group of people watching him? He should have been afraid, but Ammon appeared completely harmless.

"I am not letting you inject me with anything."

"I can think of no other way to be satisfied."

"I cannot willingly consent to it," began Gerald, attempting to sound reasonable. "It would be unethical. I have potentially damaging information, held in confidentiality for friends and clients. It would be unethical for me to put myself in a position to compromise their confidential information. It is impossible for me to trust that you will attempt to only extract my sincerity and intentions, therefore, I cannot let you inject me with that liquid."

"We may be at an impasse then," Ammon said while wiping his forehead. He looked deflated and unable to argue, but a little impressed. "I am not the only individual who needs to trust you."

Gerald decided to use his last option, the truth.

"Listen, I'm willing to tell you whatever you need to know. I am willing to be completely honest with you."

"Completely honest?" Ammon asked with sudden suspicion. "Are you not who you say you are?"

"No," Gerald held his hand up. "I am Gerald Fuger, and I am a lawyer, just like I said I was. I was completely honest about that, but there is no client, or at least, not the kind I hoped you thought. I have nothing, in any way, to do with Eugene Mallove's murder, or any prosecution of it."

He paused to let Ammon comprehend the information and anxiously watched Ammon's expression for signs of anger. To Gerald's relief, the man seemed curious instead of angry.

"So who are your clients or friends then?"

"I am not at liberty to say," Gerald tried sounding reassuring. "But they mean you no harm in any way. They want to remain completely out of the limelight, anonymous like you. I haven't even told them about you yet."

33

Gerald

"What do they want?" Ammon asked. He sounded like someone playing Monopoly who'd just drawn the card to go all the way back to the beginning. "What is the real purpose of meeting with me?"

"They want the same thing Eugene Mallove wanted, what you gave to him."

Gerald's entire bluff depended on his guess being correct, that clandestine hired thugs had murdered Eugene Mallove for what he'd had in his possession, which Ammon and his associates had given him. If Gerald guessed incorrectly, Ammon would know and Gerald's mission might fail. A fusion power generator seemed too implausible, but so did the NMG. He had to make the attempt.

Ammon paused for a good five seconds. His words brought a chill to Gerald's chest.

"What do you think we gave him?"

"A fusion generator," Gerald said without hesitation. For a moment, he feared Ammon would laugh in his face.

"What do your friends want with a fusion generator?"

"It's not my place to say," Gerald said, trying to hide his excitement. "But they know what will happen to them if they are caught with it. So you can see, it is in my best interest to fly under the radar, just like you."

"So how did you find me?" Ammon looked confused and worried. "Will others be able to follow the same trail?"

"We can discuss the details later," Gerald said as if details had little importance. "But I don't think you have to worry about anything. The whole cold fusion fiasco is part of history and no one is trying to open the case up again. I am curious though, why do you think Mallove was murdered?"

"If you think about the alternatives," began Ammon. "Destroying the generator was their prime objective. Murdering Mallove was a warning message to the world. Everyone knows that secrets will eventually be discovered. If a device was ever allowed to exist, it would escape their grasp at some time. Game over. Free energy isn't exactly in their best interest, at least, not while the oil market is so lucrative." Ammon leaned up against the wall, next to the window and rested against it. "To tell you the truth, when we heard of Mallove's murder, we thought that we were going to get..."

"The same fate?" interjected Gerald.

"Yes. We took a huge risk giving him what we did, but we knew Mallove would never willingly betray us. We just thought he would be more discreet with it. He wanted to develop it, you know, get it into the right hands who could make it happen. Apparently, he made a mistake and took it to the wrong people."

"You're lucky to be alive," Gerald said. "I wonder if they killed him too quickly, before they learned about you? Have you ever considered the possibility that they know about you, and are keeping you under surveillance?"

"After so many years," Ammon said. "We stopped worrying about that, until I saw you yesterday."

"So when do I get to see it? Is it here?" Gerald looked around at the room, the one place he knew it was not located.

"It's not here," Ammon said going to the door. "I'd like you to meet Tom, my boss. I'm sure he has a few more questions for you."

Ammon opened the door, revealing a tall man standing in a dark hallway. The light from the hanging lightbulb in the room, cast his features in an eerie light. He stood almost three inches taller than Ammon and just as thick, with muscle instead of fat. He appeared to be in his mid-fifties and had streaks of gray in his blond hair.

Before the man entered the room, he seemed to be inspecting Gerald for flaws. After a moment he came to some conclusion and smiled thinly, but with narrowed eyes. Gerald felt more confidence from Tom than from Ammon.

"Gerald Fuger," Tom said and stepped into the room. When he shut the door, Gerald felt imprisoned. "I see Ammon let you into the club. We don't have any reason to worry about you, do we? Remember where you are. No, wait, you have no idea where you are. Isn't that right?"

34

Cesar

Cesar marveled at his luck to work with such a beautiful and intelligent young lady. As a younger man, he probably would have been too intimidated or too obsessed with impressing her to get much work done. Sometimes when she looked at him, her green eyes made him pause with admiration of her presence, but he never felt any physical attraction. After the death of his wife, Cesar felt no need to form physical relationships with other women. At that point in his life, he focused on enjoying the qualities of other people, male or female. Taylor made that task easy. She also reminded him of his daughter.

Forming such a close friendship with a man like Gerald Fuger showed Taylor to be a good judge of character. Intelligent people usually felt drawn to others of the same or higher intelligence, not just interest. Although he liked to tease Gerald, Cesar considered himself lucky to know the man. When he saw Taylor and Gerald together, he sometimes wondered if Gerald had a romantic interest in her. Gerald needed a strong woman in his life. He and Taylor would be a good match, but somehow Cesar failed to see that relationship starting. Gerald should keep their relationship platonic. Cesar planned to initiate that conversation one day.

Cesar enjoyed watching the growing relationship between Taylor and Dominga. The older woman needed a younger woman to love and pamper. Dominga loved finding people like Taylor, someone who needed just a little polishing, someone who had not yet discovered the need for some vanity in her life. In Cesar's opinion, Taylor would never be truly converted. She was just what Dominga needed.

Taylor's arrival changed the whole social dynamic of his house. She helped to alleviate the friction between Dominga and Doroteo which sometimes became dangerous. Cesar thought his two friends secretly enjoyed the conflict but failed to see or care about forbidden territory. Taylor became a pleasant distraction. Her physical and mental brilliance helped return life to his friend's eyes. Although Doroteo liked Taylor, he would never show it. If not for the excitement of their work at his shop, Cesar would have chosen to spend more time at home with his new daughter and enlivened friends.

While working on the NMG, Cesar thought their level of excitement could not get any higher. Then Gerald sent his message. After Cesar read the email from Gerald, he looked at Taylor in shock and disbelief.

"I cannot believe it. Could he have found a fusion generator?"

"He found something," Taylor said, brushing her thick red hair out of her eyes. "He wouldn't be telling us this if he didn't think it was something important."

"To be honest," he said as if confessing to a Catholic Priest. "I never really believed, in my heart that there was anything to find, concerning cold fusion. It was pure hope, but I thought it would be good for Gerald to go on the hunt. He's like a bloodhound, only truly happy when he was on the scent of some poor animal."

"I don't know what to think. It seems too good to be true." Taylor sat down in a chair and gave out a long sigh. She looked tired.

"Yes," he agreed.

"All of this doesn't feel real," she said quietly, as if spoken only to herself.

After a few minutes, Cesar reread the message. He spoke slowly. "It's possible that there is something else going on."

"What do you mean?"

"I don't know. He could be in trouble. His emails are encrypted, so why is he providing almost no information?"

"No," Taylor said abruptly. Searching for implications in his email probably required more time and effort than literal translations. "He thinks he found it, but needs us to verify it, as well as pick it up. It's exactly how I felt when I called him about the NMG. If he was in trouble of some sort, he would have given a hint in his message. This message is pure, sincere Gerald."

"I don't want to get my hopes up, but what if he actually found what we need?"

"If he has a fusion generator," Taylor said and smiled wide, "and it produces the kind of power it should, we can make a ship they cannot capture."

Cesar imagined what Doroteo would say if he could participate in their conversation. He would lecture them about proceeding too quickly, or at all. While Cesar worked with Taylor on developing the new technology, Doroteo would be considering the potential security issues.

"It also means we need to take more precautions against discovery," Cesar said and wondered for a moment if they should abandon their quest. Even if he felt that to be the correct course of action, he could not relinquish the thrill of the chase. "This is getting even more serious than it already was."

Taylor's smile waned just a little bit, but she retained the same confident look she always had. While watching her pale skin become even whiter, Cesar thought she looked more alive. Did fear give her strength? That night at the house, after Cesar explained their plan of traveling by car to Salt Lake City the next morning, Doroteo spoke to Cesar.

"I'm driving down with you," Doroteo said. His tone allowed for no disagreement and Cesar saw no reason to argue with his friend, but he did have an alternate plan.

"What do you think about driving down with Taylor and accompanying me on the return trip? You could be backup."

Cesar wanted Doroteo and Taylor to spend some time together, even though he expected his friend to refuse. Letting Taylor help acquire the fusion reactor seemed only fair, but he would rather be the one to acquire it.

Doroteo responded only with a "hmmm" and gave Cesar enough time to finish his proposal.

"There should be no problems on the way there, once I get out of Salt Lake.

I'm more concerned about getting the thing."

"That's true," agreed Doroteo.

"Why does Taylor need to go at all?" asked Dominga.

Cesar looked at her with surprise and Taylor put her hand on Dominga's shoulder.

"There's no way I'm gonna miss this. Don't worry, we've got the man himself with us."

Taylor extended her right hand and squeezed Doroteo's shoulder. Cesar suppressed a smile at the sight of the girl being so affectionate with him. In response, Doroteo tensed almost imperceptibly, but remained motionless as if failing to notice the physical contact. No one ever touched Doroteo, not even Dominga.

That evening, Taylor emailed Gerald about their plan to leave early the next morning. He replied within a few minutes and let them know to bring cash, a lot of cash. They needed fifty thousand dollars total, but Gerald could only provide about ten thousand. Cesar provided the rest without going to the bank.

After seeing the large sum of money, Taylor seemed to go into shock. She had probably never seen that much cash in her life. Cesar considered the sum to be an insignificant compensation for what the scientists might be selling. Taylor recovered quickly from her reaction.

Cesar entered the kitchen at six-thirty the next morning, surprised to find Taylor sitting at the kitchen table drinking coffee and eating toast. She looked up at him and smiled with obvious excitement in her features.

"Be careful and say hi to Gerald for me," Taylor said on his way out the door. "Let us know when we can come escort you home."

"I will," he said.

As Cesar turned onto the road, he noticed Taylor waving from the front porch. Hopefully, his excitement would help keep him awake during the long drive to the Salt Lake Valley, his first visit to the area.

A light rain assaulted his car, then stopped when he reached Tacoma. Time passed slowly, giving him the time alone to help focus his thoughts, of all the ways to build the engine to power their first craft into space. He only had to stop twice for bathroom breaks.

In the middle of his drive through Idaho, he received an email from Gerald on his iPhone. Gerald gave directions to where they would meet and then take him to show him the device. When he arrived in downtown Salt Lake City, the sky began to darken and the whole valley began to glow with artificial lighting. He would have to wait until the next day to fully appreciate the Wasatch mountains looming to the east. Seeing them at dusk already made him feel small.

He drove directly to the hotel, instantly noticing Gerald in the lobby. Cesar first noticed the huge smile on Gerald's face.

"I think this is it," Gerald said after they sat in the corner of the lobby, away from anyone else. "It required some maneuvering to get them to show it to me. They don't trust me fully yet, but I think you can help with that."

"So they showed this thing to you. How do you know it is what they claim?"

"That's why you're here, Cesar," he said with a laugh. "The device they showed me was amazing. Eugene Mallove bought one from them and someone found out about it, but they failed to make the connection to Cerametrics."

"This company, Cerametrics, they make and sell the device?" Cesar felt amazement at the possibility. If true, how did they keep it a secret?

"Not exactly," explained Gerald. "The first guy I met used to be a lab assistant to Dr. Pons. He and his boss spent several years secretly developing the technology. They use their company resources, but no one else knows about it, and his boss is the president. I met them both and they took me to see it."

"So they're trying to make money off it?"

"That was the original plan, but since Mallove's murder, they are scared to death of being discovered." Gerald sat back in his chair. "I had to threaten them a bit, in order for them to show it to me. For a moment, I thought they were going to kill me."

Gerald laughed quietly after the statement, but Cesar could see that he spoke with perfect sincerity. He really liked Gerald and smiled while listening to him. Gerald spoke as if they lived in an exciting movie.

"What do they want now?" Cesar knew they wanted money, but they also would not want to have a traceable transaction.

"Of course they need money for it," admitted Gerald. "It's got some expensive components, they say, so they can't just give it to us, but they also want to introduce it to the world, just without the threat of death. That's probably why they are willing to take the risk on us, that and my amazing skills at espionage."

Cesar leaned forward and tried to remain serious. He could not relax just yet. "They don't know about us, do they? What did you tell them?"

"Just that I was working for some clients and could not disclose any of their information." A small family entered the lobby and went to the concierge desk. Their young daughter who appeared to be about eight had wild brown hair and caught Gerald's attention. She looked at him and smiled so he held up his hand and returned the gesture, then turned back to Cesar. "I do, however, think they will be sympathetic to our cause, if you think it's wise to tell them. Since we know dangerous information about them, we have some leverage. If we tell them about us, it will be in their best interest to keep it confidential. It might help them trust us."

Sitting back in his chair, Cesar thought for a moment. The reasoning helped to relieve his main concern, the safety of their secrets.

"We should discuss it with Taylor before sharing that with them." He smiled at the irony of needing permission from a twenty-something-year-old girl.

"Agreed. We don't want to risk making her angry." Gerald almost seemed more frightened of upsetting Taylor than their secret being discovered.

"What is the plan?"

"I told them you might be arriving tonight," Gerald answered. "They said we had to do it at night, but I'll understand if you want to do this tomorrow. You must be exhausted from driving all day."

"I can rest later," said Cesar. "Let's go see this thing."

35

Cesar

"That's what I thought you'd say." Gerald smiled. "I hate to ask this, but since we might need the truck, you'll need to drive. I can't drive a stick."

"No problem," Cesar said, failing to hide his disappointment at being unable to relax and let Gerald drive.

After Gerald called his contact at Cerametrics, they climbed into Cesar's truck and drove towards the west of the city, to the open desert. For miles and miles, they saw only snow and sagebrush. While passing the Great Salt Lake, the dark prevented a clear view. Cesar hoped to have some time the next day to see the enormous salt lake.

Gerald played the role of navigator. After nearly an hour of driving, they finally turned from the main road and onto a smaller one. Cesar figured that they had traveled about thirty miles away from the city.

"So, I take it that this is not the way to their company?"

"Oh, I'm sorry," said Gerald. "No, they keep the working prototype at an offsite property that one of them owns. As you can expect, they've become rather paranoid."

A crystal clear sky accompanied the cold night. Cesar forgot the last time he'd seen the sky full of stars so clearly. During the winter in Seattle, he would be lucky to see the open sky, but lights from the city would drown the starlight.

After a short while on the smaller road, they parked behind a two-story brick building set off from the main road about two hundred meters. Cesar thought the structure looked like an old school building. A light shone from some of the windows of the first floor. When he stepped out of the truck, the brisk desert wind hit him hard in the face. The cold sank into his bones and he instinctively wrapped his arms around his waist.

When they went into the building, the lack of wind felt like a heat source of its own. A taller man with thick blond hair sat at a table in the middle of the room. A shorter stubby man stood by him as if ready to welcome them to his home. From Gerald's description, he recognized them.

"Ammon and Tom," Gerald said after closing the door. The men acted casual, as if they already knew how Cesar looked. "This is Cesar, the client I was talking about."

Although both men were perfectly polite, Cesar could sense the anxiety in their faces and postures. They acted like men living their last night before a big battle.

"What line of work are you in?" asked Ammon.

For the next few minutes, they all became better acquainted. Cesar gave only a brief explanation of his history, including his flight from Mexico. He assured them that their secret would be safe with him and his friends. They listened intently and without question. Cesar thought they looked satisfied after learning of his volatile relationship with the government.

When finished with the social proprieties, they led Cesar and Gerald down some stairs to a lit basement of brick and exposed pipes. The space reminded him of the utility room of an old school. Cesar felt instant gratitude for the warmer air. He could still hear the wind from outside, but the sound felt more distant.

"We added this whole part of the room," explained Ammon as he showed them the large area filled with a random assortment of equipment. The walls of new gray brick contrasted with the chips and cracks in the older walls. In the middle of the new area, stood what he assumed to be the reason for his visit, a generator of some sort. Cesar felt his heart rate increase. The moment reminded him of when Taylor showed him the NMG. Gerald put a hand on Cesar's shoulder.

"We do some experiments at our work," said Tom. "But for the dangerous stuff, we come here. It's easier to conceal the accidents."

Cesar noticed a small open closet, like the kind in a radiology office, where the technologist goes to shield himself from the x-rays.

"Have there been any accidents?" asked Cesar casually, as he walked around the room. The two men looked at each other. Tom smiled.

"Let's just say that we've worked out all the kinks for you," said Tom.

Cesar felt an excited surge of cold blood fill his chest, and his heart accelerated to keep the blood moving. He turned to Gerald.

"For us?"

Slowly, he began to believe the view before him and what it implied. He walked to the generator and extended his hand towards a piece of the stainless steel. He put his four fingers on the metal and slid them across the cool surface.

"So this is it? A fusion generator?"

Tom nodded his head, as if introducing his firstborn infant.

Cesar recognized only some of the components on the generator. He saw several small boxes with wire coils which looked like alternators. Shiny flex pipes connected a group of segmented steel cylinders arranged in a circle, orthogonal to the floor. A large chamber sat in the middle of the cylinders, part ceramic, glass, and metal. Almost every piece had sensors connected to them. The others watched as he inspected the apparatus. A computer display showed digital readouts of several temperatures, voltages, charges and energy flow. One readout indicated five hundred watts.

"It's so quiet," said Cesar, impressed that a device could run so quietly.

"The reactor only makes noise when it reaches maximum power," Ammon said with a smile full of pride. "Then it hums."

"And what is maximum power?"

Cesar wanted to start with a quick tutorial. He wanted to see the device in action. Tom rubbed his chin.

"We've got this one up to about five hundred kilowatts, but we're limited by our power transmission system. We could generate a lot more if it didn't melt the cables."

"That's good, right?" asked Gerald. He had a hopeful look in his eyes.

Cesar nodded and smiled silently. The power would be sufficient for a start. Would he be able to understand it enough to scale it up?

For the next ninety minutes, they discussed the underlying scientific theory. Gerald stood and listened intently, but only as a spectator. He asked no questions and deferred all comments to Cesar. After only a few minutes of discussion, Cesar stopped trying to hide his excitement. The two spoke with just as much excitement to explain how their creation worked.

Both men showed equal familiarity with its operation. Surprisingly, Cesar discovered that he understood almost everything. By the end of the conversation, he had learned how the nuclear reaction proceeded, along with the by-products and radiation. They openly admitted to lack a full understanding of the operation theory and were still working to answer all the questions. Cesar understood the study of science. Most of the time, scientists achieved only a top level of understanding. As an engineer, he could live with that.

Before he became totally convinced, however, Cesar had to see the device in action. Their obvious pride and excitement began to dislodge any suspicion of deception. He just needed to see for himself, like he had with the NMG.

"Can we have a demonstration?" he asked after they finished telling him about the heat transfer system.

"Yes, of course," Tom said rubbing his chin. "Even though this alone doesn't prove anything, take a look at the fuel level readout. For the past month, we've used just five grams of the stuff, keeping this place warm, basically. I totally understand if you need to see something, more substantial."

"I'm impressed already," Cesar said, thinking about the fuel consumption.

"Ok," he said apologetically. "I'm afraid the most energy-consuming demonstration that we're set up to do right now isn't going to be very extravagant."

"What have you got?" He just wanted to see it working at a high power output, to hear it hum.

For their demonstration, they wanted to show the production of a copious amount of energy. After returning to the freezing cold outside next to the back of the building, they filled a fifty-five-gallon steel cylinder full of water then connected a huge resistance heater coil to a heavy wire and immersed it in the water. They covered the container with a makeshift lid which looked like a huge spout.

"Interesting demonstration," said Gerald, laughing and holding his arms across his shivering chest.

"We really don't want to draw attention to ourselves. Otherwise, we would make something really amazing." Tom held out his hands and motioned them to move back. "We don't want to kill you two, just yet," he said, smiling.

The promised demonstration began about thirty seconds later. They first saw some steam begin to escape into the air as a thick fog. After a minute, they watched as a ten foot jet of steam and water drops shot into the air. All four of them stood in silence and watched the geyser spray high into the air. Even Gerald refrained from commenting, from breaking the spell.

At the highest point, the jet spray rose thirty feet into the air. The freezing wind quickly froze the water and ice crystals crashed back on the ground all around them. Cesar extended his hands toward the barrel to enjoy the heat like a campfire. After just a short while, all the water had vaporized. Cesar had no more doubts.

"Yes! I've seen enough," Cesar said with a frozen smile. "Let's get out of this wind."

When Gerald introduced the topic of price, they explained the expensive costs associated with the materials and preparation of the components. The key component contained a proprietary ceramic matrix composed of palladium and other expensive materials which could only be found at Cerametrics.

Of course, they wanted to be compensated for developing the generator, however, their primary motivation was to see their creation replace fossil fuels and take its place as the primary energy source for humanity, as it already was for the rest of the universe. They also wanted the rights to it and the profits. Unfortunately, they knew the achievement of their ultimate goal lay far into the future, as long as the government failed to discover it first. Cesar said he thought they had an idea of how to make that happen, but they would have to wait.

"When we accomplish what we hope," he said to them. "Maybe we can work together on introducing it to the world. We'll definitely keep in touch. I believe together, we're both treading on this dangerous ground now."

In the future, they might bring these two men into their full confidence, but he had to let Taylor help them make the decision. Ammon and Tom's bravery had already gained his trust and respect, but sharing his other secrets with the two Mormons increased the chance of exposure for them all. Keeping knowledge of the NMG away from them would be in their best interest.

Ammon and Tom had taken a great risk by trusting Gerald, and Cesar felt great satisfaction to have given the task to him. "Choose the right man for the right job," his father always said.

"I believe you asked for fifty thousand dollars?" Cesar asked. "Is this the one we're getting, or do you have the prepackaged item back on your shelves somewhere?" No one laughed at his attempt at humor.

"We have parts for several others, but we wanted to make sure we gave you a working model."

They accepted the money and directed Cesar on how to dismantle the apparatus. Gerald helped Cesar take it apart with Ammon's assistance. Cesar noticed the pleasure on Gerald's face to help with the process even when he showed an obvious aversion to getting his hands dirty or bruised. Gerald probably preferred to let others do the manual labor. They provided several padded containers and got the whole package ready for transport in his truck, finishing just after midnight.

"If you ever need anything, please let us know," Ammon said after the truck started. "It might be a good idea to use Cerametrics for some of your other needs, just to throw people off the scent, if you know what I mean. Of course," he said, wrinkling his brows, "maybe the less contact the better. I don't know."

"When we contact you, it will probably be through one of my subsidiary associates," Gerald said from the passenger seat. Ammon nodded. Tom just stood with his arms folded across his chest as the wind tossed his hair like a salad.

Before they drove away, Cesar gave one last look at the building and felt a wave of solace about the whole event. When starting his own company, he'd recognized it as the beginning of something big. When he made the decision to run for mayor of Ciudad Juarez he'd thought that he could make a difference in the lives of many people, but that decision had changed his life the most. It had cost him his family and country. In the new phase of his life, he had seemed to stumble upon Taylor and Gerald by pure chance, by no direct effort of his own.

What would his new project cost?

"Amazing," Cesar said to himself as they drove off into the cold night.

As the building sunk into the darkness behind them, he felt the historical aspect of the moment. The building might become a historical monument one day. He felt tempted to stop and take a picture, but he just wanted to go home. He would return one day, return to the Utah desert.

36

Taylor

February 5, 2009

After Cesar left on his trip to Utah, Dominga became quieter and more reserved. She spent a lot of the time in her bedroom or on the couch, usually reading. On the night of Cesar's absence, Dominga failed to prepare dinner so Doroteo ordered pizza.

Taylor considered the option of working at the shop, but felt awkward spending time there alone, and of course, thoughts of a possible fusion reactor fought for her attention to detail. With the NMG and a high-power fusion reactor, they could build anything. No engineer or scientist on the whole planet could be as lucky. Unless she could share her thoughts with someone who could understand, they threatened to paralyze her. That left only Doroteo.

At the moment, Doroteo made a better audience than Dominga, but he gave the impression of always wanting to bring the conversation to an abrupt end. Taylor found his threatening attitude amusing and attempted to extend their limited conversations as far as possible before he could invent an excuse to exit the conversation. She required only a few conversations with him to feel more at ease. She could not allow her entire stay to remain nearly devoid of hearing him speak.

When the email arrived the next day, Dominga read it before anyone else.

"Taylor, Doroteo," she yelled from her bedroom. "A message from Gerald and Cesar. Come quick!"

"Isn't it so cute how concerned she is?" Taylor said to Doroteo on their way to join Dominga in her room.

Taylor spoke with exaggerated affection and hoped to spark some irritation. Amusement in his reaction might help calm her nerves. She felt like a doctor had emailed them with how long they had to live. The grunt of annoyance helped, but not much.

"It's good news, I think," Dominga said.

In the email, Gerald said he would be returning home the next day. Before leaving, Cesar invented a code for their communication about the event. If the message contained 'the next day' the phrase meant Gerald had found success and they would be returning immediately. If the message contained 'they would be coming home soon', it meant the whole thing had been a failure. Taylor's heartbeat resumed beating when she understood the good news.

Taylor had difficulty sleeping that night. She wanted to leave that moment and not wait until the next day. Doroteo wanted to get sufficient sleep. They only planned to meet halfway so they had plenty of time. The situation reminded her of being a child at Christmas when her parents had always failed to hide her presents. Waiting and keeping her knowledge a secret caused more anxiety than if they had managed to actually surprise her.

"We don't really have to go," Doroteo said as an afterthought, as if he had no interest in the whole affair. "I'm sure Cesar can make it back on his own."

"Doroteo, really?" Taylor said in exasperation. She stared at him as if just proposed marriage, then realized that he meant the suggestion as a joke. Instead of admitting to gullibility, she pretended ignorance. "He's your closest friend and you are not worried? Don't you want to see the fusion reactor?"

Even though she felt safe in their secure location, Taylor lowered her voice whenever talking about the nuclear reactor. The information still seemed too unbelievable and insecure.

"I suppose," he agreed lazily. "But I don't feel like driving all night. We should get a few hours of sleep first."

She eventually managed to fall asleep, but jumped out of bed without fatigue the next morning. After failing to find Doroteo she assumed he overslept so she knocked on his door. Since she'd never previously attempted to wake him, she felt curious about his possible reaction. She waited for several seconds without a sound, then decided to put all her stuff in the car and wait. In surprise, she found Doroteo sitting in the driver's seat, waiting for her. He seemed to be meditating.

Without any verbal exchanges, they started driving and Taylor watched as the wipers removed the heavy rain from the windshield. After a few minutes of silence, she decided to speak and expected Doroteo to show some sort of acknowledgment.

"I'm so cold. Can't wait for the car heater to get warm."

Doroteo made no response or indication of hearing her.

"See Dominga before we left?" she asked while still looking forward.

Doroteo grunted something incoherent and she decided to interpret the sound as a negative answer. Did Doroteo act that way when tired?

"Do you think Cesar's nervous driving around with a fusion reactor all by himself?" She asked this question leaning forward and looked directly into his eyes. After positioning herself to face him more completely, she waited for two seconds before continuing.

"Maybe."

"Doroteo," she began somewhat forcefully. "This is getting ridiculous. I need you to talk to me. I cannot ride with you the whole way in silence."

He kept staring straight ahead for a few moments, and then spoke without turning his head. "What do you want me to say?"

"OK, that was my fault. How about I ask it this way." Hearing him speak made her feel a little better. She smiled and got more comfortable, as if preparing for a nice long conversation with him. "How do you think Cesar feels about traveling with a fusion reactor, all by himself?"

This time, he looked at her, but kept the same blank expression. Taylor thought his eyes looked more deeply set in his face than usual. The whites of his eyes reflected the low light from the dashboard.

"I suppose he's not very comfortable with it."

"That's how I felt when I brought the NMG to show Gerald for the first time."

She took her eyes off his, to relieve any discomfort. She really did want to have a conversation with him and not tease him the entire time. “I felt like I was going to get in a wreck and then an ambulance was going to come, pick me up and notice what I had with me and turn it in to the authorities. If that didn’t happen, I was sure to be mugged before I ever got to the Burgerville to meet Gerald, or else the police were going to see in my eyes that I was hiding something. Have you ever felt like that?”

His look of suppressed irritation told Taylor how much he preferred to drive in silence.

Ten long seconds passed and Taylor prepared to push him more. If he remained silent, did he think she would quit? She would continue attacking him and enjoy the process. She felt a twinge of guilt for having to be so forceful, but she wanted him to feel totally comfortable with her and talking seemed like the best way to accomplish that task. If he still refused to talk after her next attempt, she would give him a little break before making another attempt. Before she continued, however, he did.

“I felt that right after I joined the police in Mexico.” Doroteo began slowly as if unaccustomed to saying more than one phrase at a time. While talking, he kept his eyes on the road. “I volunteered to go undercover, infiltrating the local drug cartel. Only a few of us were willing to do it. I thought I was invincible.”

“According to Cesar, you are invincible.”

“Ha,” Doroteo said and continued as if uninterrupted, “I soon became friends with one of the bodyguards of a low-level trafficker, and only after a few weeks, I found myself in the middle of a meeting with one of the main cartel leaders. I always knew the dangers of the job, but that was the first time I realized they would kill me if they knew who I was. I remember being,” he struggled for the right word. “Frightened.”

She would probably never hear him say that word again.

“What did you do?” Taylor asked with genuine interest.

Before his confession, she'd only wanted him to talk to her, to pass the time more quickly. Now she felt intense curiosity.

“I convinced myself that I didn’t care if I died.”

“How did you do that?”

He again paused before answering.

“There was a time in my life when I had to make a difficult choice, and I just went back to that moment.”

A voice in her mind warned that if she really wanted to have a good relationship with him, she should minimize the banter.

“I’ll understand if you don’t want to talk about it, but I would like to hear it.”

He looked at her and paused.

“Have you ever been in a fight? I mean a physical fight? Wouldn’t be surprised if you have.”

If she wanted to extract information from him, he would require her to pay with an experience of her own. She smiled at the memory and unsuccessfully attempted to hide it.

“I threatened a couple girls before, but it never came to any actual violence, unfortunately.”

“Well, have you ever thought you were going to get the shit beat out of you?

Or, let me say it another way." He paused to gather his thoughts. "Did you ever know that you were going to get the shit beat out of you?"

Taylor felt grateful for the answer to that question.

"No. I've never been privileged with that experience."

"It's at that moment that you can make one of the most important choices of your life. You can choose either to cower, or you can choose to go down fighting."

"Most people lay down and take it, I would think."

"They don't think they have a choice. Those who do are lucky." He smiled for the first time. "Fighting back is the only way to survive. Even though you may not live to have another chance, people will think twice before they threaten you again."

"What happened to put you in that position, of fighting back?"

Taylor felt a slight hesitation from Doroteo.

"I got the shit beat out of me, but my older brother never touched me again. That day, I earned his respect, but he never got mine."

"It's OK if you don't want to talk about it, but what happened to your brother? I guess you two did not get along?"

"In English, if your brother tries to kill you, what would you call it? Not getting along?"

Doroteo turned to her from the road and waited for a response.

"Did your parents ever intervene?"

"My brother was a local dealer." He turned back to the road. "My parents were terrified of him, and so was I."

Taylor waited for him to continue, but they drove for the next three minutes in silence. Would he share any more information? She wanted to know more, but she might have to wait for more details. She felt lucky to be getting any information from him.

"I don't mean to belittle your experiences," Taylor began tentatively. "But physical violence is just one way to fight back. Look at Gerald. In a sense, he's been fighting for many years. At least, he's not rolling over."

"Does he even know what he's fighting?" Doroteo asked seriously.

"He knows it better than I do, but he's just more optimistic. That's how he can be so happy, even with all this shit that keeps happening in this world. I just get so angry. Frankly, I can't understand how he deals with it. If it weren't for my projects, my distractions, it would drive me crazy. I can't even turn on the news or listen to talk radio anymore. All they talk about is the housing market collapse and how to justify the republican bank bailout, and now Obama's ready to approve another round of it. The worst part of it all is that everyone thinks it's OK to give the banks stolen money, so that they can lend it back to us? How many people lost all their savings because of what happened? How many people are stuck with a home that is worth half of what they paid? And what are the people going to do about it? They're going to re-elect the same criminals that caused it all."

37

Taylor

Taylor sat forward and took a deep breath. She needed a diversion for her growing anger.

"So, what do you really think about what we're doing?" Taylor planned on breaching this topic sometime on the trip and that moment seemed as good a time as any. "Don't worry about hurting my feelings."

"I like you, Taylor," he answered. "So you don't have to worry about me lying to you. I think what you're doing is dangerous. I'm not against taking chances, but the real enemy in this world is powerful. They control the most powerful military that has ever existed on the earth. They control the most powerful weapons and surveillance instruments. Their resources are limitless and they have billions of mindless but devoted followers."

"This world is full of people who don't want to fight back," she finished for him. "They take whatever shit is handed to them with a smile. They're the cause of all this mess. It's people like Gerald and the rest of us, who have to live in the world they've allowed to be created. Doesn't it piss you off? I don't care anymore about them. I'm in this for people like us. Who cares what happens to the rest of humanity. It's their own damn fault."

"Do you feel better now?" he asked.

"A little," she agreed. Venting gave her a momentary reprieve from frustration.

"In my opinion," he began. "Your chances are small. If you don't do anything, where are you? The same place you would have been in. Why can't you just live your life? Bad things happen to people, things we cannot control. Life's not fair. Sometimes we just have to live with it."

"And accept what is going on around us, without a fight? That's what you're saying?"

While getting on the ramp to I-90, he paused to focus on the road. Soon they would be crossing the bridge. They had another hour of night before the dawn and would be traveling over dark waters. When he spoke again, he sounded apologetic.

"Yes, you are right. I'm just saying that you still have the chance to live your lives to the best you can possibly have. Instead, you're taking a dangerous road that might be a very short walk."

"I don't look at it that way," she said smiling. "For me it's an adventure. We actually have a chance to do something really significant. I've never felt so energized in my whole life. You can sense it as well, can't you? At least, you can see it in Cesar and Gerald, and maybe even Dominga."

"Yes," he agreed. "I can see it."

"So why are you choosing to be a part of it?"

He rubbed his chin with his left hand.

"When Cesar was forced to leave Mexico, he asked me what I wanted to do. I could have stayed and had a decent life, but I was tired of the game. I thought that by following Cesar, I could take a break from all the fighting. I've been fighting my whole life."

"So..."

"Cesar," he said slowly as if still deciding to say more. "He needs my help. Friends help each other right? Why am I even telling you all this?" He snorted.

"Remember, you like me." She smiled and patted him on the shoulder then turned to face the road ahead. To give him a break from talking, she would continue filling the silence. "To be honest, I'm almost too excited to be scared. I get to work on something big and now with this fusion generator, I'm too shocked to believe it really, it's all got even bigger. Maybe I've been listening to Gerald too much. His optimism is rubbing off on me."

Thinking of Gerald caused her to smile. Doroteo laughed loudly.

"I thought Gerald was a crazy fanatic and couldn't believe Cesar would even listen to him, but now. I'm beginning to think he's either a genius or extremely lucky. I hope he's both. If this thing we're getting really is a low-temperature fusion generator, I'll never doubt him again."

"He's the biggest optimist I've ever known. It's contagious. If it wasn't for him, I wouldn't have found you guys, and I wouldn't have thought about going into space. That was all his idea."

She switched the stereo to the radio and asked Doroteo if he minded listening to music. He showed no coherent opposition so she proceeded to find an acceptable station for the background. Taylor liked music, but she never chose music as an activity by itself. Taylor thought music had only one purpose, to keep her mind focused while she worked. Unlike others in her age group, she never remembered the name of the songs she liked, or the group who performed them. If she disliked what she heard, she turned the station, but her mind usually spent its energy elsewhere.

Taylor and Doroteo listened to music on the radio while the sun appeared behind the clouds on the horizon. Doroteo drove the car as if in a trance, always looking straight ahead. He never said anything about the music, or anything except as an answer to her comment or question.

They planned to meet Cesar at a Home Depot store in Boise. So far, their only contact came from Gerald's email the previous night. Taylor agreed with the plan to refrain from cell phone contact. She also had doubts about the security of email, but they had to communicate some way and paper moved too slowly.

"Dominga said your father was a machinist?"

The unexpected question from Doroteo came after a long stretch of driving in silence. The last exit sign she noticed indicated a place in Oregon called Baker City.

"Yes," she said, feeling surprised. "He had a shop like Cesar's, but a little smaller. Before he died, he sold it so Mom could have some money to live on. He knew she didn't have the motivation to run it or keep up with the ownership. I could have, but he wanted me to stay in school."

"Was he part of the reason why you chose what you did?" He kept his eyes on the road. "What you wanted to study in school?"

When most people learned of her father's death, they usually said sorry or gave some other kind of condolence. The news made most people feel uncomfortable in her presence. Doroteo acted as if unaware of the social propriety, as if he already had extensive experience with death in his life.

"If I had a different father, then I might have chosen something else." The thought of taking a different path in her life always caused anxiety. She hated the thought of her life being dependent on circumstance. "He always wanted to show me what he was working on and liked teaching me how to do things. It's probably mostly his doing, I'm sure, but I'm glad of it."

"I'm sure he wouldn't have shown you so much, if you didn't reciprocate the interest. You must have been an interested student."

"*Reciprocate,* huh?" she said laughing. "You're English is amazing."

"I never went to college, but when I was in Mexico, I studied English on my own. When I was working for Cesar as head of security, he had to work with some people who only spoke English, so it was good for me to learn."

"Well, you've got a heavy accent, but your English is great."

"Thanks," he sounded genuinely pleased which surprised her. He seemed to be growing accustomed to her, the reward of her efforts and charm.

Two hours later, they entered Boise Idaho and took the exit that would lead them to the rendezvous point at Home Depot. They drove slowly through the parking lot for a few minutes in search of Cesar's truck. After failing to locate him, they parked. Taylor began to worry.

"I wish we could use our phone to call him," Taylor complained. "It feels like we're in the dark ages."

"Gerald was right about keeping phone silence. He should minimize evidence of visiting Utah."

"What did you do before cell phones?" she asked with sarcasm, intimating his old age. "It must have been annoying."

Doroteo ignored the statement.

38

Taylor

A few minutes later, Taylor noticed Cesar as he pulled into the parking lot. In excitement, she exited the car and waved her hands. For the first time since leaving that morning, she stood on her own feet. Her muscles screamed with the release of caged tension. Blood flowed to her legs, flooding her entire body with endorphins. The cloudless sky helped the air remain crisp and biting, a welcome change from the eternal rain and cloudy skies of a Northwest winter. When they returned to Seattle and the warmer rains, Taylor pledged to remember the cold.

As Cesar parked next to them, the smile on his face filled her with excitement, another sign of success. He greeted them with a simple, "Buenos dias". His beard seemed fuller than usual and his hair looked like he'd just awoken. She realized how well he normally maintained his grooming.

She followed him to the back of his truck. While he pulled the cover open enough for her to see, she quickly glanced around the parking lot for any spying eyes. No one else had parked in the back of the parking lot and she noticed the only other people visible were an older man with what looked like his son walking toward the store entrance.

She had imagined the moment of seeing the reactor and prepared herself to feel disappointed or uninspired. As she expected, they'd dismantled the apparatus and packaged it for protection during transport. She assumed her real excitement would come when she saw the reactor in operation, but after looking at the jumble of boxes and wrapping, Taylor felt her heart accelerate.

"Is it true?" she asked excitedly. "Did you see it working?"

"Oh yes, it's true," Cesar said proudly. "Gerald really pulled through with this one."

She put her hand on his shoulder and felt the warmth of his skin under his thin coat. Doroteo stood at the opposite of the truck bed and looked at the contents with a curious expression. His dark eyebrows drew closer together, forming a V.

"There were no problems?" he asked.

"Nothing I noticed," Cesar replied. "But I'm glad you came to meet me. Thank you."

"No problemo," Taylor said, laughing at the opportunity to use pseudo-Spanish.

"Taylor." Cesar sounded exhausted and held out his keys. "I'm so tired of driving. You'll want to talk with me about this I'm sure. Here, you can drive."

"Of course," she replied instantly, feeling glad to give him a break and to talk about what happened. It only seemed fair since Doroteo had given her a free ride. She turned to Doroteo and smiled. "Do you think you can handle the drive back without me?"

"I'll manage," he said wryly.

For the first hour of driving with Cesar, Taylor learned all he knew about the device. She enjoyed their roles being reversed. Previously, she taught him about the NMG, but now with the fusion reactor, he became the teacher. Even though they both had only a rudimentary knowledge of the fusion process, together they had enough confidence to adapt the reactor to their needs. She looked forward to putting it together. That thought reminded Taylor of an experience from her childhood. When seven years old, she had disassembled her best friend's new binoculars and enjoyed learning how they worked. Taylor remembered having as much fun reassembling them and seeing the relief on her friend's tear-filled face.

"I could not wait to tell you about it," Cesar admitted.

"Me too," she said while looking forward. She felt emotionally drained. Their task ahead suddenly felt more daunting than ever. "Tell me the story about how Gerald found it."

"In a past life, Gerald must have been a bloodhound. He explained how, but I do not understand how he traced it back to the company in Salt Lake City. I was too anxious to see the thing. He left out a lot of the details. We can ask him when we see him next."

"Maybe we should start paying more attention to Gerald," Taylor said laughing. Cesar looked confused.

"Do you not take Gerald seriously?"

"I take him seriously, usually, but sometimes his head seems to be in the clouds. I thought that this was a wild goose chase, something to keep him occupied while we worked on the NMG. I won't ever doubt him again."

"He's an idealist," explained Cesar. "Many people use that as an insult, but it can be the highest compliment."

Speaking of Gerald reminded her of something she wanted to discuss. "Sometimes I wonder if it's worth the effort. We're risking a lot on this."

"Freedom is superior to convenience," Cesar said as if repeating the pledge of allegiance to the United States flag. Then he turned to her. "Taylor, it's all about squeezing everything out of life. I could have accepted what circumstances gave me, and lived the remainder of my life in comfort, but what would it have left me? Empty memories!"

She took a moment to consider his words and felt no desire to argue with him. She just wanted to hear someone else say what she already thought. When Cesar failed to say anything else, Taylor looked out the window at the central Washington landscape. In about thirty miles they would arrive in Yakima. While Taylor watched the scenery, she noticed a large barn on the left with the sun reflected on the shiny metal roof.

"Doesn't it feel like everything seems to be coming together," she said while shielding her eyes from the bright light. "Do you think we're getting help from somewhere? I don't mean like from a God or any of that nonsense. I don't know what to think. What's the probability of all this being a coincidence? I mean, what's next aliens?"

"Didn't Gerald say something about aliens?" Cesar spoke while looking out the passenger window. He failed to laugh at her joke. "Expecting extraterrestrial help after acquiring a fusion generator and your NMG, it might be too much to ask the universe to deliver."

"Do you think that's even a possibility?" she asked, turning and looking at him with intensity. Never before in her life had she ever thought of aliens as credible. Thinking of them brought a feeling of anxiety. "If an alien contacted Gerald, would he tell us or keep it a secret? How would you react if we did actually came in contact with an alien?"

"I really don't know." Cesar shook his head.

"I've thought about this kind of stuff before, not just about aliens, but also about all the other bullshit like angels, devils, ghosts. Could we experience anything like them and have rational reactions? I don't think our psyche is capable of handling something so out of the ordinary. Sure, all that shit's in the movies and everything, but I think if anyone actually saw something remotely similar to that, their brain might refuse to acknowledge it. We'd invent some lie as a rationalization. Our mind might attempt to explain it with a twisted version of reality, some sort of shit we've already seen in the movies. Am I making any sense?"

"Not much," Cesar said, and laughed. "Maybe we can talk to Gerald about it. I think I know where you're coming from. Maybe another influence exists, that we don't understand."

"You can talk with Doroteo about it," she said and laughed with him. "I'll watch."

"That's fair," said Cesar. "How was your ride with him?"

"We had a good talk," she began. "Despite what you might think, I actually like the guy. He's tough, inside and out, and I like that."

"I'm glad," said Cesar seriously. "I was worried."

For the next hour she drove without any other substantial conversations. Cesar seemed absorbed in thought and Taylor felt no surprise. They had a lot to do when they returned home. If he wanted to work in the shop that day, however, she might get Dominga to make him go to bed instead. He looked so exhausted. Did he look forward to being reunited with Dominga?

She looked forward to working in the shop again, but other possibilities soon replaced thoughts of the shop. Her daydream began when she imagined leaving the atmosphere and entering orbit in a craft she helped to build. Taylor had always wanted to watch the blue light of the sky slowly transform into the black of space, and the stars to appear during the light of day. Slowly, the silence and the shooting white lines on the road helped Taylor begin to drift on the river of her own thoughts.

When Taylor became conscious of her eyelids feeling heavy, she began to worry. She glanced over to check on Cesar to see if he showed the same symptoms. He sat very still, with his eyes staring straight ahead as if in a trance. She looked back to the road ahead and used all of her energy to keep her eyes open.

In the distance, she saw a shimmer of light above the road, almost like a mirage. When they came closer to the aberration, it transformed into a huge hole in their lane. She tried to move her foot from the accelerator to the brake, but her body refused to obey the command. In panic, she watched as the hole in the road approached at seventy miles an hour. As the distance between them shortened, she attempted to scream, but only silent breath escaped her mouth. She turned again to Cesar. He showed no signs of alarm, his eyes devoid of life, dead open.

When they reached the black hole in the road, its complete blackness expanded to swallow the truck and its occupants. In anticipation of an impact, Taylor pushed back against her seat, the only command her body obeyed. As the truck crashed over the edge, time seemed to slow and she felt as if falling down a mine shaft with black walls. She continued to fall until all light disappeared. After falling for several moments in total darkness, she saw a light ahead and then recognized the eye.

The sound of her own scream jerked Taylor back to consciousness. She felt pressure on her shoulder and swung her head to see Cesar holding one hand on the wheel and the other on her shoulder.

"Slow down, Taylor, slow down," Cesar said calmly but with clear concern in his voice. She stiffened her hands on the wheel and pulled her foot off the accelerator. They traveled at over eighty-five miles per hour, but her heart seemed to be racing twice as fast. "Are you OK? I think it's my turn to drive."

While Taylor attempted to relax in the passenger seat, Cesar resumed the task of driving. Even with her eyes open again, her mind remained fixed on the image of falling toward that alien eye. She told Cesar nothing about her nightmare. She wanted to forget about the dream and especially about falling asleep while driving. She'd never had such problems while driving. All their talk about demons and aliens had influenced her thinking. In the future, she would avoid thoughts about aliens and focus on her work.

III: INTERFERENCE

The summit finally reached
Hurry! Enjoy the scene
Before the silence is breached

39

Gerald

While Gerald watched Cesar drive away with the fusion reactor, he felt a strange elation. At first, he attributed the feeling to the natural reaction of having participated in an event of historic significance. That explanation, however, felt inadequate. Another human emotion dominated his overall feeling: a sense of entitlement.

Before his search for the fusion reactor, Gerald had only felt like an assistant to Taylor, helpful yes, but only in an auxiliary capacity. He never felt unappreciated though and actually enjoyed following Taylor's lead. He had happily acted as a facilitator to join Taylor's genius with Cesar's resources and experience. After delivering the other half of what they needed, however, he felt more like a partner. He now could make decisions on his own and no longer felt the need to first seek Taylor's approval. But even with his new feeling of entitlement, he would never dare make any significant alterations to the group without consulting her first.

On his return flight to Seattle, Gerald concluded that they needed to recruit additional people to help prepare for the future. Although he trusted Taylor's and Cesar's judgment concerning scientific and engineering matters, he thought they should look at their options from other angles. In his opinion, all successful endeavors resulted from the efforts of a diverse team of talented people from multiple backgrounds.

After returning home, Gerald had arranged a private meeting with Taylor to discuss his recruitment plans. For the discussion, he wanted a private meeting without Cesar and especially without Doroteo, who intimidated him and who would likely disagree vehemently with the recruitment proposal. He felt confident prevailing in an argument with Taylor alone, but not with Doroteo supporting her.

The subsequent discussion with Taylor had become more confrontational than Gerald had anticipated, even without the participation of Doroteo. Taylor's first comment revealed how the rest of the conversation would proceed. "Gerald," she began in exasperation. "You're like a little child. You just can't wait to tell your secrets to all your little friends."

In the end, Taylor reluctantly agreed to let him recruit his friend, a retired botany professor from Germany, a woman named Gerda Schreiber. He refrained from confiding all of his plans with Taylor and only told her about Gerda. Having an old retired lady know their secrets seemed less risky to Taylor than someone still working and connected to the business or academic world.

On his drive to visit Gerda, Gerald reflected on everything that had happened since his rendezvous with Taylor at Burgerville. Of course, witnessing the NMG and then finding the fusion reactor had almost overwhelmed him, but the future seemed to contain even greater events than those discoveries. As usual, Gerald became lost in his thoughts while driving and almost missed exit 253 to Bellingham. He anxiously anticipated seeing Gerda's reaction to his proposal.

Twelve minutes later, Gerald pulled into Gerda Schreiber's driveway and shut off his car. She lived in a small house, in an older but clean and orderly neighborhood. The front door soon opened and Gerald waved at the older lady who stood with a quizzical look on her face. He paused a moment to meet her eyes before opening the car door. He failed to remember ever seeing her with a smile.

"Hi Gerda," Gerald said while running to her front door. In the short distance, the rain soaked his head and neck, sending a chill down his spine.

"Come in, come in my friend," she said with a distinctive German accent. "Come out of the rain and get warm." She began the word 'warm' with an interesting mixture of 'w' and 'v'.

"Thank you, Gerda. It's a typical Northwest day, isn't it."

"Indeed," she said while shutting the door behind him.

She took his overcoat and indicated for him to sit on a couch by the front window. Translucent white curtains allowed the gray outdoor light to fill the small room. He immediately noticed the various species of plants placed in every corner of the room and by all the furniture, not an unexpected sight in the home of a botanist, he supposed. Most of the vegetation had large leaves of various shapes and shades of green and blue. The warm humid air in the room offered comfort, but the plant life reminded Gerald of the cold Northwest forests.

While she went to the kitchen to get coffee, he admired a painting of a beach at dusk, hanging on the wall above her black piano. The white caps of the waves contrasted sharply with the dark water and dangerous storm clouds in the sky. The artist had filled the space between the black water and sky with the brilliant blues, pinks and oranges of a beautiful horizon. As the artist had most likely intended, the scene reminded Gerald of a brighter future beyond the harsh forces of nature.

On the piano, a wooden picture frame showed a middle-aged man with the same blond hair, blue eyes and sharp nose of his mother. Another picture opposite the man showed a woman of similar age with thick red hair. Her eyes appeared so light, that Gerald could not discern any color, although he assumed they were blue. In between the two adults, sat a single picture of two blonde, blue-eyed children, an older boy with his arm around a younger girl. Gerald thought they both looked between nine to twelve years old.

Gerda returned with a cup of coffee in each hand, steam rising into the air from the black liquid. She held the mugs with the steady hands of a much younger woman. She paused a moment to look at him with half-closed eyes, as if inspecting him for symptoms of ill health.

"If I remember correctly," she said while delivering the cup and sitting opposite him, "you like it black."

"You have a good memory," he answered, genuinely impressed at her memory from their last encounter at a cafe, a year ago.

"Thank you," she answered as if annoyed to accept a compliment. "Now, I am extremely curious as to your visit. On the phone, you indicated that you were going to be up this way, but I cannot see any reason for anyone to visit Bellingham, so I assumed you came just to see me. As you know, I am only here because my daughter got a teaching job at the University."

"Well," he said, pausing to sip his coffee, "I didn't want any phone record of a special trip just to see you."

"Interesting," she said, "considering some of your clientele. Continue."

Gerald smiled appreciatively at her sarcasm.

"Actually, I want to include you as a consultant of sorts, in a very sensitive project. But before I tell you the details, I feel the need to warn you."

"Warn away," she said and laughed, but without a crack in her serious expression. "I'm too old to be afraid of dangerous consequences."

"I'm glad you feel that way."

Gerald took a deep breath, feeling immediate relief. On the journey to see her, he had considered the option of revealing his proprietary information without any warning of the associated danger, but that option would have stolen the choice she had in the matter. Gerald felt compelled to take the chance that she would refuse participation.

"I have a friend," Gerald continued, attempting to remember his planned approach, "who shares our beliefs about society. To put it simply, this friend of mine has invented a device which can transform the world as we know it."

Gerald continued with his exposition of the events Taylor had initiated. Gerda saved most of her questions for the end of his story, with only minimal interruptions for clarification. At the end, she peered at him with only thin slits for eyes, nodding slowly. After a few moments, he began wondering if she would explode into laughter or start swearing at him in German for telling such a ridiculous story.

"Hmm," she began slowly and opening her eyes wider, her light blue irises visible again. "I don't completely understand what you want with me? I don't have a great understanding of high energy particle physics. What can I do?"

"Well, I'm afraid of proceeding with tunnel vision, but I'm more concerned about the possible consequences of going forward with this. Remember what I said about escaping into space with this thing, to get out of their reach and make it visible to the entire world? Well, what if we have to escape into space for an extended time? What if we had to build a colony somewhere? As a botanist, your knowledge would be invaluable."

"Hmm, plant growth in a gravity-limited environment and artificial atmosphere," she said, leaning forward, excitement showing in her eyes. Although she looked directly at Gerald's face, she looked through him. "As a botanist, this area of research has always interested me. How far down the road do you see this possibility becoming viable?"

"At the moment, they are optimizing the integration of the two new technologies. From what Taylor explained, they will have the ability to go anywhere in the solar system, much faster than any vehicle currently available and with a fraction of the cost. All we have to do is keep it secret until then."

"Yes, I can see why she would be concerned about sharing this information. I almost can't believe your story."

"I had to see her invention for myself," he interjected. "I will try to arrange a time for you to see it too."

"That would be wonderful," she said and clasped her hands together. "While we've been sitting here, I've been fantasizing about what you said, about how government could have a very limited influence in space."

"Or nonexistent."

They both smiled at that thought.

During the subsequent conversation, they reminisced. When Gerda lived in Seattle, they had both been a member of the Libertarian party and Gerald had enjoyed talking with her at their meetings. After she moved to Bellingham, when her daughter-in-law started teaching at Western Washington University, she withdrew from political activity. She confessed to losing faith in the political process and had allowed old age to focus her thoughts on happier topics, such as her son and his family.

"Do you know anyone else who might be useful to join the team?" Gerald asked after a lull in the conversation. He had been waiting for an appropriate time to change the topic. "I'm looking for someone with a background in human biology?"

"Hmm," she said, sitting forward. "Let me think. Like you already mentioned, this person would need to have the same belief system as ours. That's priority one."

"Yes," he agreed. "The last thing we need is someone who thinks a government agency should handle this."

"Unfortunately, all of my associates in that field are terminal collectivists, but I think my son may know someone in Portland." While trying to recall her memory, Gerda rubbed her left wrist. "She works at a pharmaceutical company there. She has a Ph.D. in biochemistry I think. I'll have to ask him what her name is. He only met her once."

"That would be great. Let me know if you think of anyone else."

"Before you go, we can have lunch together." Gerda's eyes dared him to refuse. "I have some excellent homemade soup. It'll warm you up before you return to the cold rain."

During lunch, Gerald asked about her personal life and then spent the next hour looking at pictures of her son's family. He enjoyed taking a break from the disturbing topic of subversion, but seeing pictures of her grandchildren reminded him of how much his success or failure could impact the future of the next generation. Those thoughts became another sobering motivation of how carefully Gerald needed to handle the situation.

Before departing, Gerda asked for his preferred method of communication and he told her about the secure communication channel he wanted to construct. He got the idea for it after having to arrange the physical meeting with Taylor, when he should have been able to just call or email her. He wanted to avoid leaving electronic records of their correspondence and did not trust Google, Microsoft or AT&T to protect their privacy.

"That's when I got the idea of having an associate of mine, a computer expert, build a website. He said he could have something up and running within a week."

"I will be excited to see it."

Before Gerald departed, Gerda promised again to contact her son and get the name of the woman with the biology background. Then she would text

Gerald with the woman's name. At the door, she hugged him unexpectedly and squeezed his arm. Her hand felt almost hot and the sensation caused him to smile.

"Thanks for including me," she said before releasing her grip. "I am very excited about this."

"No, thank you."

After backing his car into the street, Gerald turned for one final look at the old woman and her quaint little home. Gerda stood on her front porch with her hand extended rigidly in the air, as if in salute. He smiled, waved, then watched the old German disappear into her home.

Before returning to the interstate, Gerald pulled into the parking lot of a small shopping area so he could contact his friend, Franklin Harvey, with the message to start working on the website. Gerald had already decided to create the website, but he wanted to wait until after his discussion with Gerda. If she had rejected his offer to participate, then perhaps the website would have had to wait.

If he had a successful meeting with Gerda, Gerald would send a secret code, per Franklin's request, to register the domain and start working on the website. Gerald remembered feeling amused at the young man's excitement. Apparently, Franklin loved the opportunity to act covertly, even when he possessed very limited information about the group and their secret technology.

Gerald typed the required text message on his iPhone and paused before tapping the send button. He smiled and shook his head at the absurdity of the secret code, but after sending it, the message felt mysteriously significant.

Remember your lunch and don't forget the punch.

Three seconds later, Gerald received Franklin's simple reply, a smiley face emoticon.

When Gerald first discussed the website with Franklin, he let Franklin devise the plan himself and only required a secure and innocent-looking platform to communicate. Franklin would put more effort on the site, Gerald decided, if he devised the plan himself. Gerald remembered his contagious enthusiasm to begin working on the task.

"Cryptography is one of my specialties," Franklin had said with confidence, "and we can disguise it as an innocent website about astronomy."

Gerald had complete confidence in Franklin's ability. He had met Franklin through one of his clients. During a visit to a small company which he represented, he had seen the young man, who appeared about twenty years old, fixing a database issue. Gerald had immediately noticed the words written on his cap.

Ron Paul for President

Gerald had introduced himself and then attempted to determine how the young man felt about politics, an attitude which often predicted intelligence and the capacity for independent thought. During their brief exchange, Franklin revealed a passion for the open source software community which he saw as a subset of the freedom movement. He spoke vehemently about how the government had bureaucratized intellectual property and continually attempted to shackle free communication with unnecessary regulations.

Franklin's attitude and intelligence had immediately impressed Gerald, more than the young man's program design competition trophies. Gerald had never previously considered the open source community in that way. He needed no other reasons to hate governments than all the misery and destruction they caused.

After sending the text, Gerald's excitement about the website began to mount. He decided to wait a couple of days before requesting an update, but hoped Franklin would contact him sooner. Gerald spent the remainder of his return journey to Seattle, thinking about the best way to approach the new potential recruit, a woman he had yet to meet. He would have to do some research first and plan more carefully than he did for Gerda. Gerald needed to become acquainted with her first, before trusting and involving her with their dangerous activities.

Just before pulling into his parking space at the office, his iPhone began vibrating. He looked at the text message from Gerda and stared at the name for several seconds before shifting the transmission from drive to neutral. The woman's name felt significant.

Sadi Jacobsen

40

Sadi

March 2009

Sadi Jacobsen fell asleep on the couch again. Sometime later, her daughter's nanny, Jen, turned off the lights and covered her with a blanket. When Sadi awoke again sometime after midnight, she thought the room looked darker than normal with just a sliver of a moon visible through the blinds. While wiping perspiration from her face, the memory of the horrible nightmare felt like the sting of a wasp.

As usual, her unconscious mind decided to torture her again with a slightly different version of her son's death. He had died the previous November, the night before Barack Obama became the forty-fourth president of the United States. Even with her libertarian attitude, she had no personal opinion of the president, good or bad. The timing of his election, however, so close to the most tragic event in her life put a stain on his image. The name of Barack Obama became a constant reminder of what had happened, a name of death and tragedy. No matter where she went, she failed to escape the biting reminder. Everyone seemed to either hate him or love him, but in her opinion, he acted as a mere puppet so she refrained from talking about him.

In her nightmare that night, she found herself again driving the car on the night of the accident. Instead of just her son, however, this time her older daughter died too. At the end of the dream, Sadi stood like a statue, holding her two dead children in her arms while the cold Oregon rain pelted her head and slid down her neck.

Over the months since the accident, her nightmares had started to become less frequent and she'd begun to experience more unconscious time with her son while he lived. While recovering on the couch, Sadi wished the dream had been one of those bittersweet ones. The good dreams never left her feeling sick inside, although still sad. After waking from those dreams, at least, she could desire to fall back asleep.

The pain never went away, but at least, in her dreams she could still see him. She used to try thinking of him being with Jesus, but that offered no real comfort. The thought felt like eating sugar. It felt pleasurable on her tongue, but always left a bad taste in her mouth.

Before she fell asleep, she had been reading the American Journal of Hematology. The magazine lay on the coffee table in front of her, its outline barely visible in the dark. Her laptop sat next to the magazine and had long ago gone dark while she slept. Now a single blinking LED illuminated the table every three seconds. Her watch showed thirty minutes past midnight. Should she get up and go to bed or stay there on the couch? She wished Jen would have woken her, instead of making her more comfortable. Sleeping on the couch happened too often lately. Since the accident, she'd focused too much on her work and needed to devote more time to her remaining child, Helen.

"I need to get to bed," she whispered to herself and stretched her arms.

She began to remove the blanket, but stopped after hearing the noise. It was the noise that had been absent for several months, the sound that haunted her dreams. Somehow, her dreams had found a way to invade the real world.

In an attempt to send any dream residue back to the darkness, Sadi took a deep breath and yawned. After her senses recovered, she heard the sound of a sleeping child again. Just a few feet away from her, the sound felt all too real. Sadi knew the sound of her eight-year-old daughter's breathing like her own. Only a mother could distinguish the sleeping sounds of her children. Only her son made that sound when he slept.

The noise originated from a recliner on the opposite side of the room. From her position on the couch, she could not see the source through the darkness. "I must be dreaming," she said quietly then closed her eyes and hoped to awaken in the light of the morning. Perhaps the past four months had all been just a nightmare about to end. With her eyes closed, the only sound became the slow, steady breathing of her sleeping son.

The sound of that breathing seemed to be the only sound in existence, but she found no comfort hearing it. Such experiences only happened to people who'd lost their sense of reality. Sadi spent the last four months convincing herself that she would never see her son again. In vain, she fought back the tears. A demon had entered the real world to torment her.

"Get a hold of yourself," Sadi said aloud to the darkness.

The sound of her own voice gave her strength. Her sensations had an explanation. Her imagination had transformed it somehow. Suddenly, she felt a great urge to stand on her feet. Her heart pounded too hard inside her chest to remain motionless.

The feeling in her chest reminded Sadi of the funeral, the last time she saw the body of her son. She never had a worse moment in her life, not even the day her son died. For a long time, she could not remember him alive, just dead in a coffin. She wished she'd never looked at the body.

When her watch chimed she jumped. She instantly knew the hour, one in the morning. Being conscious of the time again felt like a slap in the face. For the past thirty minutes, Sadi had been listening to the sound, but it felt like just a few moments. The breaths came slow and steady like the waves on the beach. Sadi reached toward the coffee table and the movement caused the laptop to spring to life. The soft glow instantly saturated her eyes and washed the remainder of the room in an even more impenetrable darkness. Sadi held her breath, wondering if the change in lighting would disturb the breathing, but it continued without pause.

Pushing back her fear, she tried speaking, but only whispered instead.

"Who's there?"

Silence responded.

Sadi tried adjusting her eyes to the light, but she could only see a dark haze beyond the illuminated laptop. As she began to close the lid, she noticed a new email in her Gmail account. Instinctively, she quickly read the message.

Lunch tomorrow?
I'll text you.
-GF

The email message failed to register in her mind. A man she only knew in cyberspace had written it. He would have to wait. The sound of breathing from her dream visitor excluded all other thoughts. She closed the lid of the laptop computer and waited for her eyes to readjust to the dark again. Gathering up her courage, she spoke again, louder than before.

"Who's there?"

This time the sound of steady breathing stopped, replaced by shuffling of a little body. A moment later, a complete silence filled the room.

"Mamma," said a tiny voice, a voice silenced the previous November.

The word echoed inside her head like a hammer and her blood froze in her veins. Sadi felt completely paralyzed. The word was spoken exactly as she remembered. She listened to the sound of a child hopping off the couch and walking in her direction. The outline of his tiny form appeared out of the darkness. Fear seemed to give Sadi enough strength to sit back against the couch, as far back as she could go.

The child stopped in front of Sadi and held out his hands for her to put him on her lap. A single tear fell from each of her eyes. They burned on their way down her cheeks. She knew he could not be her son, but he appeared exactly the same as she remembered.

"Hold out your hands," said a voice inside her head. "Don't waste this time."

The voice in her mind felt completely alien. The child waited patiently. His eyes reflected the low light in the room.

"Jacob?" she said tentatively, to herself. "How can it be you?"

Sadi slowly extended her hands and he melted into her arms, just like she remembered. For a long while she held him, without speaking. All the pain of the last few months dissipated. She felt a single tear fall onto her arm. She chose to remain silent.

"Mamma," said the child as if he was going to say more.

Instinctively, she stroked his head. She felt him begin to resist, but refused to relax her hold on him. For the moment at least, she would pretend he existed. If she let him go, he might disappear. When she looked into his eyes, she noticed an infinitesimal speck of light. Did the light come from the moon or something self-generated?

As she stared at the light, she comprehended the reality of the child. She knew her own imagination lacked the strength to produce all the details in their exactness. She could feel his breath on her chin, the warmth of his skin under her fingers. With sudden sadness, Sadi knew the truth. The child in her arms was an exact copy, but not her Jacob.

With fear in her eyes and heart, she slowly let go of the boy and leaned back on the couch. For a few moments, he just stared at her and some of her shock dissipated until she gained enough courage to speak.

"Who are you?"

"I wanted to see you," he said in a perfect imitation of her son. "I wanted you to hold me again."

"You're not my son," she said quietly and spoke as if talking to an adult and not to a two and a half-year-old toddler. Sadi felt a strange conflict. She should have been afraid. She should have closed her eyes in an attempt to retreat into her own darkness. Any attempt to communicate with an apparition meant insanity. "Why are you here?"

"I miss you Mother," the child said with perfect sincerity in his voice.

When fear failed to rescue her mind from the abyss of anxiety, Sadi attempted anger. Unfortunately, that emotion could not be summoned. She felt only curiosity and a sadness that the situation had to be false.

"Why are you doing this?" she asked in desperation, momentarily holding back more tears. She felt no malevolence from the child, but wanted to feel something different than sadness. "Do you know where he is?"

The sound of a door opening upstairs stole her attention away and she realized her eight-year-old daughter, Helen, had awoken. Just as she knew the breathing of her little boy, Sadi knew the sound of her daughter's movement. The counterfeit son suddenly moved closer to Sadi, so that his face hovered within three inches of her nose. The child put both tiny hands on her cheek. They felt warm and smooth like a child's hands should be. Without thinking, Sadi pressed her hands on top of his. The touch wiped all thought from her mind.

"I need to go away again," the child said with a small pinch to her cheek.

Sadi remembered her son performing the same action. In the back of her mind, she could hear her daughter walking softly down the stairs.

"*Helen*," the child said with thick affection, turning his head towards the stairs. When the child returned his attention to Sadi, she noticed the light deep inside his eyes sparkling like sunlight on a stream.

Helen arrived at the bottom of the stairs, and would soon come into view. The child's eyes narrowed and focused on Sadi.

"When they come for you," he said. "Think of the future."

At that moment, Helen energized the kitchen light. The glow spilled around the corner, into the living room and drove away all darkness from the room, including the child. Sadi's hands fell onto her empty lap.

The blond girl of eight years stepped into the room, rubbing her eyes.

"Mom, what's wrong? Have you been crying?"

"It's nothing," Sadi replied, squinting in the light.

Helen came within reach and Sadi pulled her close. For several moments, she just hugged her daughter and stroked her hair while the conversation with her dream son repeated in her mind. The experience felt too real to be a dream, but how could it be anything else? Why did she need to think of the future?

"I'm fine, Helen," she said, getting up from the couch. "Come on, let's get to bed. You can sleep with me tonight."

41

Sadi

March 2009

Sadi held a vial of blood between her thumb and index finger. As she shook the vial, a thin film of blood oozed down the transparent wall. Although she worked with blood nearly every day, the beautiful red liquid still held some kind of power over her, like a child looking at the star-filled sky. The sight of blood always reminded her of life. She loved looking at it and wondered at how such a beautiful substance could also symbolize pain and horror. The film of blood drained too quickly back into the dark red pool.

By the apparently lower viscosity, she knew that the blood came from an anemic donor. How many times did she have to complain to the donor screening guys? Too many blood samples came from anemic donors. The undesirable property should have no effect on her tests, but she hated uncontrolled, extra factors.

For the past three years, Sadi had worked for the pharmaceutical company, Pantra, located in Hillsboro, Oregon. She loved her job and especially her most recent position as hematology project manager. The previous year the company had promoted Sadi to the new position. The promotion meant she had to follow commands from fewer people, with more freedom on her projects. Sadi focused on characterizing the drug Exdantrafir, one of their experimental anti-viral medications and for the past few weeks, she'd spent a majority of her time testing the T-cell response to an invasion of viruses which the pathogen department prepared.

Due to the disturbing experience earlier that morning, Sadi had difficulty concentrating on her work. The memory of seeing her dead son threatened to steal all her mental capacity. She failed to make any sense of the memory. Her mind felt like a spinning top with an excessive precession. No matter how much she tried, her rational mind refused to believe the experience happened. She felt tempted to stay home, claiming to be sick, but concluded that work would help her keep her mind distracted from disturbing thoughts.

"Am I losing my mind?" she asked herself before placing the vial in the centrifuge.

Maybe she just needed time? Nightmares sometimes took several days to fade into blurry memories. Before that happened, she still had to deal with the email that arrived suspiciously at the same time. She feared a connection existed between the two events.

On the drive to work, Sadi received the man's promised text message. In as few words as possible, her new friend wrote where he wanted to meet her for lunch. As she drove to work, she replied by text on her iPhone.

c u there

To help her merge back into reality, Sadi needed to talk with another human, someone other than her young daughter or teenage nanny. Fortunately, she had become good friends with one of her coworkers, a woman named Zoya and all that morning she waited impatiently for an opportunity to talk with her. Although she felt unprepared to talk about what happened during the night, she could discuss her lunch rendezvous.

Zoya, a native from Iran, had come to the United States with her husband for graduate school. After arriving, they had a daughter and decided to stay. Only after becoming very close friends did Sadi learn about her parents and how they were political leaders in the Iranian government. Due to all the foreign interference in the country, they had become targets for violence and encouraged Zoya to leave for her safety. Zoya complained confidentially about the unfortunate situation in her home country. She confessed to being afraid of openly talking about her real feelings due to all the anti-Iranian propaganda she heard in the news and entertainment media. Sadi felt sorry for her and often wondered how she would feel living in a country so intent on invasion and oppression of her home country.

Sadi could only share her deepest personal matters with a few people, Zoya being one of them. Since the funeral of their son, her separated husband seemed to lose all concern for their remaining child. Helen hardly knew him anymore. Although Sadi hated the man, she'd rather have her daughter, at least, spend some time with her father. If nothing else, that time could help Helen appreciate her mother more.

After they divorced, Sadi's ex-husband became a symbol of her old life of drugs and apathy, and the memory of him always reminded her of the old Sadi. To be completely honest with herself, she did not blame him for the grief he caused. Ultimately, she made the mistake of marrying him, just like her mother unwisely married her father. People rarely broke or escaped their conditioning and often failed to change the course set by their parents. Sadi prided herself in being one of the few who broke her own conditioning. The process began when she made the choice to continue with college. Then, when Sadi gave birth to her first child Helen, she decided that Helen would live in better circumstances, with a better example to follow.

Sadi only talked to her ex-husband when absolutely necessary and fortunately, she'd rarely had to deal with him since the divorce. After the accident, he stopped pretending to care about their daughter and by his absence forced Sadi to arrange all the funeral preparations herself. His family tried to apologize for him, but his actions mattered little to her. He had acted like a jerk as a part-time father and he remained a jerk after they divorced. She paid her lawyer extra to locate him and deliver the divorce papers. With him out of their lives, she finally felt free.

Around ten o'clock that morning, Sadi found herself alone with her friend.

"Hey Zoya," she said. "I found something very interesting on the internet."

The slender short brunette, sat in front of a computer screen on the opposite side of the room. Her ponytail spilled over the back of her white lab coat like a black snake on the snow. After a moment, Zoya turned from her computer screen and waited patiently for Sadi to finish.

"And..." Zoya said, an apparent question in her dark blue Persian eyes.

Having those eyes focused on Sadi caused a moment of appreciation. Before continuing, Sadi pushed a wisp of her dark hair from her face. She stood slightly taller than Zoya, had fuller features and looked much paler, an obvious native of the Northwest United States.

"Ever heard of the Free State Project?"

"Doesn't sound familiar," Zoya said and her smile grew wider. "Did you join a LSD addicts anonymous group?"

Sadi smiled but refrained from indulging her friend by laughing. She wanted the conversation to remain quasi-serious.

"Close, but no. It's a group of people who moved to New Hampshire to create a free society. I found their website last night."

"Another freedom organization, huh?" Zoya rolled her eyes. She spoke with a homogeneous mix of humor and sarcasm, but with eyes stained by concern. "Last year it was the Libertarian party, then something called *Freedom Force,* and now this. You know you're on the CIA and FBI watch lists now, right? Has this, Free State Project, had any success?"

Sadi took another vial of blood and began preparation for the control and test samples.

"I think they got someone elected to the legislature, but I haven't looked into it that much."

"I doubt they'll get enough people to control an entire state."

"That's what I thought," Sadi agreed. "They're not exactly following the 'baby steps' principle, but at least they're doing something."

"Baby steps principle?"

"Sorry. It's a reference from a movie with Bill Murray called *What About Bob*. It's about starting small, in manageable steps."

Sadi always had to explain her American entertainment references.

"Oh," Zoya replied. "I haven't seen it, but Bill Murray is funny."

Sadi paused again before continuing with the other topic she wanted to discuss. She knew Zoya would disapprove, but she had to tell someone.

"I never told you about this person I've been emailing have I?"

Sadi attempted to act casually, as if she simply forgot to share an insignificant piece of information. Both of them knew the information had not been shared. Zoya shook her head with negative affirmation and opened her eyes even wider.

"What person?" She emphasized the word 'person'. "Is it a man?"

"Well you're right about the man part, but I have no reason to be interested in him as a man, if that's what you mean. One of my Libertarian friends, a lab assistant who worked here before you did, said he needed someone with a biology background. I've never actually met him, in the real world. We've just been emailing each other."

"Does he have anything to do with the Free State Project?" Zoya asked. "Does he want you to move to New Hampshire or to donate?"

"No, that was just one of the things he asked me about, but I don't think it's what he's really interested in. We talk about a lot of stuff. He sounds like a lawyer."

"So, he claims to be a lawyer," she began as if still deciding what else to say. "What else does he claim to be? A model and a millionaire just looking for some nice girl, like yourself, to share his vast wealth with?"

Sadi failed to refrain from laughing and had to turn away to regain her composure.

"Zoya, it's nothing like that. He really hasn't told me much about himself yet."

"OK," Zoya said and Sadi heard some relief in her voice. "So what does he want, do you think?"

"I don't know exactly what he wants, other than to meet with me." Sadi spoke tentatively, feeling like a deer drinking water from a pool that might contain an alligator. "I get the impression he wants to get to know me more, before meeting and revealing his true intentions."

Zoya shifted her chair to face Sadi.

"Uh, is it a good idea to meet with him, before you know what he wants?"

"Maybe not," Sadi admitted.

Even if Zoya doubted her judgment, Sadi trusted the friend who had facilitated the connection.

"So, don't do it," Zoya said in exasperation. "I really don't know why you're telling me this. I know you're not going to listen to me."

Sadi disliked the frustration in Zoya's voice, but unconsciously appreciated the diversion.

"Listen, Zoya, I know it sounds crazy, but I have a strange feeling about this. I just wanted to let someone else know about it so…".

Sadi paused and Zoya took the opportunity to finish her sentence.

"So that I would have something to tell the police when you are missing. You're not going anywhere without me. Where are you meeting this man?"

"Sorry Zoya," Sadi said with real regret. "I can't bring anyone with me, but don't worry. I'm not dumb enough to meet him anywhere alone. We're going to meet in a public place."

"That is a good idea, but what if he is a crazy stalker? When he sees your beauty, it will be all over. Don't let him follow you when you are done."

Sadi took a moment to review her conversations with the man. The effort required less than a second to confirm her previous conclusions. Gerald failed to exhibit the typical characteristics of a crazy stalker. The thought had crossed her mind, but she had to trust the friend who had connected them and her own judgment.

Gerald had asked a lot of questions about her, as if just innocently curious, but he seemed to already know a lot. That worried her a little. From his writing, however, he also seemed well-educated and polite.

He claimed to require her assistance for some kind of consulting, but refused to give any specifics over email. Did he want some incriminating information about her company? Due to its political tactics, Sadi had no love for the pharmaceutical industry and she understood how often the pharmaceutical industry wrote their own rules and bought key politicians to write regulations for the industry. Despite her personal feelings for the industry, however, she loved her work with immunology and had no intention of putting her job at risk.

If another pharmaceutical company or the government intended to initiate a lawsuit against Pantra, one of their lawyers might attempt to acquire evidence through its employees. The possibility of Gerald being an attorney for the government seemed unlikely. Gerald showed obvious signs of sincerely despising the government, besides, he could have gotten all the information he claimed to need from an expert at the CDC. The government had plenty of their own experts.

If Sadi had learned anything from her formal education, she learned to trust in evidence and make decisions based solely on the facts before her face. So far, she found no evidence to cause major concern.

"So when is your meeting?" asked Zoya.

"Lunch today." Sadi turned from her samples to face her friend again. "I promise to tell you all about it when I come back."

"Where are you going?"

"Not sure," Sadi said. "He's going to text me at noon about the place."

"Why do I get the feeling you aren't telling the whole story?" she asked, sounding somewhat offended.

"I've told you all I know," Sadi said, attempting to offer some comfort.

Would Zoya attempt to follow her to her secret lunch meeting? If she did attempt to spy, she would need to sit inconspicuously within hearing distance. Sadi would enjoy seeing that, but doubted it would happen.

Sadi became consumed in her work for the rest of the morning. For a little while at least, she needed to forget about the experience with her son the previous night and emotionally prepare for the next singular experience at lunch. Just before she left for lunch, the topic of her clandestine meeting resurfaced. Zoya made Sadi promise to keep her phone handy and to call her if anything strange happened.

Zoya stopped Sadi just before she left. She squeezed Sadi's hand and held it while speaking.

"I'm sorry for being so nosy," she said with an unusually sweet smile. "It wasn't my place to pry. I know you wouldn't do anything *stupid*."

Zoya's sarcastic tone caused an involuntary smile to appear on Sadi's lips. In her friend's not-so-subtle way, she wanted to prevent Sadi from acting stupid. On that occasion, she let Zoya have the final statement. She wanted her friend to feel like she had some influence over the situation.

42

Sadi

As Sadi walked to her car, she received the next text message from Gerald. He wanted to have lunch at the PF Chang restaurant, just ten minutes away from her work. On her way out of Pantra's secured parking lot, she waved to the security guard stationed there. On that day, only a few people left the site for lunch. Most employees preferred to stay on-site for the excellent cafeteria.

"Have a good lunch, Ms. Jacobsen," said the guard.

After turning onto the main street, she checked the rear view mirror to see if Zoya had followed her. She smiled when her friend failed to appear, but then almost wished Zoya would have followed her anyway. Although unafraid of the meeting, she would have appreciated her friend's opinion of the man. At first, what she saw in the rear view mirror failed to register in her consciousness.

After Sadi turned onto the street, a dark green 2005 Mustang pulled out from the side of the road. Sadi took the next turn then glanced behind her again and noticed the same vehicle turning on the same road. Sadi shook her head and laughed at the temptation to feel paranoid.

The air outside felt cold, but refreshingly dry and clear. Sadi welcomed the sunshine, a sharp contrast to an extremely wet Northwest winter where the dreary rain attacked them, day, after day, after day. The clean, cold air helped her appreciate the warmer air inside her car and helped erase some of the strangeness of the night's experience. Some day soon, the sun would go back in hiding until spring.

In order to distract her thoughts, Sadi energized the radio and turned the station to NPR. As she drove to the restaurant, she listened as the radio hosts discussed the global financial meltdown. During the first few weeks of the most recent man-made catastrophe, she'd listened intently to everything presented to her by the major media sources. After doing intensive studying on her own, she'd grown very angry at the government for facilitating the events.

Whenever the people on NPR talked about the subject, she fought the temptation to change the station and kept listening. She never completely understood why she kept listening, since she could not do anything about the situation. Perhaps she enjoyed having a specific target for her anger. Hating the government for its most recent round of plunder felt easier than feeling angry at the universe for what had happened to her son. Perhaps if she had more freedom in her life, she would have chosen another road that night and her son might still be alive.

When halfway to the restaurant, she looked behind her again just out of curiosity and noticed the same Ford Mustang traveling at about the same distance as when she last looked. The man drove just far enough away to prevent her from recognizing his face. Had Zoya called someone to follow her, or had Gerald arranged the tail to assure that she came alone? The whole thing seemed too ridiculous, but she decided to test her suspicions anyway.

She knew of a gas station a few lights ahead and planned to pull into its parking area. After activating the turn signal, she slowed while keeping her eyes on the rear view mirror. The Mustang made no indication of turning. As the car started to drive past the gas station, Sadi noticed the driver looking straight ahead, but for one small instant, he turned to look at her. Even though the car blew warm air on her neck, that instant of eye contact sent chills down her spine.

Sadi waited until the Mustang disappeared from her view, then pulled back into traffic, towards her destination. For a moment, she felt tempted to turn around, go back to work and forget about the meeting.

"This is ridiculous," she said to herself. "I should take a sleeping pill tonight!"

Sadi noticed nothing else suspicious on the rest of her way to PF Chang's. The dark green Mustang failed to make another appearance. After that threatening experience, Sadi focused on the sunlight on her face and excitedly anticipated meeting an interesting new person.

Unintentionally, Sadi found herself hoping to find Gerald in need of more than just a professional consultant. Whether lunch turned into a professional or personal meeting, however, Sadi hoped to meet with a single man. Having lunch alone with a married man might make her feel very uncomfortable. She would have to watch for signs of marriage. Since the accident, she seemed to lose all interest in forming any new relationships, platonic or romantic. Perhaps this time she would feel different.

After arriving at the restaurant, she realized they had failed to prepare for the problem of recognizing each other. Should she carry a sign with her name? Or should she just write, “Desperate and Stupid”?

In the restaurant parking lot, she felt the same uncomfortable sensation of being watched again. She looked around, half expecting to see the green Mustang. Eventually, she failed to recognize it in the lot and told herself to stop thinking about it.

"I probably am being watched you silly schizo," she said to herself. "He's probably watching me from inside the restaurant."

Her paranoid feelings reminded Sadi of being eighteen-years-old, the last time she took acid with her sixteen-year-old brother. As usual, they took drugs while home alone and with all the blinds closed to be as dark as possible at five in the afternoon. She remembered watching all the colors seeping through the blinds like smoke and almost passing out from laughing. They had peeked from under a blanket in fear of the creatures in the room with them, the creatures they heard growling menacingly and laughing hysterically. When the evil creatures pulled the blanket away from covering them, it would be the end. She would literally die while laughing and she looked forward to such an end.

Then Sadi remembered the horrible stomach ache which followed. Fortunately, just the thought of acid could almost induce vomiting. Her reaction to the drug became one of the many reasons she failed to continue the practice, unlike her brother. He probably still did acid every once in a while, but he kept his drug addiction more under control now. The memory made her sad.

After shaking the memory of her foolish youth, she entered the restaurant and pretended to act bored. A giant Chinese Terracotta warrior statue greeted her solemnly. While momentarily appreciating the piece of history, a man tapped her right arm and spoke tentatively.

"Ms. Jacobsen?"

Taylor turned and found a tall, dark-haired man wearing a suit. How could she have failed to notice him?

"Gerald?" she asked in surprise.

The man stood at least five inches taller than Sadi, making him over six feet tall. He seemed to have enough thick hair to cover two heads, but wore it short enough to comb to the side. His dark blue suit hung on him as if he had lost ten pounds since its purchase. Overall, he looked professional and reminded her of a lawyer. His genuine smile helped ease her unconscious fear of meeting with a crazy political activist.

"Thanks for meeting me here," he said as if they often had lunch together. Instead of waiting for her reply he turned to the counter where a beautiful young girl greeted them with a smile.

"Yes, a table for two please," he said then turned back to Sadi. "I hope this place is good for you? I know it's close to your work."

"Yes, I like this place," she replied, somewhat confused at his tone of familiarity.

She had been prepared to introduce herself, but felt awkward saying it. His disarming smile momentarily erased her confusion and she felt forced to also smile.

He almost ignored her until they were seated and specifically asked to sit in a remote booth, instead of a table in the middle of the room where the girl wanted to place them.

"Sorry that I didn't introduce myself properly yet," he said confidentially after they were seated. "The name's Gerald Fuger."

Until now, Sadi had never heard his last name. While looking through the menu, she noticed him inspecting their surroundings with suspicion. For almost a minute of silence, the situation felt like an awkward first date. Sadi decided to quickly choose her favorite menu item and then begin the interrogation.

"So," she began, somewhat playfully. "Have I guessed right that you're a lawyer?"

He looked up from the menu into her dark blue eyes and smiled.

"How did you know? Woman's intuition?"

"In your emails you just sound like one. You write like one."

"If you mean I write like an above average lawyer, then I'll take that as a compliment."

He set his menu on the table and almost immediately, the waitress appeared to take their order. They both quickly ordered and the conversation continued as if never interrupted.

"I suppose it's a compliment," she said. Sadi studied his eyes to see if they contained any emotion other than light sarcasm. So far yes, but she probably had to know him better to see the difference. "I just like trying to figure things out on my own. So, let me see if I'm on the right track."

"Ok," he said as if he heard a challenge. "But I just want to warn you. I don't think you can even imagine my purpose for our meeting."

His comment caused her a momentary hesitation.

"Is that supposed to scare me?"

"No, I just like to get down to business," he said. "But let's see how close you get."

"You're interested in my work." She squinted and looked directly into his eyes again. "That's the easy part, considering all the questions you've asked me about it."

She waited for a response.

"Continue," he said.

"This next part, I'm not so sure about," she said and sipped her water. "You either share several of my views concerning politics and history, or you're a damn good sociopath who's convinced me of it, in order to establish a sense of trust and solidarity."

He continued to smile, but remained silent. If he meant to intimidate her, he failed.

"Depending on the answer to that, you could either be a government agent investigating Pantra. Or, you could be a lawyer for Bayer or another of our competitors, trying to steal some proprietary information from me. If that's the case, I'll enjoy watching you squirm when I turn out to be uncooperative."

She raised her eyebrows in a challenge.

"Are you done?" he asked after taking a bite of his food and leaning back against his seat.

She thought he looked entertained, so she tried to sound indifferent.

"To be honest, I doubt either case. I think the more likely scenario is that you're working for some non-profit cancer research firm who dislikes working with that joke of a department, the CDC. My time is limited, but I'm definitely willing to donate some of my time for a worthy cause."

"How about we start with what I'm not," he said as a polite interruption. "I may even tell you everything, but likely not today. You might not want to know everything. Ignorance is sometimes a convenient safety net."

"Ok, whittle it down some more please." The way he stressed the word 'safety' caused her to sit forward. When she felt more comfortable, he continued.

"I'm not working for another pharmaceutical company, or for the government, or for a non-profit research group. Well, that's not true, I actually do occasional work for a few non-profits, but that has nothing to do with our meeting. I'll tell you about the group I represent, but I need to lay some groundwork first.

"Let me tell you what I know about you and we'll go from there." His smile transformed into a very faint curve of his lips. "If that's OK?"

If he failed to get her full attention already, he had it then. She slowly twirled her fork around some noodles, but kept it there on the plate, approving with silence.

"You were born and grew up in Portland, in a poorer part of town. Your mother died when you were ten years old and you had to raise your younger brother, Brian, because your father was too busy with his job, along with his other activities."

"For reasons I cannot understand, not only did you go to college, but you stuck it out and excelled even. Very few people who come from your circumstances ever escape it. Not to give any credit to anyone other than yourself, but some of your courage and tenacity probably came from your mother's death. You look like her, you know. You must have been close. Her death may have made you angry. I don't know about you, but anger can be a strong motivator. That's one of the problems with people today, they aren't getting angry. Whatever the reason for your strength, you definitely have my respect."

He did not wait for her to respond or validate any of his words. In their email correspondence she had told him some of her history, but not even half of what he knew. He continued with her story like a crab boat cutting white waves for the next pot.

"You married while working towards your undergraduate degree in chemistry and graduated with honors, even after having a daughter. You and your husband separated in the middle of your graduate school at the University of Washington. While there, you earned your Ph.D. in molecular biology where you focused on infection and immunity. I read your first publication in the Journal of Hematology. To be honest, much of it was beyond me and I only finished it so that I could look intelligent for reading it, so don't try to discuss it with me. I'll look like a fool."

He paused, as if trying to decide to go further. When Gerald spoke again, he started cautiously and became quieter.

"After the death of your second child, you and your husband finally divorced."

Gerald leaned forward and focused on her eyes. He seemed prepared to stop speaking if she displayed signs of anger or sadness.

"I know your son died last year. I was sorry to learn of it and I'm very sorry to mention it. After his death, you've probably started thinking seriously about all you've been told, by your religion, by the government, and by society in general. I think you've realized that almost nothing can be taken at face value, and usually it is almost the exact opposite. As you and I have discussed online, truth can sometimes be horrible, but it must be faced and cannot be ignored. Your emotional strength and the fact that you're an expert in microbiology is just what I am looking for. I think you can make a great contribution to the group I represent."

Sadi felt like he had just invaded her home and looked through her underwear drawer. She did not feel anger, however, just insecurity and vulnerability. To be privy to that kind of personal information meant he either had connections or just knew how to dig for information. Being a lawyer probably helped too. In the short pause, she wanted to speak, but he continued again.

43

Sadi

"I just need you to know that we've done our homework on you, and I want you to take me very seriously. I believe you can be trusted. It's my job to help you trust me."

Sadi thought of seeing her son early that morning and strained her eyes to keep them dry. Did that experience prepare her for this meeting? Did the experience relate to Gerald in any way? The thought felt too improbable to take seriously and to suggest out loud.

"OK, you definitely have the upper hand," Sadi said finally, glad to keep tears from her eyes. "I didn't even try to figure out who you were. Your first name was good enough for me."

Sadi laughed to herself and forced a smile. In an attempt to appear as unconcerned as possible, she slowly took a drink.

"You're probably wondering why I needed to know so much about you?"

"You want me for some kind of consultancy, something secret?"

"Yes, we need you for your technical expertise, and if you decide to help us, it needs to be kept confidential."

"So why all the personal information? Why do you care about my political views?" That seemed to be his key factor in choosing her. He could have picked from thousands of experts in her field. Sadi leaned forward and lowered her voice. "Why do you care if I know about all the lies everyone seems to be swallowing? That can't have anything to do with my educational background."

Gerald leaned away from her, as if her proximity made him nervous. She watched his eyes as they moved from her to the rest of the room. He appeared to be worried about something, and trying to hide it. Did he feel frightened? He began speaking before resuming eye contact.

"What did you think about that group I told you about? The Free State Project?" After he finished scanning the room, his eyes locked back onto hers.

"The Free State Project?" she said in unfeigned frustration, a bit too loudly. "Oh my God. That's what this is about! I'm not moving to New Hampshire if that's what you're getting at."

"Why not?" he asked with an amused tone in his voice.

Immediately, her heart sank with immense disappointment. The whole situation made no sense. Why would this man, who appeared so intelligent and wrote so eloquently, go to all that trouble for just one person when the Free State Project needed many thousand to make a difference? Did he think she would make a large contribution? She hated the thought of being solicited, and wasting her time.

In another moment of unexpected revelation, Sadi realized a more personal root cause for her sudden depression. Unconsciously, she had let herself hope for the meeting to include the possibility of a romantic relationship. His acceptable physical appearance and intelligence helped her become vulnerable to the natural need for a personal connection. He had also violated her sense of independence, which she'd spent so long to build.

He sat with raised eyebrows, silently waiting for a response. All her negative emotions became directed at him. She had difficulty concentrating on his question.

"Why won't I move to New Hampshire?" she began. Talking gave Sadi a sense of emotional release. Internal anger transformed into words. "First, they're trying to free an entire state. There aren't enough of us who know what's really going on in the world, and who give a damn, to fill a county. Second, even if we were numerous enough for a whole state, the government would come down on us harder than they did on the South during the civil war."

Instead of shock at her anger, Gerald seemed amused by her arguments.

"Yes, but if they were successful? Would you do it?"

"I'm not itching to move to the cold Northeast, but sure, in your very hypothetical world I'd do it." His failure to recoil at her emotional outburst damaged her confidence. Before finishing, she clenched her fist on the table. "Only if I thought they had a chance."

"Even if they couldn't eliminate all the artificial laws, wouldn't it be nice just to live in a community of people who share our views?"

The argument made sense to her. If she had more than just a few days of casual thought on the subject, she probably would have more fully considered his postulate. Unfortunately, she had only looked at their website a couple of times. His arguments made no difference. She wanted to stay angry at him.

"To be honest, I would rather stay away from many of the people who claim to be interested in freedom." The disappointed look on his face gave her a slight sense of guilt for speaking rudely. "But yes, I do like associating with true libertarians."

His tone became more serious and the smile on his face disappeared.

"How much would you be willing to sacrifice to live in a place like that? Twenty thousand dollars? Fifty? A hundred?"

Her level of anger rose to its previous level. "How could I have been so stupid?" she wanted to say. Even though she refused to move to New Hampshire, he wanted her to donate money anyway.

"You can't be serious," she said. "I can't believe you're asking me for a donation."

He sat back in his seat and amusement returned to his eyes. "I never claimed to be associated with the Free State Project."

Sadi sat in stunned silence for several moments. Her anger slowly turned to a feeling of relief for being wrong in her assumptions. She also felt foolish for being so angry and required some time to relax. Would her ridiculous hope return? Hope for a possible romantic relationship? All the emotions of the past ten hours left her physically exhausted. At that moment, she felt like Gerald had sent her back to the beginning of a board game.

"Now I feel stupid for being so angry," she said in mock anger. "You seemed to enjoy watching me vent."

He laughed uncomfortably.

"I apologize for putting you through that. I really did not intend to make you feel any negative emotions."

"It's been one of those days," she said in apology. "Normally, it would have been fine."

"Good. Now, you did not answer the question. Hypothetically, of course, how much would you be willing to sacrifice? I'm sorry to put a dollar amount on sacrifice, but I think many sacrifices can be measured in dollars or at least a percentage of one's bank account."

"There are plenty of other things to sacrifice," she said and paused. "I don't believe that what you're proposing is even possible, not now at least. Even if a free society like that existed now, it would not exist for long. They'd find a way to destroy it before the world realized that it actually worked."

"First they'd send paid intruders to stir up trouble, fund some terrorist acts and claim that the free society was responsible, reinforcing the misconception that it would never work and was a horrible system. It wouldn't cost much money to do it either. They can always find cheap grunt psychopaths to do the dirty work of the elite psychopaths."

"Once they had the justification to eliminate us, it would be all over. I'm sure you can imagine how many missiles they can launch, how many tanks they can roll over us. Remember what they did to Hiroshima and Nagasaki? Remember how many people they killed, people like you and me who were just trying to make a living? Remember what the Russians did to Chechnya? What China did to Mongolia? What the North did to the South? How many kids they killed in Waco Texas? I could go on and on. If I remember right, you even wrote something similar in one of our email conversations."

"Yes," he said, looking a bit dejected. "You're probably right. History is filled with tragic events."

The look on his face reminded her of when she told her daughter the real identity of Santa.

44

Sadi

"Now, Sadi," he said and seemed to recover. "I don't want you to be angry with me, but I cannot tell you everything today. First, for your protection, and second, because you will need to consider the implications of your involvement. However, what I have told you needs to be kept confidential. I need you to promise me that this conversation stays between you and me. Do I have your word?"

"Sure," she said without pausing. "You have my word."

"Even if you get questioned by a government official?"

She gulped, but nodded. "You still haven't told me anything."

"If anyone asks you about this meeting, tell them that I decided not to tell you anything. You did not want to continue with our conversation. Understand?"

"I understand about acting ignorant, but let me get this straight. You're talking about establishing a free society? How is that even possible? I think you're sincere, but 'think' is not good enough. I don't know if I'm willing to sacrifice my security and comfortable lifestyle for a free society."

"Like I said, I'm not going into details today, but you're almost on the right track."

Up until that point, Sadi thought of freedom as just an abstract thought, an idea existing only in fantasy. Of course she wanted to live in a land of freedom. Of course she would fight for her daughter to have a better future. Even though she thought the Libertarian party had a very small chance of success, she had joined them. At least, her vote meant something.

Had her choices carried too little risk? The government had no reason to fear Libertarians. Being so few in number, they had little or no real power. The overwhelming majority of people supported the establishment, either the Democrat or the Republican face of the beast. The majority believed what the mainstream news told them about it. She liked Gerald's view, the concept of living with others in the freedom movement. How much would she be willing to invest? How much of her daughter's future would she risk? She needed time to think.

Suddenly, Sadi remembered the Ford Mustang on her way to the restaurant, then she remembered Gerald suspiciously looking at the people around them. For the first time during the meeting, she became more aware of the people in the restaurant. A group of three college-age guys occupied the booth behind them. They spoke rather loudly and she doubted if anyone could hear her conversation over their raucous chatter. Sadi spoke in a whisper.

"Do you think we're being watched?"

An unexpected smile returned to Gerald's face.

"What makes you say that?"

"On my way here," she began, "I thought someone was following me, a man in a dark green Mustang. I pulled into a gas station and he passed me, but I was sure he had been looking at me."

He sat back.

"You probably haven't spotted him here, am I right?"

"No, I haven't, and there was no Mustang in the parking lot when I got here. I checked, but forgot about it until now. Do you think he was following me, or was it just my imagination?"

"I'm afraid it might be true," he said, shaking his head as if he considered being followed a mere annoyance. "Sometimes they have a guy following me. I think they're trying to build a case against me, because of some previous issues which I really don't want to discuss at the moment, but it's unrelated to the topic we've been discussing. I apologize if they give you any trouble. Just remember that the law does not require you to talk to them. I can be your lawyer if anyone asks."

"Who are they?"

"The Federal Bureau of Investigation," he said while putting a piece of meat in his mouth.

"OK?" Sadi tentatively asked. "You're going to have to tell me about it. If you want me to trust you, I can't think of you as an outlaw."

"I understand," he said. "I didn't want to talk about it, because it's kind of embarrassing, but I guess you do deserve an explanation. A couple of years ago, some acquaintances of mine broke into the Seattle Federal Reserve office. I really had nothing to do with it, but I pissed off the FBI when I chose to be their defense attorney, pro bono. I didn't let the FBI take advantage of them and they failed to implicate me, like they also wanted. You can verify the story if you don't believe me. It's all public record."

"I'll take your word for it. For now."

His explanation failed to quell some of her doubts. She already had too many.

"If you decide not to get involved, then you have nothing to worry about. Your record's clean and the FBI will find no interest in you."

"Well that's good," she said. "I guess."

He smiled again.

"After work tonight, go home and think about a future where you own your life, without coercion from our tyrant kings. I personally think it's worth the risk. If you want to know more, please contact me. I'm pretty excited about what's going on and wish we could go over all the details now, but as I said you have to make the decision first."

"I'm sorry, but you've got to give me more than this." Sadi could not make an informed decision on what Gerald revealed. "At least, tell me how I can contribute to your group? Why did you choose me?"

From the look in Gerald's eyes, Sadi wondered if he hoped to avoid this question. Before he answered, the experience with her son that morning rushed into her memory again.

"I guess this was inevitable," he began. "The answer might not be acceptable to you, but I chose you because I think we might need you."

"You might need me? What does that mean?"

"That's hard to explain without telling you confidential information, but finding you is a different story."

Before continuing, he looked above her head in thought, slightly to his right. Sadi tried to remember what 'looking to the right' meant, inventing an answer or searching for the right one?

"An old coworker of yours, Paul, introduced you to a friend of his and his friend described the encounter to his mother, a woman named Gerda Schreiber. His mother is an old friend of mine. Gerda gave me your name when I asked if she knew anyone with a background in biology who also had libertarian tendencies."

"Yes. I remember you telling me that."

"Well, what I didn't tell you was that when I heard your name, for a reason I can't explain, I knew I had to contact you, even before I learned more of your background in biology. I don't usually base my decisions on feelings, but in your case, I couldn't ignore them. I hope that doesn't scare you. I'm not making it up as some sort of black magic pick-up line. Please don't take it the wrong way. When I learned more about you, I knew you were the right choice. All that I can say is we want people to look at things, from several different angles."

While he finished his explanation, the memory of seeing her son invaded her thoughts and nearly drowned the remainder of his words. Before responding, she picked up her glass and poured some cold water down a dry throat. A deep breath helped restore her composure.

"If I make the decision to get involved, how do I let you know? Through email?"

Gerald looked relieved by her response.

"No, email is too insecure. Log into our secure website. That will be your answer."

"Even if I want to learn more, I can still decide not to get involved?"

He nodded then looked at his watch.

"Well, our hour is up. It was very nice finally meeting you, Sadi, in person. I do hope you consider the next step. Even if not, I hope we can still keep in touch? There are too few of us."

"Sure," she said, then worried about how quickly she responded.

He removed a business card from under his suit coat, wrote on the back for a few seconds, then handed it to her. His card reminded Sadi of her divorce lawyer, a man she did not particularly want to remember. She quickly read the name of his law firm, FUGER AND FOWLER.

She turned the card over and saw what he wrote, the address of their website, a username and six random words. Before Sadi visited the website, he told her to make several different web searches, sign into a number of new websites and then do a Google search for three of the six words on the back of the card. A Google search of any three words from his list would deliver their site in the top ten choices. He did not want her to type their website directly into the web browser. In addition, she could only log into the site within a specified time of the evening.

The extra precautions seemed extreme and unnecessary, but Sadi agreed to follow them should she choose to proceed. If investigators ever searched her internet log, they would find the sites she visited, no matter what method she used to reach them.

As they exited the restaurant, Sadi had more questions than answers and the impression of experiencing an emotional roller coaster. Before going their separate ways, she searched for anything suspicious, but noticed nothing out of the ordinary. They parted with a formal handshake.

"I hope we meet again."

After grasping the car door handle, she turned for one last glance. Gerald stood in the same spot watching her. He smiled and raised a hand, then turned toward his black Taurus and disappeared inside.

45

Sadi

When Sadi returned from lunch, she had difficulty concentrating on work. Although she failed to learn much of what Gerald wanted, her mind raced through the countless possibilities. At least, she no longer suspected him of being a government agent.

The memory of being followed by the man in the Ford Mustang refused to leave her conscious thoughts, filling her with a sense of violation. Just thinking of their brief eye contact sent chills through her system. Whether the man worked for the FBI or another organization, Sadi had no clue. At that time, the employer made little difference.

"So how did your meeting go?" Zoya asked with a teasing smile. If she felt relief for Sadi's safety, she kept the tone out of her voice. "Was it a romantic connection? Are you interested in him?"

Even though the possibility of a romantic relationship had secretly been one of Sadi's hopes, Zoya hinting about it caused a flare of annoyance. Sadi fought the temptation to blame her friend for placing the thought in her mind. For the sake of confidentiality, she would pretend to play the game even if the act caused embarrassment. Failing to deny the accusations might cause Zoya to continue believing the wrong assumptions.

"Lunch was good," Sadi began. "He was not married, or at least he wasn't wearing a wedding ring."

"Was he handsome?" Zoya's knowledge of the English language contained only limited vocabulary about sexual attraction. She often used the word 'handsome' to categorize men.

"Actually, he was very handsome," Sadi said before she could consider her response and then remembered Gerald looking at her in the parking lot.

For the present, Zoya asked no other questions and neither of them discussed the topic again for the next few days. Sadi regretted mentioning the meeting in the first place and planned to avoid the topic in the future.

Two nights later while falling asleep in her room, Sadi had the distinct feeling of being watched. The sensation remained even after opening her eyes, but the room remained empty. She tried forgetting the experience and concentrated on falling asleep instead. Exhaustion usually knocked her totally unconscious without the memory of the transition. That night when she closed her eyes, swirling lights tricked her into forgetting about lying in bed. She only remembered enjoying the show her mind produced.

The twirling lights slowly transformed into a depiction of her kitchen with her brother sitting at the dining table. She missed seeing him. Over the past few years, he visited only a few times a month, rather than every week.

While she watched at the table, her brother studiously wrote on a piece of paper, probably song lyrics for his band. A hazy yellow light obscured the paper and enveloped his hands in front of him. The light felt perfectly normal in her dream and raised no alarm for breaking any physical laws.

After a long while, other people began walking through the kitchen, people from her memories. Some of them paused to admire the blank walls, and others walked as they would through a grocery store. Sometimes Sadi would glance at one of the random shoppers, but none of them gave any sign of noticing her.

Sadi knew some of them intimately, but others originated from brief encounters in public somewhere. With each of them, she remembered the exact instance of their meeting. Occasionally, a famous actor, politician or news anchor would appear. Donald Trump and John Wayne walked in together with her dead grandmother. The old lady looked confused, as if deciding to approach Sadi and ask a question. Before Sadi could talk to her, however, the old woman walked out of the room and disappeared. Sadi had no memory of ever meeting her, just seeing her picture. Hopefully, her grandmother would make another appearance.

During the entire episode, her brother wrote furiously on the paper and paid no attention to anyone around them. The fuzzy yellow light hovered over his hands and shifted in different directions.

Strangers eventually replaced all the familiar people and they all turned to face one direction, to a space between the counter and the refrigerator. She noticed other people's faces peering through the windows, all looking in the same direction. Sadi calmly followed their gaze.

A boy occupied the small space, sitting down on the ground with his back to the wall. He appeared to be near twelve-years-old and Sadi thought she knew him, but failed to remember his name. Out of all the people who walked through her kitchen, only the boy acknowledged her existence. After staring into the boy's eyes, she realized the reason for all the interest in him. Sadi was looking at the only living person in the room. All the rest of the people were ghosts. They stared at him, mesmerized by the light in his eyes, the blazing light of life.

The boy scraped his feet slowly against the ground in an attempt to push himself further in the corner, to hide in the shadows. As she watched him, the scene filled her with sadness. As children, everyone else had rejected the boy. Only Sadi and her brother gave him acceptance and friendship. The fear in his eyes felt like a stab to the heart.

The people slowly began to drift out the open window like smoke, anger filling their eyes. All the ghosts stayed outside and the thousands of eyes continued to watch the kitchen through the window. Eventually, only Sadi and her brother remained in the kitchen with the boy.

For an unknown reason, Sadi knew a method to remember the boy's name. She only had to touch his hand. Then she could simply say his name and the boy would stop being afraid. As she stepped forward, the boy cringed in terror, afraid of her approach. She paused for only a moment, but then proceeded forward more slowly as if trying to corner a frightened cat.

The more she walked, however, the farther away he seemed to be. At the same time, the hazy yellow cloud covering her brother's fingers began to grow and reach toward the boy.

"I'm not going to hurt you," she said while extending her hand.

The cloud of light grew larger and its beautiful, yellow color swirled together with blackness. Before she could continue moving forward, the cloud totally enveloped the boy, removing him from her sight.

Soon afterward, the light also enveloped her brother, leaving Sadi alone, surrounded by the light. A short time later, the dark swirls filled the entire space. The darkness grew until only tiny dots of light remained, dots in every direction. She stared at the beautiful sight for a long time and forgot the scene in the kitchen, the ghosts, her brother and the boy.

Sadi found herself floating in an endless space, with no sun or anything but the distant stars in her view. She searched in vain for the Earth, but only the endless starlight surrounded her.

At first, the blue dot just looked like all the other stars, but when the Earth grew to the size of her fingertip, she recognized her old home. As the planet and the surface features became more discernible, she realized that her return to Earth meant death. The giant orb raced to meet her and she would burn up in the atmosphere like a beautiful shooting star. Would she become a child's wish before bedtime? That destiny seemed poetic.

When the Earth filled her entire view she waited for the quick end. Her body would soon vaporize, her ashes to remain in the upper atmosphere for eternity. She had no time to despair, no time to regret the loss of time with her daughter. Amazingly, Sadi continued unscathed through the atmosphere instead of being vaporized by the plasma wind.

The speed became incredible. She flew past the clouds, faster than a bullet. After ripping through the clouds, she saw a line on the Earth, stretching as far as she could see in both directions. Soon the line became a road with a dot on it. The dot became a man, just standing there and looking up to the sky, at her.

Right before she crashed into the man, she recognized him, Gerald Fuger. She extended her hands towards him in an absurd attempt to cushion the impact and he opened his arms as if preparing for an embrace. She awoke with a jolt, just before her impact obliterated them both.

In the dark of her bedroom, she sat up in bed and wiped the moisture from her forehead, the image of Gerald's face filling her memory. She felt ready to connect to the web and give Gerald her answer.

46

Sadi

Images from the dream lingered in her head like the crowd of ghosts in her dream's kitchen window. Gerald's face became a nightmare, repeatedly rushing towards her at lightening speed. Visiting his website seemed to be her only way to stop his assault. As Sadi headed towards the stairs, she stopped by the open door of the next room to check on her daughter. Helen lay under the covers, only her blond hair visible. A pink glow from the night light filled the room with softness and the sound of Helen's steady breathing completed the tranquil atmosphere. Sadi usually slept at least ninety minutes more, but waking at four-thirty in the morning seemed a small price to pay for relief from the dream.

She forgot what time Gerald said to log onto the website. After finding his business card, she opened her laptop computer in the kitchen and brought the machine to life. While waiting, she started preparing coffee.

As instructed, Sadi chose three of the six keywords on the card for the Google search. As promised, the target website appeared as number four in the list of several million search results. She clicked the link and a cartoon-style drawing of a rocket escaping the Earth filled the main page. From the other pictures and text, a random visitor would think they landed on a site dedicated to astronomy. The images contained an impressive array of star charts, constellations and cartographic depictions of the Earth with distance vectors and scientific formulae in beautiful calligraphy. Sadi was instantly impressed.

Sadi's fascination with studying the website allowed the person approaching the kitchen table to escape her notice. When her daughter's twenty-year-old nanny, Jen, cleared her throat, Sadi jumped in surprise.

"Oh, I'm sorry," Jen said and yawned. "I heard a noise and came down to see if Helen was awake. Oh, God I'm tired. Sorry Sadi."

Sadi thought the girl looked more ragged than normal, even after just getting out of bed, then she remembered the rock concert Jen had attended with her friends the previous evening. She'd returned home after Sadi had fallen asleep. Sadi considered advising the girl to take a shower to wash the dried sweat and tangles out of her dark brown hair and the smeared mascara from under her eyes, but refrained. She had to suppress a laugh at her appearance.

"Sorry to wake you, Jen," Sadi said as she turned to shield the computer screen from her view. "How was the band?"

"Awesome," she said with a smile, rubbing her eyes. "Your brother sure had the crowd going. I think he even noticed me."

Sadi understood Jen's infatuation with her brother, an affliction that hundreds of other young girls suffered. Normally, Sadi would indulge the girl by letting her talk about the experience, but she wanted to get back to the computer.

"Let's talk later. You should go back to bed," Sadi told her and smiled. "From my viewpoint, you could use a few more hours."

"What are you doing up this early?" Jen ignored the teasing insult.

"Couldn't sleep."

"OK then," Jen said, attempting to see past Sadi to the computer screen.

Sadi moved farther in her way and let the awkward silence become an indication of who would win the contest to see the computer screen.

"Yeah, that's a good idea," Jen said with a small frown. "I'll just get back in bed."

Sadi smiled while she watched the girl walk away. She loved the girl like a sister and trusted her completely. Jen had turned into the perfect nanny for Helen. She always put her job above everything else in her life and loved her ward like her own. Sadi also liked having another woman in the house.

In some ways, Jen acted like a teenager. Nearly every month, she went to a concert for the latest rock band in town. After discovering Sadi's relationship to the attractive lead singer of a local band, Jen had bought their latest album and became their biggest fan. When Brian came over to visit for the first time after she started as the nanny, Jen had almost fainted with excitement. The memory of that event always made Sadi smile.

A few months after Sadi hired Jen, Sadi noticed the familiar smell of marijuana on her clothes and confronted her about it. While afraid of being fired for the offense, Jen told the truth about the situation. Her bold admission impressed Sadi.

Sadi took a more pragmatic approach to drugs than the general population. If Jen could do her job well, why should Sadi care about them? Since Sadi cared for the girl, she did her best to warn Jen about the dangers of drugs, especially the more physically harmful ones and to stay away from them in general. They were especially forbidden in her home. Due to her own stupid actions as a youth, Sadi refused to let the situation scar her opinion of Jen.

Like Jen, Sadi also loved to talk about the music she liked. Their tastes in music overlapped in several areas. At the beginning of their professional relationship, Jen had asked Sadi to attend a concert with her. Even though Sadi had felt tempted by the offer, she'd wanted to keep a bit of a professional boundary between them. Going to a concert and getting high with her employee seemed like a pretty good reason to decline the invitation. Besides, she wanted to keep that part of her past buried.

Sadi had attended enough of her brother's shows anyway and wanted to distance herself from his type of friends, although she still shared a love of music and enjoyed discussing the topic with him.

After Jen walked back up the stairs to her bedroom, Sadi listened until all indications of movement ceased. She turned back to her laptop screen and noticed the login box just under the address bar. While holding Gerald's business card, she read the username he wrote and typed it in uppercase letters, IRIS.

Did Gerald produce the username just for her, or did the word simply indicate a new recruit? The word either referred to the flower, or part of the eye and either could be considered a compliment. After shaking her head in irritation, she signed into the site as IRIS and a prompt asked her to create a password. A welcome message instantly appeared after she hit ENTER.

Welcome IRIS, please read this page and answer the question at the bottom. By signing in and continuing further, you agree to keep what you learn strictly confidential. Thank you for your willingness to participate!

Sadi only required a minute to read through the information on the page. The text failed to include anything specific related to the group's true purpose, but instead explained how the website should be used as a secure medium to communicate with other members. At first, she felt confused, then realized that the text intended to mislead the reader. Either that or Gerald wanted her to join a site devoted to helping people cope with addictions to sex and drugs. The clever prose would lead interlopers into believing that the members of the site only wished to hide embarrassing personal information.

After laughing quietly, Sadi began to feel better about joining. At the bottom of the page listed three options with a radio button on their left.

1 *Want to proceed!*
2 *Still need more information?*
3 *Not interested!*

After selecting the first option, Sadi held the cursor over the 'OK' button and rested her index finger on the keypad. Before clicking, she paused. Did she have intelligent reasons for accepting the invitation? Her mind answered with a 'no', but her feelings told her to tap the keypad. The action of proceeding seemed to follow the same path as the intense dream of that night and the vision of her son.

Although Gerald had failed to mention the subject of compensation, Sadi wondered if participation offered anything other than the opportunity of being part of something important, such as human freedom. Would her actions help increase her own freedom or Helen's? Was that worth the risk? The tap of her finger answered 'yes'.

After clicking 'OK', new text appeared giving her instructions about the next step. She needed to log into the site again after twenty-four hours. "Great," she whispered. "More waiting."

Sadi wondered again why Gerald chose her name as Iris. Then she closed the computer and attempted to rest from thought for a while.

47

Sadi

The day she chose to join Gerald's group, Sadi had difficulty concentrating on her projects at work. Even though the website instructed to wait twenty-four hours before logging into it again, she decided to hurry home after work and log in again. Despite that plan, however, she accidentally agreed to one of Zoya's requests.

"I'm sorry, but what did I just agree to?" Sadi looked up and asked in confusion.

"Don't try to get out of it Sadi," Zoya said while finishing up her tests for the day. Zoya refused to accept any excuse. "Your mind has not been here with the rest of us today. You need to relax with a drink. Who knows, maybe you'll meet someone."

Sadi desperately wanted to go home so she could discover the next step to the process, but she also felt an obligation to Zoya for ignoring her all day. The thought of a drink with her friend, however, felt more tempting than socializing with unfamiliar men. She disliked the idea of finding someone at a bar. By her own logic, if she felt uncomfortable making a romantic connection at a bar or pub, she would probably be incompatible with a man who did.

While Sadi sipped her drink at the bar, she avoided eye contact with any guy who happened to look in her direction. Zoya talked about her frustrations with her child's teacher. She kept one eye on Sadi and the other looking around the restaurant at all the people. Anyone in the bar would probably have thought Zoya and not Sadi wanted to meet a guy. After twenty minutes of one-sided conversation, Zoya turned her whole attention to Sadi and stopped suggesting that she try to appear more approachable to eligible men.

"Are you ever going to tell me what happened with your secret rendezvous with that man?" Zoya asked as if in resignation of never knowing.

"Didn't I already tell you about that?" Sadi answered.

"You told me he was a lawyer and needed a consultant for one of his clients," she said and brought both eyes to meet Sadi. "You left out the most important part, the part that *I* wanted to hear. Is he single? Is he handsome?"

"Yes," Sadi answered and remembered her asking the same question before. Sadi smiled, then put her glass to her lips to avoid saying more.

"Hmmm," Zoya said and thought for a second. "When are you seeing him again!"

"I don't know."

"You're enjoying this aren't you?"

"What do you mean?"

"Stop laughing at me," Zoya said, acting hurt. "Promise me you'll tell me if anything happens. I need a promise!"

"You'll be the first one to hear anything," Sadi said and erased the playful smile on her lips. "He is handsome, but I'm not expecting anything to happen."

Sadi arrived home early enough to put Helen in bed for the night. Helen really wanted to see her mother so Jen had let her play the Wii to pass the time.

"Mom!" Helen said after Sadi walked in the front door, jumping from her perch on the couch where she played MarioKart on the Wii game console.

Helen loved that game more than all the others, one of the only things she seemed to enjoy doing lately, other than drawing. She threw her arms around her mother's waist.

"Welcome back," Jen said sarcastically from where she sat the table. She looked up just enough to acknowledge Sadi's arrival.

"I was waiting for you forever!" said Helen as a yawn made her pause. "Where were you?"

"I'm sorry hon," Sadi answered. "Zoya made me get a drink with her. She had some stuff she had to tell me."

"Were you looking for a man?" asked Helen loudly as she ran back to the couch to continue her game.

Jen snorted with a laugh from the table. Sadi ignored her.

"No man tonight, dear, just a drink." Sadi sat on the couch next to her daughter and watched her play the game. "You're in third place. Good job!"

"I would be in first," she replied angrily. "Waluigi just pushed me over the cliff. He's always undermining me."

Where did her daughter learn the word, 'undermine'? Did she even know what it meant? Helen often used random new words that she heard from different sources. Sadi turned to Jen and mouthed the word, 'Undermine'?

"She was falling asleep on the couch," Jen said and shrugged. "So I said she could play the Wii until you got home."

Sadi stood and noticed a thick opened textbook and several papers scattered across the kitchen table. While Jen worked on her school work, she drank orange juice and ate some toast. Jen liked toast with butter and nothing else. She often had the same food to begin and end her day.

"Thanks Jen!" Sadi said with sincerity, then changed to a teasing, but serious, tone of warning. "All those carbs are going to catch up to you, when you get to my age."

Jen answered by taking another bite of toast, smiling and then returning silently to her work. Helen finished her game five minutes later, at ten minutes after eight in the evening. After her game they followed the normal bedtime routine of the bathroom, a final drink and two short books that Helen insisted Sadi read. As she bent down to kiss her daughter goodnight, Helen put her skinny arms around her mother's neck.

"I love you, Mom!" she said with a huge smile and a tone full of exaggerated drama, like a contrived theatrical performance.

Helen liked to put extra emphasis on most displays of affection. Sadi loved that part of her personality, but hoped the behavior would fail to transform into an excessively dramatic teenager.

"Love you too," Sadi answered and tried prying her daughter's hand from behind her neck. "You can let go now!" Sadi laughed while imagining her neck snapping under the pressure from the tiny hand.

"Is this our home?" Helen asked after relaxing her hold and slipping free.

"Of course this is our home," Sadi answered. "Why would you ask that?"

"Hmmm," Helen replied as if considering a great philosophical question. "I had a dream last night about moving to a new home, but I don't remember where."

"Do you want to move?" asked Sadi.

Helen yawned and rolled onto her side, facing the wall. Her words became a whisper.

"Oh, I don't know. It might be exciting. Goodnight, Mom!"

Usually, when Helen finished participating in a conversation, the other participant should abandon all efforts to keep the conversation going. Sadi ignored the urge to ask another question and patted the covers over her daughter. As Sadi left the room, she left the door slightly open and glanced one last time at the unconscious lump under the covers.

Sadi opened her laptop on a chair in the living room facing Jen. After logging into the site with her IRIS username, she discovered a completely different website. Either the site owner had enhanced her site permissions or the site itself had gone through a serious overhaul. Overall, the site looked pretty sophisticated. Gerald and his friends had seemed to put a lot of effort into making security tight.

At the top of the screen, a blinking mail icon indicated that Sadi had a message from Gerald. In the note, Gerald made no attempt to hide his excitement at her decision to join. For the next two hours, Jen stayed at the kitchen table and Sadi sat in the living room with her laptop, devouring all the contents of Gerald's website.

48

Sadi

April 7, 2009

A few days later, while Sadi prepared to put Helen into her bed for the night, the phone rang. She would have let the call transfer to voicemail, but Helen lifted the receiver before Sadi could stop her.

"Hi, uncle Brian!" she said excitedly, then held the phone out to her mother with a pout. "He wants to talk to you, mom."

Sadi sighed and knew she would have to talk to him. Conversations with her brother sometimes lasted a long time and she'd just wanted to put Helen to bed and relax. He usually called earlier in the evenings, or would just visit unexpectedly. Before taking the phone from her daughter, Sadi attempted to remember the last time she'd talked with her brother. It had been longer than two weeks when he called last. She should have called him.

"Hi, Brian," she said, keeping the impatience from her tone. "How's it going? Sorry I haven't called. I've been distracted lately."

"I've been too busy to notice," he said laughing. "You won't believe who contacted me."

"Who?"

"Freddy called me yesterday," he said and paused to let her recognize the name. "And he wants to get in touch with you, but don't worry. I didn't give him your address or phone number or anything."

"Freddy Carlson," she said and the image of him in her dream made her heart skip. She knew no one else named Freddy. "Is there a reason why I wouldn't want to talk to him?"

"No," her brother paused. "It's just, you remember how fond he was of you. I thought I'd give you the choice."

"Did he say what he wanted?"

"He just said he needed to see you, but he wouldn't tell me why. You know Freddy. He's in his own world."

"Well," she said and paused for a moment to give the impression of consideration. Yes, she definitely wanted to see Freddy. "Give him a call and see if he wants to visit here, but you're coming with him."

When the car pulled into her driveway the next night, Sadi watched anxiously from the window. The darkness and rain obscured the faces of the driver and passenger, but somehow she recognized her brother and Freddy sitting in the front seats. She felt some anxiety as she anticipated seeing Freddy walk through the door with her brother. Would the event feel like her past trespassing on her present?

Sadi took one last look outside and realized something unexpected. She assumed Brian would be driving Freddy to her house, but her brother sat in the passenger seat. Freddy drove some kind of luxury sedan which her brother would never choose or afford.

"Too pretentious", he would say.

Sadi had difficulty imagining the strange boy she and Brian used to know driving an expensive car. They were just a bunch of poor kids from the bad side of town and Freddy lived in an even worse condition than she and Brian. She remembered Freddy being a very intelligent kid, so why would he not have a good job and a nice car? He deserved it. She felt happy for him.

She held no grudge against Freddy, just anxiety at seeing him again. She liked him even, as a friend, that is. If they would've met by chance at a grocery store or somewhere, it would have been a pleasant encounter. They would have talked for a long time, perhaps set a time for a meeting with her and Brian. On this night, circumstances were completely different. Freddy had actively sought her and after her dream of him and her association with Gerald Fuger, the encounter seemed like an ill omen.

While waiting for her uncle, Helen sat on the couch and played the Wii, becoming totally oblivious to everything. Both of her tiny hands held tightly onto the controller and moved it almost violently.

Jen joined Sadi at the window and looked over her shoulder at the car.

"Who's that?" she asked. "Are you expecting anyone?"

"Oh, sorry. I forgot to tell you, Brian's coming over with an old friend of ours."

Due to all the strange emotions going through Sadi's head, she'd neglected to tell Jen of the planned company.

"That's Brian? Brian is here *now*?" she said somewhat in shock. "Why didn't you tell me? I look horrible."

Jen raced up the stairs to the bathroom by her room. Sadi would get a lecture about her negligence later. Jen never admitted to being in love with Brian, but she never hid her excitement at seeing him, either. Too many times in the past, Sadi had seen other girls fall into the same trap of her brother's confidence and charisma.

After the bathroom door slammed shut upstairs, Brian rapped on the door once before opening it.

"Come in out of the rain," she said before saying hello to the two men. "Put your coats over here, on the rack."

Before she had time to say anything else, Helen slid off the couch and ran to them.

"Uncle Brian, Uncle Brian," the little blond girl screamed as Brian removed his coat.

Sadi took his coat just before Helen smashed into him. While he pretended to suffocate, she hugged him hard and laughed wickedly, as if intentionally trying to kill him.

"Choking," Brian gasped in a whisper. "Need oxygen. Can't breathe!"

"Hi Sadi," said Freddy Carlson as he awkwardly placed his coat on the rack. "Thanks for letting me visit. It is great to see you."

"Good to see you too, Freddy." Sadi stood motionless, about to hug him, but he held out his hand to her and they greeted each other like a formal business meeting. "How long has it been?"

"I believe," he said, gathering the right words. "It has been eight years."

The sounds of Brian and Helen momentarily drew their attention away from each other. Brian had grabbed his niece and spun her over his head. After making her do a backflip, she landed on her feet then fell back on the couch. Before he let Helen relax, however, he plucked her from the seat again and presented her to Freddy.

"I forgot to introduce you," he said and looked serious. "This is Freddy Carlson. He used to chill with your mother and me when we were younger, but older than you."

Helen tilted her head up to him and gave Freddy a silly look.

"I'm Helen," she said in a high, squeaky voice, like a living doll whose string had been pulled.

Sadi rolled her eyes.

"Oh, come on, Helen. Act normal for once."

"Hi there, mister," she said with a new deeper voice, too deep for an eight-year-old.

"Hi Helen," Freddy said smiling. "It is good to meet you. Thank you for letting me come to your home."

Sadi liked the dichotomy between her daughter's informality and the polite address from Freddy. At that moment, Jen came down the stairs and acted surprised to see people in the house. Sadi smiled discreetly. Her brother would definitely recognize Jen's performance.

"Hey, Brian," she said as casually as she could. "What a surprise. Sadi forgot to tell me that you were coming. I saw you at your show a couple weeks ago."

He turned to her and smiled. Jen preened like a cat in the sun under his attention.

"Hey, Jen. I saw you, but I lost sight of you. Otherwise, I would have come over to say hi."

"Don't lead her on, brother dear," Sadi said quietly, hoping he could hear her thoughts.

Would their blood relationship allow for telepathy? Probably not.

"Race me," said Helen running back to the couch and grabbing a Wii remote. She offered the controller to Brian. He looked from Jen to Sadi, then back to his niece. "I think," he said hesitantly. "That you can't stop me from playing with you."

Before Brian started playing the game with Helen, Sadi turned to Jen.

"This is an old friend of ours, Freddy Carlson." she said, turning to Freddy. "And this is Helen's nanny, Jen. She lives here with us."

"Good to meet you," she said then promptly excused herself to sit on the love seat to watch Brian and Helen play the MarioKart game.

"Sorry, Freddy," Brian said while steering the virtual car with his Wii controller. "I'll be over here for a while. I take orders from this one here."

"So, what have you been doing the past eight years?" Sadi asked as they walked to the dining table. From their location, they could hear everything from the video game participants in the living room. "I want to hear about what's been up with you."

As Freddy and Sadi talked, Brian played the video game while also attempting to participate in their conversation. Helen kept scolding him to keep his eyes on the virtual road and accused him several times of not concentrating on driving. Jen sat opposite them on the love seat, totally engrossed with the game. She kept cheering for Helen and clapped her hands when Brian crashed his virtual vehicle.

"Throw that shell at him," Jen yelled at Helen every few minutes.

Sadi kept Freddy speaking for most of the conversation. He told the story of how he came to work for Mr. Smith. While learning of his good fortune, Sadi felt extreme gratification. She knew the horror of his childhood all too well. Except for the loss of her son, the problems in his life made her challenges seem easy.

"Freddy's not telling you the best part," interjected Brian while he continued to stare at the television screen.

"What's that?" asked Sadi, turning to Freddy.

"I do not know," Freddy said in a puzzled tone.

"This guy he lives with, his mansion is in the Sylvan Highlands, and Freddy has access to all his money!"

"I only use it to get what I need," he said defensively. "Sometimes he tells me to get other things I do not need. I would never steal from him."

"Of course you wouldn't," Sadi said and put her hand on his wrist. "I am so happy for you Freddy. Sounds like things are finally looking up for you. You deserve it."

"I think providence is smiling on us both."

"So how's school going?" Sadi asked. "You're going to Portland State?"

"Yes, and I will be done next year with my bachelor's degree."

Freddy told them of his plans to attend graduate school and wanting to major in something related to cellular biology. He still needed to decide on a major, but felt torn between all the different fields. Sadi advised him to enter graduate school in the department he wanted, but to keep an open mind and explore the possibilities before making his final decision.

"There's no hurry. You're in a good position," she said and smiled wide. "You don't have any kids or an abusive spouse to distract you."

"I am sorry you had to deal with that," he said gravely, not laughing with her as she intended.

"That was the past," she said. "I think we're both looking at brighter futures."

During their conversation, Freddy seemed able to relax and feel more comfortable, but he still seemed socially awkward. Sadi felt sorry for him. He would probably never feel fully comfortable in social situations. Sadi decided to concentrate on his improved position in life.

Sadi was impressed by his knowledge of biology and science in general. Judging from his questions about graduate school, he had a good understanding already of biochemistry. He also seemed technologically savvy. Being removed from all the former drama in his life probably gave him time to focus on learning. With access to everything he could ever want, his talents could blossom.

During the next pause in their conversation, she wondered about the real purpose of his visit. When talking about graduate school, she thought he just wanted advice. Then she remembered her dream of him and falling back to the Earth. She needed to talk with him alone.

49

Sadi

At nine-thirty Sadi turned to Helen and said she had to go to bed. She would have argued, but Brian said he would take her. After Jen followed Brian and Helen up the stairs, Sadi turned to Freddy. He wore a look of concern.

"So you haven't mentioned why you wanted to see me," Sadi said after they were alone. "It's been fun to see you again, but your visit was not to get advice about graduate school, was it?"

"No," he said, avoiding eye contact. "It was not the purpose of my visit. I have something to show you."

Freddy stood from his seat and walked to the front door where his coat hung on a hook. He removed an object from an inside pocket and returned to the table. For a brief moment, Sadi imagined him returning with a weapon. She held her breath as if he prepared to aim a gun at her.

"I think I am supposed to show you this," he said while sitting, but keeping his hand closed.

"What is it?" Sadi asked, taking her first breath. She saw the sides of a flat crystal in his closed palm and could feel her heart rate accelerate. A strange thought occurred to her that the object in his hand was connected to everything else strange happening in her life recently.

"Sadi," he said with a quick glance at the stairs. "I do not know how to say this so maybe I can just show you and see what you think."

Slowly, he opened his hand to reveal a flat piece of rectangular crystal. Its surface shimmered with refracted light from above the table and Sadi could see the spider embedded inside. At first, the object reminded her of a piece of acrylic encasing a real insect, but after looking closer, the spider looked like a flat piece of rock. Seeing the spider recalled her memory of the time she invented his secret code word, the trick to help him identify people when he could not see their face. Did he still use the spider code word? Had Brian had to say 'spider' when he called Freddy? She planned to ask her brother later.

"It's beautiful," she said and felt a strange desire to take the object from Freddy's palm. "What is it?"

"I have no idea what it is," he said in a whisper.

For the next moment, they both just stared at the object in silence.

While admiring the beautiful object, several questions surfaced. What did he want her to say? Was it a gift? Did he still love her? He might still be infatuated with the memory of a younger Sadi, but he surely could not love Sadi of the present. Time must have either buried his childhood obsessions or else enhanced them. Before the silence prompted her to respond, she wondered if he felt disappointment at seeing her again.

"It's very intricate," she said and gently lifted the crystal from his palm. After turning the object in her hand to see the other side, she felt an unexpected shock. The object looked exactly the same on both sides. "The detail is amazing. Where did you get it?"

"I want to tell you why I am here, but…"

He paused and looked at her uncomfortably.

"Freddy," she interjected, remembering his difficulty with language. "Whatever it is, just say it. If you say it wrong, we can fix it. That's what communication is about."

"I do not want you to think I am crazy."

"I won't. I can take whatever you have to throw at me," she said and smiled. "Believe me."

"My sister gave that to me, but when I asked her about it the next time I saw her, she did not remember giving it to me."

"That's weird," Sadi said and frowned at the memory of his cruel sister, Wanda. "I didn't think she would give you anything this interesting on purpose. Was she drunk when she gave it to you?"

"No, she was sober," he said then pointed his index finger just above the crystal surface, over the head. She noticed how he averted his eyes as if avoiding a bright light. "If you look at the eyes on the head. What do you see?"

Sadi focused on the rows of glimmering eyes lining the head, but her vision became blurry. Her peripheral vision seemed fine. Did her eyes feel tired? After a moment of contemplation, she felt fine. She rubbed her eyes and made one more failed attempt.

"It almost hurts my eyes to look at it," she said, feeling confused. "Is that what you wanted me to see?"

"Sadi, I will just tell you," he said and sighed. His voice lowered to a whisper. "This object puts me into a trance and gives me strange visions."

He looked down at the table, as if embarrassed. Under any other circumstance, Sadi would have questioned the person's sanity. From his reaction, he understood how strange the statement sounded to her.

"What kind of visions?"

A sudden chill suddenly raced through her central nervous system. Sadi thought instantly of meeting her son in the dark of the night, and her dream with Freddy and Gerald. How did Freddy and the crystal relate to all her other strange experiences?

"I took a video of myself when it put me in one of the trances," Freddy said, returning her attention to him. "In the vision I had, I was told to come see you."

Sadi sat back in her chair, looking at him with curiosity and trying to hide her feeling of shock and anxiety. For just a moment, she wondered if he had some mental condition. Sometimes when people obeyed their dreams, someone else died. For the past two hours of conversation with Freddy, however, she sensed a higher level of maturity. He no longer seemed the lost and lonely boy she'd known as a teenager.

"What do you suspect is the reason?" Sadi felt a small fear of his possible answers. "You don't have to be right, but right now, your guess is more than I've got."

"I, I," he said, stammering. "I have no idea, but I brought the video with me. If you have your computer, I can show you. It is proof. I feel the need to show someone."

"OK."

Did she really want to see the video?

Freddy opened the palm of his hand to reveal the crystal again. At the same time, Sadi heard steps on the stairs and Jen laughing. Freddy closed his hand on the crystal and when Jen and Brian returned to view, Freddy looked at them with wide eyes.

Sadi quickly intervened.

"Jen, could you and Brian leave us alone for a few more minutes?"

Brian quickly scanned her face and nodded.

"C'mon, Jen," Brian said in a tone of sarcastic mental anguish. "Obviously, we're not wanted."

Jen followed Brian to the kitchen like a puppy dog. From her peripheral vision, Sadi noticed the girl's lips stretched into a wide smile. Brian would expect Sadi to reveal to him the parts of the conversation he missed. She would normally tell her brother whatever he wanted to know, but in this instance she might retain some of the details, at least until she could invent a good way to exclude information about Gerald's group. She still needed to tell him about the vision of her son.

After Jen and Brian disappeared into the kitchen, Sadi stood and retrieved her laptop from a hidden drawer in a dark wood cabinet. The cabinet served as their entertainment center and could close to mask the presence of electronic equipment like the television set. She placed her laptop on the coffee table then Freddy gave her a portable flash drive from his pocket which contained the video file.

As Sadi watched the video, she stared in disbelief and shock as the lights splashed out of the crystal and onto Freddy's face. The mixture of the beautiful lights and the eerie, motionless state of Freddy's features made Sadi pull her arms tightly across her breasts to fight the sudden chill. The entire evening felt like another dream. In a small way, she wanted the experience to be a dream, then she could wake and continue with her normal life. After a few minutes, she concentrated on taking deep breaths.

Sadi knew exactly why Freddy felt confusion and fear for his sanity. Strangely, she felt somehow prepared to hear the story from Freddy and see the video. Seeing the video helped validate her own incredible experiences. They helped prepare Sadi for the current experience. She had no clue what the crystal or lights meant, but she knew her next action. She would introduce Freddy to Gerald and show him the video. Gerald needed to learn about Freddy and the spider inside his crystal.

At the end of the video, Freddy removed the flash drive and closed the program so that no one could watch the video again on her computer. He looked into her eyes for a brief moment, then returned his gaze to the floor and waited.

"One thing's for certain," she said, shakily. "You're not crazy. There's been some strange things happening to me lately. Strange dreams, new people. Might be related. No, Freddy, you're not crazy."

She tried to laugh, but the attempt failed to convey any humor.

"Does this mean anything to you?" Freddy asked hopefully.

Sadi thought for a few seconds before responding. Were the events related to Gerald's secret technology group? She had to check with Gerald first. Sadi intended to keep her promise to not reveal his secrets.

"Actually, it might, but I need to do some investigation first. I will get back to you about it, but not tonight."

Their eyes met only briefly, then after looking away he took a deep breath and slowly exhaled. His eyes seemed to reflect a physical and emotional exhaustion. Did he feel any sense of relief to see her reaction to his extraordinary claims? Did he recognize her respect and empathy? Sharing the burden of his bizarre experience must have been a weight lifted from his conscience.

For a moment she felt tempted to share the vision of her dead son, but promptly changed her mind. The thought of sharing that incredibly personal experience filled her with anxiety. She definitely did not want to begin weeping in front of Freddy.

"So this happens whenever you look into the eyes of the spider?"

"Whenever I try to focus on the spider's eyes, time passes and I have no memory of what happened. I only remember what happened the last time, when I took the video, when I had the vision. I'm afraid to look at it now."

"If you hadn't shown me that video, I would've had a hard time believing you, but I would have anyway. What happened in the vision?"

The question seemed to have a physically draining effect on him, as if she just punched him in the stomach. He shifted in his seat before responding.

"A strange woman appeared and talked with me, and showed me things. At the end of it all, she said to find you."

"Did this woman say why?"

"No," he answered.

"Can I see the crystal again?"

Sadi rubbed her chin and took a deep breath as if preparing to dive under water. When he first told her to look into the spider's eyes, did he think she would have the same vision? Did he intend for her to fall into the same trance? From the look in his eyes, she saw no reason to suspect ulterior motives. The Freddy from her past would never intentionally harm her.

Freddy returned the crystal to Sadi and she began a more thorough inspection, one with a new respect. While looking at everything but the eyes, she marveled at its beauty and detail. Who'd made the object? Some secret government agency? An alien? Was it a religious relic? Had Jesus or Buddha held it once? Her imagination offered a million other explanations.

"See anything?"

"Let me think about this, and I will get back to you. I promise."

50

Sadi

April 10, 2009

When Sadi's brother called again the next day, he asked about what Freddy had wanted. Sadi gave him a reason she knew he would reject.

"He just wanted to see me again," she began. "To confess his former love for me."

"Yeah, right," Brian answered. As she hoped and expected, her brother laughed. "Freddy'd never admit to that. He's still too shy about it. I could see it in his face. We had a good talk in his car. Wow, can you believe his luck? The personal servant of a millionaire who doesn't care how much money Freddy spends on himself. C'mon, what's the real reason he came to see you?"

"Can't tell you yet," she said. "And that's the truth."

Brian paused before answering.

"OK, don't tell me," he said in resignation. "So what does this mean? Is he going to be in our lives again? Is he going to be in *your* life?"

Sadi laughed into the phone.

"Like I said Brian, I can't say anything about it now, but I'll fill you in, if anything happens."

Could her brother hear the forced and insincere laughter? If Brian thought Freddy caused her anxiety, he would continue asking her questions until she told him everything.

For two days since the meeting with Freddy, Sadi had let the experience mix with all of her other recent experiences. At first, she'd accepted Freddy's visit and his news, but the video had become more frightening as the images replayed in her memory. The experience reminded her of when she took Helen on a hike to the top of Beacon Rock in Washington. For the entire following week, Sadi had dreamed of the hike and of Helen falling to her death. The nights after Freddy's visit, she would close her eyes and the blue and orange lights would shine from the spider's eyes then reach for her. In some of her dreams, crystal spiders crawled all over her bed, shooting bright orange webs of light at her face, and trapping her.

Her imagination constantly supplied explanations which kept increasing her anxiety, so she attempted to avoid thinking about them. She concentrated on her plan, transfer the investigation to Gerald and let the lawyer find the answers. All the strange things in her life began after meeting Gerald and his secret energy group. After a couple of days, she'd emailed Gerald about what happened, but excluded many of the details. He needed to make a trip down to see her for the full account.

On their website's secure chat environment, she used the username of 'Iris', the beautiful flower and he used the username of 'Aristarchus', the ancient astronomer, the first man to put the Earth in its proper place, the man everyone had ignored.

Iris: Something happened, but I don't know what it means. I think it's related to the group.
Aristarchus: OK, what is it?
Iris: I'd rather not say over the internet.
Aristarchus: What can you tell me?
Iris: You probably wouldn't believe me if I told you anyway. You really need to be here. It's kind of urgent. When are you coming back to Portland? I need to talk to you in person.

Gerald said he would visit that Friday afternoon, just two days away. Sadi offered him a place to stay, if he wanted. After giving him her address she'd felt a great relief, as if her mental suffering had already come to an end. Somehow, an irrational feeling indicated that Gerald would take care of everything and solve all of her problems.

She took Friday afternoon off from work to meet Gerald at her home and arrived to an empty house with Jen still at the community college and Helen still at elementary school. She always felt strange at home alone. Normally, she would have enjoyed the hour to herself, but thousands of emotions competed for her attention, including the new thoughts of occupying an empty home with an attractive man. When she saw his car pull into her driveway, her pulse felt stronger and seemed to skip a few beats.

When he entered her house, she first noticed his suit and professional demeanor. He had a laptop bag slung over his shoulder with his hair perfectly in place, in almost the exact same position as when she first met him at the restaurant. She wore blue jeans and a blue button blouse and felt underdressed. They had been in communication for a few months, but she still felt a little uncomfortable seeing him in person. Preparing to share an important and confusing secret failed to alleviate her emotions.

"How was your drive down here?" she asked after sitting at the kitchen table. She felt a sudden sense of déjà vu. She'd heard the story from Freddy in the same position.

"Nothing out of the ordinary happened," he said, followed by a laugh. "For me, that's saying something."

He drained half his glass of water in two silent gulps.

"Are you still being followed?" asked Sadi, mildly curious. Being watched by the government seemed less important than what she had to share. "Is it something you ever get used to?"

"I haven't noticed anything since we met," he said. "That's probably a bad thing, assuming that if they don't want me to see them, I won't."

"I guess that's a good thing," Sadi admitted. She felt unprepared to talk about the purpose of his visit just yet. "Does anyone suspect what you're, I mean, what we're doing?"

"I'm ninety-five percent assured that no one knows what we're doing," he said in a convincingly confident tone. "They're only interested in me for my past affairs."

"That reminds me," she said, attempting to appear irritated. "You haven't told me everything yet."

"OK, but first why don't you tell me why I needed to drive down here? I thought it was urgent."

"I want to know exactly what's happening in the group first. I need to know why so many strange things are happening to me. Maybe I won't *want* to share what has happened, I don't know, but maybe it's related."

He thought about her words for a moment, then squinted his eyes while inspecting her face. She would see how he reacted to an ultimatum.

"Of course, of course," he said in apology, then drew a deep breath, as if preparing to confess a crime to the police.

She smiled in triumph.

"You deserve to know everything. I'll just tell it plain and simple. I know a girl who invented something that can take us anywhere we want to go and I found an energy source to power it. We're gathering a small multidisciplinary team to help develop the possibilities, and I think we can help humanity obtain freedom."

He paused to breathe, allowing Sadi time to comprehend the information. A worried look spread across his face, as if he feared she would tell him to leave her house.

"Oh my God," she said while looking in his eyes. She attempted to break eye-contact, but had difficulty looking away. "How can I help with that?"

Instant relief appeared on his face and his next words.

"What we need are intelligent people who also appreciate the importance of freedom. We could have chosen any number of microbiologists, but ninety-nine percent of the population have no idea how important freedom is or what it even means. They think the government gives them freedom and is on their side, that the people in charge are doing what is best for them. Of course, in reality, space travel and more accessible energy sources are a threat to their influence."

While Gerald waited for her response, Sadi stared into his eyes, squinting. When she finally spoke, she began slowly.

"I really don't know what to say right now, but I know what you mean, not about space travel, but energy. I guess I never appreciated that fact, but you're right. Energy is the key to control. Who is the girl who invented this thing?"

"She's a friend from college," he answered casually. "I met her when I was in law school at the University of Oregon. I hadn't heard from her for a long time, other than email. She called me up at the beginning of the year and wanted to show me something."

Sadi sensed nothing other than a casual relationship in his tone. How did he feel about this girl? Did he feel a physical attraction to her? Why did Sadi have to consider relationship concerns? They just made the situation more complicated. She needed to focus on the information and not her lack of romantic connections.

For the next ten minutes, she listened to the condensed story of how he'd found the fusion reactor and of its delivery to the girl and their Mexican friends. Listening to the compelling story helped Sadi forget about human relationships for a little while at least. The story failed, however, to alleviate her anxiety. It also failed to explain why she saw her son, and why a woman in a vision told Freddy to visit her, and why she saw the video of the lights emanating from the spider's eyes. Too many unanswered questions.

"I need a drink," she said before rising from her chair and walking to the refrigerator. A cool liquid sliding down her throat might restore her mind to reality. As she walked, she could feel his eyes on her back. "Want something?"

"Sure, whatever you're having."

"You were right, Gerald," she said. "That's an unbelievable story. I think you're crazy to tell anyone about it. Perhaps after I explain why I wanted to see you, you will feel the same way about me."

"I can probably handle any story now," he said, laughing softly.

"I don't know about that," she said after arriving back to the table.

Before speaking, she took her second drink from the dark grape juice in her glass. She watched the red liquid slide back down the glass, almost like blood except much less viscous. While considering how to begin her story, she watched it swirl in the glass, approaching stillness.

51

Sadi

"A couple nights ago, an old friend of mine came to visit me," she began and realized the similarities of their stories. Gerald's began the same way. "I haven't seen him for over eight years. In that time, we haven't spoken or had any communication. He was a childhood friend of mine and my brother's. I don't know what emotional condition he's got, but he's different. He's got some form of autism or something, but he's high-functioning, very high-functioning."

"What are his symptoms?" asked Gerald. "Is he a savant?"

"I don't think he's a savant. When you talk to him, he's almost normal. He makes eye contact. He listens to what you're saying."

She sat back and considered again how to continue.

"There seems to be some disconnect in his brain in some ways. He lacks the ability to connect things. He can't connect faces to names, actions to reactions. On top of it all, he's had loads of other problems to deal with, like growing up through the foster care system and all the abuse that came with it."

"Poor guy," Gerald said with sincerity. "It's good that he had you as a friend."

"Yeah, we were his only friends. The only ones I knew of."

"So why did he contact you after all this time?"

"He said that he was instructed," she said then paused, "in a dream, to find me."

"Let me guess," he said with a big smile. "It wasn't just some random dream, or a subconscious desire to see you again?"

She continued as if uninterrupted.

"He acquired a strange trinket, a crystal with the image of a spider inside. If he looks into the spider eyes, it can put him in some sort of a trance. When he visited, he brought the crystal to my house and showed me. He knew how crazy the whole thing would sound so he captured it on video."

"He captured his vision on a video?"

"No," she said. "He recorded himself going into a trance. I saw it for myself. There were strange lights coming out of the spider eyes. It was very disturbing to watch. It frightened him so he came to me for help."

Gerald sat back against his seat and took a sip of juice.

"He might have made the video to trick you, but you would have considered that and not felt the need to call me. What about this experience made you think it was connected to our group?"

"He said his dream had something to do with the solar system, or he saw the solar system in his dream. I can't remember exactly what he said."

"Wow," he said, shaking his head and smiling. Gerald set his glass on the table and ran his hand through his thick brown hair. "We have to visit this guy. I'd like to see this video for myself, and the crystal."

"OK, I know you haven't had much time to consider it, but what do you think it means?"

She almost wished he would have no explanation. Did she want to hear the answer?

While she looked at his face, Sadi recognized the opposite reaction than what she expected. He seemed to be excited about the news. He had an instant response.

"Lately, I'm more open to strange hypotheses than I usually would be," he said and scratched his chin. "This crystal seems too advanced for anything the government can produce. What do you think? Can this crystal thing be made by man? Do we have the capability for such a device?"

"I don't think so," she said and instantly disliked the direction of his question. "When I looked into the spider eyes, I could not focus on them. It felt very strange, but I saw no vision. None of my explanations can account for the lights."

"If the object can do what you say, and it was not made by humans," he began talking to himself, "it must have been made by something else. Aliens? Some other intelligent life on Earth that we don't know about? But why did he contact you?"

"It's got to be your group, the group."

"Wait a minute," he said. "We may be taking this too much at face value."

"What do you mean?"

"You say you haven't seen Freddy for a long time, and he has mental issues? How do you know he's not being manipulated? I'm not saying you shouldn't trust him, but sometimes, people like that can be taken advantage of. What if the video was created with really good graphics? But then the question changes. Why would someone want to do that?"

"To mislead the group," Sadi said, finding some comfort in the alternative explanation. It failed, however, to explain her other recent experiences.

"To undermine what we're trying to do." Gerald laughed and shook his head. "I like the alien explanation better. This could be a bad turn of events. There's only one way to find out. Let's give your friend a call and make a visit. Is that what you had in mind?"

"That was my plan," she admitted. "He gave me his phone number and told me to call later in the afternoon." Sadi stood from the table and found her phone by the refrigerator. "Should we call him now?"

"Sure."

She felt anxious calling Freddy, but Gerald's presence offered some comfort. After learning about his living circumstances, she wanted to see where he lived and meet his boss, the wealthy old man.

After a single ring, an older man answered the phone.

"Hello," said an old voice, filled with concern and fragile as rice paper.

"Uh, hi," she said and cleared her throat. "I'm looking for Freddy Carlson."

"He's not here. Who is this?"

"I'm a friend of his, Sadi. I..."

"Friend?" the old man replied with a tone of disbelief and suspicion. "He's never mentioned your name, Sadi. What kind of friend? How do you know him?"

His angry tone caught Sadi by surprise. She looked to Gerald and shook her head in confusion.

"I'm an old friend from when we were kids. He came to see me a few days ago."

"He did?" Sadi listened to silence for several seconds. When he started speaking again, his tone became softer. "Sorry, I didn't mean to be rude. May I ask why he visited you?"

"I'm sorry, but he might not want me to share that. Can I speak with him first?"

"He can't come to the phone right now. What do you want from him? Are you one of his sister's friends?"

The old man began to grow impatient again.

"No, I'm definitely not friends with his sister." Sadi thought she understood the old man's concerns. Freddy had a horrible sister. "Like I said, my brother and I were practically his only friends, a long time ago. He just wanted to see us again."

He paused again and she listened to the sound of breathing.

"This may sound forward," he said. "But what do you do for a living?"

"I am a microbiologist at a pharmaceutical company," she said in a tone of humility.

Sadi despised people who loved to flash their credentials. She worked with some of those people. The old man's question sparked an idea.

"One of the reasons why he came to see me, was to ask for advice about graduate schools. He's interested in biology and knew about my line of work. I wanted to come and see him, tonight if possible. Would that be all right?"

"To tell you the truth," he said and his tone changed again, back to concern, almost panic. "I don't know where Freddy is. Do you have any idea where he might be?"

"What?"

"He's missing. He never came home last night."

"Oh my God," Sadi said with shock.

"It's never happened before. The police won't do anything. I have a private investigator looking for him, but he doesn't have any good leads yet."

Sadi held her hand over the phone and turned to Gerald.

"He's missing and his boss is frantic."

If the old man refused her request to visit, would she ever see Freddy again? Would her questions be answered without Freddy? She felt instant guilt for worrying about her own desires, rather than her friend's safety.

"Let us come over. Maybe we can help."

"If you help me find him, I will be in your debt."

52

Sadi

After Mr. Smith gave Sadi directions to his house, Sadi sent Jen a text message saying she might not be home until late and to bring Helen home from her gymnastics class. At five in the afternoon, she and Gerald left her house in his car. The sun appeared only as a vague blur behind the dark clouds. As they drove through the light rain, Sadi wondered if they could help find Freddy and if the old man would blame them, and what Gerald really thought about her story.

They entered the driveway where Freddy lived and had to wait for the gate to open before they could drive all the way to the tall archway which covered the entrance. On the short drive, they saw the old man peeking through the windows at them. Sadi knocked and Gerald stood slightly behind her to the left. Gerald's silent presence helped Sadi to feel less anxiety. What did Gerald feel about her? Did she care what he thought?

The old man opened the door and introduced himself as Bill Smith, Freddy's employer.

"Hi, I'm Sadi Jacobsen and this is my friend, Gerald Fuger."

Before arriving, Sadi considered claiming Gerald as her brother. If she introduced him as her lawyer friend, the old man might be suspicious about their true motives, although he would never guess their real motives. The man looked suspiciously at Gerald for only a few seconds before letting them into the house. He asked no other questions about Gerald's identity.

"Come inside."

He led them into a large sitting room, with a piano and some simple furniture. The room seemed too small in such a large mansion. Sadi and Gerald sat on a small couch and the old man chose a Victorian chair opposite them. He quickly explained how Freddy took care of the house and most of his affairs.

"I have come to depend, very much, on that boy," he said, his old voice cracking. Sadi wondered whether he would start crying or coughing.

"He spoke very highly of you, sir," Sadi said.

"He's grown on me," the old man said and looked at Sadi with clear eyes. "I'm very worried because he's never stayed away overnight. If he ever did, I know he'd tell me beforehand or at least he'd call me. I know he would. Was there any other reason why he came to visit you the other day? I've been unable to reach his sister. I wouldn't be surprised if she was involved."

"If his sister was involved, what do you suspect she might have done?"

"I don't know," he said. "It's the only lead I have to go on. She wouldn't want to disrupt his position here with me, because it benefits her. She would not want to jeopardize that."

When Sadi first saw the thin old man, she expected him to be slightly incoherent. To her amazement, he acted and spoke very confidently, although with the frailty of old age. His sharp eyes seemed to notice everything before them. She liked him instantly and when they made eye contact, she decided to be completely honest with him. Lying to him felt like a foolish decision.

Up until that point, Gerald remained silent and let Sadi handle the conversation. He sat forward then.

"What were the very last things you remember him saying to you, Mr. Smith?"

"Nothing out of the ordinary," he began and slowly pounded his leg with his fist. "He was going to his college class, then he had a lab scheduled. He usually arrives home by two or three. If he planned to come home later, he would have told me."

"Do you know how to get in touch with his lab teacher?"

"Already had her contacted," Mr. Smith said, his voice filled with disappointment. "He attended the lab as normal, and finished early. According to her, Freddy acted the same as he always did."

"So your private investigator talked to his lab teacher?"

"Yes. He also went through the downstairs rooms, the ones Freddy uses, looking for clues. He is checking on some things, he says, but he doesn't have any solid leads. He's going to check on Freddy's sister. I told him not to let her know we can't find him."

"Do you mind if we have a look through his things?" Sadi asked before she had time to consider the propriety of the question. "Sorry."

He stared at her like a cat preparing to pounce on a bird. Did she just ruin the opportunity to help? Would he kick them both out of his house?

"Freddy didn't visit you just for your advice about graduate school," he said finally. "Did he, Ms. Jacobsen?"

"Not entirely," she said quickly, and laughed at allowing herself to feel intimidated by an old man. "What I mean is, that was only part of his reason, but I wouldn't feel right about sharing it, unless I had his permission first."

"Now you're worried about his privacy?" asked the old man. "You just asked if you could go through his private things. If you cannot tell me everything you know, at least tell me something."

"It's very different," said Gerald, "than what you might think."

He sat back in the chair and smiled for the first time.

"I know Freddy, probably better than anyone on this Earth. I wouldn't be surprised by anything you'd have to say."

Sadi felt the need for a private conversation with Gerald about what they wanted to tell Mr. Smith. On the drive, they neglected to prepare for the possibility of telling him everything that happened to Freddy. She and Gerald made eye contact and she wondered if he had the same questions. They all waited for her to speak.

"Mr. Smith," she said slowly, still not fully knowing what would escape her lips. "Freddy was having strange dreams, dreams in which he was instructed to find me. That's the truth, but I know it sounds weird. Has he said anything about that lately?"

The old man sat forward in his chair.

"He hasn't said anything about dreams, but he *has* seemed more worried than usual. I just assumed it was due to school. Could his dream have been stress induced?"

"This was no normal dream," Gerald interjected. "It was more of a trance, externally induced it seems."

"Now you're making even less sense," the old man said in frustration.

"I know it doesn't make sense." Sadi tried to sound comforting. "He took a video of it happening and showed me, otherwise I wouldn't have believed it either."

"If that's true, there must be a reason why he was told to meet you. What are you and Gerald involved in? What's the connection between you all?"

He reminded Sadi of a judge trying to settle a dispute.

"Gerald's just a friend," Sadi said quickly. "He was going to help me figure this thing out. That's all."

Mr. Smith looked at them both, with obvious distrust. Before he could interrogate them further, Gerald turned to Sadi.

"Tell him about the ornament that Freddy showed you."

"What ornament?" Mr. Smith looked from Sadi to Gerald and back to Sadi again.

She had doubts about revealing the crystal with the embedded rock spider, but Gerald gave her no other option.

"Freddy brought a crystal to my house to show me, a little bigger than the palm of my hand. It had a flat spider made of rock inside it. I don't suppose he ever showed it to you? I know it sounds crazy, but I saw the video he took, with my own eyes. Light was coming out of this crystal thing. He believes the crystal put him in a trance and showed him the vision. It might be a clue that will lead us to him."

"No, he has not shown this thing to me," Mr. Smith said in anger. "How am I supposed to believe you?"

"You're not," said Gerald with sympathy. "Were we to find this crystal, it might be more believable for all of us, including myself. Like you, I just have Sadi's word to go on. I came here to help her find her friend. Perhaps you could search through his rooms for this crystal for us?"

Gerald's words seemed to appease Mr. Smith and the muscles in his face began to relax. He placed his cane on the floor in front of him and started to stand so Sadi stood and extended her hand to help him.

"Thank you," he said without emotion. "Now, you two please stay here while I go look for this thing."

After the old man left the room, Gerald stood and walked to the window.

"What are we going to do if he doesn't find the crystal ornament?" He stared through the window, into the night. "Any ideas?"

"I'm wondering what we're going to do if he does find the crystal," said Sadi.

She tapped her right-hand fingers on the chair arm, then looked up to Gerald at the curtains. Would she have been able to persuade the old man this far by herself? Gerald had more experience with investigations involving people. At her work, she had become an expert investigating viruses. Hopefully, she could make a contribution to the search.

"The future holds too many possibilities to plan for them all. Let's just go with the flow." Gerald returned to sit next to Sadi again. "Maybe we can fit together what's going through Freddy's mind. You said he was worried. What would a person like Freddy do if he was worried?"

"When we were younger," she said and attempting to remember Freddy from the past. "He would have hid somewhere, but now, he seems more proactive. He's smart and is probably trying to figure this thing out on his own. If Mr. Smith doesn't find the crystal, Freddy may have it. Maybe it made him do something?"

"Did he think it had anything to do with aliens?" Gerald asked. "If so, how would he go about verifying it?"

"Hmm," she began. "Maybe he went to a place where he thought an alien could contact him? Someplace high and isolated?"

"Good thought. A peak might be a good place to start. I'm not really dressed for hiking, but I can be flexible. I really would like to see that video," Gerald said shaking his head.

"Don't laugh," Sadi said as a new thought materialized. She doubted they could find the video. "Could it be some kind of ghost?"

He looked at her strangely, as if preparing to ask about her sanity.

"I don't believe in ghosts."

Experience as a researcher taught her to always consider every possible angle before dismissing any possibility. She hated the idea of making a type 1 error, rejecting the actual truth. Of course, she also hated to accept a falsehood, but that meant abandoning the truth right in front of her face. After the death of her son, she refused to believe that a human life ended with the death of the body.

"This world has a lot of unexplained things in it and especially after seeing that video, I'm willing to entertain any idea."

"A ghost, huh," Gerald said, breaking eye contact. "Hmmm."

Sadi waited while the synapses in his brain chose his next action. She turned to the curtained windows and waited. Their discussion ended abruptly when Mr. Smith's voice called to them from the hallway. He entered the room and aimed his cane at them. Sadi felt like a child again with the teacher telling the class to open their books.

53

Sadi

"Come with me downstairs," the old man said. He waited only a moment before turning and disappearing into the hallway. "There's a light coming from under Freddy's bedroom door, and it didn't feel like a good idea to enter by myself."

Gerald stood first then extended his hand to Sadi. She accepted his help and watched Mr. Smith walk away, wondering if she really wanted to enter the room with strange lights. As they followed the old man down the stairs, Sadi imagined finding the door already open. She shivered at the thought.

After reaching the bottom of the stairs, a new thought temporarily replaced her anxiety. If Freddy claimed the whole lower level, he had more space than her whole house. The realization made her smile. In the basement, they entered a long dark hallway with several rooms on either side. A faint blue and orange light shot from under the last door on the right, as if from a strobe light. Mr. Smith extended his cane again, aiming the instrument towards the light.

"I didn't notice the light until after I had looked through some of the other rooms down here. My eyes are not as good as they used to be."

Both Sadi and Gerald stopped behind the old man, waiting for him to make the next move. As he lowered the cane, Sadi noticed his hand shaking from age rather than fear. He used his cane like an invisible laser pointer. After a moment, Gerald stepped forward.

"I suppose we can't just stand here."

He passed Mr. Smith and slowly approached the door. After reaching the end of the hallway, he leaned forward and listened for a moment, his eyes on the floor. Silence filled the hallway as they watched Gerald begin to slowly extend his hand. Before making contact with the door handle, the light extinguished. Mr. Smith looked to Sadi and then to Gerald who turned to face them both.

"Maybe we should call the police," Sadi whispered and placed her hand on Mr. Smith's shoulder.

She felt a strange need to physically connect with another human. Did her fear originate from inside her mind or from what lay beyond the door? With her hand on his shoulder, Mr. Smith gained the courage to start walking toward the door. After reaching the door, he hit his cane on the solid wood. The hard sound destroyed the silence.

"Who's in there?" the old man asked in anger and they waited several seconds for a response. The sound of the knocking seemed to echo in her mind. The echo in her ears soon transformed into silence again.

"Is this Freddy's room?" asked Gerald.

"It's the room he sleeps in," the old man answered. "All the rooms down here are his. I don't come down here much."

"Well," said Gerald unexpectedly, placing his hand on the door knob. "Here goes nothing."

He turned the knob then slowly pushed the door completely open. After waiting a moment, he leaned forward to see into the room and then stepped inside. Mr. Smith followed at a tentative, but steady pace. He extended his arm for Sadi to hold. For a brief moment, she felt like a stereotypical, frightened girl walking behind the men, the men who had not seen the frightening video.

Mr. Smith flipped a switch on the wall to energize the lights and the huge room suddenly felt less frightening. Sadi noticed a bed immediately to her right and small windows on the wall ahead of her and to the right. Several tables lined the walls, each table holding some piece of equipment. She noticed two microscopes, several computers and other instruments she failed to recognize. Freddy's room appeared untidy, but clean.

"I don't see anything," Gerald said after inspecting the room for a moment.

"Where was that light coming from?" asked Sadi.

"Well, we all saw it." said Mr. Smith. "Perhaps..."

His voice abruptly stopped, as a blue light stole all their attention. The light originated from inside the top drawer of a dresser next to the bed. The light shone through the cracks and flickered like a candle.

Gerald used both of his hands to slowly pull the dresser drawer completely open, holding his face away as if a creature inside would jump at them. Sadi felt more curiosity than fear. If the drawer contained a ghost, it was a tiny one.

Gerald placed his right hand inside the drawer and removed the crystal with the embedded flat spider. He raised the object in the palm of his hand to eye level, blue and orange light shooting up from his hand. As he tilted the crystal sideways, to see the source of the light, Sadi shot her hand towards him and grabbed his wrist.

"Don't look into it, Gerald," she said.

"The light is coming from inside the head," he said as if speaking to himself.

Despite her hand on his arm, he turned the crystal sideways and the light shone on them all. Sadi felt an invisible force pulling her head so she also faced the crystal. Intense curiosity overpowered her futile resistance.

IV: THE INTERLOPER

When by the tiger chased
Better find somewhere safe
Or your life, soon erased

54

Taylor

While standing around their prototype engine, Taylor made adjustments and Cesar typed into one of the computers connected to all the sensors. They kept the engine on the operation table, as Taylor liked to call it, but the apparatus looked nothing like an engine. It looked more like a jumble of white tubes and multicolored wires encasing stainless steel cylinders of twenty-centimeter diameter.

"What's the output now?" asked Taylor as she adjusted a set screw. She looked over to the computer where Cesar sat, but he had the screen turned away from her.

"Just another quarter turn and we should be at the maximum," Cesar said in excitement. "There you go. Keep it right there. It's modulating around twenty amps. Let's see how long it can hold."

From the wide smile on his face, Taylor assumed that Cesar was enjoying the experience of success. Taylor also enjoyed the experience, meaning she had a look of deep concentration rather than smiling.

"What does the temperature monitor read? I want to make sure temperature control is holding steady as well. That's probably more important than power, at least for now."

When she saw the temperature, she smiled at last, but only briefly.

"When we're coming back into the atmosphere, you can worry about overheating, and I'll worry about power output." Cesar sneered, half teasing, but with a serious tone. He reminded Taylor of her father.

She turned to look at the sunlight streaming from the window high above them and then jumped at the sight of Doroteo right behind her.

"Holy Shit, Teo," she said out of shock, but then attempted to appear calm. "Will you stop sneaking up on me."

She expected to see the usual satisfaction he felt at catching her off guard. A few days after she started sharing his home, Doroteo said he would teach her basic survival skills. He did not ask for permission. As her first lesson, she needed to own her space, the five to ten feet around her. People could enter her space, but only after she allowed their entry. Whenever possible, Doroteo liked to trespass.

Instead of showing any sign of victory, however, he waited for Taylor to regain her composure. He stood silently, as if waiting to say something. Cesar concentrated on the computer and ignored them both.

"Hey," Doroteo said finally.

Taylor held steady eye contact with him, preparing to reply, but he discreetly handed her a piece of paper. She took the paper from his leathery grasp.

Someone's been in here. They might be watching or listening.

Doroteo turned away and approached the engine, pretending to inspect it. After Taylor read the note, she felt the blood drain from her face. Her skin became paler than normal. Calmly, she walked to Cesar, handed him the paper and went back to the engine to stand by Doroteo. Cesar glanced at the paper and paused for no longer than a hundred milliseconds.

"Let's go get something for lunch," he said. "I'm starving."

Taylor looked at her watch just as the digital readout turned from ten fifty-nine to eleven. They usually ate lunch between twelve and twelve-ten every day. For the next ten minutes, they stopped their tests and waited for the power-down procedures to complete.

Doroteo extinguished all the lights in the shop and motioned for her and Cesar to stay by the exit until he rejoined them. A single ray of sunlight shot down from a window near the ceiling and the light made the particles in the air sparkle. In the lower light, Doroteo removed what looked like a handheld stun gun from his pocket.

Taylor leaned close to Cesar's ear and whispered.

"What's he doing?"

"When we get out of here," Cesar said while keeping his eyes on Doroteo.

Doroteo removed a small instrument with a red LED light from his pocket and held the object in his hand. The LED blinked with a frequency which changed with his location in the shop. As Doroteo walked casually around the large shop area with the small instrument, the scene reminded Taylor of the movie, "Ghostbusters" when the character Egon Spengler searched for ghosts with his hand-held instrument. Taylor felt an unexpected irritation at failing to remember the name of the device from the movie. After a few minutes of inspection, he stopped at a bench where their radio sat.

After a moment of staring at the radio, Doroteo walked back to Taylor and Cesar. She followed him outside while Cesar locked the door. They all climbed in Doroteo's dark blue Dodge Ram and as usual, Taylor sat in the extended cab.

"Is this secure?" asked Cesar after shutting the door.

Doroteo looked more angry than she had ever seen him.

"Of course," he said with a thick accent.

Taylor never knew what to expect from Doroteo's manner of speaking. He alternated from using an almost unintelligible Mexican accent or sounding like a typical native suburbanite.

"Teo, what did you find?" Taylor asked.

As they pulled onto the road, Doroteo kept his eyes focused ahead of him.

"I didn't find anything at the shop," he began and Taylor heard no more anger in his voice. "I just wanted to make sure the place was clear before we left."

"What made you suspect the possibility?" asked Cesar.

"While driving up just now, I found a car parked down the street," he said, his anger returning. "I made eye contact with the man inside right before he looked away." Doroteo shook his head and slowly blinked his eyes, possibly as a sign of frustration. "At that moment, I knew. The man drove away while I was parking."

"Who was it?" Cesar asked.

"FBI." Doroteo answered with obvious certainty in his voice.

Cesar nodded his head in agreement.

"Made eye contact eh," Cesar said and smiled. "Losing your touch a bit."

Doroteo grunted under his breath, but said nothing.

On their way to Taylor's favorite sandwich shop they discussed the worst possible scenarios. By Doroteo's estimation, the agent could have been listening for two to three days at most. At first, Taylor felt extreme paranoia of her secret being discovered, but after recalling the past few days, she remembered saying nothing incriminating.

If the FBI heard them talk about the NMG device or the fusion reactor, they would still have had no direct evidence of their activities. They only talked about power transfer, computer control and efficiency optimization. Their conversations and work had focused on the specific design details, not the overall picture or science behind the new technology. They never used the term fusion, only generator and engine.

Despite her attempt to consider the situation with optimism, Taylor felt sick inside. Being investigated by the FBI caused enough concern even if they had no evidence, yet. How long before the FBI raided their shop and confiscated all her hard work? Why did the FBI show interest in them?

As the best scenario, Doroteo had caught the agent at his first attempt of surveillance. Another possibility involved the CIA. Taylor remembered Cesar's story about how the CIA warned him to stay out of trouble. Maybe they were just checking on him. Even in that benign situation, the CIA still might have heard something and decided to investigate more. She decided to stop thinking about the possibilities and let her friends handle the situation. They had much more experience than Taylor.

After arriving at the restaurant, Cesar and Taylor ordered a sandwich, but Doroteo just sat with them and had water. He attempted to look bored while watching for someone snooping nearby. While eating in a booth furthest away from all the other patrons, they spoke quietly about all the possibilities.

"We can talk all day about what we think they have on us, but how to figure out what they *do* have on us, or what they suspect?" Taylor spoke while chewing a large bite of her barbecue chicken sandwich. "How are we going to do that?"

Doroteo looked at her without emotion.

"We capture him and make him tell us. That's how."

Cesar frowned, but remained silent. Taylor quickly finished chewing the bite of her sandwich.

"Capture a FBI agent?" she said in disbelief. "And then what? Kill him when we're done?"

"If you want," Doroteo answered in perfect seriousness.

"What's your plan?" Cesar asked, as if simply trying to determine what movie to see that night.

"Wait a second," interrupted Taylor. She looked at the two men as if they were two hit-men planning a murder. "We can't capture a government agent. That's kidnapping. Besides, if we do capture him and we get the information, then what? We let him go and warn him to not include it in his next report?"

Cesar reached over the table and put his hand on hers. Taylor realized how loudly she spoke and then looked around the restaurant to see if anyone turned to watch them. When the older man spoke, he talked to her gently like a father to a child. Did Cesar begin to think of her as a daughter?

"Taylor, remember who you're talking to here. Doroteo and I have been in much worse circumstances than this before."

"Yeah, but you were the government."

Instead of providing comfort, their nonchalant attitude caused more impatience and paranoia.

"There are bigger sharks in the ocean, Taylor," he explained. "Little fish in the government can be eaten just as easily, and often more frequently. Remember, government officials don't usually make the important decisions."

His words failed to placate her.

"How are we going to get the information out of him?" She whispered even quieter. "Torture him?"

Doroteo leaned closer.

"Is that how you think I get information from people?" he asked almost threateningly.

Another person might have cowered before those four black eyes, but Taylor knew to hold steady eye contact.

"I haven't really thought about it until now, so you tell me."

"It won't come to that Taylor," said Cesar. "But it may not be pretty either. Just trust us. We cannot go into detail here. Let's wait and listen to Doroteo's plan."

"Wait a moment," she said in surprise. Among all her other questions, she had neglected to ask the obvious one. "If they had no bug in the shop, how do you know they were listening to us? Did they have something in the phone?"

"Our voices are vibrations aren't they?" Cesar said. "Vibrations transmit through walls and windows which can be electronically enhanced. They have many ways now."

"Unless you can prove otherwise, they can hear you," Doroteo said while looking away.

They spent the rest of their lunch break discussing all the possible problems with following the plan. Taylor mostly listened and reserved many of her concerns for later thought. After a while she felt a little better about the situation. She had never been involved with anything like what they considered. The movies always made her laugh with how unrealistic their surveillance and intelligence activities appeared. The movies looked fun compared to their plan.

55

John

FBI Agent John Pratt had thick dark brown hair, naturally tan skin and dark brown eyes. He liked to keep his hair short, his fingernails trimmed and his skin tight through exercise. When people looked at him, he always appeared happy and pleasant. He spoke politely to people and everyone thought he liked them, but he kept his real feelings deeply hidden. In reality, very few people held his respect. Those who found themselves on the other side of his wall knew his domineering, critical and manipulative side, the aspects of his personality that made him an effective FBI agent.

Agent Pratt sat at his desk staring at all the papers strewn over its clean surface. If anyone came by his desk, they would see him reading, diligently working. In reality, he only stared at the closest paper while attempting to suppress the previous twelve hours of his personal life and invent an escape from his current predicament. During the past several nights, he only slept for a few hours. His new girlfriend's three-year-old child chose the night to cry, ask for drinks, watch movies, basically everything but sleep.

Before he allowed them to move into his apartment, his girlfriend accepted full responsibility for her child. He would not be a babysitter or handle the child's needs. He lied about liking children and invented an excuse to avoid any responsibility. At that time of his career, he could not allow himself to become emotionally attached to children. They would make him soft and he needed to be hard, like the criminals he prosecuted.

Like an idiot, he assumed she would take their contract seriously. After they moved into his apartment, he discovered the woman's true irrationality. Her agreement basically meant nothing and she secretly expected him to do everything he verbally refused to do. When he failed to obey her unconscious expectations, the tension began.

If he only knew how annoying the kid would become, he never would have let them move in with him. Every day, he waited for the perfect opportunity to end the relationship. When he failed to invent a good excuse, he imagined possible scenarios where they had to leave, like death or abduction. He could only hope.

Agent Pratt worked in the Counterterrorism Division at the Seattle Washington FBI field office, the second assignment in his eight years at the Bureau. He loved many of his job duties, but hated writing reports and analyzing data for other people. He spent twenty percent of his time collecting data, the fun part, and eighty percent in analysis and writing reports, the mind-numbingly boring parts.

The top papers on his desk related to his most current case, the two loner, extremist college kids. The papers contained information such as pictures, college transcripts, and their most interesting Gmail messages. Both of the kids attended the University of Washington and had different majors. As far as Agent Pratt knew, they never met each other.

He spent much of his time recently gathering information about several other similar suspects, hoping to group them together somehow. They crossed into the terrorism radar by all the time they spent searching the internet for explosive devices. Unfortunately, judging by their grades and types of classes, none of them had any understanding of science. In Pratt's opinion, none of them showed any indication of possessing sufficient motivation or intelligence to carry out a violent attack, no matter how much they bragged about it to their loser friends.

Pratt's boss wanted information about as many loner-anarchists as possible, in the hopes of catching one of them with homemade explosive devices. If Agent Pratt had any luck, he would apprehend those vermin extremists in the act of exploding something, or a failed detonation at least. In his other fantasies, explosives destroyed one of their all-night beer and porn bashes, leaving the world with fewer losers. In that case, he would miss the pleasure of sending the kid to jail, but the senseless destruction would be better than nothing. So far, his efforts were showing absolutely no possibility for any future detonations.

During his recent information gathering activities, Agent Pratt contemplated the next phase of his strategy. When should he use FBI resources to help one of the kids acquire explosives? Were any of them worth the effort? The FBI had to be careful. Such tactics could backfire. His superiors would not tolerate another fiasco like the 1993 World Trade Center bombing when the FBI infiltrated the terrorist group and supplied them with explosive. The FBI got terrible publicity from that incident when the explosions actually took place.

If Pratt would have handled that case, the public would never have discovered the truth. Not that the exposed truth mattered anyway. As long as the mainstream media never validated the story through exposure, the public would never believe the story when an independent source eventually exposed it. Agent Pratt despised the typical arguments against such tactics. He believed the rationale adopted by the intelligence community. Instead of allowing the enemy to recruit potential terrorists, the FBI and CIA should proactively control the situation and recruit the extremists first.

When Pratt suggested his plans to the director of the Seattle office, they failed to become part of the agenda. His boss wanted something more low-level, something to give the office a good image without the possibility of bad press. Pratt had little hope of success with these small-time losers, but he did find some hope in a new case he had acquired. His boss did not need to know about following his plan anyway.

His phone rang and he recognized the phone number of his boss. A phone call meant a request to visit. Otherwise, the Director would have used email. Without answering the call, Agent Pratt rose from his desk and went to the office of the Director.

"What's up Jason?" asked Pratt as he entered the office.

"Shut the door and have a seat."

56

John

Pratt shut the door as requested and sat in one of the chairs in front of the director's desk. The director of the Counterterrorism division, Jason Smithson, had been heading the department for five years now. Before he became the director, he worked as an agent like John and they remained good friends since his promotion. He had blond hair, light green eyes, and wore a white shirt tight against his muscular arms.

"I've been reading your update on the college kids," Jason said while looking at his computer screen. "You've got to have more on these guys than this. You're my best agent. I'm counting on you. I'm not sure if you've been using our informants to their full potential."

Agent Pratt sighed and sat back in his chair.

"It's probably true sir, but I really don't think these kids have it in them. I'm getting sick of reading their pathetic emails. To tell you the truth, I hate these kids more than I hate Muslims."

"All the more reason to get the little shits, wouldn't you say?" the director said and smiled. "From their emails, it sounds like they do have it in them. You need to give me more. Figure out a way to push them over the edge. I cannot include this lack of progress in my report. You know how it goes."

The director looked directly at his friend, waiting for a response.

Agent Pratt met the intense gaze from his boss without flinching. Only Agent Pratt could have that kind of exchange with Jason Smithson, at least the only agent at their office. Even more than their friendship, John Pratt and Jason Smithson shared a common cause. They both intended to rid the world of extremists, anyone who fought or would fight against them, against the establishment. While the other agents scrambled to discover how to please their boss, Jason and John read the same page from the same book.

"Sir," he began. "Some of my lack of progress is because of the time I've spent on Gerald Fuger lately."

Agent Pratt waited for a response and almost expected an unpleasant one.

"Good old Gerald," said Jason while shaking his head. "I know it's good to keep tabs on that guy, but he's been a dead end for a long time now, ever since you failed to convict him with the Reserve break in."

"I know, I know," Pratt replied in response to the blunt rebuke. "But, let me tell you what I haven't included in any of my reports yet. He's been talking a lot to our old friend, Cesar Sanchez, and there's something new, a recent college graduate, a genius in mechanical design, another extremist that he's been talking with."

Jason Smithson sat forward and looked interested.

"Oh, they'd love to bring that guy down." Agent Pratt imagined the director licking his lips.

Ever since Gerald Fuger's indirect involvement in the Federal Reserve building break-in, he's been on 'the list'. Unfortunately, Gerald had been a dormant volcano since the incident. He still had great extremist potential, but he knew how to keep a low profile. Pratt had been following Gerald Fuger like the Japanese sought the blue tuna. Big fish like him never changed.

"The girl who moved in with Cesar Sanchez is quite a beauty," Pratt said while imagining what he could do with her. "but she's a smug little bitch. She works in his shop now and seems to be just like Gerald, an extremist. Her brother committed suicide after coming back from Iraq. She's pretty pissed."

"Perfect," Jason replied sarcastically. "Sounds like the birth of another tumor on society."

"There's been a lot of secret communication between them all."

"I don't doubt it," said Jason. "He's smart and knows we're watching him. What makes you suspicious of Cesar and this girl?"

"I've been at their shop and they're up to something." John sat back in the chair and glanced above Jason's head at the picture of him with Bill Clinton. "I'm not sure what they're making, but I'm going to find out. Are you ever going to tell me about Cesar and why we're not supposed to touch him?"

"I can't say because I don't know. It's classified. Over my head." Jason Smithson turned to his computer and punched some keys. The director took a deep breath and cleared his throat, the sign he planned to change topics. "I also wanted to talk to you about the Hezbollah case. In your report, you did not give me an update on your lead of their funding source."

While they talked about other cases, John Pratt's mind kept drifting into fantasies of placing Gerald Fuger into a military detention center for interrogation. If he only could have the chance to interrogate him, what would he learn? The fantasy felt like too much to hope. His experience with Fuger as a new lawyer proved the man's skills and his understanding of how the legal system worked, including all its loopholes.

The Law Firm of Fuger and Fowler had several suspicious clients including, at least, one mafia family, an Islamic trust fund and some remote business operations on Indian reservations. He seemed to be supporting all the people Agent Pratt hated, institutions he considered un-American. As a final affront to any decent citizen, Fuger had the audacity to be a member of the End the Fed movement and some anti-United Nations groups. After being involved with the Federal Reserve break-in, those associations were unforgivable.

By successfully prosecuting Gerald Fuger, Agent Pratt would add negative stigma on those anti-government groups. Pratt needed to make an example of him, send a message to others involved with those groups. They and the goddamned Muslims were enemies of the USA.

Sometimes, Pratt would find himself daydreaming of shooting a bullet through Fuger's head. He would find a back alley somewhere, dark and alone then first shoot him in the stomach. Before all his blood escaped from the punctured aorta, Pratt would finish the deed with a bullet to the head. His body would never be found.

That kind of end seemed too easy for Fuger. People needed to know what happened to him. Agent Pratt had fun fantasizing about killing him anyway. The act would leave Pratt with nothing other than personal satisfaction. He needed to be recognized for the indictment. To get complete satisfaction and further his career at the Bureau, Pratt had to put Fuger behind bars.

Pratt hoped to use the new development in the Fuger case to learn more about Cesar Sanchez. He used to be the governor of Ciudad-Juarez in Mexico and somehow managed to escape the drug cartel upheaval and relocate to the United States alive. From the reports he found in the media, Pratt knew Cesar should have been assassinated like his wife and sons. Something suspicious must have happened to prevent his death.

At the end of their conversation, he left Jason Smithson's office with more assignments, probably intended to divert his attention from what he wanted to do, investigate Gerald. He would need to spend more time at work. Would his new girlfriend get tired of never seeing him and move out of his apartment, and take her obnoxious kid? That little girl ruined their fun nights together.

He spent the next few hours cleaning up the mess on his desk and preparing to close some loose-ends. He needed to schedule another trip to the University of Washington campus to follow-up with the fanatical anarchists. Before leaving, he would need to acquire some petty cash for one of his informants, a janitor who had access to their dorm room. While thinking of his inevitable conversation with the janitor, Pratt prepared for frustration. If a grenade sat on the table in the kid's apartment, the idiot would lift the grenade to look for anything interesting underneath. For this reason alone, John only accepted pictures from the man and never his assessment.

Pratt had only one thing he could trust in the world. Money. People obeyed money, the only action Pratt could expect from the average citizen. If he spent sufficient time, he could always find someone to do what he wanted, for the right price. Money ensured discretion. If anyone discovered the janitor's underhanded dealings, he would look like a creep no one could trust or believe.

Before he left for the university the next morning, John Pratt visited their surveillance device expert, or as they all affectionately referred to her, the bug girl. When people came into contact with Charlie, the short, solid girl, they first noticed her hair. Perfectly straight, auburn bangs stopped just above her eyes. Her hair always looked like a waterfall, frozen in time.

"Charlie, remember that little favor?" he asked.

"Depends on whether you're gonna dump the girlfriend or not," she said and smiled, her clear braces glistening in the light.

John ignored the impulse to wretch at the thought of any romantic connection with the woman. He smiled instead.

"How many sexual harassment charges do I have to file Charlie," John smiled and laughed convincingly, punching her in the right arm.

"So are you ready yet for me to make that placement?" she asked in a serious tone.

"We need to hold off on that, for a while."

"What happened?" she asked.

"Unfortunately, I've already got what I need," he said in a regretful tone of losing the need for her services.

He had no intention of telling her or anyone else what really happened, that Cesar's friend, the rough-looking Mexican thug, had caught Pratt spying at their machine shop. From that brief look into the man's dark eyes, Pratt knew he had to be careful and back off for a while. After investigating Doroteo's profile, Agent Pratt decided to change tactics and use a more sophisticated approach when dealing with a former chief of security.

After he finished talking with the bug girl, he left for the university. On the drive, he imagined several possible confrontations with the Mexican. The man would probably pose an interesting challenge, but Pratt felt confident in his abilities to prevail in almost any conflict. Success all depended on mental and physical preparation. Maybe one day he would have the opportunity.

57

John

April 3, Friday

On his way home from work Friday night, Agent Pratt stopped at one of his favorite pubs. He usually went by himself and avoided becoming too familiar with anyone there. He enjoyed the anonymity. If he recognized anyone, he would try to avoid eye contact and sit somewhere far away.

He liked to look at the women, the pretty ones, have a few beers and watch whatever game happened to be playing. When he had the opportunity to talk with an attractive woman, he usually invented a unique name and occupation he thought would interest her the most. Most women responded positively to his strong and confident demeanor more than his fabrication, but they usually bored him in the end and he would tell them politely to get going. If no female caught his attention, he stayed less than an hour before going home to his girlfriend. He resented feeling obligated to spend time with the woman and her kid who severely damaged his sex life.

On that night, he met a woman. She wore an expensive strapless dress, dark blue and tight. The fabric strained to contain her feminine form, especially her large breasts. She approached Agent Pratt and seemed sincerely interested in learning everything about him. He had difficulty inventing a fictional persona when her scent and golden skin intoxicated him more than the alcohol in his scotch. His physical reaction to her felt like a separate heartbeat.

After an enjoyable thirty minutes of conversation, she claimed to require fresh air and suggested to go somewhere more private, but failed to mention any place specific. The location seemed an unimportant detail to Pratt. He could easily handle going anywhere with her, for a few hours.

On the way to his car, he experienced extreme difficulty attempting to walk and think simultaneously. For the last few steps, he even required her assistance. He looked up at her and felt like a puppy looking at the little kid who wants to buy it.

"Whoa there big guy," she said, laughing at his drunken behavior and leading him to the passenger door.

The door seemed to open at just the right time, just before he fell into the car. On his way down, he hit his head. She laughed at him again, her mouth opening so wide he thought she would swallow him whole. He laughed at the strange and frightening sight, but really wanted to close his eyes and cry instead. By the time she shut his door and opened hers, his laughter transformed into quiet snoring.

"Barely made it to the car," she said while breathing a sigh of relief.

She looked around the vehicle to see if anyone had noticed, but no other human came into her view. A taxi drove past and then quiet.

The woman stared at Agent Pratt for several minutes, searching for signs of consciousness. After feeling assured of the drug's effectiveness and her safety, she retrieved his wallet. Careful not to leave any fingerprints, she made sure to follow the Mexican man's instructions and wear gloves. She removed all his money and credit cards from his wallet. In disappointment, she only found fifty-five dollars in cash, but the Mexican had given her seven hundred dollars for the job. He told her to take the cards and then cut them into pieces and discard them far away in a public trash receptacle.

No one watched as she drove away and no one would have cared if they did. On the drive, she removed her wig and tried to ignore the feeling of anxiety about her final task of the night, to meet the Mexican and receive the rest of her money.

John Pratt dreamed of a disturbing trip to a dentist wearing grease stained overalls. While lying in the dentist chair, flat on his back, the dentist and his assistant probed, poked, drilled and talked. John tried to follow their conversation, but a large rubber dam separated his upper and lower teeth. He could barely manage to concentrate on breathing, let alone listening. The dentist and his assistant acted as if they worked on a car engine.

After the dentist and his assistant faded to nothing, John watched as a thick nebulous fog rushed past him like a river. Different colors of black swirled above him. He had never felt such a sensation. For what seemed an eternity, he floated in all the new colors. After another long time he began to enjoy the sensation. Nothing could disturb him in all the black.

After floating for a long time, he felt his environment changing again. An increasing physical pressure began to squeeze him. He never felt such amazing pressure. In the darkness, he felt himself smiling and that also felt amazing.

The pressure and his feeling of euphoria intensified and almost brought him to the point of oblivion, but then the shaking began. A light began to fill his vision and coalesced into vague shapes, like figures from a Picasso painting. The main figure, a tall, skinny man with a pointed hat like a wizard stood in the center of a congregation containing millions or billions of people.

The wizard stood much taller than everyone. A glowing green fog spewed from the tip of a staff in his left hand, the source of all light. The people swayed around him as if with some invisible current, illuminated by the green light above them. Part of the fog swirled above the old man, part swirled around the crowd and the rest disappeared in the black sky. The attention of the entire crowd focused on the wizard. John watched from far away.

"John," said a voice from the sky, a whisper too loud to ignore. "Shoot them. Kill them."

John looked above him, toward the source of the voice, but he could only see the green fog ascending into the sky.

"Who said that?" he whispered, afraid of attracting the attention of the wizard.

The wizard turned towards the sound and his angry yellow eyes shone like a bright laser. John wanted to pull some of the darkness around him, a shield from the light.

"John," the sky whispered again, even more intently. "Flee! Come to me."

58

Taylor

April 3, Friday

It was Friday night just after dark, the third day in April 2009. Doroteo told Cesar and Taylor to wait at a foreclosed home at the end of a poorly paved private road. While he went to get the FBI agent from his contact, Taylor and Max waited in the empty house, in the dark. If all went according to plan, Doroteo would arrive with the unconscious government agent. If he wanted to abort the plan Doroteo would call, otherwise they were supposed to wait. He told them not to use any cell phones since their call records could be used later as evidence against them should the FBI suspect their involvement. Taylor spent the time attempting to build confidence in her two new friends' plan.

According to Doroteo, his drugs would help them extract information without the need for the physical violence or coercion. She felt some comfort, but it failed to erase her shock at the plan itself. Any mistake could destroy her future. Any piece of evidence left exposed might lead Taylor and her friends into the comforting embrace of a federal prison. Would she be sent to the Guantanamo Bay detention center as a terrorist? Maybe she should study Islam in preparation.

"Please explain to me again why they won't suspect us?" Taylor asked. "I know Doroteo seems to have no concern about the plan, but I'm still not used to kidnapping government agents and drugging them."

Cesar sat down on a chair that had been left in the upstairs bedroom, but Taylor remained standing. While waiting for him to answer, she tapped her left shoe with the heel of her right shoe.

"The FBI are a government agency," he began. "Is that enough or do I need to give more explanation?"

"Normally, that would be all I needed to hear, but with our safety on the line, I need more."

"OK, so you're not convinced," he said and laughed. "To give them credit, the FBI are good at what they do, offense. They have the money, the manpower and all the other required resources to plan effective offensive strikes. Fortunately for us, they have a huge bureaucracy to weigh them down. It's very effective at making them ineffective, especially at defense."

"I'll have to take your word for it."

Taylor could feel him looking at her, but could not see his eyes in the low light. When he exhaled loudly, she knew he had more to say.

"The most successful private companies, which aren't subsidized by the government, are led by the skilled and ambitious people who rise to the top. In the FBI and other government agencies, those in leadership are usually those with the best connections and not necessarily those who are most qualified. It's mostly politics, who-you-know, what you're willing to do. Their priorities are set by political agenda. Their organization was designed to protect the top criminals, the people who control the money and capital. The bureaucracy won't expend the time required to find out what happened to one agent stupid enough to let himself get caught. Doroteo thinks the guy will be too embarrassed to tell anyone about it, and especially if he ever wants to get promoted."

"Yes," she said impatiently. "I get that, but this guy won't remember any of it right, because of the drugs?"

"Taylor," he began quietly. "You've never taken any illegal drugs in your life have you?"

"Of course not." Taylor looked affronted. "I'm not a shithead!"

"All this media attention about the government torturing people for information. The debate if it is ethical or not." Cesar tapped the stick in his left hand on the wooden floor. The noise seemed to replace the darkness. "A bastard's trick, a red herring. That's all it is. If they want real information, they'll use drugs."

"I know. Psychological warfare."

"Doroteo's got his own special concoction of hallucinogens and other drugs to keep this guy in the perfect state. He'll tell us everything we want to know." Cesar laughed slightly. "He'll even sell out his own mother and father if we wanted him to, but I'm afraid it won't be as dramatic as the movies. Sorry, but at least, it should be entertaining."

"So he's not going to remember anything?"

"Not much. Just remember what we told you and what he does remember will not include us."

Eventually, they heard a car driving slowly down the gravel driveway. They listened as a car door opened and closed and then steps towards the house. When the door opened downstairs, Cesar put a finger to his mouth. They both stayed in the room and kept the door closed. When the intruder began ascending the steps, Taylor became conscious of her heartbeat pounding loudly in her chest. The motion felt loud enough to be heard in the stillness, but Cesar appeared calm. Even though she knew Doroteo walked up the stairs, only the sight of him entering the room would remove all doubt.

The noise stopped outside the door, followed by two quiet knocks.

"All is well," Doroteo said quietly from the other side. "You can open the door."

After Cesar opened the door, Taylor forgot to breathe and thought a giant humpback stood before them. She stared at them in horror until the giant mass became distinguishable as Doroteo and another man slumped over his shoulder. Doroteo stepped forward and gently unloaded the man on a cot in the middle of the room. In an attempt to regain her composure, Taylor silently took a deep breath. Had she actually become an accomplice to an abduction? In disappointment, she expected to be more excited than afraid.

Cesar closed the door and joined Doroteo at the cot. For a few moments, the two men just stared at the unconscious man. In the dim light, Taylor noticed a dark bag covering his face. She stood far back, afraid of interrupting the scene and waking the man. If he woke, Cesar or Doroteo would handle the situation, not her.

Cesar removed a small LED lamp from his jacket and energized it, casting the room in a soft bluish glow. Doroteo sat and sighed in relief.

"Just give me a moment. I'm not young anymore."

"You and I both, my friend," said Cesar, patting Doroteo on the shoulder.

59

Taylor

Taylor took a tentative step closer and stared at the unconscious man. He wore blue jeans and a polo shirt. It looked blue, but in the dark she had difficulty determining the exact color. While inspecting the man, Taylor realized how heavy he must have been for Doroteo to carry up the stairs. He seemed at least six feet tall and muscular.

"You carried this guy up the stairs?" she said quietly, with a new respect for Doroteo. "He must be at least two hundred pounds."

"I could not have done it," said Cesar.

She turned to Doroteo and spoke as quietly as she could.

"What if this guy wakes up, but pretends to be asleep and he's listening to everything we say?"

When he answered, Doroteo still seemed to be breathing faster than normal.

"Yes, we'll have to be careful about that. From what he was given, we have about another hour, give or take, before he'll even start to regain his senses, but they won't all come back at once. He'll be disoriented and not able to think clearly."

Taylor took the last step to the cot and stood directly over him. The only way to overcome her fear would be to stare at the cloth covering his face. She listened to his shallow breathing and watched the slight rise and fall of his chest. The scene felt like a group of vultures waiting for an injured animal to die.

They had to wait about thirty minutes before they could continue with the plan, the next injections. If they administered the drugs to him while still asleep, Doroteo said it could be dangerous.

"Have you discovered this man's identity?" Cesar asked.

"Not yet," Doroteo answered. "But he's our man. I recognized his face."

Cesar slid a pair of gloves over his hands and reached inside the man's back pocket. After retrieving a wallet, he opened it. The man's badge reflected the LED light.

"Special Agent John Pratt," he read. "Just as I thought, from the Counterterrorism Division. That narrows it down a bit. At least, they don't think we're committing some sort of crime."

Both men laughed, but Taylor gulped.

To pass the remainder of the time, they discussed the FBI Counterterrorism program. Doroteo argued with Cesar about the real goals of the FBI. They disagreed on small points, but basically agreed on their main objectives, to legitimize the war on terror, by keeping it in the news and basically causing a lot of smoke. Building an effective illusion required the injection of money, manpower, and activity.

"What is the drug we're going to use on this guy, on Agent Pratt." Taylor wished the man's name remained a mystery. Would she be able to convincingly deny knowing his name if the police ever questioned her about him?

Doroteo turned from the FBI agent.

"We will first give him a drug called Amobarbital. You might have heard of it. It's not the best stuff, but it's easier to acquire than what the intelligence community uses, and it works. I've also added a trace amount of LSD. This combination works well."

Hearing Doroteo talk about illegal drugs made her laugh. She began to associate Doroteo with every illegal activity. After purchasing a dangerous and illegal nuclear reactor, they kidnapped a government agent. Next they would be injecting LSD into their victim. What was their next crime? Murder?

"Wait a minute," she said. The truth serum part made sense, although it reminded her of a cheap mystery novel, but why the LSD? "Is the LSD supposed to help him talk to us, or forget?"

"Both," said Doroteo as he tried to hide a smile. "LSD is just to make it an unbelievable experience, to distort his memory if government psychiatrists ever attempt to uncover what we've done. I've got another drug to help him forget almost everything."

"Taylor," began Cesar. "You know this is how real information is forcibly extracted from prisoners, don't you? This is how I got them to tell me where they were holding my daughter."

"Will there be some kind of permanent damage to him? I mean, I've heard these kind of drugs can change a person."

"Probably not, but what does it matter?" Doroteo asked with some impatience. "We have to find out what he knows. He could ruin all your work, your future and mine. Stop worrying about this man, and worry about what you need. He may be just doing his job, but we have a responsibility to defend ourselves."

Taylor almost allowed herself to continue arguing with Doroteo, but she felt unqualified for the task and decided to just let the professionals do their work. She gritted her teeth in preparation for capitulation.

"You're right, Doroteo."

"I know," he said, an expressionless look on his face.

His irritated tone reminded her of their serious situation. Despite how calmly he talked, she could see anxiety in his kinesics. Never before had he ever acted so irritated towards her. Did the stress of the situation reveal his real feelings? She shrugged. Maybe she would talk to him later.

For the next few minutes, no one spoke. They just watched the man for signs of consciousness. Cesar noticed the first body movement, from his fingers.

"He's almost ready to receive the next dose. Don't worry, he's not close to being conscious yet, but we should proceed soon." Doroteo spoke to Taylor and his tone returned to normal. "Let's go over what we're going to do next."

For the next few minutes, they explained Taylor's role. She would do all the talking, as a whisper. Her native accent had a smaller chance of being remembered than a Mexican one. Having a female interrogator would also help him feel more relaxed. Taylor suspected another motivation from the two men, to give her the experience. She felt like their daughter, on her first hunting trip to kill a moose.

"Oh, one other item," said Cesar.

He opened his backpack and removed an electronic metronome. He started the device at a very slow setting, about twenty beats per minute. The rhythmic tapping chimed quietly in the room. Taylor imagined a mouse hitting a cow bell with a little rock. They listened to the steady tick of the metronome for about thirty seconds and no one said anything.

"This helps me concentrate and helps them feel relaxed," Cesar said.

"Wow," she said silently in amazement. How many times have they done this?

In ten more minutes, the first signs of consciousness became apparent. In the dim light of the LED lamp they could see the man's fingers begin moving more and then he started moaning with his head slowly turning left and right. They all hovered over the cot as if inspecting a patient ready for surgery.

Taylor switched her attention between Doroteo and Agent Pratt, waiting for one of them to intervene before the FBI agent awoke or said something. She fought the urge to throw her elbow into them so they would begin. She imagined the agent jumping off the bed, pulling his gun and shooting like a crazy outlaw from the Wild West.

In the next moment, he groaned loudly. Taylor thought she heard words from under the cloth covering his head. Cesar and Doroteo leaned forward to listen, but Taylor took a step backward.

"I think it's time Doroteo," Cesar whispered.

The agent's hand slowly began moving towards his face. Doroteo reached out and stopped his hand from going any further. Cesar stepped close to Taylor and whispered in her ear.

"You're up Taylor."

She felt like an actress who suddenly forgot her lines. Cesar must have noticed her hesitation.

"Tell him everything's going to be all right," he continued. "That we're going to take care of him. Remember, you're our voice and you'll be his whole universe."

"Ok," she whispered while her heart pounded. Cesar scooted her chair next to the cot and Taylor sat down then leaned over the FBI agent. "Everything is OK. Just relax." After speaking to the man, she instantly felt more confident. Cesar nodded in approval.

"Where am I?"

After Agent Pratt asked the question, he mumbled something else which Taylor failed to comprehend. She waited in silence for the man to respond, but he seemed to fall back asleep.

Doroteo stepped over to his bag on the floor a few feet away, and retrieved a syringe and vial. With only Cesar by her side, she felt more exposed to the government agent who might jump off the cot and strangle her. When Doroteo returned to her side, she felt better. Agent Pratt made no other move. Doroteo gently pulled her away and whispered in her ear.

"I'm going to give him the Amobarbital now. It will start working in just a few minutes, then we'll be able to question him. As long as you keep him talking, he'll tell us whatever we want to know, but it might be hard to keep him focused and awake. Just keep him talking."

When Doroteo stuck the needle into the back of the agent's thigh, he jerked and made a weak attempt to pull his leg away. He lacked the strength to resist. Taylor placed her hand on his shoulder and cringed upon contact, not out of fear, but from an instinctive and personal dislike for him. The man on the cot received payment to fight against their freedom. If a rabbit placed a paw on a sleeping fox, would the rabbit feel the same?

60

Taylor

"It's going to be all right. You should feel better in a few minutes Agent Pratt."

They wanted her to call him Agent Pratt so he would focus on his work. A few minutes later, the FBI agent appeared totally relaxed on the cot again. Doroteo moved his chair to the other side of the agent, opposite Taylor. Cesar sat at his head with Doroteo and Taylor on either side. The scene felt like a group of friends warming themselves around the flames of a fire.

"Hey," the Agent said suddenly, shattering the quiet scene. He spoke in a voice louder than any of them had used since entering the house. "Hooo issss therrrr?"

Taylor heard him smack his lips together as if trying to prevent saliva from gushing from his mouth. In order to understand him, she had to concentrate. His voice seemed to have difficulty penetrating through the cloth.

"Where'm I?"

"You're safe," Taylor whispered. "How do you feel?"

"How'd I feel?" he asked in a tone approaching laughter. "Greaeaeaeaeat, aven fel this good for a long time. What ya gave me? Give me mooooooore!"

"It's the medication. When you fell, you hit your head pretty hard."

"Head dosn hurt," he said, confusion replacing the tone of laughter. He reached for his head, but Taylor stopped his hand at his chin.

"Don't touch," she began, but a cry of panic interrupted her.

"Oh my god!" he almost screamed. "I can't see. Where's th'light? Where's th'light?"

"You can't see because your head is bandaged," Taylor said and had to suppress a laugh. "You shouldn't touch it."

"Oh my god! I'm blind! I'm blind!" In his panic, he failed to comprehend her words. He sounded depressed about being resigned to a future of darkness. "I'm neverrr gonna see again, am I! This is the end for me."

"Don't cry," Taylor said. "It's going to make your head hurt more. Listen to me! You're not blind. Your head is bandaged. That's why you can't see. Your eyes are fine."

"I'm not blind?" he asked in a tone of disbelief.

The next instant, he spoke with relief in his voice and he started laughing.

"Ahhhh. Thank you, doctor. Thank you! I owe you my life. Whatever you want, just name it."

"You're welcome," she said and smiled at his promise to give her what she wanted. "We'll get to that later. For now, I just want you to relax."

"My head dosn hurt," he said in more relief. "I'm healed! You fixed me!"

"No," she said sternly. Her responses came easily and instinctively. "Your head does hurt."

"Alright," he said in quick agreement.

While fighting the temptation to laugh, Taylor felt regret at not being able to video record the experience for future enjoyment. A video could be used against them in court. One more injustice of the situation.

"Try to stay with me. Just keep talking. It'll help. Can you do that?"

"Shore, alright. Am I in a hospital?"

The agent suddenly jerked his head to the left, aiming his face above Doroteo.

"Whoa! Whoa! What the hell are you?"

He spoke with fear in his voice, as if a frightful creature appeared above him. He reached up and grabbed at the air, at the horror induced by LSD. Taylor never prepared for hallucinations. She looked to Doroteo and Cesar for guidance. They just smiled and nodded for her to continue, as if applauding a theatrical performance.

Taylor paused to regain focus. The rhythmic dinging of the metronome filled the silent gaps in the conversation and made time feel like a marching band. Taylor found herself following the pace along with the FBI agent. Taylor's brain produced the next few lines of the script.

"What have you been doing lately Agent Pratt?"

"Going to college," he said, snickering and swatting in the air. Taylor moved her hand to his forearm. If he decided to fight her, she lacked the physical strength to restrain him. "Gonna get the kids. Gotta get 'em."

"What are the college kids doing?"

"Planning a bomb," he said and his tone changed to foreboding. "Gotta catch'em in the act. Oooooh, it's gonna be good."

"What else have you been doing?"

"Checking up on my old friend," he said. "We're not good friends really. No, not really."

"Who is this friend who's not really a friend?"

"Watching," he said and trailed off into quiet.

Taylor squeezed his arm to keep the words flowing.

"Lisssning tooo..."

"Listening to what?"

"His friend, good old Sanchez and some girl. Tlayer's her name I think, like Tlayer Slift. Ha ha ha. Funny name, pretty girl. Yes, very pretty girl. Would not mind a night with her, nope. Probly shoodn be saying that to nother woman. Ha ha ha. Are you jealous?"

His comments about them and about her especially, transformed her amusement to anger. She took a deep breath to calm herself, but before she had a chance to respond, he resumed speaking.

"Hey, I'm not supposed to be tellin you this? I am Eff Bee Ayee, don you know? Fe..der…al Byo…row...of…"

He enunciated as if chewing the words.

"I know," she interjected. "I'm an agent too."

"Knew it," he said and nodded his head triumphantly. "What's your name? Not fair you get to know mine and I don't know yours."

"We'll get to that later. What else have you been doing lately?"

He continued speaking about his leads on some Islamic terrorist cases and how he needed to trace all their funding sources. He hated that part of his job, mostly due to associating with Muslims. He hated Muslims, but his superiors wanted to crack these kind of cases. They would give more publicity.

Extremists and potential domestic terrorists from the United States interested him more than the stereotypical Islamic terrorists. Taylor had a hard time understanding his feelings and opinions. They consisted mainly of hatred and anger, much more than any desire to protect the public or bring criminals to justice. Her own anger originated from horrible experiences in her family, but Agent Pratt seemed to have been born with them.

"So what do you have on these little shits," she mimicked the way he talked about them. "Gonna stick em in jail, if all goes well."

He laughed stupidly.

"Hey, you're my kind a girl, I think. You're gorgeous, aren't you? I get the feeling you are, probably gotta boyfriend too."

"I'm nothing special," she shrugged and looked to Cesar across the bed.

He shook his head in disagreement and she felt her cheeks flush.

"Nuh uh," Agent Pratt scolded her, shaking his head under the sheet. "You are one hot agent. I can tell. Ha ha ha."

He spent the next twenty minutes talking about his progress on other cases while constantly asking about her physical appearance. Whenever he strayed from her chosen topics, she could usually redirect the conversation. Eventually, she returned the conversation to Gerald and his friends again.

"Tell me again, why do you hate Gerald so much?" she asked as casually as possible.

"Gerald Fugging Fuger," he said with contempt, the first instance he seemed serious. "Fugging Fuger is a goddamned extremist, like all the others, maybe worse. For what he did, he should be in jail. We'll get him."

Agent Pratt waved his index finger from side to side.

"What did this guy do?"

"He wants to eliminate the Federal reserve to take out the money supply. Can you believe that? There's not much worse you can do."

He spoke next in sync to the metronome.

Tick…"What"

Tick … "a"

Tick … "shit"

"Lots of shitheads want that," she said and smiled sincerely.

She felt the same as Gerald on that topic.

"Fuger planned the Federal Reserve building break-in, the whole goddamned thing, and got away with it. He let his friends take the blame."

"How did he do that?"

"Cause he's an asshole lawyer. That's how." He suddenly stopped talking and grabbed at some invisible thing in the air. Taylor let him grab at nothing for a few seconds. "Whoa, come back here you. Come on, just a little closer."

"What else did he do? Is he up to anything now?"

"Don't know, but he must be. Gotta find out what his friends are doing at that machine shop."

“So, what are they up to?”

“I’ve been liss’ning,” he whispered and laughed quietly. “Lisssennninnng, they don’t even know.”

“For how long?”

“Long enough to hear some strange shit.”

“What kind of shit?”

Her tone became suddenly angry and Doroteo put his hand on her shoulder.

“A jet engine that's not a jet. Too quiet.” He put a finger to the cloth at his face. “Shhhhhh”

“That doesn’t make any sense.”

“It doesn't make any sense,” he sang. “No sense, no sense, no sense. Gotta keep lissssennninnng.”

Taylor kept silent for a few moments and Agent Pratt fell asleep. This time she let him sleep. She sat back and Doroteo leaned forward.

“Very good Taylor,” he said. In the low light, she could see the outline of his smile. After the brief display of praise, he patted her on the back. “I’m going to give him the next drug now. It’s going to be harder to talk to him, but it will erase the remaining memory of the night.”

Doroteo rummaged through his backpack for another vial of liquid. When he inserted the syringe into Agent Pratt's other leg, the man only flinched, but remained asleep.

The metronome marched forward.

Tick

Tick

Tick

Tick

Cesar stood and motioned for Taylor to come with him into the hallway. Once out of the room, Cesar leaned close to her and spoke with a tone of relief.

“He doesn’t know anything.”

“Sounds like it, but I still want to know two more things. What exactly has he heard, not just what he thinks he’s heard, and what he plans to do.”

“Never satisfied are you?” he asked, looking directly into her eyes.

Suddenly, they heard talking from the other room so Taylor turned to go back. Before she could leave, however, Cesar grabbed a hold of her arm.

“Just don’t put too much emphasis on our true interests.”

After returning to the room, she found Agent Pratt calling for her. Doroteo held onto his arm.

“Pretty lady, pretty baby. Talkin to you. Yoohoo. Talkin toooyoooo hooo. Why sooo quiet?”

Taylor quickly sat down and patted his shoulder.

“Don’t freak out. I’m right here. You were telling me about what you heard in that machine shop.”

“No more talking, until you say sorry, and why am I floating in the air? Not fair. Hey, fair, air. Ha ha ha. I’m a damned poet. What a trip!”

“Stop being such a bastard,” she said in the hopes of getting his attention. “I have nothing to be sorry about.”

“Bastard,” he said and licked his lips as if the word tasted like a sweet sucker. “Hmmmm. Give me one second. Rastard, no that doesn’t work. Lizard, no no no. Hey, I got it, conjastard. Ha. Conjastard rhymes with Bastard."

He laughed triumphantly and continued until he started coughing.

"Listen to me, Agent Pratt," she said once his coughs subsided enough for him to hear. "You need to stay focused for just a few more minutes, OK? Just finish your story and we'll be done. You can get back to sleep."

"Not tired anymore," he said while yawning. "Not tired at all. You are an amazing nurse agent. I feel all better now. What time is it?"

"Don't interrupt me," she said barely louder than a whisper. Impatience told her to yell at the man, but she feared to break the stillness. "What exactly did you hear in the machine shop?"

"Ha," he said loudly. "Don't know what they made really, but they'rrrrr excited about it. Talking about space a lot. Sir Space-a-lot, like from the legends. Oh mannn. I am on a rollllll. Are you writing this down? This beautiful poetry just keeps flowing out of my mouth, like a damn river. I should have been a cyclist, no I mean a lyracal, you know one of those guys who writes music, a lyracle. Damn it all to hell. That's not it!"

He raised his hand and began conducting a silent symphony to the metronome beat.

"You mean a lyricist," she said impatiently.

"Oh, thank you, pretty agent nurse. Thank you so much," he said and started crying again. "You saved me! Now I can be a leereesist, just like I always wanted."

While he cried great sobs of relief, she waited to talk again. All his irrational behavior stopped being funny and transformed into an annoying spectacle.

For the next thirty minutes she attempted to discover what he planned to do. No matter how nicely she asked or how much she threatened him, he refused to tell her his plans. No one ever irritated Taylor that much without severe repercussions. Eventually, he agreed to tell her, but only if she let him whisper the secret in her ear.

Agent Pratt said their discussions about freedom and the absurdity of the government made him too angry to hear anymore so he planned to break into the shop himself. He admitted to being intimidated by their security guy and even had doubts of finding anything incriminating. He only cared about putting Gerald in jail somewhere and had no interest in the Mexicans or Taylor.

After hearing his plan, Taylor returned to the topic of his target Muslim groups, her final act in their performance. Doroteo said that people remembered the beginning and end of conversations more than the middle. If Agent Pratt successfully recalled any part of their interrogation, they wanted him to remember the end which excluded them.

When Agent Pratt started repeating a little poem he called, 'Allah and the dollah', Taylor decided to end the conversation. Under any other condition, his poem would have made her laugh.

"OK Agent Pratt," she said. "That was a beautiful poem you sang about. You're going to be a great lyricist. I bet you're thirsty, yeah, really thirsty."

He stopped repeating the poem.

"Yes, I am."

"I bet your throat feels like a cactus, doesn't it?"

"Oh my god, yes! Please, just give me something to drink."

Doroteo reached inside his bag and removed a small glass of liquid with a cap. After removing the lid, he handed the container to her. She held the liquid for a few seconds, staring at the contents in the LED glow. The sedative would become an unimpressive end to a very strange evening. She dreaded the thought of lifting the cloth from his face and helping him take a drink.

"I'm going to be real gentle," Taylor said as she slipped her hand under his head and helped him lean forward to drink. When the cold water touched his lips, he breathed deep. In one gulp he drained the liquid.

"Oh yeah, oh yeah!"

"I'll give you more in a minute," Taylor said and returned his head to rest on the cot. "We don't want you to have too much too fast."

"Anything you say, doctor agent!"

Taylor heard no more from him. Slowly, his left hand slipped off his chest to hang lifeless at his side. They all stared at the body in silence until he became totally still and breathed quietly. Taylor felt herself relax. Her friends would bring the remainder of the show to a peaceful end.

"So you're going to take him outside some bar?" asked Taylor in the dark. She stood at the window, looking at the trees which surrounded the private drive.

"He's going to be confused when he wakes," Doroteo said. "It'll be a while before he begins to suspect that anything strange happened. Hopefully, the woman from the bar will help provide a convenient and pleasant answer to his lost memory of the evening."

While Doroteo worked on putting his things away, Taylor watched the night. After a minute, she noticed a distant light through the trees. In panic, she recognized a car slowly rolling down the long drive.

"Um, guys. Someone is coming."

61

Taylor

"What?" they both asked in unison.

"Someone is driving towards the house," she said and ran to extinguish the LED light.

"¡Mierda," Doroteo said in anger then joined Taylor on the opposite side of the window.

Together, they watched a small pickup truck drive slowly down the drive. Doroteo's car sat in the driveway, just out of their view. Cesar had parked on the street, beyond the trees he and Taylor had passed on the way to the house.

"Probably just some stupid kids," Cesar said.

"Wait here," Doroteo said. "I'll take care of this."

He left the room and Taylor heard him run down the stairs in just a few steps. Cesar stopped the metronome and joined Taylor at the window. The absence of the metronome tick made her feel momentarily disoriented. What would Doroteo do?

Taylor attempted to appear calm and ignore the annoying sensation of her throbbing heart. From the outside, the window must have appeared dark with no occupants, but Taylor felt exposed and trapped. The timing of the truck's arrival seemed like too much of a coincidence. The vehicle could have appeared during the interrogation, when no one watched.

"What's he going to do?"

"I have no idea," he answered and Taylor thought she heard a bit of amusement in his tone.

"Worried?"

"A little," he admitted, looking straight into her eyes. "But, let's let Doroteo worry about it."

They returned their attention to the approaching pickup truck which looked like a Ford Ranger. The truck stopped about thirty yards from the house.

"Damn it!" Taylor whispered quietly. "They see the car in the driveway."

"Look," Cesar said and pointed.

The truck resumed its forward motion and stopped again at the edge of their vision. The lights in the cab suddenly burst to life, revealing a teenage boy and girl. The boy opened the door and stepped out while keeping his hand on the door. Through the window, Taylor heard their muffled voices.

"No one's home," the boy said.

"But the car," the girl said, pointing through the windshield. "Someone's here."

"Too dark for anyone to be home," he responded. "The real estate agent left a car here to make it look like someone was here, to scare people away. Come on. It's more fun this way anyway."

The girl swore before exiting the truck. When the door shut, the cabin light extinguished. The girl joined her boyfriend as he approached the house, vanishing from sight. The girl said something else, but Taylor wondered if she heard the words correctly.

"Hey, that looks like an undercover cop car?"

"You're just being paranoid," the boy replied.

Cesar walked slowly to the door, but stopped as the floor creaked. He motioned for Taylor to approach the door from another angle.

"You weigh less," he said barely audibly.

She took a couple tentative steps, but heard no reaction from the floor. In the quiet, she heard every noise, her boots moving on the floor, her breathing, her heart beating. She opened the door to the hallway and listened. The teenagers were whispering just outside the front door.

In the silence, they waited. Cesar stood like a statue in the middle of the room, afraid to move. Agent Pratt breathed softly and rhythmically.

If the kids came up the stairs, she would let Cesar take control. She felt confident in his skills and instincts in dangerous situations. Taylor only feared being caught. Hopefully, Doroteo could resolve the situation without hurting them.

The sound of their failed attempts to open the locked front door replaced all other sounds. When the sound stopped, the kids would either try the back door or leave. Forty-three seconds later, however, Taylor heard a door in back of the house slowly open and close. While holding her breath, she watched for a light to appear from the bottom of the stairs, but the house remained dark. As she listened to their conversation, her anxiety began to decrease.

The teenagers spoke quietly about where to 'do it'. They failed to explicitly define what 'do it' meant, but the action obviously involved some sexual act. The girl just wanted to hurry and then leave. Taylor shook her head and failed to stop herself from silently laughing.

Were stupid teenagers going to ruin her plans because of sex?

Suddenly, a bright light shone through the window behind her and from the bottom of the stairs. Taylor turned towards the window and extended her hand to shield her eyes from the intense light.

"Shit, shit, shit," the boy said in panic.

"Oh God. Is it the cops?" the girl asked. "If my dad finds out, he's going to kill me."

Taylor heard them walk quickly to the front of the house, probably to look out the window.

"What the hell," the boy said, with a tone of surprise and anger. "It's my truck lights."

"What..." the girl began to say, but a loud noise from the back of the house interrupted her.

Taylor and Cesar listened to a loud scraping sound and heavy footsteps from the back of the house. Even though Taylor knew that Doroteo made the noises, they caused a feeling of fright to race through her entire nervous system. She had a momentary fear that one of the teenagers would have a heart attack. She turned to Cesar and noticed his mouth stretched into a huge smile.

"Holy Jesus," the girl shrieked in panic and blood-chilling dread.

The boy said something with similar alarm and soon afterward, the front door opened and slammed shut. Within seconds, the truck drove out of their sight, leaving the house in darkness once more.

V: PROBE

The specter from the sky
Takes you for a ride
How high can you fly?

62

Gerald

Gerald lay on the couch of his childhood home and stared at the ceiling. He watched as random patterns in the popcorn ceiling shifted into strange creatures and faces. The scene looked like a demonic, cloudy sky. Thousands of faces showed different expressions, some showing fear, some crying, and some laughing. He watched in mild curiosity as they floated in and out of recognition.

A raging fever of a hundred and three degrees Fahrenheit fought to control an invading virus. To help fight his fever, his mother gave him a large dose of acetaminophen. An hour after the first dose, she gave him another large dose of ibuprofen. While watching the faces above him in the ceiling, he listened to the muffled phone conversation between his mother and grandmother. His skin felt like a hot fire. The possibility of death no longer produced anxiety.

The faces appeared to shift, as if observing invisible activity in different locations of the room. Some of the faces even talked silently with each other, sharing interesting secrets. Occasionally, they would pause conversing and look down at him, but only for a brief moment then they would return to their secret conversations. The whole experience felt extremely strange and disturbing. Watching the faces in the ceiling occupied his attention while leukocytes in his body fought the virus.

Twelve-year-old Gerald attempted to remember the most recent events in his life and why they used to feel so important, his school project due the next week, his best friend moving to another state, the prettiest girl in school showing no interest in him. His memory felt far away, as if his experiences in school occurred several years in the past. Nothing in his life mattered to him anymore. For the remainder of his life, he felt content to lie on the couch and watch the sky.

The heat emanating from his skull became his only memory, his only sensation of the outside world. The heat spread from the top of his skull to the rest of his body, but stopped before reaching his cold hands. Young Gerald placed cold fingers on his forehead and enjoyed the sensation, the only physical pleasure in his life.

Eventually, he slept and dreamed of a pleasant car ride with an old man and a beautiful woman his age. No one spoke as they drove on a dark road in the middle of the night. While they traveled, he enjoyed watching the windshield wipers remove small rivers of rainwater from the glass. As he watched the trees speeding past in the darkness, he never worried about their final destination.

While her newborn son squirmed in the bed next to her, the hours flowed past like a river of honey. Sadi attempted to recall a longer night in her life. Perhaps the memory of a longer night would give her hope for an end to the current one. For the moment, however, her only memory became the previous uncomfortable moment. The new tiny human cried every few minutes and would only stop when Sadi rubbed his back and pulled him close. When exhaustion finally overpowered her senses, the action became automatic.

Sadi loved her infant son more than anything in the world, but the reason for that love temporarily eluded her awareness. Would her love continue through the night? Could she function as a mother without the emotional connection? Fear of losing that connection to her son consumed her thoughts when conscious and haunted her dreams when she slept. As she alternated between the conscious state and the unconscious, she imagined being trapped in a continually revolving door, unwilling or unable to make a decision.

Eventually, she slept and dreamed of a pleasant car ride with an old man and a man closer to her age. No one spoke as they drove on a dark road in the middle of the night. While they traveled, Sadi enjoyed watching the windshield wipers remove small rivers of rainwater from the glass. As she watched the trees speeding past in the darkness, she never worried about their final destination.

As he lay in the hospital bed, Bill Smith thought about how close he came to dying and wondered how many more years he would live. Every few hours, a nurse would visit and examine his physical condition after the recent heart bypass surgery. The nurses kept his body heavily sedated with medication for pain and sleep. Occasionally, the burning pain in his chest would explode, imprisoning all his thoughts and then the nurse would come and increase his pain medication and he would sleep.

At one point, he heard the voice of his son and Bill opened his blurry eyes to see a man standing by his bed, his son. When he attempted a response to the voice, he forgot the question. Only silence escaped his lips. After a while, the man vanished, leaving Bill alone with only his thoughts for company.

Several times, a woman wearing a brilliant white dress appeared by the bed. She looked like his wife at their wedding, but since she died a long time ago, he doubted the validity of his senses. A daughter might look like the woman. Did he have a daughter and just failed to remember her? He asked why she came to him and what she wanted, but she would just smile. While looking at the woman, he could also see the lights on the ceiling through her face. He missed his wife.

Sometimes the room darkened and his eyes dimmed and he could see the inside of a car sliding silently over a dark road. He sat with a younger man and woman, their stone faces facing forward. When he looked out the window, he saw dense trees moving quickly past his view, soon replaced by other trees. In the car he felt calm. The pain from surgery damage vanished.

63

Sadi

"Sadi. Wake up."

Gerald's voice exploded out of the darkness, ripping her from unconsciousness. She paused for a moment before opening her eyes, fearing what she might see? Did Gerald lie beside her in bed? What happened after Freddy's bedroom? When she inhaled the scent of new leather and felt the soft crunch of her seat, her fear vanished. With no memory of how she arrived in her present position, she somehow found the courage to open her eyes.

Sadi opened her eyes to see a dark forest through a car window. Instinctively, she extended her hands and squeezed the steering wheel, enjoying the sensation of endorphins entering her blood stream. She used the few seconds after opening her eyes to assess the situation. Somehow, she had unconsciously driven an unfamiliar car and parked on the side of an isolated road in the forest with Gerald Fuger.

LED lights from the dashboard cast a soft glow on the new leather interior of an expensive car. Sadi turned to her right to see Gerald sitting in the passenger seat and then to the back seat where Mr. Smith sat, his head tilted back, either sleeping or dead. A sudden feeling of panic soon passed after she recognized signs of the old man beginning to regain consciousness.

"What are we doing?" Sadi asked finally after returning her attention to Gerald.

At the sound of her voice, he removed his hand from her shoulder.

"I have no idea where we are, or how we got here. I woke up to find you and Mr. Smith asleep."

Before Sadi could respond, she heard the sound of Bill Smith moving in the back seat. Both she and Gerald turned to face the back seat and watched as the old man turned his head from left to right in an attempt to assess his situation.

"What are you doing driving my car?" He asked the question with a tone of irritation and obvious mistrust, intimating an abduction situation. "Where have you two taken me?"

His quick recovery surprised Sadi. He acted more aware of his surroundings than she or Gerald.

"We both just woke up too," Gerald said, turning to Sadi. "I don't remember how we got here, and that's the truth. Do you remember anything Sadi?"

"You were awake before I was," she said to Gerald in an instinctive attempt to defend herself from the old man's accusations.

"OK, I don't mean to accuse you both," said Mr. Smith as if interrupting two children in an argument. "We were in Freddy's room, looking at that crystal thing.

Does anyone have it?"

"I do," Sadi said before consciously considering the question. "It's right here."

She immediately felt the object on the seat between her legs. Slowly, she lifted the crystal into view, holding the object away from her. The crystal surface scattered the LED light of the dashboard onto the ceiling. No unnatural light emanated from inside the object.

"Don't look at it," Gerald said in warning. "That's when my memory ends and everything went fuzzy. We need to find our location."

Gerald turned to look through the front window as if he could determine their location from the view. In the following silence, Sadi listened to the soft vibration of the engine and the sound of light rain hitting the windows. The sensations helped soothe her anxiety. After a moment, Gerald reached his hand to the steering column and energized the headlights. The bright light illuminated tall evergreens on either side of the narrow road.

"Does anyone have a phone with them?" asked Mr. Smith.

With the crystal in her hand, Sadi looked at her feet, then her lap and all over the car for her purse. She imagined a frantic Jen, unaware of her location or time of return.

"I don't have my purse with me," she said in frustration. She always carried her phone in her purse.

"I don't have my phone with me either," said Gerald.

"We were taken here for a reason," said Sadi after trying to calm herself. "We need to figure it out."

"Ms. Jacobsen," Mr. Smith said and leaned forward. "You're the one in the driving seat. What do you remember?"

Sadi placed both hands on the steering wheel again and closed her eyes. She remembered the dream of lying in bed with her newborn son, but did not want to talk about the experience. She spoke with her eyes closed.

"I can't even remember getting in the car."

"I remember having a very vivid dream," Gerald said. "I remember being sick when I was ten or eleven. My mother gave me a ton of painkillers to fight a fever, but all the drugs made me hallucinate. I remember staring at the ceiling and seeing faces there. I don't know if it means anything, but I woke you two up after coming out of it myself."

"Maybe we should drive a ways to see if anything shows up," Sadi suggested. "Maybe we're pointed in this direction for a reason?"

"Maybe we stopped here for a reason," said Gerald. "I'm going to get out and have a look around."

"Do you think that's a good idea?" asked Mr. Smith.

"We came to help you locate Freddy," Gerald answered and opened the glove box in front of him. He lifted several papers and eventually retrieved a small flashlight. "Oh good, a flashlight. You two stay here, until I get back."

Before her fear could materialize, Sadi opened her door enough to feel small drops of rain pelt her hand. Mr. Smith looked out the window, as if he contemplated joining them too, but he only watched as they exited the car.

"Don't worry," Sadi said before shutting the door. "We won't abandon you."

"Thank you," he said, shaking his head slightly.

Sadi had difficulty determining his tone. Sarcastic? Grateful? She almost felt like an unpaid servant.

On their walk to the front of the car, Sadi shivered from the cold air and rain hitting her arms. Too bad she failed to bring a hat. While holding her arms tight against her breasts, she watched as Gerald scanned the area with his flashlight. Out in the cold without a coat, she would last maybe one to two hours before acquiring hypothermia. The thought of Freddy out there somewhere in the cold wetness caused a more severe shiver than her physical reaction to the cold.

"This is insane," Sadi said. "Even though I already saw this crystal thing in action on Freddy, these surreal experiences are hard to deal with."

"I'm trying not to think about it and focus on finding Freddy," said Gerald while shining his flashlight off the side of the road and into the thick undergrowth of the forest. "Poor old man thinks we've kidnapped him."

On the left of the car, the forest sloped upward and the right sloped downward. Sadi saw nothing but moss-covered trees and a fern covered forest floor. If either of them stepped off the right side of the road, they would tumble about fifteen feet before crashing into thick blackberry bushes.

"I'm not going to lie! I'm kind of scared," she said and attempted a weak laugh. "And not just for Freddy."

"Do you think Freddy's out here somewhere?" Gerald pointed the flashlight at the blackberry bushes below them and clutched his chest for warmth with his left arm. "Are we supposed to go looking for him, through that?"

Sadi could feel Gerald's growing frustration. Up until that point, Sadi thought he acted like a boy scout on an adventure. Sadi had no experience with boy scouts, however, or camping.

"There's nothing here," she said and walked to the passenger door. "We should start driving again. I think you should drive though."

"See anything?" asked Mr. Smith after they returned to the warm interior of the car.

"No," Gerald began. "I think Sadi had the better idea. We're going to drive a little until we see something."

When Gerald started driving he kept their speed at a very slow ten miles per hour. Sadi wanted to travel faster, but just watched out the window. After less than a minute, Sadi noticed a dirt road a couple hundred feet away on their right.

"Look, a road," she said, pointing.

An old mailbox at the beginning of the dirt road indicated a private drive with a single destination. The mailbox leaned sadly to the left and appeared unused for several years. Recent car tire tracks led down the road, slightly washed away by the rain. The single set of tracks indicated one car's entry without an exit.

For an unknown reason, Sadi knew they arrived at the right place. Gerald entered the road without agreement or protest. In any other circumstance, trespassing on private property would have caused anxiety, but their current situation felt different.

As they moved slowly down the long road, no one spoke. They traveled about two thousand yards while looking through the windows for signs of life or evidence of Freddy's presence. When they arrived at an almost ninety-degree left turn in the road, Gerald stopped the car and extinguished the headlights.

"Look up there," he said pointing to the trees to their left. "I think I saw a light."

Sadi turned her head and Mr. Smith sat forward squinting.

"What kind of light?" Mr. Smith asked.

"I don't know. I don't see it anymore."

"I think it's a barn," Sadi said after her eyes adjusted to the absence of the headlights. She saw the outline through the trees, but no lights. "It might be time to call the police."

"No," Mr. Smith and Gerald said simultaneously. Mr. Smith finished, "I don't have any reason to believe you two, but I do. We were brought here for a reason. It seems to me that if whoever delivered us here wanted to kill us, they could have driven us off a cliff."

Against her will, she agreed with his argument so Sadi made no protest. She made the suggestion to involve the police instinctively, but knew they had to resolve the situation themselves. She had a daughter to consider and would act irresponsibly by risking her own safety. Gerald chose to remain silent about his motivation, but Sadi knew he wanted to keep out of any government spotlight, no matter how small.

"You're right. I was just getting scared."

"We'll be OK," Gerald said, looking directly into her eyes. "I have a good feeling about this. Well, that's not exactly true. At least I don't have a bad feeling about it anymore."

"Yes," said Mr. Smith from the back seat. "I think Freddy's here too."

For the next few minutes, they watched the barn for signs of movement before deciding to drive onward. For the remainder of the road, they drove slowly and without headlights. Despite his claim otherwise, Gerald acted frightened and only Mr. Smith acted as if unaffected by any feeling of foreboding. Maybe after such a long journey in life, he possessed less fear of the end.

Their current path ended in a clearing with several hundred acres of open field behind the old barn. From what she could see in the very dim light, the crop resembled alfalfa, but Sadi had no direct experience with farming. In the dark of night, the barn stood silent and wet.

"Looks like this is an entrance to that road over there," Gerald said, pointing to the small road winding to the right from the barn. His finger followed the direction of the new road to a speck of light on a hill miles away. "Looks like a farmhouse way over there. Must have been the light I saw. This barn's probably being used as extra storage. Doesn't look very inviting, does it?"

Gerald parked the car directly in front of the barn, then killed the engine.

"So what do we do?" asked Sadi.

Of course they needed to check the barn, but that action had an obvious problem. From what Sadi knew, they had no method for protection, other than a solid flashlight. What if an angry farmer discovered them? Being shot by a farmer with a shotgun seemed like a pathetic end to her less-than-illustrious life. On the other hand, what if they found nothing in the barn? That possibility felt almost as frightening as physical danger. Freddy would still be lost and they might have to consult the crystal again.

Before Sadi gave any indication of feeling mentally prepared, Gerald opened the door. He walked around the front of the car and opened Sadi's door for her. Before exiting the car, she slipped the crystal into her right pocket again. With the crystal out of physical contact Sadi felt strangely more vulnerable.

"I don't think anyone wants to be left behind," Gerald said while holding the door for her.

"Thank you," the old man said when Sadi helped him exit the vehicle and stand.

The light rain restored the chill almost instantly to her bones. She hoped the cold Northwest wetness failed to give the old man a cold.

"Seems to me that we should be looking for Freddy's car," said Mr. Smith crossly. "I don't see any other car here."

"Where did those other car tracks lead?" Sadi searched for signs of the other car tracks they saw at the beginning of the road. "Did anyone see them?"

Gerald shone his flashlight down the road where they came to reveal two sets of tire tracks. Their pair of tracks stopped where Gerald parked. Sadi watched the flashlight beam illuminate the other set of tracks which led to the back of the barn.

"If that's Freddy," Gerald said and shined the light on the face of the barn, "then he went around the back."

"That's got to be him," Mr. Smith said quietly and with a tone of relief. He lifted his cane in the air, pointing to the door. "We should look into the barn first."

"I think you're right," Gerald answered. "Let me go first."

64

Sadi

They followed Gerald silently through thick, wet grass to the barn door. The sounds of their movement mixed with the sound of the rain on the leaves around them and the slight breeze in the trees. They stopped at the door and Gerald put his hand tentatively on the old and rusted latch. He handed his flashlight to Sadi then placed one hand on the latch and the other hand on the door frame.

The latch unclasped with a loud, resounding click. At the harsh sound, Sadi's heart temporarily stopped the flow of blood and Gerald froze into a silent statue. He soon recovered and continued to swing the door open even with the loud squeaking of the rusty hinges. After opening the door just enough for him to step inside, the creaking stopped and Sadi let the silence repair the damage to her nerves.

"Hand me the light," Gerald said.

He shot the narrow beam into the barn, but from his position, only Gerald could see inside. While Sadi and Mr. Smith waited impatiently, Gerald stood motionless and silent. After waiting for several seconds, Sadi tentatively placed her hand on his shoulder to check his emotional condition. Did he see something to cause fear?

"Gerald, what do you see?" she asked. "Is Freddy in there?"

"Don't move," he answered quietly. He spoke so softly, Sadi could have mistaken his words for occurring only in her imagination. When he spoke again, his voice rose to a higher volume. "I think he's in there, but he's not alone."

"What do you mean, not alone?"

"What's wrong?" Mr. Smith spoke loudly, causing Sadi to cringe and squeeze Gerald's shoulder in panic.

She turned and placed her hand on her lips, then shrugged her shoulders, hoping to indicate ignorance. Before she turned to face Gerald again, she noticed the light from his flashlight extinguish. He slowly exited the doorway and turned to face his companions again. As they huddled in the dark and rain, Gerald told them what he saw. He spoke so quietly that Sadi feared Mr. Smith would be unable to hear him, but the old man acted as if he heard.

"I believe that your friend is in there," Gerald began, addressing Mr. Smith. While speaking, he paused twice to turn and check the door. Sadi felt her anxiety grow during the time required to explain the situation. She followed his gaze both times and imagined a dark apparition flying from the dark interior of the barn.

"The floor's covered with hay and he's asleep in the middle. The problem is," Gerald paused again to listen.

“What the hell is in there with him?” the old man demanded.

“There’s a bear sleeping next to him,” Gerald said and attempted to smile, but his attempt lacked any hint of tranquility. He gulped before finishing. “With a cub, I think.”

“What kind of bear,” Sadi asked before taking time to consider his claim, as if the detail made any difference. “Let me have the flashlight.”

Gerald handed the flashlight to her.

“Does it matter what kind of bear?”

“I don’t know,” she said in irritation. The situation seemed too ridiculous. Gerald obviously misinterpreted his senses. “Is it a big bear, small, what? This whole thing is crazy. I know there’s no polar bears around here, or grizzlies. Is it a panda bear?”

“OK, OK,” he said, taking a deep breath. “It was dark brown, maybe not as big as a grizzly, I don’t think. My experience with bears is very limited.”

“A bear?” Mr. Smith said to himself. His grip on Sadi’s arm tightened. “I don’t know if we should shine the light in there again.”

“If you want to look,” Gerald said, “shine it on the floor, close to the door.”

Sadi stepped ahead of Gerald and Mr. Smith followed her with his cold hand on her arm. She shone the flashlight at her feet then moved the beam across the entrance threshold. To her amazement, she saw the bear, and Freddy lying beside the huge creature with a bear cub lying on the other side of them. For a moment, she watched the scene with curiosity, but then imagined the bear waking.

A new desire overpowered all her other senses, the desire to run and keep running. Sadi had never experienced such a strong urge, but found difficulty tearing her eyes away from the strange scene. For one very long second, she watched in a state of petrification. The light rain fell on her unprotected neck, sending shivers down her spine and deep inside her chest. Part of the bear hid the human face, but she recognized Freddy's blond hair.

After a deep breath, Sadi resumed some control of her senses. She extinguished the light and stepped back to discuss their options. The scene left her mind with too many questions. She waited for one of the others to speak first.

“We could drive the car to the barn door,” said Mr. Smith. “Shine the high-beams on them and blast the horn. Maybe that'd scare the bears away.”

The old man's words surprised Sadi again. The slow movement of his physical frame and weak voice betrayed a quick mind.

“It might put Freddy in danger,” Gerald responded with concern.

“Is it possible to wake him without waking the bears?” Sadi asked with little hope for a positive answer. Bears possessed more sensitive hearing than humans and would certainly wake with less stimulation. “If only we had some kind of weapon. I’ve got pepper spray in my purse, but I don’t have my purse, sorry.”

Gerald whipped his head upward, looking above Sadi and Mr. Smith with open mouth and wide eyes. As Sadi turned, her blood froze again. Instinct again commanded her to run and hide, but her feet felt like a tree, firmly attached to the ground. She watched as a bright point of light slithered through the trees toward them. The scene would have resembled someone approaching from far away, holding a flashlight, except the light traveled high in the air, flickering when the trees blocked her view. Sadi felt more fear of the light than she felt towards the bear, an irrational fear she failed to describe.

"What the hell is that?" Sadi whispered as quietly as possible while remaining audible. "It's coming our way."

"It's something tall, or floating." Gerald said and placed a protective hand on Sadi's shoulder, slowly pulling her close. "We should get back in the car."

"We're not leaving Freddy," said the old man defiantly, but even he appeared frightened. "We've got to get in the barn. If those bears haven't hurt Freddy, they shouldn't hurt us."

With his frail hand on her arm, Mr. Smith pulled Sadi towards the barn and opened the door wider. The hinges squeaked in protest. Together they disappeared inside. In the dry, dark interior of the barn, the cold hand on her arm reminded Sadi of Mr. Smith's presence and the physical connection provided some comfort.

Without taking his eyes off the light, Gerald followed them into the darkness then quietly shut the barn door. He stayed close to the door and watched through the cracks, the light illuminating his face. As the light intensified, her view of the barn interior improved and reminded Sadi of their extreme danger. Did some nonhuman entity find amusement in setting the scene for a twisted horror show?

While breathing as quietly as possible, an unpleasant smell assaulted her senses, a mixture of old hay and wet animal hair. The sensation contrasted sharply with the smell of fresh air from outside. Sadi had never stood so close to bears, not even at the zoo. Her imagination alternated between being eaten alive by a protective mother bear and the unknown of the approaching light in the trees. The light caused a mixture of irrational fear and curiosity to explode deep inside her mind, overpowering all other instincts, even the urge to run and hide.

As the light from outside intensified, Sadi and Mr. Smith watched Gerald as if in a trance. Awareness of the bears escaped her immediate memory.

"What is it?" Sadi whispered.

She pulled Gerald's sleeve to get his attention, but he failed to respond to her touch. In the soft glow, he looked like a statue. After releasing his sleeve, she turned away from the barn door, from the white light shooting through the cracks. Would the light put her into the same trance? She turned to the Mr. Smith who still appeared conscious.

"What's going on?"

"I don't know," he answered flatly. "Are there people coming our way?"

"That's not a normal light," Sadi answered in resignation while frantically searching for any other explanation.

Unfortunately the experience felt too real, not abstract enough for a dream. She found the old man's hand and clasped hard.

65

Sadi

When the light began moving up the walls, Gerald's head swiveled upward, smooth and mechanical like a robot. Together, Sadi and Mr. Smith followed his gaze and watched the light enter the barn through the cracks in the walls. The image of Sadi's daughter suddenly flashed through her mind. Would Helen ever see her mother again? The thought caused her head to ache. In panic, she grabbed Gerald's arm and shook him.

At her touch, Gerald showed signs of life. He stopped watching the light and made brief eye contact with her, then Mr. Smith. Sadi saw his eyes full of questions, but a new sensation stole her attention, a vibration at the base of her neck, resonating from her brain stem. Sadi moved her head upward in reaction, to refocus on the light. The white light traveled slowly over the barn roof, illuminating a loft with hay spilling over the edges.

"It's moving towards that opening," Gerald said.

He pointed to the wall above the loft to an open window near the arched ceiling. While watching the light, Sadi understood what Gerald experienced. The light became her entire focus, displacing all concern, worry and anxiety. She had no more desire to look or run away. All three of them watched like an audience sitting in a movie theater as a bright object appeared in the empty window space. At first, its intensity blinded her, but after a few moments, the features became discernible.

The levitating object resembled a giant, polished chrome bullet with an extremely sharp tip and just small enough to fit through the window. The object slowly turned to face them before beginning its descent, the sharp end pointing in their direction and the back end hidden from view. Before her eyes adjusted to the light, Sadi thought the entire object shone, but the mirror surface simply reflected the light emanating from its rear, from thousands of tiny protruding filaments. The strands of light resembled fiber optics, but finer than hair and brilliant white light escaped their entire surfaces. The strands gently waved in the air, responding to an invisible current.

The light filled the room as if from the shining sun, but Freddy and the bears lay as motionless as Sadi and the men standing next to her. The object stopped ten feet above Freddy, its cylindrical body aligning horizontally and slowly turning to face the three erect humans before becoming completely motionless. Even the strands of light stopped flowing. The entire scene resembled a photograph, a single snapshot of time.

The still scene lasted only a second before the object began a vertical motion towards Freddy and the bears while the sharp tip continued to aim at

Sadi and her two companions. During its descent, the strands of light extended further until they reached Freddy's face. The old man tightened his grip on Sadi's arm, but said nothing.

The filaments of light approached within inches of Freddy's face and ears, and for a few moments, appeared to probe him affectionately. The mother bear moved her giant paw slightly, but stayed asleep.

When finished examining Freddy, the probe began moving slowly towards Sadi. She no longer felt like the member of an audience. Instead, she felt like a patient on an operating table, naked and without anesthesia. Her heartbeat intensified as the distance between them narrowed. Her heart felt ready to explode when the sharp tip stopped within a foot of Sadi's face. While the tip motionlessly hovered at eye level, she imagined the thing rushing forward and piercing her head. The filaments of light stretched towards Sadi, Gerald, and Mr. Smith simultaneously, immersing their faces in light.

66

Sadi

Sadi stopped counting the strands of light. Each one glowed with a slightly different color than its neighbor. From a distance, all the strings blended into a brilliant white light. Up close, Sadi could distinguish the color of each strand separately. The experience transformed Sadi's fear into a deep appreciation for the perception of color. For the moment at least, Sadi felt content to stare into the light.

After an unknown amount of time, the tendrils of light began to ripple like waves around her nose, eyes, ears and lips. She watched as they danced like the trace of an oscilloscope, flowing like beautiful hair in the wind. The waves increased in amplitude and frequency until the light coalesced into familiar faces. She recognized the face of her daughter first.

At first, the images began as topographical maps and then transformed into the more detailed images she recognized. Contour lines became finer and finer until they disappeared altogether and Helen's face became real. Watching the construction of an artificial Helen caused anxiety. Sadi's mind refused to accept the final product as her real daughter, but also failed to recognize any difference.

The barn soon became a distant memory and Sadi found herself in a new location, a place of cold and gray, the front steps of an immense Catholic cathedral. The building caused a flood of memories to nearly overpower her senses. One set of memories hit harder than all the others, her mother's lectures about having faith in Jesus. If she only let Jesus into her heart, he could save her from the horrible, wretched fate of the sinner.

Sadi looked down and noticed a gray dress falling just past her knees and then to her daughter. Helen held tightly onto her hand, afraid of being lost in the crowd which flowed past them into the cathedral. Sadi enjoyed the warmth of her daughter's hand, a stark contrast to the cold of her surroundings and the stone faces of the people.

She looked at the line of people stretching to eternity behind her then tilted her head to the sky and noticed cement gargoyles watching lazily from their perch on the cathedral walls. The frightful demons watched the people like birds of prey, ready to attack at the first sign of death or weakness. She understood how the weakest wildebeest in the herd felt being watched by the pack of hungry lions.

After reaching the top of the steps, the cathedral doors hungrily waited to swallow them. Traveling through the doors felt like entering a dark cave. Soon, they left the gray and cold of the Northwest winter, but Sadi found little comfort being away from the hungry eyes of the gargoyles.

"Stay close dear," she said to her daughter.

"Don't let go mom."

"Don't worry. I won't."

As they walked slowly down the main aisle, Helen faced forward with her head down and Sadi looked from left to right in search of two empty seats. Huge murals of Jesus and his twelve disciples lined the walls. Almost every scene included a depiction of Jesus in agony. One showed Jesus with thorns covering his head, digging into his flesh. Others depicted Jesus praying under a tree or on the cross with his eyes toward heaven. In all the paintings, his face contorted with pain and suffering and grief. The eyes of Jesus followed them down the aisle like the gargoyles, burning as a living hot coal.

Sadi saw space for them both to sit on the right side of the front row. After getting comfortable, she and Helen sat very still and quiet. None of their neighbors exhibited any acknowledgment of their presence, keeping their heads bowed to avoid disturbing the stillness. The pew stood high and several feet in front of them with a white robed priest sitting to the right of the pew, the hood of his robe resting on his shoulders. He reminded Sadi of a character from a horror movie, a man with dark eyes and mouth sucking light from the surroundings.

When the priest rose from his seat, the crowd woke from their sleep. Everyone's head simultaneously rolled upwards and faced the podium. The man smiled ceremoniously then placed both hands on the pew with outstretched arms. His smile widened as he scanned the entire room and his eyes penetrated every member of the audience. When their eyes met, he paused momentarily and his smile vanished. The smile returned after moving to the next person. Helen squeezed her hand until the pressure caused pain.

"My brothers and sisters," the priest said as he slowly backed away from the pulpit. "The time has come!"

The man turned so he could see both the audience and the stained glass window behind him. All eyes turned from the priest to the colorful glass. As Sadi peered into the light, the glass rippled like a reflection on wavy water. One moment, Jesus stood in the clouds, angels by his side and demons below his feet. At the next moment, the scene changed and the crowd gasped.

A multicolored Jesus emerged from the glass and entered the great hall of the cathedral. Behind the floating Jesus, Sadi noticed a familiar figure standing in the crowd of angels who remained in the glass, her boy Jacob. He looked the same as the day he died. The floating Jesus looked down at Sadi and smiled as if he felt sorry for her, like he looked at a lost child. With outstretched hands, Jesus called to them all.

"Come, follow me!"

At the sound of his voice, the crowd exploded in cheering and rejoicing. People rose to their feet, triumphantly extending their hands into the air. Some started shouting. Her boy in the glass smiled wide.

"Hallelujah!"

"Praise the lord!"

"Oh, blessed Jesus!"

In unison, everyone except for Sadi and Helen began moving toward Jesus and the stained glass window. For a moment, Sadi only felt fear. She held tightly onto her daughter's hand, to stop her from disappearing into the crowd. When

Sadi returned her attention to Jesus, he started moving backwards in the air until he disappeared into the window. The people ascended the steps to follow Jesus and soon disappeared with him.

When Sadi saw the people enter the window, one thought solidified in her mind. She could follow them and finally reach her son. Sadi no longer felt fear. Helen held onto her hand as they both moved forward with the masses. When she finally reached the stained glass window, her son and the heavenly host vanished in a blinding light.

After the light dispersed, Sadi saw a dry and dusty road in an arid mountain range. All kinds of trees lined the road, oaks, junipers, cottonwoods, and cedars. Dust from the road hovered in the air around them, moving lazily with a light breeze. The dust stung her eyes and Sadi felt sand crunch between her teeth.

Sadi walked with the crowd from the cathedral. She failed to see her son or Jesus, just the long and dry road so she kept walking, squeezing Helen's hand from fear of losing her. Did the masses travel in the right direction? Did Jesus lead them? People talked in hushed tones all around her and Sadi tried to listen to what they were saying, but she could only distinguish one word, repeated reverently.

"Jesus, Jesus, Jesus..."

After an eternity of walking, the road opened before them like a dry river delta. Sadi looked up from the ground and noticed the crowd ahead approaching a large and imposing mountain face, a cliff whose walls seemed to ascend into space. Sadi wanted to stop and consider her surroundings, but the people acted as a strong river current and pushed her forward.

A dark hole at the base of the wall stole her attention, a large opening in the rock which resembled an old mine entrance. The people disappeared inside the mountain through the hole as if a ravenous beast swallowed them. As Sadi watched, she unconsciously resisted the forward motion of the crowd. When Helen squeezed her hand hard enough to cause pain, all thought focused on her daughter.

"Mom," Helen said. "I don't want to go in there."

"Jacob was with Jesus," Sadi said in despair. "We have to follow him."

Helen released Sadi's hand and several people instantly filled the space between them. The crowd swept Sadi along with them, leaving Helen standing still. Sadi yelled for her daughter to come back, but Helen refused to move and after a few moments, disappeared from Sadi's sight. With some effort, Sadi stopped and pushed against the crowd until she reached Helen. She wanted to scream at her daughter in anger, but somehow retained control of her emotions.

"Helen, what is wrong with you? We've got to follow Jesus."

"I'm scared mom," Helen said and put her hand over her eyes to hide the tears. "I didn't see Jacob."

Sadi crouched down, forcing people to walk around them.

"He was there, standing with Jesus," Sadi said. "Jacob was with Jesus. I saw it."

"Jacob was with Jesus," Helen repeated in an attempt to make her mother happy.

Through tears, she forced a smile.

"Yes, Jacob was with Jesus." Sadi lifted her daughter to rest on her hip.

"Here honey. I'll carry you so you won't have to walk on your own."

For the moment at least, she had the strength to carry her daughter. Walking felt good. Returning to the flow of the crowd and succumbing to the current required so much less effort than fighting the current or even standing still. When they reached within a hundred feet of the mine shaft, she noticed an ornate wooden frame surrounding the entrance. The people entered without hesitation, knowing those ahead of them were doing the same thing. Sadi felt a similar comfort, but the idea of entering the darkness without a light caused a momentary hesitation.

"Got to have faith," she said to herself just before the darkness extinguished the light.

67

Sadi

Once inside the mineshaft or tunnel, Sadi enjoyed watching the reflection of the daylight on the crowd ahead of her, but with every step their outlines grew fainter. The sensation of noise soon replaced the light, the shuffling of feet, and the muffled words from thousands of mouths. Behind her, the light of the world shrunk to a smaller and smaller circle. After only a few minutes, the light became a pinpoint of light, a single star in the darkness.

The air of the tunnel became colder and the smell of wet clay intensified, causing Sadi to shiver and hold her daughter tighter. Helen and Sadi shared the only source of heat. The hard ground provided their only connection to the world.

"Jacob is with Jesus," Sadi said quietly to herself every few minutes.

When Helen began repeating the words, Sadi received the emotional strength to continue moving forward. She walked for a long time in the tunnel, feeling like a refugee from the world outside, the world of the sun. To occupy her mind, she focused on the concept of community, being a member of the group, sharing the same experiences with the people around her. After a while, however, doubts began to infect her conscious thoughts.

Where were they going? Why did Jesus disappear once outside the cathedral? Why did Helen deny seeing Jacob? The people around her would have the answers. Otherwise, they would not have entered the tunnel. Sadi extended her hand to the person in front of her.

"Excuse me?" Sadi said after feeling the shoulder of a shorter person, a woman with a small frame. "When will we reach Jesus? How far is he?"

"We have to push through the darkness," the woman said while still facing forward. She spoke as if addressing a child. "When it is the darkest, when we're on the brink of despair, then we'll see Jesus."

Sadi could not see anything. How could the tunnel get any darker?

"How do you know?"

"Each must follow their own path."

Sadi considered asking the woman another question, but thought she might have better luck with someone else. She turned to the person on her left and felt the elbow of a tall man. His arm felt thin and weak.

"What are we doing here?"

"Everyone must follow Jesus," he said with a comforting and gentle tone, like a loving grandfather.

"Yes," she said in relief at hearing a more friendly response. "But where are we going?"

"It's not the destination, but the journey."

Although his tone appeared to contain empathy, he spoke without turning his head, as if speaking to the person in front of him instead of Sadi. The woman to their right spoke unexpectedly.

"Fear and doubt are of the devil! Don't let him inside your heart. Praise the Lord!"

"Praise the Lord!" repeated several other people around them.

Instead of providing comfort, a sudden fear wrapped its cold fingers around her heart, temporarily stealing the warmth from her daughter. The mention of the devil made the hairs on her neck stand erect. Did the devil put fear in her heart? Did he hide somewhere out there, in the darkness of the cave?

"No!" she said more loudly than she intended.

The sound of the word felt like a water hammer in her veins. The source of the fear came from the realization of her predicament, not from the devil. She slowed her pace and people had to push past her. The darkness of the tunnel suddenly felt absolute.

"We're inside a mountain," she said to herself. "In the dark."

Her arms felt so tired from holding Helen. When she considered the idea of setting Helen down on the ground, she felt a horrible panic. The thought terrified her more than the darkness around her or a possible demon just inches from her face. What if Helen wandered away? She might be lost forever. Sadi pulled her daughter more tightly against her ribs. The fear infused additional strength into her arms.

Where had Sadi taken her daughter?

Sadi came to a complete stop then turned to look behind them, but failed to see any point of light. The light of the shaft entrance had diminished to nothing.

"What's wrong mom?" asked Helen.

"I don't think we should be in here Helen."

Sadi no longer felt comfort from sharing the same predicament with those around her.

"What do we do?" Helen asked. "Please don't let me go."

Sadi paused for a moment and attempted to think rationally. The first and easiest option had an uncertain outcome, to just follow the crowd. The other option carried less uncertainty and required much more effort. She believed in the existence of the entrance with certainty, just not its exact location without the light.

"Where's your faith?" asked a voice from inside her head, like a faint whisper in her ear.

"Faith in what?" asked a different voice.

Should she choose to put faith in her neighbors and those pushing from behind or her own thoughts and feelings? Did her fellow travelers base their decisions on facts and rational thought, or were they just following the person in front of them? Sadi suddenly felt like a domino, placed in a line with only one purpose, to fall.

With the people pushing to get past her, she recalled her experience in the cathedral with the stained glass window, Jesus and her son. If she returned, would she ever find her son again? If she abandoned her faith by returning to the world of light, her son might be lost forever.

"No," she said to herself. "By turning back, I am not abandoning Jacob."

"What was that Mom?" Helen asked.

"Come on Helen," Sadi said with resolve. "We're getting out of here."

Sadi set Helen on the ground and held her hand tightly.

"Don't let go dear," she said.

Sadi extended her right hand and began pushing against the current of the crowd. At first, she experienced extreme difficulty moving while also attempting to avoid doubts about her direction. To help focus her mind, she concentrated on one conclusion. Going against the crowd would lead back towards the cave entrance. If she ever wanted to see the light of day again, she had to push against the crowd.

After what felt like an eternity of pushing and struggling, a faint star finally appeared in the distance, the light flickering when heads blocked her view. Sadi never experienced such a feeling of relief. As they walked, the star grew larger and larger until the light felt like heat and began to burn her eyes. When they finally reached the entrance, Helen began to cry and warm tears fell onto Sadi's hand. They hugged each other as the light welcomed them back. Soon, the light grew too bright and they had to close their eyes.

68

Sadi

Sadi opened her eyes and found herself back in the barn, staring at the bright light of the probe. Hot tears slid down her cheek from the cave dream. She still felt immense relief at escaping with Helen from the dark tunnel, but the memory failed to warm the chill of the cold barn air.

The filaments soon began to pull away from her face, returning into the back of the shiny hovering object. For several moments, she watched the beautiful glowing filaments. Slowly, she regained awareness of her surroundings. Gerald stood by her side, facing the probe without expression or movement. She wanted to nudge him in the ribs to see if the action would restore his consciousness, but she feared to move. After a few moments, she gained enough courage to look away from the probe. She saw Mr. Smith crouched down by Freddy's side in the middle of the barn floor, no bears in sight. To her relief, his open eyes indicated life and Mr. Smith seemed well too.

A moment later, the probe began to slowly ascend and the action jolted Gerald back into awareness, his eyes opening wide. No one spoke as they watched the probe ascend slowly above the loft. While she watched the lights move away from her, Sadi finally understood her strange reaction to them. She felt the same reaction when looking at a beautiful painting or her child's eyes. Those experiences completely filled her finite human awareness. All other thoughts vanished.

The probe stopped a few feet above the loft and Sadi jumped in surprise when it quickly rotated and disappeared from her view, leaving a streak of light burned onto her retinae. The streak of light became the only light in the dark barn. The image looked like a tracer bullet or the trail of a shooting star and slowly disappeared. The sudden collapse of air made a loud snap.

Before her eyes readjusted to the dark, Gerald turned to Sadi.

"Are you OK?"

"I'm fine."

She wiped the tears from her eyes, hoping he would fail to notice the evidence of her emotional state. For some reason, she felt embarrassed. The experience felt too personal. A moment later, Sadi energized the flashlight and noticed the look of exhaustion in his face. No tears slid down his cheeks, but he looked like he had been running from a pack of hungry wolves.

"What happened to you?" she asked with concern.

"I don't know," Gerald said, then abruptly turned to the old man crouched beside Freddy. "How's your friend?"

Sadi still felt the despair of the cave and the great relief of escape, but from the look on Gerald's face, he experienced just as much trauma, maybe more. He refused to provide any details. For the present, she would avoid asking him about the experience.

Before responding, Mr. Smith made eye contact with Sadi and she saw the countless questions in his old eyes. What just happened? What was that thing?

"You both were staring at the lights," Mr. Smith said from his position beside Freddy. "For about ten minutes straight, neither that thing, or either of you moved. I've never seen any living thing remain so still. If I would have stayed there, the same thing probably would have happened to me, but I moved away when those strings started reaching for me. What did you see?"

She saw fear and distrust in the old man's eyes.

"I saw my son," Sadi said quickly. "He died last year."

He looked at her for a moment then shook his head.

"I am sorry. We can talk about it later."

"What happened to the bears?" Gerald asked and Sadi felt relieved to discuss a different subject.

"They left about a minute after those strings tried to get me," he said. "It was very frightening, and strange. I was counting on them being afraid of the lights, but they just woke up and left without looking back. I've been trying to get Freddy to respond ever since."

"Is he OK?" Sadi asked, and quickly joined Mr. Smith on the other side of Freddy.

"I don't think he's hurt," he said. "He's just not responding. Maybe if we try to move him? I want to get out of here."

Sadi helped the old man pull Freddy into sitting position. He gave no opposition, but just looked at them with blank eyes. Gerald stayed in the same position, watching them.

"Gerald," she said quietly to get his attention. "Gerald, are you OK?"

"What?" he asked and looked into her eyes. Before continuing, she heard a long sigh. "No, I'm OK."

Before Gerald could move to join them, a noise from outside stole her attention, the snap of a twig. Even Mr. Smith heard the sharp sound. Sadi continued staring at Gerald, listening for more noise, evidence of some creature out in the darkness. Did the bears wait outside for them? The thought made Sadi shiver and hug her breasts for warmth. She fought the urge to run to the door and hold it shut so that nothing could come into the barn, but she stayed motionless, afraid to make any additional noise.

After a few more seconds of silence, Sadi heard the sound of a human running away from the barn door, then leading down the road. She felt instant relief knowing the sound originated from a human rather than a bear, but then her relief transformed into fear again. Who watched them?

Gerald gained enough courage to turn and peer through the cracks in the barn door and almost immediately, a bright light appeared through the door, illuminating Gerald's outline. His illuminated image at the door reminded Sadi of the time before the probe's arrival, only this time the light grew fainter rather than brighter.

A noise from the floor returned her attention to Freddy. The light brought him to life. In less than a second, he jumped to his feet and ran to the barn door, knocking Gerald out of the way before throwing the door open and escaping into the night. Before her mind offered a logical plan of action, she just listened to the sound of Freddy running in the same direction as the first person. She looked from Mr. Smith to Gerald.

"I'll go," Gerald said then stepped out the door. Before running after Freddy, he turned back to them. "Stay with Mr. Smith."

69

Sadi

After Gerald disappeared from her view, Sadi stepped closer to Mr. Smith who placed his cane on the ground in preparation to stand. While she helped him to his feet, he looked up at her with confusion in his eyes. What caused Freddy to move so fast and without warning?

"Should we go after them?" Sadi asked. "They might need our help."

"Yes, definitely!" Mr. Smith held onto Sadi's arm as they moved towards the barn door. They traveled at a faster pace than she thought possible. While they walked, a million thoughts fought for her attention. Sadi avoided any attempt to answer questions and focused on how they could find Freddy and Gerald.

At least, she still had the flashlight. As they walked, she pointed the beam ahead of them. Once outside, she looked up at the overcast sky and felt the light rain on her face again. The cold sent a sharp convulsion through her body, but she welcomed the familiar sensation. The water helped reconnect Sadi to the world she understood. When she attempted to listen for sounds of running, she only heard the light patter of rain.

"Go ahead without me," said Mr. Smith. "I'll catch up."

"No, I'm not leaving you. We'll go at your pace."

"I don't suppose Gerald left the keys?" said Mr. Smith as they walked past the car.

"I doubt it," she answered.

She considered asking for his opinion about why Freddy ran away, but decided to focus on the path ahead. They walked in silence, listening intently for any noise other than their own. Although she felt concern for Freddy's safety, she felt more worried about Gerald and the old man. From Freddy's most recent behavior, Sadi had the inexplicable impression that he knew exactly what to do.

After the turn in the road, the barn disappeared behind them and Sadi could see a dull red light through the trees, far away. The light appeared different than the light from the probe, probably originating from a car's brake lights. Strangely, she almost wished to see the beautiful, multicolored strings of light again. Would she ever?

"What's that light?"

"It looks like car brake lights," Sadi answered.

Sadi mentally prepared herself to pull Mr. Smith into the trees at the first sign of danger, making sure to keep a good hold of him. The thought of entering all the spider webs, wet moss and ferns of the Northwest forest almost seemed like a worse alternative than encountering the object again. Then she remembered the bears. They lurked out there somewhere too. She decided to extinguish the flashlight. When the light disappeared, Mr. Smith gripped her arm more tightly, but said nothing.

After considering all the horrible possibilities, she almost stopped and ran back to the car, to wait for Gerald and Freddy to resolve the situation. She felt afraid, but not the same panic as she felt inside the barn. That kind of fear had paralyzed her. With Mr. Smith depending on her to help, she felt the courage to keep moving.

The road had one last turn before they reached the light source, about fifty yards away. Without warning, another light burst to life next to the red light through the trees, the familiar bright light from the probe. The explosion of light illuminated all the trees in the forest while ascending from the ground. Sadi and Mr. Smith stopped momentarily to watch as the light ascended above the trees. A moment later, the light extinguished completely and disappeared from view and Sadi heard the same sound of collapsing air again. She returned her attention to the road in front of them until her eyes readjusted to the darkness.

"Was that the same object?" Mr. Smith asked.

"I think so," Sadi answered and started pulling him forward again. She never considered the possibility of more probes. "I hope it's gone for good now. Come on, we should keep going. We're almost there."

Mr. Smith resisted enough to stop her from moving.

"I can't see very well and especially at night. We shouldn't take any unnecessary risks. If they're in trouble, it might be good to not let them know we're here."

"OK," she said. "We'll go slowly and quietly."

Sadi let Mr. Smith lead the way and they slowly approached the final bend in the road before coming into view of the car, the source of light. At the turn, Sadi stopped and turned to Mr. Smith.

"I can see better than you," she said. "Wait here while I have a look."

She left Mr. Smith on the side of the muddy dirt road and crept closer to the turn so she could investigate the scene. At the first view, her mind struggled to interpret the chemical signals from her eyes. She saw a large SUV with red brake lights illuminating the trees on the side of the road, then Gerald and Freddy. When she recognized Gerald, he turned and made eye contact with her. He started walking forward to meet her so she ran back to Mr. Smith.

"Gerald's coming," she said and held onto his arm again. "It appears safe. Let's go meet them."

"Freddy's with him?"

"I saw them both," she answered then started leading him around the turn.

They met Gerald after coming into view of the light.

"What happened?" she asked then looked past him to the dark blue Ford Explorer parked on the side of the road.

The light from its red tail lights flooded the scene in an eerie glow. The passenger door hung open and a leg dangled out the side, along with an arm. Through the open door, Sadi noticed another man in the passenger's seat. Freddy leaned against the vehicle, over the body and appeared to be searching for something.

"When I got here," Gerald began and started walking toward the vehicle. "These guys were in their car, ready to drive away, but that flying thing hovered over their windshield and shone strange lights on them. That's when they went unconscious. Then the probe got very bright and started floating up above the trees. It got so bright, I had to close my eyes."

"Do you know who they are?" asked Mr. Smith.

"I don't know," Gerald answered. "Freddy's been looking through all their things. He won't talk to me. I don't know what he's looking for. Maybe you can talk to him?"

Mr. Smith walked slowly past Sadi and Gerald, and approached the vehicle where Freddy bent over the unconscious driver. Before he arrived close enough, Freddy backed out of the car, holding a gun in the air and Mr. Smith stopped. Freddy turned to face them, the gun gripped firmly in his right hand, pointed to the sky. Mr. Smith spoke first.

"Freddy," he said slowly. "What's going on?"

In the following moment of silence, Sadi realized the rain had stopped.

"Do you know who these men are?" Freddy asked and glanced briefly back to the car. He spoke more confidently and forcefully than normal.

"I have no idea," the old man said.

"Do you Mr. Fuger?" Freddy asked after turning to Gerald. He kept eye contact with Gerald while awaiting for his answer when he would have normally looked away.

"They're probably the FBI agents, keeping track of me. They want to catch me doing something illegal."

"Do you know that they can ruin all your plans, and put some of your friends in prison, or worse?"

Sadi noticed Gerald's body become rigid while answering, but his tone remained casual.

"Yes, I know."

"These men are in a position to take away our freedom at least. That is certain."

"Unfortunately, they always have that option."

Freddy pointed the gun to the unconscious man's head.

"We would be justified in taking their lives."

The corners of Freddy's mouth straightened and his index finger tightened on the trigger. Sadi gulped. Her eyes opened wide.

"Freddy," she said. "What are you doing?"

"That may be true," Gerald interjected, ignoring Sadi for the moment. "But you're the one with his finger on the trigger."

"We are all in the same predicament," Freddy said.

He kept the gun steady.

Mr. Smith turned to Gerald and Sadi, the red brake lights highlighting every wrinkle on his face. He spoke with anger in his voice.

"What is going on here? Who are you two with?"

Gerald chose to ignore Mr. Smith and kept his focus on Freddy.

"That is not our only option!" he pleaded as though Freddy pointed a gun at his mother. "If we kill them, it would be almost impossible to remove all traces linking us to their deaths. Their car probably has a tracking device on it. They would be led right to this spot and they'd find evidence linking us to them. We don't have any credible alibi."

"But it might give you enough time to accomplish your goal."

"There's got to be another option," Sadi said.

As much as she abhorred the idea of killing the unconscious men, she experienced difficulty disagreeing with Freddy's conclusion. If someone threatened her freedom, she had the right to defend herself and her daughter. Instead of killing the men, she would rather overdose them on some drug to destroy their memory of the evening, but they had no such drugs with them.

"Fortunately for them, we will spare their lives," Freddy said, smiling strangely. After lowering the gun, he wiped the trigger and grip of the gun with his sleeve then reached over the men and put the gun back in the car glove box. He turned back to Sadi and sighed. "Sadi, give me the crystal."

Sadi slowly approached the car and saw the other unconscious man in the passenger seat more clearly. Both men lay against their seats, facing forward with closed eyes. They wore jeans and t-shirts. In the darkness, their features were indiscernible. As she came closer, she feared to make any noise and fought the urge to run the other way. Would her proximity wake them?

She removed the crystal from her pocket and extended her right hand to Freddy, the crystal in her open palm. After taking the crystal, he held the object close to the man's face like a mirror, an inch from his nose. Sadi jumped back when blue and orange lights shot towards the man like electric arcs in a plasma. The light connected to the man's eyes, holding steady for about twenty seconds and reflecting off Freddy's face like the flames of a flickering fire. The man sat up suddenly with the light still connected to his eyes. Everyone except Freddy stepped back.

The man sat motionless until the lights slowly dissipated into nothingness and then fell back into his seat again, unconscious. Freddy moved around the SUV to the next man and performed the same operation on him. When the lights disappeared, Freddy remained motionless, staring at the dark crystal. Mr. Smith stepped to the open driver door, resting his frame on the cane.

"Freddy? Are you OK?"

At the sound of Mr. Smith's voice, Freddy turned from the crystal, a glazed look in his eyes. When he spoke, he no longer had the same tone of confidence and authority in his voice. He talked as if confused and almost afraid, but aware of the surroundings.

"Mr. Smith, you should not be in the cold like this," he said finally. "You will get sick."

Freddy closed the passenger door and returned to the driver seat. He lifted the man's hand and leg into the vehicle, then shut the door.

"Freddy," said Mr. Smith quietly. "Will you explain to me, to us, what is going on?"

"I will try to explain it all, but after we get out of here." He gently placed his hand on the old man's upper arm and started walking tentatively down the way back to the barn. "We should not be here when they wake up."

Sadi and Gerald stepped in line behind Freddy and followed them back to the barn. Sadi wanted to ask Gerald about what happened, but decided to postpone her questions until they could talk confidentially. On the walk, no one spoke. Sadi listened carefully for evidence of the bears.

"I parked at the back," Freddy said after they arrived at the barn.

He led them to his car behind the barn, a two-door hatchback which looked like a Subaru. He opened the passenger door for Mr. Smith.

"We'll just follow you," Sadi said.

"Come back to my house," said Mr. Smith before letting Freddy shut the door. "We all need to talk about what happened here tonight."

His tone reminded Sadi of her father, when he used to scold her. She felt guilt for not telling the old man everything. When they entered the car and began following Freddy on the dirt road, she felt safe for the first time since reaching the barn.

70

Sadi

On the drive back to Mr. Smith's house, Sadi just wanted to go home, see Helen, lay in bed, and wait for the next day to ask all her questions. She felt emotionally and physically exhausted. For the first few minutes, they drove in silence and enjoyed the comfort of being on the dry side of the glass. She watched the trees flying past the car and water drops sliding sideways across the glass. Eventually, the heat increased enough to drive all the cold from her bones, even through her wet clothes.

Gerald broke the silence first.

"Well, we know one thing," he said, and Sadi detected a bit of triumph in his voice.

"What is that?"

"We're not dealing with ghosts here."

He turned to her and his smile soon vanished. Sadi gulped.

"So what are we dealing with?" she asked without wanting to hear his answer out loud.

"That thing was not from Earth," he said as a statement, not conjecture.

"Some kind of alien spaceship?"

"They're either tiny little guys," he said, sneering. "Or, that thing was some kind of probe."

"It couldn't be a military thing? Could it?"

She doubted whether the government had any device so advanced.

"It's probably safe to assume," he began, "that if the government had that sort of thing, they wouldn't need regular humans tracking us as well."

"Unless those guys were the ones controlling it," she said gravely.

"Then why would it chase them to the car and knock them out? I saw it. They were scared to death."

"Good point," she agreed. What answer scared her the most? Aliens or her fellow humans? "Any ideas about what it wants? For some reason, that probe or whoever controlled it, wanted us there."

"From what you told me of Freddy, the spider in the crystal was designed specifically for him, something he couldn't resist." He turned from the road, making momentary eye contact. "What is Freddy normally like? Does he always have multiple personalities?"

Sadi recalled Freddy holding the gun to the man's head.

"He's normally shy and timid."

"That's not what I saw."

"After Freddy put the gun away, he looked scared, almost normal."

“Well, he seems to know where we are,” said Gerald after the next moment of silence. “Maybe he has GPS? I still don’t know where we are. Do you?”

“Not yet,” she said and tried to laugh, but failed. “I’m still trying to figure it out.”

She looked outside again, but saw only trees and an overcast night sky. Eventually, she would see a sign and know their location. She desperately wanted to call Jen and hold Helen, and feel normal again.

Sadi considered asking Gerald what he saw under the influence of the lights, but then she might have to share more of her dream. Did she want to share such a personal experience? What would he think of her? She decided to ask anyway.

“What happened to you in the barn, after that thing came to us?”

He looked over to her momentarily, then back to the road. He spoke slowly, as if searching for the right words.

“I had a dream, a very disturbing dream. I did not like it.”

“Do you remember it well?” she asked casually with her eyes on the road ahead of them. “I’ll understand if you don’t want to talk about it.”

“I really just want to forget it,” he said and smiled. “Maybe we can talk about it another time.”

“I can understand that.”

“You had one too?" he asked as a statement and not a question. “About your son?”

“Yes. I don’t want to talk about it either,” she said and laughed. “But what do you think the dreams meant? Did that thing give us the dreams or was it just a natural reaction to the light?”

“I think it was testing us,” Gerald said without hesitation. He tightened his grip on the steering wheel and stretched his arms. “Freddy was testing us too, I think.”

A new thought hit her mind like a hammer, an idea inspired from a television show she used to watch. In the show, creatures took people into the water, killed them and made clones then returned the clones back into society. At first, the clones felt confusion and disorientation, unaware of what happened to them. She remembered enjoying the show, but now cursed herself for filling her head with such irrational ideas, digging its claws into her mind and interfering with her capacity for rational thought. She needed to remain rational.

“A test, huh?” she said, pressing her lips together. “I’ll have to think about that.”

“Have you ever thought about us being guests here on Earth?” he asked after a few seconds. “Maybe our real home is out there, somewhere?”

“Are you talking about religion?”

“Not really. I’m talking about the origin of our species being from somewhere else.”

“The thought might have crossed my mind once or twice.” How did he want her to respond? Memories of the cave and the joy of her escape inspired her next question. “Are you religious?”

“No,” he said emphatically. “Are you?”

“I don’t know,” she answered. She usually avoided thoughts of religion and usually abhorred talking about the subject due to its inconsistency with her reality. Religion always brought painful memories. Her father would often use the deadly weapons of religion, guilt, and fear, to get what he wanted. "My parents are Christians and I've always considered myself one. We would go a few times a year, but my brother and I stopped when we moved out. The last time I went into a church was for my son's funeral."

"Not a very good association, I would guess," he said after a moment of silence. "Religion puts a bitter taste in my mouth."

"My brother and I used to joke about being anti-Christian," she said in an attempt to lighten the mood. "You probably wouldn't understand."

"I can understand that," he said and smiled. "I used to be anti-establishment, or at least that's what I thought. It was exciting going to protests, fighting the evil corporations, the greedy capitalists."

"That's funny," she said. "Now you're a lawyer, defending them. Just kidding. If you weren't anti-establishment back then, what were you?"

"Just someone in search of purpose I guess, like most of the young. The real leaders of the world always provide the young with a distraction to fall behind. Most people end up joining what they're fighting against. It would be nice if more people could use their brains and consider the possibility of false-opposition."

"Reminds me of watching the news lately," Sadi said, glad for the change of topic. She still felt unprepared to discuss the events of the night. "It's all about the protesters blaming Wall Street, but Wall Street was just following the path paved by the government, like water down a canal. It's frustrating to watch. I usually have to turn it off."

"I know what you mean," he said. "The news and entertainment industry spend a lot of effort blaming capitalism and greed, and never the real root causes of the problems."

"Government," Sadi finished for him.

"What made you see the light?"

"I went to work with an international aid group in Kivu, the Congo," he began. "What I saw made me sick, but really opened my eyes."

He paused and Sadi wondered if he planned to continue.

"What happened?" she finally asked.

"What everyone sees on TV or in the movies of third world countries, is all about the poor and the destitute, receiving food and clothing from rich westerners. What they don't see is all the money and supplies that our wonderful government and corporations give to the corrupt governments. The people get just enough to eat, so they don't revolt. The governments, however, get all the financial support they need to keep the people in their present condition. That's the truth I discovered, and then it went downhill from there, to the history of our country, the history of religion, and learning about those who control the money supply. The whole thing used to make me so angry. Now, I try to focus on making a better future."

"What's the purpose? How do we benefit from keeping them in poverty?"

To hear about the corruption from someone with direct experience made the story feel more real and not just some news report. She always felt sad and angry that the government forced her to help fund the cause of so much sorrow.

"Large companies from Western countries, and China and Russia even, get access to the target country's natural resources at very low cost, but they have absolutely no incentive to raise the people's standard of living because that would increase labor costs."

"In a free market system, the corporations wouldn't be able to get away with it. There would be too many competitors, but thanks to governments, large corporations have fewer competitors. On the other side of the coin, big banks make huge loans to these countries because they know the loans will be repaid by the governments they control, funded by you and me of course. Those that profit from the financial system are the only winners."

"Don't you love the circular nature of it all? The absolute best part is that we're stuck with the final bill, in the form of inflation and taxation."

"And my children and grandchildren will pick up the tab when I'm gone," Sadi finished. "At least, we benefit from it now, right?"

"*We*," he said and emphasized the word. "You and I don't benefit from it at all."

"Sorry," Sadi said, forgetting to be precise with her choice of words. "You can't say we don't get any benefit from it. I mean, the things we buy are cheaper right? Americans who work for these companies get some of the profit. I'm not saying it's a good thing, but 'we' do benefit from it."

Sadi smiled and wondered if he would scold her again for the repeated use of 'we', when the word usually referred to an ambiguous group of individuals.

"In the end," he answered. "I would say we, you and I, pay more for it through taxes and inflation and wars and not to mention all the bloodshed and suffering. Overall, the only net winners are the corporation owners and the banks. The majority of the people like you and I, are always the net losers."

"Well, in the short term, we benefit," she said, refusing to agree completely. "But I see your point."

In the following silence, Sadi attempted to stop thinking about their conversation and the strange events of the past few weeks, and focus on seeing Helen and Jen again, to restore some form of normality to her life. Could she ever return to her fantasy world again, a world where decent people toiled to keep her family and friends safe from the thieves, murderers, rapists and human traffickers? Now, Sadi had found another threat to her imaginary world, that probe.

Humans liked to imagine a comfortable world. They unconsciously suppressed information which contradicted their imaginary fantasy land. Sadi fought the same temptation and also the natural urge to let others deal with problems and find answers. The public education system never taught her how to think for herself, but to accept prepackaged explanations and solutions. Sadi had taught herself how to gather evidence and make her own conclusions.

The establishment manufactured a self-promoting version of reality, the official version where generous humans and governments provided necessities to poor people and labored to provide education and security. The feel-good story allowed the average citizen of planet Earth to continue with their lives, worship their gods and ultimately allow the establishment to continue without significant opposition.

"You and I can't stop it," he said sadly. "Those who try to stop it are ridiculed, marginalized and even killed. People are fools to think we can stop it. If we can just educate the masses, they say. I'm sick of trying to educate people. We need to take more immediate action. We need to band together. I want to live in a society with people like you and me."

Sadi made no answer, but just nodded.

On the remainder of the return trip, they traveled in silence and Sadi watched lights, trees and buildings fly past her sight. Her mind returned to the experiences of the night and then what Freddy might reveal to them. Finally, they pulled onto a familiar road, highway twenty-six heading southeast. They would soon be passing the road leading to her house. As they passed the turn, she wondered when she could go home.

71

Sadi

They arrived at Mr. Smith's house at twenty minutes past midnight. Sadi and Gerald went inside and waited in the same room in which they first had waited when the evening began. Sadi found her purse on the couch. Ten messages blinked on her phone, four from her brother and the rest from Jen. She dreaded listening to them so she decided to call instead.

She excused herself from the room as she entered the number to Jen's cell phone. While waiting to hear the sounds of a connection she hoped Jen chose to not call the police, making an official record with the authorities of the abnormality. Jen answered the phone immediately.

"Oh my God," Jen said with panic in her voice. "Sadi, where are you?"

Sadi felt too exhausted and made no effort to make up a story.

"We're fine Jen," she said quickly and then slowed her speech, hoping to indicate a stable situation. "Everything's OK. Sorry to worry you, but I can't talk about it now. I'll tell you the story when I get back."

She had no intention of telling Jen the story, or even a tiny part of the real situation. She planned to concoct a plausible explanation on the way home. As a lawyer, Gerald could help engineer a believable explanation to cover any subsequent questions.

"OK, I'll wait for you to get home," she said with a tone of relief. Before Sadi could respond, Jen became excited. "Your brother called several times. Have you called him yet? Want me to call him for you?"

"Yes, that would be nice." Sadi felt a strong urge to return to the room with the others, but she could not cut the connection yet. "Is Helen asleep?"

"Yes," Jen said flatly.

"You didn't call the police did you?"

"I was going to give you another hour then I planned to call."

"I should be home in a couple hours, so just go to bed and we can talk in the morning."

Jen would probably wait for her anyway. When she returned to the room, Gerald still waited alone. He sat erect and breathed steadily as though his energy had returned. Did she look as undisturbed?

"I wish I felt like you look," she said. "I'm exhausted, and you look like you just took a shower and are ready for the day."

"It's kind of exciting," he said and smiled. "Now that we're out of the elements, back in a warm and comfortable mansion, I feel better. To think we actually came in contact with an alien, and it didn't kill or abduct us! That's pretty lucky."

"An alien is not the only option," she said, amazed that he looked for humor in the situation. "It's the most likely explanation, but we should keep our minds open to other possibilities."

"Agreed," he said, still smiling. "But for now, let's just go with the alien explanation because it is the most likely, in my mind at least."

"Ok, so where does it lead us?" she asked. "What does it want?"

"Well, it's not the typical alien invader you see in the movies, the ones where they want to kill humans and take our resources." Gerald shifted in his seat. "At the time, I was scared, I have to admit. Scared out of my mind. However, thinking back on it, the probe did not threaten us. Did you feel that it was malevolent in any way?"

Sadi considered his question. Her dream or vision felt more like a test rather than an experience meant to intimidate, scare or manipulate her. Her dream involved familiar experiences on Earth and of humanity, not of space and alien creatures. When she decided to escape the artificial cave and move toward the light again, she felt like her life had a purpose. Escaping the dark cave felt like passing a test, accomplishing an important feat. She smiled at the memory of entering the light, but also felt the anguish of seeing her son. He tormented her dreams, never within reach.

"No, I don't think it was malevolent," she said finally.

"Since it used Freddy to contact us, I think,..."

Gerald stopped talking when he heard Freddy and Mr. Smith approaching from the hallway. Both he and Sadi turned their heads to the entrance of the room. The old man entered first, followed closely by Freddy. He looked exhausted, more than Mr. Smith even. They both sat next to each other on the same couch. The scene reminded Sadi of a parent bringing her child to a store clerk to return a stolen piece of candy. He looked embarrassed. She felt pity for him. Her doubts about his identity evaporated.

"We've discussed it," Mr. Smith began. "Tonight is not the night to discuss everything. I think we're all too tired, especially Freddy."

"We understand," Sadi said in total agreement.

While waiting for Freddy and Mr. Smith to return, Sadi had allowed an unconscious tension to build. She drew a deep breath and felt the tension dissipate.

"OK, but before we go," cut in Gerald abruptly. "Freddy, can you tell us quickly what that thing was? We can discuss the whole thing tomorrow."

They all turned to Freddy, even Mr. Smith. Freddy looked to the ground.

"I am very sorry that all this happened," he said and then looked up at each of them. He opened his hand, displaying the crystal with the spider. "The crystal was a gift from my sister which I could not refuse, because I desperately wanted it. Perhaps if I refused the temptation, all this would not have happened."

"Don't blame yourself, Freddy," Sadi said. "There's no way anyone would have expected this."

"Like Mr. Smith said," interjected Gerald. He spoke politely and compassionately, but Sadi heard impatience in his voice. "We can discuss all the details and conjecture later. We all just want to know what you think that thing was."

"Something controls it, controls this," Freddy looked to his palm and gently transferred the crystal to his other hand. "It is not human, but I do not know if we can call it an alien. I do not know what it is or what it wants. It knows everything about me, I think already."

Freddy stopped speaking and the silence seemed to consume the room.

"Do you remember what happened?" Sadi asked, leaning forward. Curiosity overpowered her desire to leave. "Were you being controlled by it tonight?"

"It did not control me. It is hard to explain," Freddy said, briefly looking into her eyes. "After waking up in that barn, I could see our predicament in perfect clarity, the probe and the FBI agents outside. I saw the entire situation from every angle imaginable. I had all the information I needed to make an informed decision. Your thoughts and potential actions were all in front of me."

"Were you given any information about the group I represent?" Gerald asked. "What do you remember?"

When Freddy spoke again, he looked to the ground and seemed unaware of anyone else in the room.

"I felt like a different person, but it was me. It was me. I do not know what to think. I am sorry."

"Do you know anything about my friends?" asked Gerald again. "Please, whatever you know needs to be kept confidential."

"I'm sorry, Mr. Fuger," interrupted Mr. Smith. "It's time for you to go. Freddy needs to rest. We'll call tomorrow and we can arrange another visit. Come on Freddy, it's been a long couple of days hasn't it?"

Mr. Smith placed his cane on the floor and Freddy helped him stand. Before Gerald could ask again, Sadi stood and spoke.

"Of course," she said. "We understand."

"Goodnight Sadi," said Freddy. He paused as if wanting to say something else, but then changed his mind and left the room without looking back. "Goodnight Mr. Fuger."

"I'm just an old man," he began while walking them to the door. "My time on Earth is nearly over so I don't plan on getting involved with what you're doing. That thing we saw is obviously something for the young to handle. I don't know what your group is involved in, but you better not hurt Freddy. He's all I've got."

"We don't want to hurt anyone, especially Freddy." Sadi put her hand on his shoulder. "Believe me. He's a very good friend of mine and I would never hurt him."

"I believe you," Mr. Smith said. "Let's talk tomorrow. Have a goodnight."

72

Sadi

April 11, 2009

Sadi woke up the next morning around nine to a bedroom full of the foggy, diffused light of a hazy outside. The warmth and comfort of her bed contrasted with the cold, wet memories of the previous evening. She never slept that late, even on a Saturday. When Gerald delivered her home, she had offered him a place to stay, but he'd insisted on going back to his hotel room. He'd already paid for the night and did not want to impose. She felt too much physical and emotional exhaustion to worry about any implications.

She hurried down the stairs to the ground floor to see Jen with her laptop computer opened on the bar in the kitchen and Helen sitting in front of the television in the adjacent living room. Helen saw Sadi first.

"Hi Mom," she said without showing any concern or curiosity about any abnormal activity.

Jen had successfully kept Helen unaware of her mother's long absence. Sadi felt grateful for that.

"Good morning dear."

She knelt on the ground in front of Helen and hugged her for longer than normal after just a night's separation. While holding her daughter, Sadi remembered the experience in the cave and shivered at the thought of releasing Helen's hand in the darkness. Thankfully, eye contact with her daughter helped to melt the horror of the experience. The memory of her son attempted to force its way into her conscious thoughts, but she pushed that thought away. She lacked the energy to think about her son or what the dream might mean. She needed food.

"Gonna tell me what you were doing last night?" asked Jen, looking up from her laptop. "Did you forget your phone or something?"

Sadi already had a story prepared, without Gerald's help, an explanation very close to the truth.

"I'm really sorry Jen," she said with an apologetic tone. "The friend that visited on Tuesday with Brian, was missing. His employer was really worried and asked for our help. We met at his house and then went out all night looking for him. Both Gerald and I left our phones at his house, and his employer did not have one. We didn't think we would be gone that long."

The possibility of two adults simultaneously forgetting their phones seemed highly unlikely, but they really did forget their phones. Sadi wanted to include as much of the truth in the story as possible. Since she also planned to spend more time with Gerald anyway, her story needed to include him and be consistent with any future activities. In any event, would distorting reality ultimately keep Helen and Jen safe?

"Who is this Gerald guy?"

"He's a lawyer and wants me for some consulting work, and I also thought, I might ask him for some legal advice for Freddy who was a former ward of the state. His mother and sister might make trouble for him, so he might need some legal representation."

To complicate the situation and hopefully divert Jen's attention, Sadi purposefully added the legal information which should help shift the focus away from the events of the previous night. Jen held Sadi's gaze for a few seconds before acquiescing and returning attention to her laptop. Sadi stared at the back of Jen's head for a moment, pondering several questions. Did Jen question the completeness of her story and just lack the strength to challenge her? Should employees question the motives of their employers? Why did she care?

For the next couple of hours, Sadi followed her usual routine in an attempt to temporarily forget about the previous evening. She needed a break from the memories, needed to put them in the back of her mind and heal from the damage to normalcy. She could resume trying to understand the implications of recent events when they visited Freddy again.

When she checked the website just after eleven, she found a message from Aristarchus.

Aristarchus: Call me whenever, or just respond and I'll be over.

Did Gerald choose that username or did his inventor friend? Did she also choose 'Iris' as Sadi's username? When would Sadi meet the inventor?

Before responding, she considered the implications of his visit. If he met Jen, the girl would undoubtedly have more questions about their true relationship. That result seemed inevitable. She decided to just send an electronic response.

While waiting for Gerald to arrive, Sadi washed a load of laundry. As she chose the wash settings, Jen appeared in the laundry room, excitement showing in her wide, brown eyes.

"Sadi, you have to come see this. It's amazing."

Sadi started the washing machine then followed Jen out of the room. At first, her heart raced with panic at what might have aroused such excitement. Her mind began to associate excitement and recent events, strange metal objects hovering in the air, inches from her face.

"What is it?" Sadi asked after arriving in the kitchen.

"It's a video of this amazing singer in the UK. Her name's Susan Boyle."

Sadi sighed in silent relief and smiled. Jen often experienced tremendous excitement when she discovered an interesting video on the internet. Sadi usually gave her best effort to appreciate them and refrain from criticizing too much. Jen's laptop lay open on the bar. The Firefox internet browser showed a YouTube video on pause.

Sadi watched as a man named Simon Cowell, one of the judges of the talent show, introduced a slightly overweight woman on a stage with maybe a thousand people watching in the audience. Sadi enjoyed the singing performance, but the melodramatic reactions of the audience and judges provoked a strong desire to laugh out loud. She shook her head slightly and tried to smile as if the performance impressed her half as much as it impressed the audience.

"Wow!" Sadi said when the video stopped. "She's really good."

"Isn't she? Look how many hits this has gotten so far."

"Doesn't really sound like your kind of music," she said, hoping to divert attention from the reaction of the crowd. "Are you going to buy anything from her?"

Jen turned her attention from the screen.

"No, but that was awesome, right?"

"Pretty amazing," she said flatly, but smiled wider.

"You're not impressed," Jen said, frowning and rolling her eyes melodramatically. "Alright, spit it out. I can tell you want to ruin this, like everything else I get excited about."

"No, I really do think she's a good singer, but don't you see what they're trying to do?"

"Let me guess," she said sarcastically. "She's not actually singing? It's a recording?"

"No, but you are being duped!" Sadi suppressed her genuine smile, but not entirely. "Her performance is real, but how they're showing the reaction of the crowd and judges is to manipulate your reaction. The show could have chosen any decent singer and put them in the same position and you would have had the same reaction. It's just a marketing strategy to sell a product. That's how the entertainment industry works. They give this woman a lot of exposure to make her famous and then a bunch of people will buy her songs."

"Well, I think she's a good singer," Jen said indignantly.

"Come on, push play. I want to hear it again."

Sadi laughed affectionately and placed her hand on Jen's shoulder.

"No you don't," Jen answered, faking emotional damage, but failing to hide a smile. She clicked the play button and they listened to the song again without any further discussion.

Sadi usually noticed attempts by the media to manipulate the public and she became even more sensitive to them after meeting Gerald. Correspondence with Gerald increased her skepticism of the world. She suspected ulterior motives in almost everything. Would her paranoia grow out of control after the alien encounter? Would she feel debilitating paranoia, make false conclusions or see false connections?

Gerald arrived at a few minutes before two in the afternoon. When Jen heard the door open and his voice, she came downstairs from her room and pretended to look in the refrigerator for something to eat. Sadi knew her true intentions, to spy on her new male friend. While living together, she and Jen became almost like sisters, more than the normal employee-employer relationship. Sadi knew how Jen thought.

"Gerald," she said in introduction. "This Jen Andrews, Helen's nanny."

While Jen gave Gerald a rather long and comprehensive visual inspection, Sadi averted her eyes to avoid the temptation of laughing.

"Good to meet you, Jen," he said. "I'm Gerald Fuger."

Gerald walked inside and Sadi shut the door. Jen nodded in approval, smiling deviously. Behind his back, she stuck both thumbs in the air for extra emphasis. Sadi said, 'shut up' with tight eyes.

"I hope you don't mind," he said loud enough for Jen to hear clearly. "I called Mr. Smith an hour ago and he is expecting us anytime. He says Freddy is ready to talk now. Oh, and we shouldn't eat before we come over."

"Oh good, thanks. Let's leave now then."

Sadi acted appreciatively but inwardly felt a small, but strange annoyance that he would call Mr. Smith. She had more of a relationship to the situation than he did. Did she feel a need for more control over the situation or just dislike the idea of following his lead?

"I was hoping to meet your daughter, Helen."

"Of course," she said and the request dissolved her annoyance. She turned to Jen.

"I'll go get her," Jen said and ran upstairs, quickly disappearing from sight. A few moments later, she returned with Helen hiding behind her back.

"Why are you being so shy?" Sadi asked. Helen peeked around Jen and looked at Gerald with irritation. Jen probably forced her to leave some activity.

"Hi Helen," he said, smiling and crouching down to her level. "Wise choice to not trust me. I'm a lawyer."

His joke failed to earn even a small smile. Helen strained to keep her lips as straight as possible and Sadi waited impatiently for her daughter to say something embarrassing.

"You're not funny," Helen said without emotion.

Sadi frowned, but Jen snorted a laugh.

"Well it was nice to meet you too," he answered without showing any indication of emotional damage. He remained crouched. "Do you know why I love kids?"

"No," Helen said. "Why?"

"Because children always tell the truth. In my line of work, that's very refreshing."

Helen looked at him then to her mother.

"I guess it was good to meet you," she said, then began slowly walking backwards, towards the stairs.

73

Sadi

At Freddy's house, Mr. Smith opened the door just as Gerald began knocking. The sight of him restored all her memories of the previous evening. Sadi had begun to think of the night as a dream like the cave, but at that moment, the reality of the memories felt like a slap across the face.

Mr. Smith led them straight into the dining room and shut the doors so that Sadi felt totally isolated from the rest of the house and the world even. A large platter of food sat on the huge table in front of her, containing raw vegetables, fruits, sandwiches and several dips. The setup looked a bit unbalanced, a simple spread of food set in a lavish dining room. Freddy asked what they wanted to drink and then quickly filled their ornate crystal glasses with their drink of choice.

"I dispensed with my cook and the other staff a few years before Freddy came," Mr. Smith explained.

"After retiring from the government and my other activities, I found it unnecessary to keep them since it was just myself and I didn't care about impressing anyone anymore. You must forgive Freddy for this inelegant assortment. He thinks more about substance than the display."

"Most people like sandwiches, and vegetables are good for you," said Freddy, looking to both Gerald and Sadi. His eyes lingered on Sadi longer.

Sadi sat by Gerald on one side of the table while Freddy and his boss sat on the other side. The setup reminded her of a job interview, but with food instead of paperwork.

"Thanks for lunch," said Sadi.

"Yes, thank you," Gerald quickly agreed. "It looks good and I'm hungry."

"It is the least I can do after what you all went through last night, for me."

"What exactly did happen last night?" Gerald asked before they could continue with more chitchat. "How did it all start?"

"What do you mean?" asked Freddy. "How did I get to the place you found me, that barn?"

"That's a good place to start."

"I finished with my lab," he began and set the crystal on the table in front of him. The surface shimmered with a rainbow of refracted color. For a moment, they all stared at the crystal in silence.

"I wanted to know what this was all about so I thought that maybe if I went to a place, far away from civilization, something different might happen."

"What were you expecting?" asked Gerald.

The scene reminded Sadi of cop television shows where police officers interviewed suspects in an interrogation room. Would Freddy feel too much anxiety with so many eyes focused on him? The crystal on the table soon became a great distraction. Sadi split her concentration between attempting to look away from the table and waiting for a light to appear. Would she see a bright light and then wake in a strange place? Hopefully, the closed door would prevent the probe from appearing.

"If I was away from anyone else, out somewhere by myself, perhaps whoever, or whatever controls this thing would come to me."

"That's a pretty brave thing to do," Sadi interjected. The thought of entering the barn with the probe and the bears put a chill in her blood and caused Sadi to shudder, even in the warm room. "I wouldn't have dared try that alone."

"Not very smart if you ask me," said Mr. Smith, with the hint of a scolding tone, "but, we already had that discussion."

Freddy looked to his hands on the table as if Mr. Smith's words caused shame, but then quickly continued.

"I could not keep this from my thoughts, every time I closed my eyes, it was all I could think about. It told me to visit you, Sadi, so I did, but I was afraid to show you, Mr. Smith. I had to find some answers."

"Did you get answers?" Sadi asked.

"I drove west, past Buxton," he continued. "I felt strange while driving, like being put on cruise control and seeing the car steer by itself, only I remember steering. I can only describe the journey as walking in the dark with only the step ahead illuminated. I wanted to follow the light."

"So, it led you by controlling the available information." Gerald spoke more to himself than to Freddy. "That's interesting."

"It was dark when I finally got out of the car," said Freddy, undeterred by Gerald's comment. "I walked alone into that barn and then the probe appeared, right in front of my face. That is when my vision went black."

Freddy looked up from the table, and made eye contact with Sadi. She recalled the time when he stood outside the Ford Explorer and pointed the gun at the government agent's head.

"It took me on a journey in my mind."

"Where did it take you?" asked Gerald as he leaned forward.

"We traveled toward the sun," he said and his eyes grew wide. "We went to Mercury I think, to some structure and then crashed into it, into a black tunnel filled with light. I cannot accurately explain the experience."

"Does this structure actually exist?" Sadi asked and shivered at the mention of a dark tunnel. "Because when the probe came to me, I had a dream, at least Gerald and I did. Nothing in my dream was real."

"I do not know," he said. "I think it is real though."

"Were you told why? Why you?"

"I do not know. I think it wants me to go there. I think that is why it wanted me to visit Sadi, so I could come into contact with your group."

Mr. Smith sat forward as if on cue, as if Freddy gave him the baton to take the lead of the conversation.

"Before we go any further, it's your turn to talk."

Gerald and Sadi looked at each other for a moment then he returned his attention to Mr. Smith.

"I don't really have a choice do I?"

"I don't need too many details."

"She's gonna kill me," he said quietly, taking a deep breath. "A friend of mine came to me with an invention of hers. It can take us into space and revolutionize the aerospace industry."

He neglected to mention the fusion reactor.

"They're looking for people who share the same beliefs," Sadi interrupted before Mr. Smith could ask a subsequent question. "People interested in ending our oppressive system."

"If you haven't noticed," Gerald continued. "The Earth is run by some really dangerous psychopaths and there's no place to escape their influence."

Gerald sat against the back of his chair and let his words sink into the minds of his audience. During their statements, Mr. Smith stared at their faces, listening intently, but Freddy shifted his attention between them and the crystal on the table.

"After what Freddy told me, what you say fails to surprise me." Unexpectedly, the old man chuckled as he talked. "So am I right to assume that you need to keep this from the government, from the military I imagine?"

"Exactly," said Gerald. "I'm only telling you because of this alien incident. Now, we all share dangerous secrets."

"We don't know it was an alien," Sadi interjected.

"You wouldn't have told me," said the old man and laughed again, with more sarcasm, "if you knew my identity."

"Your identity?" asked Sadi. When she turned to Gerald, she saw the same confused expression that she felt herself. "Are you someone different than who you told us?"

Mr. Smith's eyes narrowed.

"I did not lie to you. My full name is William Benjamin Smith."

He paused after speaking and silence filled the room.

His name meant nothing special to Sadi. Gerald touched his chin with his right hand and looked up at the wall, but made no verbal indication of recognition. After a moment of waiting, Mr. Smith continued.

"I am the former Secretary of Agriculture for the federal government, part of the presidential cabinet. I'm one of the dangerous people you mentioned, at least I used to be."

"Really!" said Sadi in surprise, feeling a momentary panic, as if she just confessed all her secrets to the chief of police. His calm expression, however, erased the sensation of panic.

"Your name does sound a little familiar, but what do you mean, you used to be one of the dangerous ones?"

When the old man sat back in his chair, Sadi knew he planned to give them a detailed explanation. Both she and Gerald sat in silence as he talked. His story had a similar trance-like effect as the multicolored lights of the probe. After many years in different government positions, he became the Secretary of Agriculture.

Mr. Smith had acquired a lot of money in his positions due to all the government subsidies distributed to farmers and corporations, especially those he owned. He became very proficient at enacting laws which transferred vast amounts of money from the general public. He had acquired friends almost at the same rate and helped them receive a disproportionate amount of government handouts.

Personally, Mr. Smith owned thousands of acres in north and south America. Currently, his son governed most of the business and planned to take complete control when his father finally died. His son eagerly waited for that day.

"If I could, I'd sign it all over to you Freddy, but you'd never survive my son's wrath, or the wrath of his friends. You would literally be dead in less than a month."

Mr. Smith shook his head in disgust, but Freddy appeared untroubled by the announcement. When he spoke again, he addressed Gerald.

"Yes, you are correct, Mr. Fuger. There are very dangerous people running this world."

Mr. Smith then described all the guilt he had experienced from the years of stealing money from the public to give to his friends and the friends of his fellow politicians. He required several years after leaving government service to finally accept the true purpose of his political work, stealing money from the general population via the government structure and giving the money to those with political connections.

"For almost a year," he said. "I was so depressed that my health started degrading. I spent several years afterward trying to think of ways to undo some of the damage I'd done. I finally realized that I could do nothing significant to reverse the trend. The beast is out of any single person's hands. For a long time now, I've been looking for a way to make good use of all my money. Up until now, I've been unsuccessful, and it's too late for me I'm afraid. I'm just a bitter old man."

"You are not a bitter old man," said Freddy, returning to the conversation with vitality. "I have never known anyone better."

Mr. Smith put a withered old hand on Freddy's shoulder.

"If only time could erase the past."

"Until now?" asked Gerald with narrowed eyes. "You said, up until now."

"I don't have much political clout anymore," said the old man, his gaze remaining on Freddy. "But what I do have is at Freddy's disposal. If Freddy wants to help you, I will help you too."

74

Sadi

"Let's go get some coffee," said Sadi after leaving Mr. Smith's house. "There's a Starbucks near my house. I can't go home just yet. I need some caffeine."

In addition to caffeine, Sadi needed to discuss how their new information affected Gerald's group and more importantly, her life. The interrogation of Freddy completely changed their situation. They needed to discuss the next plan of action. Sadi needed to resolve the anxiety of an extremely uncertain future. Her body and mind craved a distraction, but the desire to just go home and take Helen to the park felt like a trivial activity.

"That's a good idea," he responded.

At the coffee shop, Sadi ordered her favorite steaming hot mug of sugar, cream and caffeine. She usually saved that kind of sugar rush for special occasions and always felt guilty for inflicting her blood with such high levels of glucose, but she needed some compensation for the trauma of the previous night. Gerald ordered an iced tea and sipped the liquid during their discussion.

"What do you plan on doing next?" she asked after they sat at a table by the window facing south. Gerald held his cup with both hands and she looked outside. The sun peered through the clouds on the horizon. In less than an hour, the light would sink into the pacific ocean.

"I really don't know," he said. "I can hardly wrap my head around it. Eventually, I'll have to tell the others, but right now, I can't think of a way to do it."

"Can't you just tell them what happened?" Sadi asked. "Maybe they can help you work it out."

"I don't like bringing a case to someone until I have it figured out. Right now, we don't know how Freddy fits into the picture. Does the alien only want Freddy or all of us?"

"I know you and Freddy think it's an alien, but can we make that determination right now? It just doesn't feel right. I don't know."

"Maybe it just scares you, so you're trying to think of other explanations?"

She looked at him, ignoring the urge to reply with a tone of irritation. She disliked others assuming they knew her thoughts even if they were correct. From his tone, however, he meant no offense.

"Don't try to figure me out," she said and smiled. "For now, we can call it the alien, but I'm just not convinced."

"Sorry," he said in apology. "It's just the lawyer in me. I'm also looking at it from a different angle, I guess. The idea of an alien is kind of exciting. Maybe it's just the boy in me."

"If you had any kids," she said, "your approach would be a little more cautious."

"Probably," he admitted.

"I just feel bad for Freddy," Sadi said in an attempt to change the course of the conversation. "He looks scared. I'm going to help him figure out what's going on."

"And you'll keep me informed, right?"

"Of course!" she said and paused while swishing the sweet liquid with her tongue. "Do you know what scares me the most about it?"

"What?"

"I didn't think about it at the time, but when we were looking into that machine, what was looking back at us? I felt more concern for what it would do to me. My imagination is getting the better of me. Whatever it is, it took control of us. We just started driving like he did, and went where it wanted us to go, without any resistance. What if it's controlling Freddy? When he has that crystal, who's making his decisions? You saw how he looked at it with such intensity. Even when he looks authentic, is he being sincere?"

"Hmm," he said. "Losing control scares most everybody, but I think we need to treat this like a court case and put the creature on trial. All we can do is consider the evidence before us, and base our decisions on that. Fear can cause people to think irrationally, but I'm not saying you're acting irrationally."

"Alright, Mr. Defense Attorney," she said and her eyes widened as if accepting a challenge. "What evidence are you talking about?"

"Instead of listening to our instincts, we should listen to our senses," he said as if starting a philosophy lesson. "Most people instinctively fall back on fear and paranoia and react from that. We can only base our decisions on evidence. What do we know about this thing?"

"It did not try to hurt us," Sadi said.

"And it could have," he replied. "We know that for sure. It could have told Freddy to kill those two men and us. It could have driven us off a cliff."

"Maybe, maybe not," said Sadi, placing her cup on the table. "We just don't remember. What if we made our decisions consciously? But I agree, if it wanted to abduct us, it could have."

"Who's to say that it didn't abduct us, and perform experiments on us," Gerald said and laughed.

"You've been watching too many movies."

"I don't watch movies," Gerald replied with a hint of pride in his tone. "But I know about them. Abduction is a popular idea because it scares people. In my opinion, a creature intelligent enough to travel here is probably peaceful and might even find us boring. They would definitely find cows and pigs a less-troublesome food supply than humans."

"More meat on them," Sadi agreed.

"That wouldn't make a very exciting movie, aliens coming down in the night and stealing cows for food."

"For a guy who claims not to watch movies, you sure know a lot about alien movies," she said in mock triumph. Before he could respond to the accusation, however, she continued with a more serious tone. "What if we're just thinking like humans, but normal human motivations don't apply? It might be like a little child trying to understand two adults who are sexually attracted to each other."

"Hmm," he said, pausing for a few seconds as if the question stopped his conversational momentum. "That's an interesting concept and you're probably right, but its motivations may not matter. All that matters is what it does. Don't you think?"

"Not really," she said. "It could be acting falsely, in order to manipulate us. We shouldn't take everything at face value. That's all I'm saying."

"OK, you're probably right," he continued. "Let's finish with the evidence first and then we can try to determine its possible motives. We know it can hurt us if it wants to, and for the present, let's assume it can get us to do what it wants. For me, that gives us the leisure to act as if it means us no harm."

"For now, maybe," she said without feeling convinced.

While listening, Sadi imagined Gerald speaking to a jury and judge.

"Can Freddy be right, that it wants us to take him into space?" he asked, his eyes narrowing. "And that's why it involved us?"

Instead of answering his question, she considered an alternate scenario.

"Can we say it doesn't have the capability? It doesn't have a ship or vessel to take Freddy on its own?"

"That might be a good assumption," he said. "It's definitely technologically advanced enough to do it on its own, but... if it knows about our group, how long has it known?"

Before she could respond, he exhaled sharply and placed his cup on the table.

"Oh damn," he said with surprising irritation.

"What's wrong?"

When Gerald continued, he spoke more to himself than to Sadi.

"What if it's been directing our thoughts or actions for a long time? Maybe it gave Taylor the idea for her invention. She's not going to want to hear that. Maybe it led me to the fusion reactor?"

"Is Taylor the name of the girl who started all this?"

While waiting for his response, she recognized the tension in his facial muscles. His irritation, however, seemed to be directed at himself and not her.

"I didn't want to tell you her name yet, for your protection of course. I guess it doesn't matter, considering what we just went through."

Questions about Taylor hijacked her thoughts like an irritating but catchy song. Did Gerald feel an attraction to the girl? Sadi imagined several possible images of Taylor and attempted to fabricate images of short fat girls with greasy hair.

For the next several seconds, they both looked out the window in silence. While considering his new concern, the beautiful colors on the horizon attenuated her anxiety. She knew how he felt. She would feel extreme disappointment to be denied credit for her accomplishments. She needed to help him feel better.

"It doesn't make sense for the alien to be responsible for your group. If it wants Freddy, why bother to use you or Taylor to make the transport vessel? If it needed a human to do the work, it could have had Freddy do it easily. What about this? Take the alien, or whatever it is, out of the picture and everything happened because of you and Taylor? Would it make a difference?"

"I hope you're right," he said and laughed. His look of concern melted. "I guess it was my turn to think irrationally, but I really do think you're right."

"Freddy is really smart," she continued. "He has the resources to do whatever he wants. If the alien wanted to, it could have him build it. Maybe it's been looking for someone who could take Freddy into space with them?"

"Hmm."

While his mind processed her words, Sadi recognized relief in his eyes and then experienced a sudden realization. She accepted the possibility of an alien controlling the probe and the crystal. The idea no longer frightened her. All the stupid horror movies she watched as a kid must have warped her sense of reality. They caused an irrational and artificial fear of the unknown, an emotion which Gerald obviously lacked. She resolved to keep Helen away from any horror movies.

"When are you going to tell them?" she asked. "I mean Taylor and the others about what has been happening?"

"Let's learn more from Freddy before we tell them anything," he said while rubbing his chin. "Besides, they're very busy working on the prototype ship. They don't want any distractions."

"When am I going to meet them?"

"Once they get the prototype done, we're going to have a test flight." He drew his largest gulp of tea since taking his first sip. "I think that would be a good time. If all goes according to plan, it'll happen in a couple months. They are putting all their time and resources into it and they have no red bureaucratic tape to slow them down."

75

Sadi

For the next few minutes, Gerald talked about how Freddy might be able to help their group. At first, he thought the extra money at their disposal would completely change the situation. During the night, however, he failed to discover significant ways to use the money. They had already obtained most of what they needed and now needed mainly to focus on individual tasks. Taylor and Cesar needed to complete the prototype ship. Gerald needed to help Sadi and Freddy solve the mystery of the spider.

As she listened to Gerald, the reality of their situation began to infect her thoughts again. She needed to seriously consider her level of involvement and whether the situation potentially put Helen, her brother, or Jen in danger. Did she have the right to risk their future?

"There's something that's worrying me," she said while he paused to yawn.

"What's that?"

"At first, it was all exciting and all. You know, meeting you secretly at PF Chang's, being followed by the FBI. But after what we just went through, now it's real."

"Yes, it is."

"I've got a daughter and brother to think about," she began. "I might be putting them in danger."

"What are you saying?" he asked with obvious concern. "You can't back out now, not after what's happened."

"I don't want to back out," she said and shook her head. "I think it's beyond that point now and I still want to help. I still want to be a part of this."

Gerald sat against the wooden back of his chair.

"I'll admit it, last night was pretty intense, but so far, your only crime has been to associate with me."

"Ha ha," she said in response to his joke. "But what about those agents following us? That was the FBI! I need to remain on the sidelines."

"I understand, really," he said more seriously. "Just focus on Freddy and I'll remember to leave your name off any declaration of independence we sign."

"That's all I'm asking," she said. "Thank you."

"If we succeed and get Taylor's invention and the fusion reactor into the public awareness," he said, "it's going to change the world. Energy independence for the masses just might allow a new system, one based on individualism. You, your daughter and everyone will be able to live a more complete life, a life of their own."

Sadi already understood the potential result of the group's success, but hearing the description of a brighter future for her daughter felt like ice on a sunburn. She loved talking to people like Gerald about the world. People who desired the collectivist ideology vastly outnumbered individualists like herself. She needed to associate with people who shared her view of the world.

"You're not trying to tell me what's best for my own child are you?"

"I'm really taking everyone's best interest into consideration, Sadi."

He failed to recognize her sarcasm.

"I know Gerald," she said, putting her hand on his wrist. "I was being sarcastic about that last part. I think what you're trying to do is very noble and I'm glad to be a part of it. It's just that this is big and I have to distance my family a bit. Everyone has to make their own contribution, right?"

"Sorry," he said and smiled. "Sometimes I think I'm being too negative. We have it pretty nice here! Compared to other places on the planet, we live in general comfort, even the poorer people do. I know the world's not perfect and I don't expect it to be perfect, but when I think of what it could be, that's what motivates me. Sometimes I let it make me angry."

"Powerful countries like ours have always been responsible for so many wars, so much violence and suffering. While we sit here with our drinks in this warm cafe, children are dying from starvation because our government or our corporations supplied their government leaders with another round of financial support. If our vampire politicians stopped taking our money through taxes and inflation, we could actually make a difference in the world. As it is now, we can donate our money to help feed the poor and build schools for them, because the system is not designed for them to feed themselves or even have a job after getting an education."

Sadi considered making a comment, but decided to let him continue ranting.

"To live in a world without taxes, without wars, no one telling you how to spend your money. Can you imagine? We wouldn't be slaves to the banks! We could pay off our houses in less than a lifetime! We could travel without having to show our papers! We could build something on our property without getting the proper authorization and without feeding the overpaid, bureaucratic system. We could drive any speed we wanted and put natural selection back to work. Idiots wouldn't have to wear seat belts."

Gerald smiled wide during his last comment and Sadi silently suffered a painful memory, the accident which took her son's life. While he talked, Sadi rested her head in her hands and concentrated on acting extremely interested.

"That's why so many people read books and watch movies," she said. "To live in a better world, or at least a more interesting one."

A young man at the table behind Gerald kept glancing away from his girlfriend to stare at the back of Gerald's head as if listening to their conversation. Sadi met his eyes a couple of times in challenge and he quickly looked away.

"Of course, you can't say this to people," Gerald finished. "They've been too indoctrinated by the psychopathic collectivists who own the world. They've never seen anarchistic solutions to social problems or if they have, some authority figure ridiculed it. By the time people are adults, they can only imagine solutions involving laws or taxes or politicians. As you know, their laws don't work and they cause other social problems and the collectivists always have more laws or more taxes ready to implement."

"Feel better," she said and smiled. "I stopped trying to talk to people about this stuff. Sometimes I feel like the only honest person at a criminal convention, trying to tell them that stealing is wrong. It's frustrating, but now we might have some hope! Are you ready to go? I need to get home."

"Sure," he said. "Like we already agreed, we really need to discover more from Freddy. I think he holds the key to all of this and I think the alien wants the same thing we do."

"Or, it wants us to think that," Sadi said silently then rose and walked out of the cafe with him.

76

Sadi

Sadi returned home at nine thirty to find Helen in bed, and Jen watching the previous week's episode of *Celebrity Apprentice* on her laptop. Sadi felt grateful to find Jen awake. She wanted to be with another conscious human, preferably a female.

When Jen noticed Sadi enter the room, she put the video on pause to give a status report of the day. While they spoke, the still image of the show faced them, Joan Rivers arguing with country music singer Clint Black. Jen's addiction to semi-reality television shows provided Sadi with her only source of information about the activities of the entertainment world. The current episode of the program would be aired on the major network the next night. Jen always liked to watch the previous episode prior to the new one.

"Sadi," Jen said before turning from the screen. "You were out pretty late with that man. What's his name again?"

Jen stretched the word 'pretty' like a rubber band ready to shoot from her finger.

"Gerald," Sadi said in confirmation.

"Yeah, Gerald. He's pretty good-looking, wouldn't you say?"

Sadi smiled and attempted to dismiss the insinuation with a laugh.

"It's not like that. We're just working on something together, but I can't talk about it."

"That's not what I see."

"OK, Jen," Sadi said, amused and a little embarrassed. "What do you see?"

"I don't see anything," she said holding up her hands and acting as if wrongly accused of a crime. "I just think it's strange that I haven't heard of this man until today. How long have you been keeping him a secret? Are you going to try and convince me that you're not interested in him?"

"I am not interested in him," she replied. Sadi attempted to display a stern look, but the suspicious expression on Jen's face inspired a change of tactics. "Jen, I think it's best if we don't talk about him right now. I've had a long two days and need to get some sleep."

Jen smiled in triumph and then returned to face her laptop. After a quiet click, the two characters returned to life, arguing. Their voices quickly faded as Sadi began walking away.

"I'll get it out of you," Jen said loudly, with her eyes fixed on the computer screen.

"Goodnight Jen."

Sadi checked on her sleeping daughter then entered her own bedroom and shut the door. She extinguished the lights and pulled the covers over her. On that night, she energized the television at the foot of her bed with the volume set to zero. She hated to wake in the night with the television flickering light on the walls, but hoped the light would help purge darkness from her mind.

VI: TRIBULATION

Before the next awful bite
Relax, take a break
And see a good sight

77

Sadi

Just prior to four in the afternoon, Sadi looked at the clock on the corner of the computer screen and contemplated going home a bit early. She would normally leave work sometime between five thirty and six, but that afternoon she had felt uncomfortable since lunch and glanced at the clock every few minutes. She'd worked on nothing particularly stressful in the lab or her office. Her day had actually passed pretty smoothly so why would she feel so much anxiety?

From her purse twenty feet away, Sadi heard the familiar vibration of her phone. In a strange way she knew Jen waited for her to answer. Before answering the call, however, Sadi just stared at the phone as if it had fangs dripping with venom. If she touched the phone, the snake might strike. Sadi waited for three long rings until she gained enough courage to strike the snake.

"Hi Jen, what's…," Sadi began to say.

The strange, abnormal sound of Jen crying stopped Sadi from continuing. Her blood turned to honey.

"Ran off," Jen said through her sobs. "She ran off..."

"Calm down Jen," Sadi said as calmly as possible. "What are you talking about?"

In her mind, Sadi already knew what happened, but she clung to the small possibility of an alternative conclusion. After an effort to breath deeply, Jen spoke more slowly, attempting to enunciate.

"I was at the store register when Helen ran off," she said finally. "The fucking lady at the checkout wouldn't let me go."

"Where are you now? How long has it been?"

She asked the first two available questions while fifty more waited impatiently on her lips. A panicked voice in the back of her mind screamed so loudly she could hardly think. While holding her phone to her ear, she grabbed her purse and escaped the office, leaving the door open. Without saying a word to anyone, Sadi left work and practically ran to her car. Later she would unsuccessfully attempt to remember the journey to the mall. She talked to Jen on the phone while driving.

"I'm in the mall security office," Jen said. "They're out there looking for her. Luckily, I had her picture on my phone."

"How could you let this happen?" Sadi made the hasty accusation before she could stop herself. Instantly, she heard Jen's sobs resume. "I'm sorry Jen, we'll find her. I'm gonna find her."

When Sadi arrived at the mall, she saw a security guard at the entrance, watching the shoppers enter and exit. Sadi ran to him and introduced herself as the mother of the missing girl.

"Where is she?" she asked frantically. "Have you found her yet?"

"No ma'am, but don't worry," the guard said unconvincingly. The twenty-year-old security guard spoke as if bored, as if parents lost their children all the time. His hat hid any evidence of hair, but he had the beginning of a beard and a goatee. "We'll find her, just go to the office. They can guide you to it at the information desk, just inside."

Without knowing how, Sadi knew the location of the information desk. While running through the mall she felt like some superdrug had enhanced her senses. She noticed every person in her path, every face and the clothes they wore. She smelled their perfume, saw pimples on their faces, the pieces of food in their teeth. She saw everything except what she wanted to see.

After entering the security office, she noticed Jen first then the two other mall employees. Energy from her adrenaline rush crashed painfully when she failed to see her daughter in the room. Jen met Sadi's questioning gaze with bloodshot eyes and silence, apparently afraid to say anything.

"I'm sorry," she said finally, almost too low to hear.

Sadi had no remaining emotional energy for anger towards her daughter's nanny. She sat on the ugly brown leather couch next to Jen and placed her right arm protectively around the shaking girl. After a short embrace, Sadi pulled away, but left her hand on Jen's shoulder.

"We'll find her," Sadi said, assuming the role of comforter. Anger would only hinder information extraction. "Tell me again what happened."

"I needed to get some things," Jen began. While speaking she seemed to regain some of her confidence. "I brought Helen with me. I've taken her shopping with me a thousand times, but she's never run away from me before."

"Did you notice anyone suspicious following you, or watching you or Helen, or anything out of the ordinary?"

"I didn't notice anyone," she said and then explained in more detail.

While Jen stood in line at the checkout of a clothing store, Helen ran into the main mall walkway. Jen thought the transaction would take just a minute, but the store employee had an issue with her cash register. When she finally left the store with her purchases, Helen had disappeared. In total, Jen searched with the mall security for an hour and twenty minutes. She called Sadi after forty minutes of searching in vain.

Between each word, hundreds of horrible explanations filled Sadi's mind. Waiting felt like a knife in the gut. Doing nothing felt like a hammer to her head. Instead of sitting in the office, Sadi needed to return to the main mall area and continue the search.

"Jen, take me to the store where it happened."

The mall authorities wanted Sadi to wait for them to locate Helen, but if she continued to sit without a physical outlet, her heart would explode or she would faint. She ignored their request and led Jen out the door of the office. With one of the mall employees following, Sadi and Jen wound their way through narrow hallways and eventually returned to the main mall area.

As they methodically visited each store, Jen stayed close by her side and talked almost constantly, but her voice sounded like the buzzing of a fly to Sadi. She nodded in acknowledgment without understanding the meaning of her words. After the first hour of searching, the voice of hope in her mind slowly began to grow silent.

They searched all the stores and talked with all the staff of each store until Sadi depleted all her search options, and then a new thought revived the voice of hope in her head. Did someone find Helen and take her home or to the police station? If so, why would they not take her to the mall authorities? Maybe an elderly person found her and just failed to consider the most obvious course of action. Maybe if Sadi went home, she would find Helen and the nightmare would end. She told Jen her plan and started leading her to the mall exit, in the direction of her car. At the exit, she decided to call home first. Why did she neglect to consider that option? She called, but no one answered.

"Maybe we should call the police first," Jen suggested. "Maybe they found her."

"Got to get home," Sadi said to herself as if Jen's words had no meaning. "Got to get home. She might be there. You stay here for a while longer and go back to the office."

"Are you sure you can drive? I don't want you to get in an accident."

"I can drive Jen," she said. "I'll meet you back at the house."

Sadi drove much faster than the speed limit, faster than any time in her life. She drove as if daring the police to give her a ticket and mentally prepared to race them to her house. That option would save a phone call to the police anyway.

When she pulled onto the driveway of her home, her feeling of hope sunk even deeper inside her chest. No unrecognizable car sat in front of her house and no light escaped any of the windows.

"Helen, Helen," she yelled after crashing through the front door. She ran to the upstairs, energized every light in the house and opened every door. She picked up the home phone and scanned through the phone numbers of the recent calls, nothing but her call from the mall.

Jen entered the open front door just a few minutes later, shutting the door loudly behind her.

"Is she here," Jen yelled after failing to see Sadi.

Sadi did not answer, but ran down the stairs towards to the phone.

"Are you calling the police?" asked Jen.

"No," Sadi replied while dialing.

78

Sadi

After accepting the absence of her daughter in the house, Sadi thought of an alternative explanation. Did her missing daughter relate to Gerald's group or the alien? Would she find her daughter in some barn like they found Freddy? Did the probe have an interest in Helen? Maybe she had incorrectly concluded that the experience was a test for her. Now the dream felt like a foreboding to what would happen. For an unknown reason, other alternatives felt too horrible to even consider. Sadi grasped the new thought as tightly as she'd held Helen in the tunnel of her vision.

She waited for three rings before anyone answered.

"Hi Sadi," Gerald said. "It's good to hear from you!"

"Hi Gerald, I'm so sorry to call you. I, I don't know what to do."

As Sadi began to speak, tears started falling down her cheeks for the first time that day. The sound of Gerald's voice broke the emotional dam.

"What's wrong?" asked Gerald after waiting a few moments for her to catch her breath.

"She's gone, Helen's gone," she almost shouted between sobs. Her legs felt so weak with barely enough strength to support her weight so she sat down at the kitchen table. "She disappeared at the Mall. I don't know what happened to her."

Over the next thirty seconds, Sadi managed to explain the story. At some points she experienced difficulty breathing. She glanced once at Jen and cringed at the sight of her tears.

"Do you want me to talk to him?" asked Jen, her hand on Sadi's shoulder.

Sadi extended her hand, palm toward Jen as a request for silence while she finished telling the remainder of the story. Talking helped more than it hurt.

After finishing her story on the phone, Sadi waited a moment for Gerald to respond. The moment of silence passed like an eternity. Any attraction she previously felt for him, dissipated like the morning fog, replaced by a need for Gerald to take control of the situation and retrieve her daughter. Only Gerald would know what to do. The situation could not be handled by the police. Sadi had no faith in them anyway.

"I'm in my car and on the way now," Gerald said. "Other than calling me, what else were you planning to do? It seems to me that you should listen to your mother's instinct. What is your head telling you to do?"

"Nothing, my brain is empty," Sadi said. All the muscles in her body felt tense and her head pounded. "I feel helpless. What do I do? Every minute feels like she's speeding farther away from me. I can't lose her too. I've got to get her back."

"OK, this is what I want you to do."

Gerald spoke as if giving instructions to a class of high school students. While listening to his instructions, she heard the slam of a car door and a car engine roaring to life through the phone. The sounds of Gerald driving to help them provided her only comfort since answering the phone call from Jen that afternoon.

"I'm going to call Mr. Smith," Gerald began. "You need to drive over there and wait for me. Mr. Smith knows the best PI around. He has the resources you will need. Will you do that?"

"OK," Sadi said and took a deep breath before continuing. She imagined the oxygen entering her bloodstream and flooding her brain. In a normal situation, asking a near-stranger for help would cause horror, but she felt no anxiety at the action. "Do you think that thing had anything to do with this?"

"I don't know, but,..."

"But what?" Sadi demanded.

"But it does seem like too much of a coincidence. We can talk about it later, just let me call them. You just go over there. Can I talk to Jen for a moment?"

Sadi handed the phone to Jen.

Jen said "yes" and "alright" and then cut the connection.

"He says that you know how to get to this Mr. Smith's house, but I need to drive."

Surprising herself, Sadi complied with an "OK."

To Sadi, Jen staying at the house made more sense, but visiting the old man with Jen felt like the right action. Helen knew her phone number and would call if she could, whether at home or somewhere else.

When they arrived at Mr. Smith's house, the gate opened before they could request entry. He met them alone at the door and when she failed to see Freddy she wondered if he waited inside for them. Did Mr. Smith lose Freddy again?

"Oh my dear," said Mr. Smith with as much sympathy as imaginable from an elderly man who hardly knew her.

He used one arm to wrap around her and pull her inside his home. She refrained from returning his affection too vigorously from fear of breaking his ribs if she hugged too tightly. As Jen held onto her other arm, the sensation reminded Sadi of when her son died. Jen had stayed by her side during that whole horrible affair. The current experience felt much worse than her son dying. At least, Sadi had known her son's fate.

"Don't you worry, we'll find her," Mr. Smith said as he guided them to the same waiting room where she and Gerald waited. "I already talked to Mr. Swenson, my private investigator. He will find your daughter."

"Thank you, Mr. Smith," Sadi said, allowing herself to feel momentary relief. Did his confidence, however, contain mere hope or his true belief in finding success? Nothing would help really, until they found her daughter.

"Hi, I'm Jen Andrews," said Jen. "Helen's Nanny."

Mr. Smith shook her hand as if in a business meeting.

"I'm sorry we have to meet under these circumstances."

"Me too."

Sadi turned her attention to Jen for a moment and saw tears just waiting to fall behind those beautiful brown eyes. When Jen noticed Sadi looking at her, she turned away before making eye contact. Like Sadi, the girl wanted to avoid any other emotional disturbances which might initiate another flood of tears.

"Excuse me for a moment," Mr. Smith said, leaving his cane against the piano.

He disappeared for a few moments and returned with two mugs full of steaming liquid.

"This will help calm your nerves," he said while giving them the drinks.

The herbal tea tasted of lemon and other spices. The hot and wet sensation on her dry tongue sent a warm shock through her entire nervous system. The taste and smell combined into an intoxicating, almost magical substance. She declined his suggestion for her to sit and instead paced back and forth across the room, watching the window for signs of Gerald's arrival. After a few trips across the room, she joined Jen on the same couch where she sat with Gerald during their initial search for Freddy.

Mr. Smith turned to Jen.

"Miss Andrews," he said with an old voice full of concern. "I would like to speak with Sadi in private for a few minutes. Do you want to explore the house?"

"I guess," she said after seeing a nod of approval from Sadi.

"The kitchen is just down the hall to the right," he said, pointing in the direction with his cane. "If you're hungry, feel free to have whatever. Thanks dear."

As Jen walked out of the room, Sadi noticed hurt in her eyes and confusion for the dismissal, but she looked away to avoid eye contact. Current circumstances, however, overshadowed her concern for Jen's feelings. After she left the room, Sadi waited for the old man to speak and hoped he would have some answer for her.

"I left a message on the phone for Freddy to come home as soon as possible," Mr. Smith said with no concern in his voice. "He's with a group from one of his classes and should be home soon."

"Has this anything to do with the probe?"

"I don't know," he said and shook his head. "But after you called, I went to Freddy's room and found the crystal, but it was dark and silent. I'm sorry, but I don't dare to touch it."

"That explanation is the only thing holding me together. I don't want to think of any other explanation. That sounds totally stupid, hoping for an alien abduction."

"How can it not be related?" he said and placed his hand on her shoulder. "I'm sure it's related and your daughter is safe somewhere, just like Freddy was, but I didn't want to take any chances this time. That's why I called the PI. He really is good. With Freddy, and him, and your friend Mr. Fuger, we're sure to find her."

Sadi looked from the floor to meet his eyes and wiped the tears from her cheeks. The feel of his cold hand on her shoulder, however, failed to transfer any comfort.

"Do you really think so?" she asked after inhaling deeply.

"I really do."

"Do you think I should have called the police?" Sadi asked.

If she neglected to call the police and failed to find her daughter, would they suspect her of foul play? That possibility would definitely get in the way. Sadi felt a strange and irrational civic responsibility to make an official report. If necessary, she would make one. Sadi looked at her watch and noticed the time, ten fifteen. Her daughter had been missing for almost seven hours.

"If you want something done," Mr. Smith said with bitterness, "don't call the police, call a private investigator. The police will tell you to wait and let them handle it. They're paid whether or not they are successful, not to get things done. If you're not famous or rich, you'll be put on a list and it will turn into a case history, not an investigation. Even the government, if they are serious about accomplishing something, will contract with the private sector. They are only the illusion of organization."

A light from the window caused them to turn their heads. While Mr. Smith rose from the couch, the gate buzzer rang and he went to answer the call.

"Come on in, Craig," he said after opening the door.

When the man entered the house, Sadi felt immediate intimidation by his size. When he extended his hand in greeting, Sadi paused to admire the giant fingers, almost twice as long as hers and three times as thick. She felt relief when his grip failed to crush her hand.

"Craig Swenson Ma'am," he said with a straight face and intense blue eyes which seemed to glow on his somewhat dull face, like the inside of an agate. She noticed a slight accent to his voice, Norwegian probably. "No need to introduce yourself, Miss Jacobsen. Mr. Smith already told me about you. We'll need to go some place comfortable, but away from the windows. Bill, what about your study?"

Craig led Sadi to the study while Mr. Smith went to the kitchen. When he met them in the study a few moments later, Jen entered behind him. Her eyes widened at the site of the giant man sitting across the table from Sadi. Mr. Smith sat by the private investigator and Jen sat by Sadi.

Craig Swenson set his laptop computer on the table then reached into his jacket and retrieved a small voice recorder. After setting the device in the middle of the table, he started the recording. His giant fingers rested on the keyboard in front of him and Sadi wondered how he hit only one key at a time. They all waited for him to speak first.

"OK, there are two realistic possibilities," he began as soon as he got comfortable at the table. His get-down-to-business attitude made her feel better. He would waste no time. "Helen was either deliberately chosen or a random target. Do you know of anyone who would want to take your daughter, a relative, a friend, an ex-husband or someone with whom you've had a relationship?"

"I don't think so," she said and turned to Jen who shook her head. "The only one who might fit that description would be my ex-husband, but he has shown no interest in Helen, or me for that matter. I haven't talked to him for months."

For the next few minutes, Craig quickly and methodically reviewed all of her past acquaintances, relatives, and friends. The experience felt like a doctor reviewing a list of medical symptoms. While speaking and listening to her answers, he typed without looking at the keyboard and after the first few minutes, she stopped noticing his typing.

"This is a very strange case," he continued, "because it happened at the mall. It is very difficult to take an unwilling child through crowds of people. I suspect an accomplice who got in Helen's confidence."

He leaned over the table and stared directly into Jen's eyes.

"Tell me what you remember. I do not want you to leave anything out, or to say you don't remember. You have to remember. Now start with why you were going shopping, how long you had the trip planned, and who knew when and where you were going."

His intensity seemed to frighten Jen, but somehow she managed to maintain her composure. No one knew of her visit to the mall, not even Sadi and she had planned the trip that morning. She told him about all the people she'd noticed at the mall, every face from her memory. While Jen told her version of events, Sadi felt as if she watched her through a telescope, as if no one else existed in the room. She recognized a hint of fear in Jen's voice. If the man intended to scare the information out of her, the tactic appeared to work.

Mr. Swenson became very interested when Jen told him of a little girl who talked to Helen. The event had happened in a previous store, but Helen never saw the girl afterward so she assumed it to be just a random meeting. He made Jen tell him everything about the little girl, her age, height, what she wore, and who accompanied her.

"No one seemed to be with her," Jen said. "But Helen is very outgoing. She always talks to other kids."

"In cases like this, nothing can be taken for granted."

During the interrogation, Sadi noticed the man's professional and courteous attitude. He gave them sympathy when he could and never strayed off topic or let their emotions sway him from pursuing his line of questioning. A few times, Jen would start crying or tears would come to Sadi's eyes. He gave them only a moment to compose themselves before bringing them back to topic.

"Save the tears for later," he said several times, and, "I know it's hard, but you have to stay focused."

Sadi felt like a sheep being herded by an Australian Shepherd dog. After about thirty minutes of intense interrogation, Craig claimed to have acquired several leads to start following.

"You won't have to call the police," he said reassuringly to Sadi. "I'm going to talk to a friend of mine on the force. I'm not going to let them put you through more hell than what you're going through."

Like a child being scolded by a parent, Sadi silently nodded.

"Is there a..." Mr. Smith began, but a noise at the study door stopped the rest of his words.

The door slowly opened and Freddy appeared. He quickly glanced at all the people sitting at the table. His eyes seemed to freeze when they reached Sadi.

79

Freddy

As soon as he entered the house, Freddy instantly felt the presence of several familiar individuals: Sadi, her nanny, and Mr. Smith's private investigator, Craig Swenson. Since the incident with the alien probe at the barn, Freddy had acquired an extra sense, a strong connection to the emotions of people in his vicinity. He soon learned that each person had a unique emotional signature. Until he understood the new ability and its purpose more fully, he would keep the knowledge to himself and tell no one, not even his employer. He hated to give people more reason to think of him as being different.

He thought he felt prepared to see the two women, but when he saw their physical appearance, the smeared mascara and tear-filled eyes, the blood in his veins froze so that he could not move. Sadi emanated pure panic, and the nanny emanated more sadness and frustration. The sadness, anxiety and panic in the room felt like drinking a cup of vinegar. They soon became his own emotions and almost choked him to death.

Mr. Smith relayed what happened in as few words as possible, but Freddy already knew what happened, just from what he felt from Sadi. Hearing the horrible situation in words felt like the strike of a hammer on the nail already in his chest. When Sadi looked at him, he already knew what she wanted to ask.

Before she could say anything, however, he turned to Mr. Smith.

"I am so sorry," he said. "Maybe there is something I can do? I, um, I will be back in a few minutes."

Freddy attempted to project a tone of hope, but he felt totally helpless and the emotion interfered with his ability to speak. The flood of emotions drove away all rational thought and he had to escape their presence in order to think clearly. He silently shut the door and ran down the stairs to his room. After closing the bedroom door, he turned off the lights and entered his smallest closet where he could sit in the quiet of total darkness.

He needed to enter the calm abyss he'd discovered as a kid when a traumatic event happened to him. With his back to the wall, he sat on the ground and hugged his knees to his chest and started counting his breaths. After counting to five, he began to feel a little better. The darkness and quiet seemed to seep into his body, helping to purge his mind of anxiety. The emotions of those in the room above him never completely disappeared, but at least he felt able to focus on the dark and quiet.

After fifteen breaths, he saw a light begin to grow from under the closet door. He counted to twenty-five while watching the familiar blue and orange light flicker and dance. The light continued to grow in brightness, destroying his cherished darkness and illuminating everything in the closet.

In the two weeks since the barn incident, he had stayed away from the crystal, but left the object on top of his dresser. Occasionally, he would glance at the rainbow surface, but never into the eyes of the spider. During the nights, he often dreamed about the spider moving inside the crystal like a living, two-dimensional creature. Until that moment, the crystal showed no sign of activity.

When Freddy opened the closet door to his room again, he shielded his eyes with one hand, partly from the brightness and partly from fear of falling into another trance. With his hand blocking the light, he slowly approached the dresser with the crystal lying on top. As soon as he touched the crystal, a singular point of light burst to life in his mind and extinguished just as quickly. In the darkness following, Freddy felt different. He experienced the same burst of light that he had on his way to the barn.

80

Freddy

After the burst of light, Freddy felt the same as when he chased the FBI agents after waking at the barn. The burst in his mind erased all fear and anxiety. Freddy felt an enhanced ability to think, with total clarity and focus. He perceived the situation in its entirety. He felt totally alive and in control of his thoughts.

Soon after feeling empowered, however, an anger began to grow deep within his mind, the kind of anger to cause sickness, like a migraine caused nausea. Knowledge of what might have happened to the poor girl became the source of his anger. The injustice of the situation stung the most, injustice to Helen, injustice to Sadi and injustice to all the other victims of similar crimes. The emotion became too intense. Freddy needed an outlet for his sudden rage.

Freddy knew of only a few types of people who would steal a child, and unfortunately the alien could not be counted as a suspect. That would have been too easy. From all the emotional evidence he felt from the people in the study, he suspected only the alien's indirect involvement. One possibility became clear. The alien had appointed the task of finding Helen to him.

What would happen to her if he failed?

He required a few moments for his eyes to adjust to the low light, to a room illuminated only by the LED lights of his computer equipment. At that moment, he failed to perceive the alien's motivation. How could the motivation matter though, if the poor girl became permanently scarred or died? He attempted to direct his anger at the alien, but could only feel anger towards the abductors.

"How does this relate to Gerald Fuger and his other friends? Why did the alien connect us?"

Freddy asked the questions quietly to himself and the sound helped him escape the darkness of his thoughts. The answer to those questions felt insignificant compared to the other questions in need of an immediate answer. Eventually, he would climb that other steep trail of questions.

He first needed to examine the possible motivations of the abductor. All of the possible motives caused Freddy to feel extreme anger, even the most benign one, a deranged parent who wanted Helen for their own daughter. Freddy choked through all the other possibilities relating to sexual predators and worse.

He needed to focus on the evidence and rely on logic and not allow fear or hope to interfere. The kidnapper took the girl from a crowded area which meant they gained Helen's confidence long enough to take her. Only a convincingly-friendly woman or younger person could have accomplished that feat, not some degenerate man working alone.

Did the abductor target Helen specifically? He or she could have chosen a much easier place to take the child. He saw several good reasons to abandon that possibility. The abductor would have chosen a child from a less fortunate situation. They usually targeted children of the poor and ignorant, or runaways, or those with drug addictions, whose parents relied on the government. He knew from experience how many neglected children existed, children left to take care of themselves without anyone to watch over them. Abductors could easily acquire those children. Sadi also had the means and intelligence to make a comprehensive search.

In a normal situation, he would have experienced less difficulty making the conclusion, but he needed to consider the alien. Why choose Helen? The reason to that question seemed obvious. The alien knew he would be motivated due to his interest in Sadi. Why choose him? What would result from the search? The alien obviously wanted a particular final result. The future resulted from too many variables, however, for Freddy to make a conclusion.

Before leaving his room and returning to the study, he made a detour to a walk-in closet in another basement room where Mr. Smith kept two pistols. Freddy never saw Mr. Smith hold a gun, but he had found them one day on the top of a shelving unit while searching for one of Mr. Smith's canes. When he saw the guns the first time, he resisted the temptation to touch one. Several days later, he revisited them. They scared him, but he felt compelled to visit them and one day he actually touched one.

Freddy opened the closet door then retrieved the box holding the guns. After opening the box, he stared with wide eyes at the two weapons and imagined the feel of the cold metal in his hands. The sight of them reminded him of the barn incident when he aimed the gun at the FBI agent's head, prepared to pull the trigger. He expected the memory to sting, but instead felt an excitement to hold a gun again. He wanted to feel the recoil of shooting a heavy bullet.

After removing the gun from the box, he squeezed the grip tightly with his fingers. Without consciously realizing his actions, he quickly released the clip and checked for bullets. He hid the gun in his inside jacket pocket and grabbed a handful of bullets. He stuffed the bullets in his other pocket while walking towards the stairs. On his way to the study, he practiced drawing the gun quickly from his jacket like the gunfights in old western movies. Should he feel bad about enjoying the action? Why did he feel compelled to get the weapons?

Could he trust himself with that kind of power? Would he fear to use the weapon if the situation required it? He understood the irrational fear so many people felt towards weapons, an artificial and programmed fear concocted by the media. Instead of portraying weapons as tools for self-preservation and personal empowerment, the media never failed to associate guns with horrible human actions. Whenever a human used a gun to murder another human, the media called the act a shooting. Instead of calling the human a murderer, they called him a shooter, or a gunman. In television programs and movies, protagonists often claimed a higher moral position by refusing to use a gun. They eventually prevailed against the evil humans with guns by sheer luck or miraculous help from a god.

81

Freddy

Freddy took a deep breath before placing his hand on the door to the study. When he opened the door and looked at the humans sitting around the desk, all their emotions flooded his mind again, but he swallowed them like a foul taste in his mouth and entered the room with an intense look of concern. They all stopped talking and turned their heads to stare at him. Sadi looked at him with moist eyes then returned her gaze to Craig who continued speaking to her. Freddy considered sitting on the couch, but decided to lean against the wall instead. He could smell the leather-bound books on the book shelf next to him.

He listened as Sadi answered Craig's questions and vice versa. Even with so many ugly emotions emanating from the woman, Freddy found Sadi as beautiful as ever. Occasionally, he gazed too intensely on her, then shifted his attention elsewhere just before anyone noticed.

While watching the scene, Freddy made a surprising realization. His new ability to sense the emotions of others had become much sharper than at the barn. Before anyone performed an action like speaking, crying or turning their head, he detected the preceding subtle emotional change, and correctly predicted the action.

"Of course, you won't be able to work for a while," Craig said at the end of his interrogation. "I suggest you spend your energy finding Helen, rather than self-pity or worrying about her. Do you have any sleeping pills?"

Sadi could not answer, so Jen answered for her.

"I have some."

"I would suggest taking them tonight Ms. Jacobsen. You're going to need rest to think clearly. That's what Helen needs you to do."

"Sure," she said as if coming out of a trance. "Yes. You're right, for Helen."

"What can we do?" asked Freddy.

His words brought all of their attention to him. Mr. Smith exhibited a feeling of surprise. Craig turned toward Freddy.

"Nothing for now," he answered, intending an end to the discussion.

"What are you going to do tonight?" asked Freddy.

Before the private investigator answered, Freddy perceived a growing impatience from the large man. Craig Swenson wanted to begin his investigation which Freddy impeded.

"Tonight, I'm going to the mall," he said, staring at Freddy as if challenging him to ask another question. "I can get the security guards to let me look at the surveillance footage."

Freddy nodded and attempted to appear satisfied. After Craig stood from the table he led them all out of the room, Freddy at the end of the line. At the front door, Craig turned and placed his giant hand on Sadi's shoulder.

"We've got some good leads to go on," he said. "Hopefully, tonight I can make some progress. Don't give up hope because I haven't."

The giant man opened the front door and stepped outside, expecting to leave them all inside the house. The man felt more frustration when he noticed Freddy following him into the cold spring night. The tall archway protected them from the falling rain.

"Can I talk to you for a moment?"

"Yes."

"Do you think the people who took Helen are with the child sex trade?"

Craig looked at Freddy in surprise. At the beginning of the interrogation, Craig had already made that conclusion.

"Most likely," Craig said. "But if you cared at all for Miss Jacobsen, it would be best not to talk about that."

"Of course," Freddy said and nodded. "What about trying to find one of the customers, someone who would pay for a little girl like Helen. That would be the fastest way to find her, I think."

"That would be a bad idea," said Craig Swenson as his eyes tightened.

While he answered, Freddy felt the intention to frighten him.

"Why?"

Before Craig responded, Freddy decided to let the man remind him of his role in the situation. Craig played the role of private investigator and Freddy played the role of the non-private investigator. People liked to put other people in their proper place.

"It's dangerous for one," he began, sounding indignant. "I also don't want you ruining my investigation and scaring any suspects away."

"I just want to help find her, just as much as you do. I will not ruin it."

"Even if you could contact someone connected to their organization, getting them to trust you would take days or even weeks, and that would be too late."

Craig's frown softened a bit and he put his giant hand on Freddy's shoulder. His grip felt strong and firm, and strangely comforting. His emotions changed from annoyance to sympathy.

"These people don't just accept any potential client who comes knocking on their door. It's a business and they will not take an unnecessary risk. Believe me, you don't want to get involved with these people anyway. They're protected by more than just the organized crime ring. They're connected to very important and dangerous people, business leaders, government officials and even federal agents. If they suspect you are a threat, they will have no problem getting rid of you, Sadi, Bill and Helen, and no real investigation will ever take place. The media will never report it and you'll be forgotten, end of story. I know how to handle this, without scaring away all the disease-ridden flies."

"Thank you for all of your help," Freddy said. He decided against asking further questions. "If there is any way I can help, please let me know. I am willing to do anything."

"I just might," he said, removing his hand from Freddy's shoulder. "But for tonight, I need to work on this alone, without any distractions. I'll keep in touch, good-bye."

Freddy returned to the house and found Jen sitting in the waiting room, on the piano stool. She waited for him to return so she could relay a request from Mr. Smith.

"They're back in the study, waiting for you."

The emotionally exhausted girl sighed and felt a temptation to ask Freddy a question. She felt an additional sadness from being excluded. Freddy paused before turning away from her to join them in the study. He felt sorry for the girl.

"Sadi's friend Mr. Fuger shared confidential information with us, information he wishes to remain secret," he began. "You and the investigator cannot know of it, yet. But do not worry. If he does not find Helen, I will."

He left the girl, briefly enjoying the small sensation of hope he instilled in her. When he opened the door to the study, he found Mr. Smith and Sadi sitting at the table in the same positions. Without the private investigator, the room appeared larger. He already knew what Sadi wanted of him and dreaded her reaction at his disappointing answer. Sadi turned to him with desperation in her eyes, tears glistening on her beautiful cheeks.

“Does this have anything to do with the alien?” she asked as he sat across from her in the chair formerly occupied by Craig Swenson.

She sounded like a woman pleading for her life. As he attempted to prepare the best response, the hope she felt in him became a stinging distraction.

“It is related,” he said. Freddy only knew one thing for certain. The alien used the crystal to enhance his senses. But for what purpose? Did the alien care about what happened to Helen? "That is all I know."

“What about the crystal?” she asked. “If we look into the spider’s eyes, will it tell me where my daughter is?”

“I already tried in my room,” Freddy said in an attempt to show sympathy, then realized that Sadi only comprehended a negative response. "Maybe it will answer you."

He removed the crystal from his pocket and placed the object on the desk just as her cell phone began vibrating. She quickly removed her phone from her purse, looking in excitement at the caller ID. Freddy experienced a sharp pain of jealousy when he heard her say hello to Gerald Fuger. The memory of how she looked at Gerald became a bitter reminder of his childhood, how Sadi existed just beyond his reach, nothing more than a friend. He quickly removed the painful thought from his mind and waited for Sadi to finish talking with Gerald on her cell phone.

Freddy decided to act as if he had a real hope for the crystal to answer her call. If the crystal failed to provide any answers, as he expected, her disappointment would hopefully transfer from him to the alien. A light had already been lit in his mind. He expected no further assistance from the alien via the crystal. While waiting for Sadi to end the phone call, Freddy wondered how the alien felt about the suffering it caused. Did some strange invisible creature sit in the corner of the room with them, watching their performance with amusement? He glanced around the room and wondered, but he felt no other emotions from anyone other than Sadi or Mr. Smith.

When Sadi finished talking to Gerald, she slowly set the phone on the desk and returned her attention to the space between them, staring at the crystal with fear overwhelming all her other emotions, fear of looking into the eyes of the spider and seeing nothing. Freddy could feel her anxiety as if his own.

She reached across the desk and pulled the crystal to stop just under her face then focused on the eyes of the spider. She stared at the beautiful little gems for a good twenty seconds, blinking as she struggled to focus. Freddy watched with little hope of seeing any signs of altered consciousness or psychological takeover, but hoped anyway. The horror of seeing the disappointment in her eyes felt almost as potent as her real emotions. Mr. Smith looked to Freddy with a sadness in his eyes that Freddy had never seen before. His boss had hoped for the crystal to provide the answers too, even more than Sadi.

"Ms. Jacobsen," said Mr. Smith after another few seconds. "You should go home and get some sleep. Craig will handle the police and everything. He's really the best. We'll find her."

Sadi did not hear him, but lifted the crystal with her right hand, holding the surface between her face and the ceiling. Her hand shook while holding the thin object.

"Where's my daughter? Please, where is she!"

Silence filled the room like a midnight tide.

82

John

April 4, Saturday

Agent John Pratt shivered in the cold of his car. After blinking back an overwhelming headache, he gathered the strength to open his eyes. At first, he could only see a foggy view of the street through the windshield. The early light of dawn caused the fog to glow and become more pronounced. After focusing his blurry eyes, he saw the pub from the previous evening. A note on the next seat thanked him for the fun evening. The author wrote in red lipstick and signed the paper with the mark of a kiss.

He tried remembering the woman's appearance or any events of the night, but failed on both accounts. Should he wish to forget her appearance? Sometimes the influence of alcohol made the frightening women appear gorgeous, one reason why he never drank too much. Agent Pratt rarely drank enough to impair his judgment anyway. A good agent should always be on his guard. The woman must have been beautiful, to get him drinking.

As much as he wanted the memory to be just a pleasant and random encounter, something about the memory felt wrong. Normally, he had two drinks and then went home, but when the woman sat next to him and started talking, he had to buy another and then another. While recalling the memories, his thought processes became fuzzy and became a psychotic fantasy where thousands of dark-eyed Muslims hid in the shadows of a giant maze. Unfortunately, none of the images in his mind even remotely resembled a naked woman.

When he tried to identify the strange images and feelings lingering in his peripheral memory, they remained just out of reach. Maybe he just needed to take a shower, have a coffee, and recover from his damned headache. Alternately, if he waited too long, memories of a dream would fade like the morning fog.

Agent Pratt started his car and waited for the heat to drive the cold from his bones. After closing his eyes, he focused on breathing and made a mental list of his questions without an answer, his memory gaps. Did he go to her apartment in her car or did he drive? Did he get a taxi back to his car? How long did he spend at her place? Did he just spend the night in his car?

If he drove somewhere, he should have remembered, but his memory of reality ended somewhere in the middle of their conversation. He looked to the control panel of his car and the odometer still showed only twenty-two miles since he filled up his gas tank, just as he remembered. Unless they walked somewhere, or she lived nearby, then he must have gone in her car.

After eliminating all the benign explanations, he had to entertain the most disturbing question. Did she put a drug in his drink? If she gave him a drug, she probably had different intentions than date rape.

"Think John," he said while rubbing his forehead. "What's the motive?"

If he could just ignore his horrible headache, he could think clearly. After another minute of thinking and rubbing his forehead, he remembered the first motive to consider, his wallet. When he opened it, he noticed the missing money and credit cards.

"Damn you bitch!" he said in anger, holding the palm of his hand against his forehead. Although his head hurt worse after the outburst, he felt better at finally having a motive. When she opened his wallet, did she notice his badge? In a strange way, he admired a woman who would steal from an agent.

Before he could continue his investigation, his phone started vibrating in the passenger's seat. With pain in every movement, he turned his head to see the phone and noticed his girlfriend's number on the screen. The thought of talking to her made his pulse pound harder in his temples. He retrieved the phone and noticed several missed calls, all from her. When he returned home, he would hear a long lecture and needed to prepare a good story.

Should he use the opportunity to end the relationship? If he could consider that question without too much anxiety, did the lack of concern indicate a weak emotional attachment to her? If he felt no emotional attachment, then why did he care about a horrible lecture? His life seemed much more complicated than his job. At work, everything looked black and white. Terrorists were evil! Ignorant citizens were good! He let the phone continue vibrating. What would one more unanswered call matter?

Following the expected lecture from his girlfriend, he showered and took a nap. He lacked the energy to invent a good story, so he told her the truth, excluding the part about the woman. He had no memory of what happened and some terrorist had drugged him. Let her chew on that story for a while. Even if he had more time and energy he probably would have told her the truth anyway. No matter what story he told her, she would not believe him anyway.

During his nap, he dreamed of racing through crowded city streets, like the 'Grand Theft Auto' video game. Instead of shooting and running over strangers, however, he killed and maimed everyone he ever knew, his parents, old girlfriends, the college kids. He took great pleasure smashing into them.

Later that afternoon, he returned to the bar, intending to get a description of the girl and eventually discover her identity. When he arrived, the only occupants surrounded a single table. The bartender, a short blond guy with straight hair looked busy, preparing for the rush of weekend revelers. Agent Pratt recognized him from the previous evening. He went to the bar and sat on a stool.

"Hi," he said as cheerfully as he could manage. "I was here last night. I don't know if you remember."

"Welcome back," said the bartender with a hint of sarcasm. "What can I get ya?"

Agent Pratt ordered a beer, but just as an excuse to talk.

"Do you remember me from last night?"

"Yeah, I remember you," he said with his back to Agent Pratt.

"Remember that girl I left with?" he asked with a sarcastic sneer. "What a piece of work!"

"You didn't know her?"

The guy turned and looked more interested.

"Why? Did it look like we knew each other?"

Pratt hoped the man heard the sarcasm in his voice.

"She seemed interested in you," he said with a smile. "Didn't look like you minded."

"She might show up again tonight. That's why I'm here, I lost her damn number." Agent Pratt paused to take a sip of beer so the man had time to consider his words. "How often does she come around here?"

The guy stopped wiping the counter for a moment while he stared off into space.

"Actually, never seen her before. I would have remembered her."

"Shit," Agent Pratt said and forgot to hide his anger. "I was hoping you would know her name."

"Hell, I don't even know your name," the man said laughing. "And I've seen you a bunch of times. I see so many people here, but only remember a few, mostly the women, if you know what I mean."

"I hear ya," he replied genuinely and smiled.

"Sorry I can't help you," the barman said with a tone of finality.

He gave Agent Pratt an awkward smile then went back to preparing the bar for the evening's customers.

Agent Pratt drank the rest of his beer in less than a minute. While staring at the last few drops in the bottom of the glass, he thought about his next move. Upon arriving at the establishment, he failed to see any video surveillance equipment outside the bar. From where he sat, he noticed two video cameras inside the bar. If he identified himself as a FBI agent, the barman would probably let him see the surveillance footage without showing a warrant. He only considered that option for a moment. He would not reveal his true identity, but keep his alter ego, a financial analyst. As such, he could not ask for private information like the video footage.

He had other options, but none of them would work. A fellow agent could visit the establishment and ask to see the footage. A pair of agents would have no questions asked, but he could not accept that option yet. If one of his coworkers discovered what happened, that a woman had drugged and robbed him, he would find himself with a whole shitload of other problems. He might as well quit and become a truck driver. As usual, he would need to invent an excuse.

Before sliding off the stool, he casually glanced at the seating area again and mentally reviewed what happened to him there. After entering the previous night, he failed to recognize anyone, so he sat by himself near the same location as his present one. He remembered the first moment he noticed the woman, when she sat and crossed her legs towards him. She smiled and he said "Hi". The sight of her thighs and breasts urged him to order a drink for them both. The mixture of her skin and the scent of her perfume became the closest thing to a magical potion as he thought possible. As expected, his memory started to become fuzzy after that first drink.

"Damn!"

As he focused on the memory of her perfume, he wondered if the substance included a human pheromone. Intelligence agencies would use a woman with such a substance, but usually for another intelligence agent suspected of duplicity. That possibility seemed unlikely. Jason Smithson knew John would never betray him or the agency. Sure, Agent John Pratt often bypassed established protocol, but only to accomplish agency goals.

After he returned home, he would collect a urine sample to submit on Monday, without a name attached. If a drug had been used on him, he should be able to detect the components. The identity of the drugs in his system would help shorten the list of suspects responsible. With any luck, the woman would try to use one of his credit cards. He could hope for good fortune, but Agent Pratt would have no such expectation. Hoping for luck wasted time.

Unbeknownst to his girlfriend, he put a vial of his urine in a small paper bag and hid it in the back of a rarely used drawer in the refrigerator, behind some expired shredded cheese. That night, he took his second shower of the day. While washing his legs, he felt a small stab of pain in his left thigh. "What the hell," he whispered. When he touched the tender area with his finger, he felt the pain again.

"Damn bugs!"

83

John

After registering at the office on Monday, Agent Pratt quickly followed his Monday morning routine then left for the drug testing lab. He could not consider sending the sample to the official FBI crime lab. That route involved too much paperwork. The proper bureau channels became a bureaucratic nightmare. He would be required to associate the sample with an official investigation and then invent a million little lies to cover his tracks. Just considering that route gave him a headache. He would not risk exposure. Using the local drug testing lab made much more sense. He knew someone at the lab who would do the test and give the results only to him without leaving any record.

For the present, he would utilize the law of parsimony and believe the simplest motive, theft. He could not, however, discard the worst alternative. Whoever drugged him could have used the robbery as a ruse and extracted information from him. Although that possibility seemed too ridiculous, he knew of many individuals and organizations who wanted that kind of access. Gerald Fuger occupied the lowest position on that list of possible suspects. Fuger lacked the courage.

While waiting for the drug analysis results, he focused on his main work tasks. Before beginning the agency priorities, however, he arranged for a trace to be put on Fuger's car. Any request for brick agents to follow Fuger would be rejected so a trace became the next best option. The airlines already notified Pratt if Fuger booked a flight, but he often drove to relatively far away places like Vancouver B.C., Portland or Spokane and Pratt wanted a record of where he traveled by land.

When Agent Pratt received the urine sample analysis the next day, his jaw literally dropped as his worst fear became reality. The mass spectrometry analysis indicated the presence of amobarbital and midazolam. Immediately, one conclusion failed to make sense. Those drugs had to be injected to have the desired effect, but he should have evidence of an injection. Then he remembered the tender spot on the back of his leg. He felt the area again and then examined the rest of his body and found another tender spot on his other thigh.

"Stupid bitch," he swore and pounded his fist on his desk.

Agent Pratt knew enough about the use of psychoactive drugs and needed no one else to confirm his fears. The presence of the benzodiazepines in his urine would account for his memory loss. Most likely, they used Versed, but they could have used other drugs. They obviously knew what they were doing and probably hired some girl from another city. Spending time to locate her would be a waste of time, but he should still check the video from that bar.

The new information helped Agent Pratt to eliminate several types of suspects and narrowed the scope of his investigation. In a small way, he felt excitement to have the opportunity to investigate his own case. Rage also helped.

As a FBI agent, he interfered with people's lives. They did not interfere with his life. Someone stole information from him, government property. Most likely, he would never remember the events, even if he went to the department psychiatrists.

A citizen or one of the dirty Muslims had violated his beloved system. Agent Pratt resolved to punish that serious infraction and make an example of the perpetrators.

84

John

April 10, 2009

Agent Pratt's phone buzzed. The agent who monitored the location of their special targets called and left a text message.

"Gerald Fuger, heading south," the text said. "Your orders?"

Pratt lifted the phone from his desk and connected to the agent.

"How long ago did he leave?"

"He's on I-5, heading south. He just left Olympia about an hour ago. If he's going to Portland, he should arrive in the next hour or so."

"Thank you," Pratt said, but before he could cut the connection, the voice on the line stopped him.

"Do you want me to call the Portland office to track him there?"

"No, I'll take care of it. Thank you, Agent Roberts."

Pratt needed to spend all his time and energy investigating his own case, discovering who abducted him, not those on his wish list like Gerald Fuger. He needed to find those responsible for violating him. For a brief moment, he considered dropping the trace on Fuger and let him have an unmonitored vacation in Portland, but then decided to take advantage of the opportunity rather than waste it.

The previous time an agent had watched Fuger in Portland, he met with the woman from some pharmaceutical company. Agent Pratt had investigated Sadi Jacobsen's background himself and found her totally benign, except for an interest in the 'End the Fed' movement. Unfortunately, she had no history of legal entanglements. An intelligent and attractive woman such as Sadi would likely be one of Fuger's romantic interests.

From whatever angle he viewed the situation, he failed to see a logical connection between his drugging and Gerald Fuger. Only the most dangerous and bold criminals would dare drug and abduct a government agent, unless they did not know him. That kind of action required someone with resources and no fear of the government. Not only did Gerald lack the guts to do something so bold, he also loved to hide behind the law and his suspicious clients on the reservation. He worked too openly. Until other evidence presented itself, he would treat Gerald Fuger as a separate case.

He dialed the number for the Portland office and hesitated a moment before hitting the send button. In preparation for the conversation, he took a deep breath and practiced smiling.

"Hi Chuck," he said. "How's the wife?"

Pratt treated Chuck like most other people, as a friend, but he had no real interest in a social connection with the man. Pratt only pretended to like the guy. He knew the usefulness of having reliable social contacts. Knowing them on a first name basis became necessary. Sometimes, when Pratt visited Portland, he spent time with the guy and acted like they shared the same interests like golf, football, and global warming. He only knew the talking points on those subjects, but personally found them tiresome. Other than rugby, lacrosse and hockey, Agent Pratt had no further interest in sports.

"I'm doing good, as usual," Chuck responded cheerfully. "How's the girlfriend? Gonna make her a respectable woman yet?"

They both laughed.

"Getting there," said John just as cheerfully. "Hey, sorry to cut this short, but I need your help with tracking someone. We're not a hundred percent that he's going to the Portland area, but it looks like that and if so, he might be there in an hour. I just need to know who he's meeting and where."

"Do you need a decoy team?" asked Chuck, changing his tone from jovial to serious.

"No, I just need some pictures. Let me know if you have any problems acquiring his signal. He's not dangerous. It's Gerald Fuger. He should be no problem."

The conversation finished shortly afterward. He wanted to spend the least amount of time working on Fuger and let the Portland team get the information he wanted. When he had more time, he could follow-up. In the meanwhile, he planned to enter the field.

One case kept stealing Agent Pratt's attention, a terrorist organization led by an illegal alien from Somalia. He lived in Seattle with a fake identification and currently spent time recruiting citizens and other illegal aliens, all Muslim, to destroy a Jewish synagogue. The FBI had been building the case against him for over a year and successfully inserted one undercover agent as the leader's confidant. Another one of the man's friends worked for the FBI as an informant. The Somali man trusted the agents completely and responded favorably to most influence from the FBI.

Pratt knew the bureau could easily provide the organization with bomb materials, either real or fake, and they would have already attempted the act of terrorism. Before they let him attempt to bomb the synagogue, however, the FBI had another plan. Pratt wanted to use them as bait for a bigger criminal, a money laundering organization the FBI had failed to infiltrate. In a stroke of luck, Agent Pratt discovered a secret back door to the organization. The Somali man had an uncle in the money laundering organization and Agent Pratt had an informant who had access to both of them.

If men from the terrorist organization arranged the abduction, then what did they want to know? They would only attempt such a desperate act if they felt threatened. They might have discovered the undercover FBI agent or the informant, or both. As a result, they would want to discover any others.

Agent Pratt needed to check on his informant. If the group had abducted him, they would know the identity of his informant and the undercover agent. If Agent Pratt failed to discover the answers, he might be the one who ruined the investigation, and all because of some woman. No one could ever discover what happened.

Fortunately, no one had murdered the undercover FBI agent yet, but Agent Pratt found no reason to worry about the man's immediate safety. The group should do what he would have done in the situation, use the spy to feed misinformation back to the bureau.

That afternoon, Agent Pratt arranged a meeting with his informant to answer the pivotal question. Had the man's position been compromised? If the informant worried about his safety, that information might be evidence that the organization knew his identity and acquired the information from Agent Pratt.

They met at one of his favorite locations, a Barne's and Noble bookstore. He liked the privacy of a specific location in the store, the end of a secluded aisle, two comfortable chairs conveniently hidden from the public. He dressed in sandals and old jeans with holes near the knees. A beige baseball cap and a slightly dirty shirt that provided the appearance of someone who needed a shower. With a just a dab of oil rubbed over his face then wiped away, he completed the picture of a vendor at a hemp festival.

He arrived at the bookstore thirty minutes before the appointment. After checking his favorite aisle, he chose a random book, sat down and started flipping through the pages. He hardly noticed them, thinking instead about all the possible suspects he wanted to investigate.

Without looking away from his book, Agent Pratt noticed his contact enter in the aisle. The very dark Somali man stood just under six feet, two inches shorter than Agent Pratt. He wore a buttoned shirt with a dark plaid pattern, no hat, and appeared as a casual customer. His short-trimmed beard and dark eyes would cause the average citizen to feel slightly intimidated, even though his demeanor indicated refinement. He sat across from Pratt and opened his own hardcover book to the first few pages. The book hid his facial hair and only allowed his dark eyes to show. Neither man made contact or acknowledged the other man's existence.

"Well, I'm here," said the man after about thirty seconds of silence. "I thought we were finished meeting."

He spoke with a slight accent, diluted by several years of living in the United States.

"Did I ever say you were finished?" Pratt spoke and continued without waiting for an answer. "You must have forgotten that you owe us, whatever we need, whenever."

"I do not owe you or anyone else anything," he said. "I cannot change what happened in my youth. That is not who I am anymore, it's just what I was born into. Now I am a contributing member of your society. I've paid back my debts, sevenfold."

"A worm cannot change into a butterfly," snorted Pratt. He loved insulting the Muslim. "It stays a worm. It will always be a worm."

"Just tell me what you want," the man answered in resignation.

If the insult had a negative effect, the man refused to give Agent Pratt the satisfaction of seeing an angry or insulted reaction.

"I shouldn't need to remind you that we also know about your father's current involvement with Al-Shabaab."

Agent Pratt enjoyed this part of their meeting and never failed to recall the facts.

"Not to mention that we could throw him and your cousin into a Somali prison hell. That's when you'll see how your bloody Allah rewards his faithful servants. Muhammad would be so proud to see such suffering in his name."

The man visibly winced at Pratt's blasphemy. Agent Pratt kept a steady gaze on the eyes of his victim, to enjoy the reaction. Al-Shabaab, a Somali terrorist organization claimed many sympathizers among Somali-born US citizens and residents. Several organizations and the man's family offered support for them. He had more connections than Pratt could even count. Agent Pratt enjoyed access to a gold mine and every FBI agent wanted some gold nuggets like him in their pocket.

With all the man's connections and those from all the other intelligence agencies, Agent Pratt figured they could throw all the lawbreakers and terrorists in prison, or just kill them to save the paperwork, but that method would be too childish. How could the FBI profit from eliminating them? In addition, some other scum would crawl from under the rocks to fill the holes in the market. The FBI could act more intelligently, manipulate the current system rather than wasting time locating and fighting new players. Agent Pratt considered the situation as win-win. Keep this man on the end of a hook or throw his family in prison.

"You can insult me all you want and my religion," he said indignantly. "Your words have no power. They will only condemn you."

"Thanks for the warning," Agent Pratt answered and changed his tone to one of concern. "Now I have a warning for you, but I don't want you to get the wrong impression. I'm only concerned because your safety is beneficial to the both of us."

"What are you talking about?" The man attempted to hide his sudden interest.

"Do you sense lately, that they are treating you differently, like they know you've been talking to me?"

The man sat back against his seat and stroked his short beard. Pratt had difficulty concentrating while watching the man play with his beard. He needed to watch for signs of deceit.

"I have noticed no such behavior," the man answered as if offended.

Pratt noticed other emotions in his informant's facial features, concern and insincerity. The man might have noticed irregularities about his treatment, but denied his true feelings. Pratt felt confident in his instincts. The man planned to investigate on his own.

"That's good," Pratt answered, pretending to be relieved. "I need you to tell me if you suspect anything. That's the only way I can help you."

"I will keep my eyes open," he said. "Why do you suspect this thing?"

"We may have an agent who is secretly trying to help your uncle," Pratt said. "I need you to discover who that is and what he told them. Hopefully, I am wrong."

"What kind of organization do you belong to? That you cannot even keep control of your fellow agents?"

The man attempted to cover his anxiety with a smile.

"It's the game we all play, my little Muslim friend."

85

John

The next Monday, after meeting with his informant, Pratt called Chuck, his contact at the Portland office. He spent so much of his time during the weekend working on his own investigation that he nearly forgot about having Fuger followed the previous Friday night.

"Did you get any feedback from the two agents following Gerald Fuger?"

"They haven't submitted their report yet," Chuck said, as if annoyed to check on another investigation rather than his own. Pratt decided against demanding an urgent response.

"When you find out, please forward it to me," he replied, "and thanks for helping me out on this one Chuck."

"No problem," he said. "I'll try to get back to you after lunch."

"That would be great. Thanks."

While waiting for the status report, Pratt kept busy, attempting to forget the frustrating weekend with his girlfriend. Her child ruined two good nights of sleep. When her daughter woke them after midnight and wanted to watch a Disney movie, he expected his girlfriend to refuse and put her back to bed. To his surprise, however, she agreed. In his exhaustion, he also agreed, even though he hated all Disney productions. He assumed the girl would fall asleep after only a few minutes, but she stayed awake in their bed for the entire movie. Agent Pratt forgave himself for being unprepared on the first night. When the same thing happened on the next night, he attempted to excuse himself to go sleep on the couch, but his girlfriend accused him of lacking spontaneity. To avoid a very long and annoying argument in the middle of the night, he watched another movie of exaggerated purity.

In his tired condition he also met with a couple of other contacts, but failed to gain any useful information about his suspected abduction. The stagnant investigation increased his frustration almost enough for him to contemplate an act of desperation, to take the evidence to his superiors. He would never make such a confession, however, so he decided to let his unconscious mind work on the case for a while. He would use conscious mental effort for what his boss wanted.

Chuck returned his call after lunch, as expected.

"What have you got?" he asked, trying to hide his impatience for having to wait.

"John," he said and Agent Pratt cringed at the tone of disappointment. "I don't know what happened."

"What do you mean?"

"Well, the two agents who followed Fuger, they got nothing."

"Nothing?" asked Pratt, more confused than angry. "They don't have any pictures or any contact information, or both?"

"The two I sent are rookies," he explained hesitantly. "But very competent. I don't understand it. I'll have to talk to them more. They're both embarrassed."

A million questions appeared in his mind.

"Was their presence detected? Did Fuger elude them? What?"

"No, nothing like that. They lost their cameras, and don't remember what happened."

For the next ten minutes, Pratt extracted all the information Chuck had acquired from the two agents. He sent Agent Pratt the GPS log from their vehicle which revealed a strange story. Gerald drove to his hotel, checked in, then went to the home of a woman named Sadi Jacobsen. Pratt already knew about her. Fuger's next destination introduced another character into the story, some rich old guy. Pratt wrote down his name and would examine his identity later.

After the old man's house, they drove about thirty miles away to the wilderness, to some small farm where they stopped for a couple of hours. The two agents returned to homebase after the farm. Something happened at that site and Pratt doubted that two FBI agents, rookies or experienced, just fell asleep as they claimed.

Another option became apparent. Maybe they lost Fuger on some small forest road and were too embarrassed to admit it? Despite his anger, he felt compelled to admit the difficulty of remaining inconspicuous as the only other vehicle on an isolated road, in the night. That explanation would have satisfied him, but they claimed to fall asleep, a more embarrassing confession.

The story reminded Pratt of what had happened to him. Only memory-tampering drugs would explain memory loss. For the next few moments, Agent Pratt enjoyed an intense anger. Although the evidence failed to directly connect Gerald Fuger to his abduction, the coincidence existed. Agent Pratt never let a good coincidence go to waste. If Gerald Fuger played a part in his memory loss, Pratt would find a way to kill him. Fuger would just disappear from the face of the earth and no one would ever discover what happened to him. Sending him to jail involved too much work.

"Chuck," Agent Pratt said after asking all his questions. He used a tone of neutrality, as if the news failed to affect him emotionally. "Just send me the report and please get the agents' urine and blood analyzed and have them checked for injections. I want to know if they were drugged and by what. Tell them I may want to talk to them once we get the results back. Let's give this high priority. I can take it from there."

While waiting for the results of the drug tests, Agent Pratt experienced difficulty focusing on his work. The next day, his boss took Pratt to lunch. They usually ate lunch together once a month, but they had gone just the previous week. His boss must have noticed the change in his behavior. Pratt should have hidden the emotional impact of his abduction.

Director Smithson chose a table in an isolated corner of the bistro. After the waitress took their order, he looked intently at Agent Pratt across the table.

"How's the girlfriend working out?" he asked casually.

"It's about to be over," he said. "That's how it's going. I used to get sleep. Now we wake up twice a night."

"You're finding it hard to throw out a woman with a little girl."

Smithson laughed hard at his friend and employee. Instead of a smile, the director received a cold stare.

"I don't think it's very funny."

"OK," said his boss, suddenly acting seriously. "Tell me what else is going on. You're not the type to let personal matters interfere with your work. You and I are stamped from the same die."

Although Pratt neglected to prefabricate a cover-story, one came instantly to his mind.

"It's all these assholes I have to work with." He ran his fingers through his hair in a convincing simulation of someone at the point of exhaustion. While talking, he imagined the two agents botch the simple task of watching Gerald Fuger. The image of them asleep in their vehicle helped maintain a convincingly emotional outburst. "I'm approaching some critical points in some cases, but I have to deal with some real goddamned idiots."

"Do you know what makes and breaks men?" Smithson asked.

Pratt turned from his view of the front window and met his boss's eyes.

"If I listen to your bullshit advice, can we talk about something else?"

Despite his tone of annoyance, Agent Pratt felt sincere interest in his words. Smithson rarely gave advice or said the same thing twice to anyone. He expected them to remember.

"The people who succeed in this life," Smithson said. "They give everything they've got to get it."

"Yes, and…" Pratt began, but his boss continued as if uninterrupted.

"Those at the front of the race put all their concentration, interest, and soul, if it exists, into what they are doing. Their personal lives come second, if they have any to begin with. They're devotion always keeps them one step ahead of the rest."

"Are you saying I'm letting my personal life interfere with my work?" he asked incredulously. "I don't have a personal life when I am working. I wouldn't have even mentioned it. You're the one who asked about it."

Director Smithson laughed and shook his head.

"That's not what I'm saying. I am telling you that devotion is a two-edged sword. If you let it, it will break you. It's my job, as your boss, to keep that from happening. What I am telling you, is that I better not see you at the office for a few days."

Agent Pratt became silent for a moment and looked down to the last cut of steak on his fork. Taking time off would not deter Agent Pratt from continuing to work as his boss knew. Smithson had given him an unspoken command. Do whatever he needed.

"Ok," he said before consuming the piece of steak.

Chuck called Pratt's cell phone the next day from the Portland office.

"Hi Chuck," he answered while driving. "The drug tests come back yet?"

"Yeah, we got em," he said with obvious disappointment. "The results came back with nothing. They're clean. No trace of any drugs capable of inducing an altered, psychotic state, and no injection points on their bodies."

"Damn," Pratt spat without attempting to conceal his emotions.

His mind already accepted the original explanation of drugs. He just waited too long to take urine samples. Someone associated with Gerald Fuger drugged the men. For the moment, he considered no other explanation. He planned to visit the site where they lost their memories.

86

Helen

While Jen, Helen's nanny, waited in line at the cashier, the little girl with light brown hair who had talked to Helen in the previous store, approached her again. Helen recognized the girl when she touched her shoulder.

"Hi, Helen," she said with a genuine smile, showing her desire to become friends. "Come wait with me outside."

Helen looked back to Jen in line then to the open area just outside the shop.

"OK," she said.

"We can wait for her out there."

Helen followed the slightly older girl outside, planning to sit in the empty couches there, but the girl kept walking. Even after Helen yelled for her to stop, she kept moving. When Helen started running after the little girl, she failed to notice her direction, towards the exit of the mall just around the corner. She looked once behind her to the shop where she left Jen.

"Hey wait, where are you going?" she yelled again.

"My little sister just ran outside," the girl answered without looking back. "Come on, I got to go get her."

The little girl ran to the door of the mall exit and held the door open for Helen.

"Hurry, so your nanny won't notice that you were gone when we get back. We'll come right back in, I promise. My sister took my favorite Bakugan, the one I wanted to show you."

Helen had a large collection of the popular Japanese ball toys, Bakugans, and wanted to see the one the girl would get. She paused, however, in front of the open mall door and stared outside with disappointment, preparing to refuse and run back to the store where Jen waited. Fear of retribution from her nanny overpowered the urge to see a cool new Bakugan toy.

Before Helen opened her mouth to share the disappointing news with her potential new friend, she felt a strange new sensation. Her fear and trepidation suddenly disappeared, replaced by a feeling of comfort. The new emotion spoke to her like a voice in her mind.

"Go outside," the voice said softly. "It's going to be all right."

With her fear suddenly erased and replaced by a strange tranquility, Helen felt no concern about following the girl. After exiting the mall, Helen noticed a car parked next to the curve with ugly thick exhaust escaping the tail pipe. The girl ran to the open back passenger door and slid inside the dark interior. Helen approached without hesitation. When Helen saw no other little girl inside, she stopped and rested her hand on the car door.

Extremely dark tinted windows blocked the bright sunlight, making the interior too dark to see clearly, so Helen took a closer look and noticed the absence of any other little girl or driver. She began to turn and look behind her, but felt a push instead. She landed in the backseat with her legs still sticking out of the car. She turned just in time to see a man pushing her feet inside the car and shutting the door. The older girl held tightly onto Helen's shoulder, keeping her in place.

"It's OK," she said and repeated the words several times while the driver returned to his seat.

"Let go of me," Helen said in panic, attempting to free herself from the tight grip and failing to extend her hand far enough to reach the door handle. As the car jerked into motion, an angry voice from the front seat stopped any other attempt to move.

"What took you so long, you little shit?"

"Where are we going?" asked Helen before the girl could respond. "Please take me back."

The man in the front seat ignored her.

"Don't make me ask again Daryn," the man said angrily. "What took you so long? Did anyone see you?"

"Sorry, Mr. Becerra. I did my best. I hurried! No one noticed me, I promise!"

"I've got to get back to my nanny, or else I'll get in trouble," Helen said directing her words to the girl next to her.

"Keep her quiet, or so help me."

"Yes, Mr. Becerra."

The girl named Daryn placed her hand on Helen's leg just above the knee in an attempt to calm her. She opened her mouth to speak, but a hand from the front seat stopped her with a hard slap on her forehead, causing Helen to jump. The girl silently placed her hand on her forehead to rub the sting away, but Helen squealed in fear. She attempted to back into the corner, but the hand reached quickly from the front seat to also hit Helen. The force of the blow knocked her head back against the seat. Her eyes flew wide open and she froze in place. Tears silently rolled down her cheeks.

Not in her entire life, had anyone ever hit her. She felt her blood pulsating through her veins and sat in silence. She felt like an animal in a trap, waiting to be killed and eaten.

"Get your seatbelts on and shut up."

While they traveled, the man played loud, harsh music on the radio, the kind her mother would never let her hear. The singer used forbidden language to the rhythm of a loud drum beat. Helen could feel the drums vibrate her chest and seat. While the loud music played, the girl whispered so only Helen could hear, but Helen paid no attention. She only cared about not getting hit again. Talking brought the slap so she planned on staying quiet. She only made movement with her eyes.

For the first several minutes, the loud music caused difficulty thinking. She required several more minutes to shut the horrible words from her mind and concentrate on a topic of her choosing. The little concentration she managed to muster, she used to remember the feeling of peace she experienced in the mall. By the end of the thirty-minute car trip, she managed to immerse herself in the feeling. Although the memory of getting hit never completely vanished, she could breathe calmly.

At the end of the trip, the man parked the car in a dark garage, shutting the door behind them. After opening the car door for Helen, he stood in an angry silence and waited for them to exit. Daryn gently pushed Helen on the shoulder in the direction of the open door, a sharp contrast to the strong grip at the mall. The older girl acted as if nothing out of the ordinary had happened.

“Come on,” she said with a smile on her face. "It's all right."

As Helen stepped out of the car, she noticed the single lightbulb hanging from the ceiling and then the old tools on the walls around the garage. The lightbulb barely shone enough light to show their surroundings. A piece of cardboard covered the only window on the wall with bright light entering the garage around the edges.

“It's all right Helen,” the girl said again. “I want to show you my…”

“Go tell Mrs. Becerra what happened,” the man said, interrupting the girl in mid-sentence. “Then get to your room. I want to have a little talk with our new friend.”

Before disappearing into the house, the girl glanced back at Helen with a worried, but sincere smile. Helen stood by the car while the man shut the door quietly. When the door shut, Helen felt like all connections to her past also closed. Fearing to look into the man’s eyes, she stared at his shoes instead.

He placed his hand on her shoulder, squatting and meeting her at eye level. He gently lifted her chin so that she looked at his face. His touch made her feel sick, but she feared to show any sign of resistance.

"Just breathe," said the tranquil voice in her mind.

“You’re going to like your new home,” the man said in an almost kind tone.

The physical sound of his voice reminded her of how imaginary the one in her mind sounded. That voice told her to breathe, so she concentrated on breathing. Since the man's words failed to call for a response, Helen just waited. For several seconds, they just stared at each other. His grip tightened on her shoulder and started to hurt, but his warm smile remained.

“Afraid to talk, huh? In the future, you will be afraid *not* to talk.”

87

Helen

Helen wanted to ask her abductor what he wanted, but her mouth failed to open. After waiting another moment for her to speak, he stood and pushed her gently toward the door to the house. Once inside, she noticed the dirty and messy interior, a strong contrast to the perfectly clean environment of her home where her toys only occasionally littered the living room floor.

The door from the garage led to a kitchen with dirty dishes covering every table and counter surface above the yellow linoleum floor, with old dirty clothes in the corners. The kitchen smelled of dirty dishwater. They passed through the kitchen and into a large, generally cleaner living room.

If visitors to the home only saw the living room, they would have had a higher opinion of the caretakers, probably assuming the rest of the house to be in similar condition. Two large, dark leather couches sat across from a new large screen television set in an expensive entertainment center. A round coffee table with a tinted glass top sat in the center of the room.

A woman with blond hair and a cigarette between her fingers sat on one of the couches. Her skin looked old, but she looked about the same age as Helen's mother. When the woman saw Helen and the man enter, she put her cigarette in the ashtray on the coffee table in front of her. She looked pleased, but with no smile.

"Not bad," she said as Mr. Becerra pushed Helen forward for a closer inspection. The woman extended her hand and touched Helen's hair. When she touched her cheek, Helen flinched and the woman pinched her cheek hard enough to cause pain. "Don't resist me child when I'm checkin you out. It's gonna get you hurt. What's your name?"

"Helen Jacobsen," she said quietly.

The woman turned Helen in a complete circle.

"Yep," she said with pleasure in her voice. "She's just what we were looking for. Listen to me, Helen. Next time, you are to speak so I can hear you better, understand?"

Helen nodded.

"Take her to Daryn's room," the woman said after turning to the man.

She spoke to him like an employee. Mr. Becerra took Helen to a room at the end of a hallway in the basement which smelled of mold. When he opened the door, Helen resisted the pressure of his hand on her shoulder to step inside the room.

"Well get in," he said and shut the door after pushing her roughly inside.

The sound of the lock actually caused Helen to feel a little better, as if the locked door protected her from the kidnappers. She stood motionless in front of the door and stared at the older girl sitting on the end of a dirty bed, the girl who helped put Helen in her current, horrible situation, her fellow captive. Daryn stood and walked to the door, placing her left ear on the hollow wood and listened to the retreating footsteps from the hallway. The stairs creaked as Mr. Becerra ascended to the upper level. Both girls stopped listening when he shut the door at the top of the stairs.

"OK, Helen," the girl said cheerfully. "He'll leave us alone for a while."

Helen made no response, but just stood still, inspecting her surroundings. The dirty room had one bed against the wall, just under a small and tightly shut window. Several dolls littered the ground around a small table against the opposite wall. Paper and crayons littered the white scuffed surface. The only light came from the window above the bed.

"Don't worry, I'm not going to hurt you," Daryn said, stepping forward.

After recognizing the girl's sincere sympathy, Helen began to cry, great sobs and tears pouring down her cheeks. Daryn rushed instantly to her side and embraced Helen with both arms. They embraced for several minutes. Neither of them spoke and to Helen's astonishment, the girl began to cry as well.

During their embrace, questions materialized in Helen's mind. Did the girl have no friends? How long has she been here? How to help her? Her brain failed to provide any answers, but the tranquil voice from the mall returned.

"Just wait," the voice said and Helen stopped crying.

"Mr. Becerra said I was going to get a new friend today," said Daryn when they let go of each other. She wiped her tears away and talked as if their emotional breakdown never happened.

"A new friend?" asked Helen, wiping her own eyes.

"Yeah," the older girl said. "It's going to be great. We can play dolls. You like dolls don't you?" Daryn skipped to her bed and picked up a pair of Barbie's from the ground. "This one is named Helen. I named her before I met you. Isn't that cool? And this one's Charlie. I know it's not a girl name because she's a tomboy."

Daryn extended the doll named Helen in her hand towards Helen. She took the doll, but kept her eyes on the older girl. Daryn broke eye contact and smiled at the doll in her hand.

"Hi Helen," the girl said in a mock older woman's voice, speaking for the doll. "I'm Charlie."

88

Mr. Becerra

Mr. Becerra joined his wife in the living room then retrieved the pack of cigarettes from the coffee table and popped a cigarette between his lips. After lighting the end, he sat back and took a long drag of smoke. He removed his favorite baseball cap from his head, the cap from his favorite local pub and placed the cap on the coffee table in the place of the cigarettes.

"We struck gold with that one," he said. His smile of satisfaction glistened on the oily skin of his face. "Just what Mr. Lewis has been looking for."

"How was the slip?" she asked. "Smooth?"

"Like butter," he said, taking another drag of smoke. He watched her flip the page of her magazine, the latest copy of Vogue. "That little shit pulled it off just like I taught her. She's gonna get a big thank you tonight."

"That's good," Mrs. Becerra said dismissively. "You better not lay a hand on blondie. That's the deal. He wants her fresh."

"You don't need to remind me," he said with a hint of derision in his voice.

"Good," she said ignoring his tone.

"After we hand her over, we'll be set." He attempted to catch a look at his wife in the eyes, but she concentrated on the magazine. "You still excited about the plan?"

"The gettin-out-a-here plan?" she asked, finally tearing her eyes from the magazine and looking to the window, to the darkening gray outside. "Of course, but Mexico? We'll fry our asses off."

"Yeah," he said. "But we'll be frying our asses off on the beach. That little girl just bought our tickets."

"I'm gonna give them a call," the woman said, placing the magazine on the couch beside her, face down to mark her page. "I'll bet you anything they'll want her tomorrow night. The sooner we're rid of her, the better."

"It's a shame isn't it?" he said.

"What is?"

"Daryn might only have a friend for a day," he said and laughed.

"We promised her a friend," the woman replied. "But we never said it would be forever."

Mr. Becerra stood and retrieved the phone for his wife.

"What do you think's gonna happen to the girl?" he asked with the phone extended in his hand.

Mr. Becerra could imagine a million wonderful things he wanted to do with their new captive. He also knew her most probable fate once she left their care, but he wanted to hear his wife give her prediction out loud. He loved hearing her talk about that sort of thing. In anticipation, he felt the saliva pooling on the sides of his tongue. She looked at him with a wry smile on her face.

"For the money they're paying for her, it's not gonna be pretty. Those bastards are sicker than you. That girl won't last the night."

89

Freddy

Mr. Smith talked to Sadi and Jen after Craig left his home, attempting to provide some comfort. He shared his confidence in Craig's ability to find Helen. They just had to wait. Craig would probably find the right clues in the security video footage at the mall security office, sufficient to lead him to Helen that night even. Mr. Smith used Craig Swenson for several years and the man always had success. He professed complete faith in his private investigator.

Gerald called Sadi after reaching the bridge over the Columbia river from Vancouver Washington, just twenty minutes later. Freddy watched as Sadi frantically punched at the buttons, trying to find the correct one to answer. Every phone call felt like a stab wound to Sadi, and Freddy cringed at the mixture of hope and foreboding filling her whole body. Did the phone call bring good or bad news? Had someone found Helen? Alive or dead?

Gerald arrived at eleven-thirty. Mr. Smith told him most of the story, but with Jen present he excluded the part about the crystal. Gerald asked many of the same questions Craig had asked and Mr. Smith answered all his questions quickly and quietly for fear of reopening the fresh wounds. In the end, Gerald asked for the name of the investigator, so he could contact him to ask more questions. He then suggested that Sadi and Jen should go home and get some sleep. To Freddy's amazement, she agreed. Jen led the way to the front door and Sadi followed with a dazed expression, full of exhaustion, fear, and sorrow.

As Sadi, Jen, and Gerald drove away, Freddy watched with a small twinge of jealousy. He had no future with the girl he used to love and maybe still loved. With his new sense, he felt the attraction between Gerald and Sadi. Even in the tragedy, he could still feel their mutual feelings. If the worst happened and they never recovered Helen, Sadi would probably never recover and lose all interest in life. Even if her future omitted him, Freddy committed to keep this horrible thing from happening to her.

"Freddy," Mr. Smith said after they left the house. "I know you want to help, but we should let Craig handle things tonight. He needs time to think about it, by himself."

"I know," Freddy said and looked down at the ground. He felt so tired and emotionally drained.

"Are you sure the alien won't help us find her?" Mr. Smith asked after a pause. He looked straight into Freddy's eyes, as if he suddenly distrusted how Freddy might answer. "The alien caused this didn't it?"

"I cannot explain how I know, but this is a test for me. To what end? I wish I knew."

“A test?” Mr. Smith said, rubbing his chin in thought. Freddy felt confusion emanating from the old man. “I have no experience in my life to help me think about this. At the barn, I felt no malice, but kidnapping a child is probably the worst thing someone can do. What is your guess as to the purpose of the test?”

"The purpose depends on the outcome, I think. Helen is either rescued or not." Freddy hated to talk about the possibility of failure. "What are the consequences of her rescue? I am not sure if that will help me find her. There are too many possibilities. I need to visit my room and think."

"I need sleep," Mr. Smith said, suddenly looking very tired.

The old man had exhausted too much of his energy to ask any more questions and left Freddy alone in the waiting room. When Freddy returned to his room in the basement, he sat on the bed with the crystal in the palm of his right hand. He stared at the crystal surface for ten full minutes before recognizing the overwhelming desire to close his eyes, fall back on his bed and succumb to the melatonin in his blood.

After laying on top of his bed and closing his eyes, images of Helen in different situations played in his mind, each situation worse than the last. Monsters held the poor girl captive, abusing her worse than his foster families had abused him. Freddy imagined he could feel her waiting and hoping for someone to rescue her. He remembered hoping for someone to rescue him too. He fell asleep with the crystal laying on his chest, dark and lifeless.

When Freddy woke up early the next morning, he felt no better than the previous evening, not even physically rested. Fortunately, he forgot the specifics of horrible dreams. He and Mr. Smith waited for communication from Craig. He called at eight thirty with a progress report. Craig spent a good portion of the evening at the mall, watching the surveillance video from the stores. He had several more hours of video to review before he would be satisfied and he might need to review the video a second time.

Mr. Smith cupped his hand over the phone and turned to Freddy with a slight smile on his face.

“He saw Helen speaking with another little girl,” he whispered. “Craig thinks she had something to do with it.”

At the end of the phone conversation, Mr. Smith gave all the information he learned. Craig saw a man with the little girl who had talked with Helen. He had not yet seen the man’s face, but he could clearly see the unique baseball cap which had the logo of a local brewery named Breakpoint Brewing Company. The cap indicated very good news, the man lived in the area. Craig asked Mr. Smith and Freddy to research the brewery and find all the places where one could purchase a cap with their logo.

Craig Swenson had two major leads to follow that morning, acquiring more video footage from the male suspect and taking the little girl’s photo to social services. Maybe he could determine her identity, if she had a record of some kind. From his previous experiences, he had little hope for cooperation from social services. They had so many layers of bureaucracy which impeded a private or police investigation. If he got lucky, he would acquire a good picture of the man with the little girl and take it to his contacts in the police department who would be more than happy to help him. Kidnappers were likely to have a criminal record of some sort, and hopefully the guy had lived in the area a long time.

Mr. Smith sounded hopeful during his progress report. Hearing the optimism from his boss caused Freddy to feel better as well. Freddy felt energized at the prospect of helping with the investigation. He ran downstairs to his laptop and started searching the internet for all the information about that brewing company.

Freddy discovered only three stores which sold the cap with the brewery logo. He called each one to see if anyone made a recent purchase, but no one claimed to know anything so Freddy visited them and asked all the clerks. No one remembered selling any of the caps recently and he located the caps in the inventory of only one store. He emailed the disappointing results of his investigation to Craig.

Effort spent on the investigation helped conceal his severe anxiety, but when he completed Craig's assignment, his anxiety grew to almost unbearable levels. He needed something else useful to do. While considering his options, he felt an inexplicable, but undeniable impression. Just wait. At the moment, he could do nothing. Did the impression originate from him? Wait for what? The impression became another source of concern. He felt like a prisoner, waiting for the guards to come and take him to the electric chair.

He had a required lab at school that afternoon, but planned to make only a brief appearance to satisfy the attendance credit. His lab partner would have to take more of a proportional share of the work for once. In order to secure a good grade for himself, he usually did more than his share of the work. His lab partner failed to pay as much attention to detail as he liked. If he let his partner follow the instructions her way, he would probably receive a worse grade. At the moment, however, his grades felt trivial.

Craig called again a few hours later, just as Freddy prepared to drive to his lab. As usual, Mr. Smith picked up the phone.

"Hi Craig," he said with urgency in his voice. "What have you found?"

While Mr. Smith talked with Craig on the phone, Freddy could hear disappointment in the big man's voice. His boss liked to keep the phone volume high and Freddy could hear some of the conversation. The private investigator found some better footage of the man with the little girl, but doubted whether any could be used for identification. At the moment, he planned to take what he had to the police station. Hopefully, the police photo manipulation software could enhance the images for a positive identification.

The excitement Freddy felt that morning began to dissipate a bit after the conversation with Craig ended. He hoped Craig would find her of course, but his feelings indicated a different plan, with Freddy as the key participant. The abductor had Helen for only a day and Freddy hoped they had a few more days to find her. While Mr. Smith explained what Freddy already knew about the conversation, he could feel the true emotions of Mr. Smith. Fortunately, they matched his outward appearance, optimism and complete faith in Craig's abilities.

Before Freddy left the house for his lab, he went to his room for a book he forgot to put into his backpack. As he passed the dresser, the dark crystal laying on top drew his attention. The eyes of the spider showed no light of their own, but reflected the artificial lights in the room, just like any other piece of glass would.

He felt a sudden and extreme hatred for the crystal. The object symbolized what happened to Helen. Did Sadi feel the same? He slung the backpack over his shoulder and hid the crystal in his pocket, out of sight.

After arriving at his lab, Freddy decided to stay for half the time rather than leave immediately. His lab partner usually let him take the lead, but when he failed to initiate the routine lab preparations, she awkwardly took the lead. After twenty minutes, he turned to his partner, a shorter brown-haired girl with a permanent smile on her face. He liked her.

"Erika," he said, feeling no need to fake any discomfort. "I need to go, sorry. You can take it from here right?"

"I think so," she said without taking her eyes off the glass buret. A solution of sodium hydroxide slowly dripped into their acid solution. A moment later, she stopped the flow and looked into his eyes. She wanted to ask why he needed to leave, but then changed her mind, not wanting to pry. "I'll be fine. I hope you feel better."

He forced a smile, then turned and walked out of the lab. Erika watched him until he disappeared from her sight then returned her attention back to the titration. Her brief concern for him became the only positive emotion Freddy felt. In the parking lot, he just sat in the car, angry at himself for taking personal time when he should have been helping Sadi.

He removed the crystal from his pocket and held it tightly in his hand, watching the sun slowly approach the horizon through the window, passing between sparse cloud cover. He had only two and a half hours before the sun would disappear behind the horizon, starting the process of night. That event seemed important. After slowly opening his palm to reveal the crystal, he looked into the eyes of the spider. Despite the distaste he felt for the object, he hoped to become entranced, but waited in vain for the alien creature to give him instructions. Although still unable to focus on the spider eyes, nothing seemed to happen.

While watching the eyes, someone knocked on his window and he jolted as if caught daydreaming. He turned his head to see a familiar person standing outside his window, his lab partner Erika. For a moment, he just stared at her blankly.

"Freddy, Freddy," she asked, her voice muffled by the glass. "Hey, what's wrong?"

He started the car then rolled down the window, using the time to assess the situation. While Freddy sat in his car, Erika had completed the remainder of the lab.

"Nothing is wrong Erika. I am OK."

"Have you been sitting there this entire time?" she asked and the smile returned. "You were just staring at that thing. What is it?"

"Just a car ornament," he said, quickly placing the crystal between his legs on the seat, out of her sight. "I, I am OK."

"Our lab is over. Can I do anything for you?"

After convincing her of his stable condition, she left him. He watched as she entered her car and drove out of the parking lot, towards the setting sun. The previous forty minutes had passed in a mere instant. He had no memory of the time, but he knew one thing, what he needed to do, what he needed to do quickly.

90

Freddy

Freddy felt an uncomfortable sensation, like the instinct to eat when hungry. The sensation urged him to drive south, get on interstate five and just drive. Before leaving the parking lot, however, he checked the glove box to find the gun with the silencer he made for it. He searched his memory, but failed to account for how the gun arrived in that position. Seeing the weapon brought a feeling of reassurance and he had to fight the temptation to reach for the gun and grip it tightly. He shut the glove box in an attempt to shut the thought from his mind.

Before following his instinct to travel in a southward direction, he decided to go against his instinct and take a detour, to Sadi's house. He pulled onto SW Broadway towards the interstate heading north, towards Hillsboro where Sadi lived. The urge to drive south attacked him more harshly, but he ignored the intense sensation. He had to get Sadi. Was it just an excuse to see her?

After arriving at her house, he ran to the door.

"Freddy?" a confused Jen said, after answering his heavy knocking.

"Hi. Can I come in?" he asked in a hurry. "I need to see Sadi."

"Of course," she said.

Jen led him to Sadi and he noticed her pitiful condition. Her eyes had no more life in them. She wore the same clothes as the day before, with her dark hair pulled into a messy ponytail. After seeing him, she made a weak attempt to open her eyes wider, as if the small action required a tremendous amount of energy.

"Any news?" she asked while attempting to suppress the small bead of hope at seeing him. "Do you need to sit down?"

"No thanks," he replied. "I need you to come with me."

"What have you found?" she asked, a sudden bolt of energy animating her features.

Freddy looked from her to Jen, then back.

"It might be nothing, but you should come with me."

He widened his eyes and nodded his head toward Jen so only Sadi could see. At the realization, she nodded and then ran to a closet by the front door to grab a jacket.

"What do I need to bring?"

"Go get a small, but sharp knife."

Freddy whispered so only Sadi could hear him. They left the house and Freddy saw Jen watching from the front window.

"Have you found her?" asked Sadi after shutting the passenger door.

"I might know where she is."

His answer had the power to crush her hope so Freddy chose his words carefully. He reached under his seat and removed the crystal, then handed the object to her. He kept his eyes on the road while feeling her extreme apprehension at touching it.

"Where is she?" she asked while looking at the crystal.

Did she speak to him or the crystal, or both of them?

"We need to drive south. That is all I know, for now."

He initially felt the need to get on interstate five southbound, but that direction suddenly felt wrong. Instead, he decided to take the Hillsboro Highway south. Freddy glanced out his window at the setting sun and estimated just another hour before sunset. Dusk seemed like a critical turning point in the evening. They needed to reach their destination before losing too much daylight, but not too soon either.

"Can I call Gerald and tell him where we are?" she asked. "He went to get some food."

"No," Freddy said rather bluntly, cringing at the man's name. "We should not let anyone know where we are or what we are doing. I was supposed to do this alone, I think."

"But you came to get me?"

"Yes," Freddy said and nodded.

They drove a long time in silence and just looked out the window. Time seemed to pass so slowly. Freddy felt immense anxiety to hurry, almost overpowering his fear of what they would find at their destination. The effect of so many different chemicals entering his blood stream produced a strong desire for physical movement so he stretched his arms and legs while driving. As Sadi watched the terrain fly by them, he felt the hope he inspired.

The alien gave him much more than empathy. His life made him very good at empathy already. When he saw others experiencing emotional trauma, he always felt a similar effect to some extent. At least, he guessed their emotions. After the barn experience, however, he actually felt the emotions of those near him and not just what he imagined. Along with feelings, came a glimpse of future actions. Emotions motivated action.

After a long interval of silence, Sadi suddenly felt a mixture of fear and confusion. Before she spoke, Freddy turned to face her in anticipation of a question about upcoming violence.

"Freddy," she said and flinched after meeting his eyes. "Why do you need a knife?"

"It is just a feeling I have," he said apologetically and decided to delay revealing the gun to her. "Sorry if it makes you nervous."

"Do you know where we're going?" she asked.

"We are going to Salem," he said as the answer materialized in his mind.

He unconsciously pushed a little harder on the accelerator. At their current speed, they would arrive in a little over thirty minutes, just as the sun would set. His answer failed to satisfy her underlying questions. He waited patiently for her to form the next words.

"How do you know all these things? What happened to you at the barn?"

"I can feel the emotions of others," he said flatly. "I do not know how or why.

It hit me like a ton of bricks after I woke up at the barn."

"Can you feel my emotions?" she asked tentatively, as if she feared the answer.

"Yes," he said while looking at the road ahead. "I am sorry, but I cannot control it. Emotions give me clues to future actions. That does not explain everything, but it is all I know."

His answer had the opposite effect on Sadi than he predicted. She felt immediate pity for him. Her next words needed no response and they drove the remainder of the journey to Salem in silence.

"Hmm," she said. "Thanks for telling me Freddy."

When they finally entered downtown Salem, he still had no idea of their final destination. His instincts told him to keep driving. He turned when the feeling urged and drove straight when the feeling vanished. Did he imagine the sensations? Did he bring Sadi on a wild-goose chase?

The situation changed when they passed an elegant, five-story hotel on the right. Freddy suddenly felt sick to his stomach. Vile humans occupied the building. Their emotions sickened him and he wished he could spit the feelings from his mouth. The negative emotions contrasted sharply with the beautiful building where the abductors held Helen captive.

"What's wrong?" asked Sadi as she noticed the glistening sweat on his forehead.

"We need to find a place to park," he said, choking back the disgust enough to answer. "This is the place."

"Where are we going? Where do we stop?"

The traffic light turned from yellow to red in front of them and he stopped the car obediently.

"We need to park on this block."

"There's a place."

Sadi pointed to an open parking space down the right side road. After the light turned green, he continued driving straight and came around the block to park where she indicated. They both exited the car then Freddy walked around it and opened the passenger door. While Sadi waited on the sidewalk, he removed the gun and silencer from the glove box. After slipping the silencer in his pocket, he secured the weapon deftly in his pants over his hip and covered it with his jacket, all without Sadi noticing. He removed a Boston Red Sox baseball cap from the backseat then shut the door. After placing the hat on his head, Freddy pulled the cap down low to conceal his face.

After shutting the door, he looked to Sadi and noticed her watching the buildings around them and the traffic. Freddy took a deep breath then turned his attention to the western sky. The sun looked like a glowing marble sitting on the horizon.

91

Helen

Daryn took control of all the dolls after Helen lost interest in playing with them. For several hours, Helen just sat on the floor and watched as Daryn made the Barbie dolls talk and do normal girl things. Helen regained her motivation after a while, partly from boredom, to participate in another tea party. She still felt completely disoriented in her new surroundings, but being away from the adults and in a room with another little girl made the experience more bearable.

Daryn filled every moment with chatter, speaking either as the dolls or as herself so Helen just had to listen if she decided to remain silent. Sometimes during the activities of imagination, Helen thought her new friend treated her just like one of the dolls. As the older girl talked, Helen's mind raced through a million different ways to escape, but every scenario ended with one of the Becerras catching her. They frightened Helen more than becoming separated from her mother. Her only comfort came from imagining the police or her mother breaking down the door and rescuing them. She hoped they would spend all their time in the room.

After the first tea party, Daryn showed Helen all of her possessions. Introducing her to all the toys required quite a while, at least a couple of hours. At the beginning, Helen winced as Daryn proudly handed the old, dirty toys to her. She usually liked to keep her hands clean. Helen feared to upset the girl so she pretended to inspect and admire all of them. In addition to missing her mother and Jen, Helen began to miss her own toys.

When Helen noticed the room becoming noticeably darker, she waited for Daryn to energize the overhead light, but she made no indication of noticing the lower light levels. She just continued to play as if unaware of her surroundings. Helen ignored the desire to ask for more light. Maybe the single light above them did not work.

The lower light levels caused Helen to recognize another physical sensation, the need for food. Her stomach began to ache and she tried remembering the last time she ate anything. Before going to the mall, she had a peanut butter and jelly sandwich. Jen promised to get her a treat from a kiosk at the mall once she satisfied her need to shop, but they never made it that far.

The memory of being with Jen made her want to cry again, but she stopped herself and focused on their games. Besides, asking for food probably meant an unpleasant meeting with one of the adults again. At that point, Helen would rather die of starvation than see them.

A short while later, Helen recognized another, more urgent impulse, to visit a bathroom. How long could she ignore the uncomfortable feelings before she had to act and leave the room? She did not have to wait long for the answer. They suddenly heard footsteps on the stairs.

At the noise, Daryn immediately rose from the floor and stood to attention like a soldier in the military.

"Stand up when he comes in," she said while extending her hand to help Helen to her feet.

Helen quickly stood and they waited for the door to open. Never in her life had she ever heard anything as scary as the sound of the approaching footsteps and then the turn of the door knob. Mr. Becerra poked his head in the room and his eyes fixed on Helen, then Daryn. He held a can of Coors beer in his right hand and leaned against the door frame on his left shoulder.

"Bathroom time," he said in a friendly and caring tone, but Helen recognized the man's insincerity as if he talked with a bad speech impediment.

To her relief, she found a bathroom just down the hall from their room. She would not have to go upstairs and interact with the woman who scared her more than the man.

Before shutting the bathroom door, Helen glanced back and found Mr. Becerra looking at her with a smile on his face. This time, the smile looked sincere and made her feel even more uncomfortable. On their way back to the bedroom, Helen expected Daryn to follow, but Mr. Becerra shut the door behind her and took Daryn with him up the stairs. The look on Daryn's face disturbed her almost as much as her abduction at the mall. Her face turned to stone, reminding Helen of a zombie from the movies her mother never let her watch.

Helen listened with her ear pressed against the door. When the noise of them ascending the stairs vanished, Helen felt brave enough to energize the light. To her surprise, the light caused a small feeling of hope. She climbed from the bed onto the dresser to look out the window. From her viewpoint, she could only see the dark gray clouds in the sky. She tried to open the window, but failed to hear even a small creak of movement.

Helen sat on the bed for a long time, staring at the clutter of old toys, clothes and dirty carpet. She felt like crying, but fear and confusion acted like an emotional damn. She listened with dread at every noise from upstairs and imagined what the noises might mean.

At the same time, every sound brought the possibility of Daryn's return, the only person in the whole world who shared in her misery, who understood her position. The person who lured her away from her family now became her only friend. Without Daryn, Helen sat alone with demons behind every shadow. Without her, Helen would be all alone.

After an hour passed, Helen began to feel drowsy so she laid down on the bed. The pillow had once been white, but over the years of unwashed use, the fabric turned gray and dirty, and smelled bad. She fought sleep as long as possible, afraid of what might happen if she closed her eyes.

Helen woke several hours later when the lights extinguished, leaving the room in almost complete darkness. Helen opened her eyes in panic and watched a small shadow slowly approaching the bed.

"Hi Helen," Daryn said in a robot's voice, cold and emotionless.

Without changing her clothes, she joined Helen in bed, laying motionless on her side. Helen waited for the girl to say something else, but she remained quiet.

When Daryn began to cry in barely audible sobs, Helen forgot her fears and the sadness of losing her mom. She forgot the terror of being shoved into an unknown vehicle, forgot the despair of watching the familiar shopping center fall away into the distance. She only wanted to comfort Daryn and make her feel better.

Helen put her tiny arms around her new friend and held tightly. Daryn's crying stopped soon afterward and they both fell asleep. Daryn slept without moving. Helen dreamed of her mother having tea with Mrs. Becerra and laughing.

92

Helen

Helen failed to hear the creaking of the stairs the next morning as Mr. Becerra descended to the basement. He opened the bedroom door and used an angry hiss to wake both girls from a deep sleep. A bright gray light leaked into the room from the window. After opening her eyes, Helen instantly noticed the man, sending her heart into a sudden sprint.

"Time for breakfast," he said in a commanding tone then disappeared down the hall, leaving the door open.

Both girls went upstairs in the clothes they wore the previous day and silently ate breakfast at the kitchen table. Daryn shoved dirty plates out of the way so she could place their bowls of plain oatmeal on the table. The oatmeal had no sugar or any other additives, but satisfied Helen's hunger. She failed to recall a longer interval without eating or oatmeal ever tasting so good.

They ate their breakfast while Mr. Becerra watched the news in the living room, the back of his head to them. Helen kept her eyes on the food until Mrs. Becerra reappeared.

"Thank you for breakfast," Daryn said and put her hand on Helen's leg and squeezed.

"Yes," Helen said quickly, but kept her eyes on the table. "Thanks for breakfast."

"You girls need a bath," she said in a stern voice.

Mrs. Becerra made them both take a bath together with the bathroom door open. Mr. Becerra stood in the doorway and watched while his wife thoroughly scrubbed them. In the middle of the procedure, she turned around to face him.

"Get out of here," she said angrily. "Don't get any ideas."

Helen cringed at her angry tone, but the man just laughed and silently walked away. When Mrs. Becerra turned back to the girls, she squinted at Helen. For a brief moment, Helen thought the woman had done something nice for her, but the look in her eyes claimed otherwise. They made Helen colder than the air on her wet skin.

"You're clean. Get out and dry off while I do your hair."

She gave both girls a towel and brushed their hair, starting with Daryn.

"Thank you, ma'am!" Daryn said.

"You need to look real good for a meeting with a man later this afternoon," she said after starting on Helen's hair. "You're to be polite and do whatever the man tells you. Do you understand?"

"I, I," Helen stuttered. "I don't know."

While waiting for the woman's response, Helen forgot to breathe. The woman shook her head and laughed sarcastically as if she just asked a horse to repeat her words.

"Smile and nod your head," she commanded.

The woman smiled with wide eyes, nodding theatrically as a demonstration of what to do. Helen's heart accelerated, but she nodded her head and tried to smile.

"Good job," Mrs. Becerra said in a tone lacking any hint of praise. "You're gonna be in a real nice place, so you gotta look real good. You'll meet a real nice man named Mister Lewis. Now show me what you're gonna do when you meet him!"

"I am," Helen started to say and tears began forming in her eyes, but Mrs. Becerra stopped her.

"No words, just nod, and you better wipe those tears away, real quick. You hear me?"

"Yes, Ma'am."

Mrs. Becerra gave the girls a set of new, surprisingly clean clothes then left them alone. To Helen's relief, she closed the door and let them dress in privacy. Helen's hands shook as she pulled the pretty, satin dress over her head. Daryn dressed quickly and wordlessly then helped Helen with the rest. She smiled and hummed while pulling up the new stockings and then the shiny new shoes on Helen's feet. Helen felt like one of the dolls.

When both girls finished dressing, they returned to their room for a few hours. After the door shut, Helen recovered her morale enough to attend another tea party with Daryn. During their imaginary exercise, Helen asked a question.

"What's going to happen?"

The question wiped the older girl's smile from her face.

"I don't know," she said in irritation.

After several moments of looking angry and offended, Daryn's expression changed to excitement. She ran to a drawer and removed an old Japanese Bakugan toy.

"I almost forgot that I had this," she said in excitement. "You like Bakugans, right?"

Helen held the spherical toy that transformed into a robotic monster. The object reminded Helen of the previous day when Daryn showed her the same toy. She spent a couple of seconds pretending to admire the thing.

The next sound made them both turn their heads towards the door. Helen stopped breathing. The door to the basement opened and the stairs creaked as heavy footsteps descended them. Daryn positioned herself protectively between Helen and the door. When the door opened, Mr. Becerra appeared with two glasses of a strawberry-red liquid.

"Brought you some Kool-Aid," he said with a smile, extending the clear plastic cups to them both.

Daryn drank the liquid without a moment's hesitation, but Helen looked at the cup with apprehension. She never drank Kool-Aid in her life. Hearing the name caused a vague feeling of something sinister.

"Do you have a problem?" asked Mr. Becerra, his tone turning to anger and eyes narrowing.

"Thank you," Helen said and started to sip the sweet liquid.

Surprisingly, she enjoyed the cool fluid sliding down her throat. Mr. Becerra waited until she drained the entire cup. After he took the empty vessel, Helen felt a tingling sensation all over her body. Never before in her life had she felt so good.

Helen spent the next two hours in a mixed state of warped consciousness and sleep. As she watched a million different colors swirling around her head, she had no time to feel bad or wonder about her location. She felt like water in a small stream, slithering down a mountain slope, sunlight randomly stabbing her in the eyes. She felt no more fear, just wonder as the amazing sensations passed through her.

At one point, her mother's face floated in the sky, high above. A flock of birds flew through her giant cloud face, ripping the beautiful face apart.

93

Freddy

As Freddy and Sadi walked towards the hotel where the kidnappers kept Helen, all the emotions Freddy felt when they drove past the building began to creep into his mind again. The combined emotions of malicious and ignorant humans, mixed together, created a net unpleasant concoction, like smelling a mixture of fresh flowers and rotting meat. The horrible sensation intensified his anger like nothing else in his life.

Freddy enjoyed the anger. The emotion felt like drawing fresh air into his lungs after escaping an outhouse. The emotion provided the strength to place one foot in front of the other.

Helen's emotions became clearer. Freddy recognized her unique emotional signature, reminding him of the unpleasant memories from his childhood. He remembered the feeling of being powerless, frightened and alone, surrounded by people who cared nothing for his welfare. He felt none of those emotions for himself anymore. He felt in control of himself and the situation, even though he remained ignorant of the future.

His mind refused to consider any conclusion to the evening different from locating and saving Helen. His feeling of confidence, however, brought an unexpected feeling of paranoia. Did he suffer from delusion? Could he trust his emotions and new senses? Only the barn incident supplied any significant confidence so far.

When they turned the corner and the hotel returned to view, Freddy stopped to study the building. The fifth floor instantly drew his attention, the top floor. As he stared at all the windows on the fifth floor he noticed that the last light of the sun would soon leave the hotel in shadow.

"Is Helen in there?" asked Sadi, afraid of a negative answer.

"Yes," he said.

As Freddy peered at the top floor, he could feel Sadi's confusion and concern for the immediate future. She wanted to ask him several questions, but chose to remain quiet for fear of ruining whatever guided him. Freddy only had one good, solid feeling at the moment, her confidence in him. He decided to focus on that single positive feeling.

"We have a small obstacle," he said.

"What?" she asked quickly.

"We need to quickly check in and get a room, but we want to avoid getting caught on their security cameras, and not use real ID. Do you have a fake ID?"

He knew her answer before she spoke, but waited for her response anyway.

"I don't have a fake ID."

"That is OK," he said. "We will work around that."

His plan required a room on the top floor, anonymously acquired. Since they had no fake forms of identification, Freddy would have to test the validity of a popular belief: 'You can buy anything in this world with money'.

Freddy brought a huge bundle of cash, more than a person should attempt to carry at any particular time and probably more than the legal limit. With enough money, no one would ask for a credit card or identification. Rich people got away with murder and all sorts of corruption with what money could buy. Money had its own way of doing things.

Freddy turned from the building to stare intensely at Sadi. She needed to become less noticeable, less identifiable. With her hair pulled back like usual, everyone could clearly see her face. She needed some cover. Freddy wore a baseball cap which concealed his face well enough. People in general, however, noticed a pretty woman more than an average man.

"Sadi," he said tentatively. "There is one thing I think you should do. Can you let your hair down, to cover your face at all?"

He watched as Sadi untied her hair, shook her head and arranged several strands over her face. She had no bangs so her eyes were still visible, but she looked quite different. He enjoyed watching the transformation, a momentary reprieve.

"Is that good?" she asked.

"Perfect," he said without emotion.

"So what's the plan?" she asked with curiosity and not a challenge. "How are we going to get a room without identifying ourselves?"

"I have enough money to get a room without an ID," he said confidently. "I will enter first and go to the front desk. You come in a few minutes later, but just go sit in the lobby until I can meet you at the elevator "

She looked at him in surprise, but remained silent. He could feel her complete confidence in his abilities. She felt as prepared as if they spent several months planning. Her dependence caused him to feel even more pity for her. He hated to feel powerless and dependent on others.

As planned, Freddy walked alone into the hotel lobby, feeling as if he walked past a group of feasting jackals. He hoped none of them noticed him so he walked while facing the ground and his hat pulled low over his face, but not far down enough to raise suspicion. After sensing his emotional effect on those in the lobby, he adjusted his gait to minimize their notice.

The front desk came into view almost immediately on his right. A plump, short woman with a pretty face stood behind the desk, looking down at a computer screen. Despite her cheerful appearance, he sensed her impatience. She planned to go home in just a short while and wanted nothing unexpected to occur.

He approached her slowly. When he arrived at the desk, she failed to acknowledge his presence so he pretended to admire the painting on the wall to his right, an abstract piece of boxes with sharp corners and pastel colors. A few milliseconds later, she looked up from the computer screen and he whipped his head around to meet her eyes. She jumped in surprise.

At the instant of eye contact, Freddy knew the woman had an awareness of illegal activities occurring on the top floor above them, but since those activities failed to affect her, she did not care. As long as she received a steady paycheck, they could do whatever they wanted. Her attitude of indifference added to his anger, but he forced his lips into a smile.

"I would like a room," Freddy said, but before she could ask a follow-up question, he placed five hundred-dollar bills in front of her. "Is something on the fourth or fifth floor available, facing west preferably? I love a good view."

She swallowed before answering. His question made her anxiety levels rise.

"Would you like the Emperor Suite?"

He looked intensely into her eyes and recognized the word 'Emperor' as a code word. She mistakenly suggested the Emperor Suite instead of following the guidelines to wait for the guests to make the specific request. He needed to act confused and refuse the suggestion. If he agreed, procedure required that she notify her manager which would delay her from leaving for the night and caused a feeling of annoyance. Freddy glanced at the list of rooms on the wall behind her and failed to see any room listed as an 'Emperor Suite'.

"No," he said, acting confused. "Nothing special, just whatever this will get me."

"OK," she said innocently while cursing herself for her blunder. "I'll need to see a credit card."

She experienced difficulty maintaining eye contact with him when she just wanted to look at all the money on the table. Freddy reached his hand to his back pocket and acted as if he just made a disappointing discovery.

"Oh, sorry, but I forgot my credit card. Is this enough? I do not need a receipt."

He looked casually at the money on the table between them, raising his eyebrows as if slightly annoyed.

"Yes, this will cover it," she said quickly, finally understanding what he meant. She pulled the bills towards her and they disappeared behind the desk.

Freddy recognized Sadi's proximity before she appeared in his peripheral vision, walking past him towards some couches in the lobby. The woman behind the desk failed to notice her. She focused her full attention on the money and how she could maximize her share. She would give him a good room, the least expensive option with whatever discounts at her disposal, then she could claim the remainder of the money.

The woman quickly completed the transaction and extended his room access card in her left hand, an apartment on the fourth floor. As he took the room access card he smiled politely, but felt anger at the woman for profiting from him. Without saying another word he turned and joined Sadi at the elevator.

Even though Sadi missed a shower for the past few days and in general looked disheveled, standing by her made Freddy's heart skip a beat. Her dark hair hanging around her face caused her eyes to appear more mysterious and beautiful than usual. He felt a sudden temptation to put his arm around her in an attempt to offer comfort. He knew the action would be an appropriate gesture, but he lacked the courage to make the attempt.

They both waited impatiently for the elevator and Freddy realized why he probably should have visited Salem alone. Sadi's proximity might hurt his ability to concentrate. He needed to focus on Helen and her captors, not fight his sexual instincts. He felt like standing in a pond full of alligators with only one friend. When the time came for them to separate, he would be even more alone and would have to face all the sharp teeth by himself.

His heartbeat quickened when the elevator door opened. He let Sadi enter first, then followed her inside. When the door closed, he felt a momentary relief. They successfully completed the first step of the hotel infiltration and no one had taken any special notice of them except for the front desk attendant and she would be going home in a few minutes. Freddy let his body relax for a moment and took a deep breath to prepare for the next step.

"Freddy," she said, putting her hand on his shoulder and holding tightly. She spoke in a whisper, slowly but saturated with impatience. "Where's Helen? Is she on the fourth floor?"

As the elevator carriage approached the second floor, Freddy considered his words carefully. They only had a few moments in the elevator to talk. The elevator door would open on the third floor for an old man who would ruin any further verbal communication.

"Helen is not on the fourth floor," he said and pointed to the third-floor indicator light which just illuminated. "I will explain when we are safely in our room. A man will be entering soon."

As expected, the elevator door opened and the tall man in his late sixties stepped inside the carriage. After pushing the button for the first level, the old man tipped his head to Sadi in acknowledgment.

They encountered no one on their walk to their room on the fourth floor. They walked silently on light blue carpet decorated with elegant red swirls and circles. Gold-painted trim ran horizontally down the middle of each wall, separating the white surface above from the ebony below. The beautiful hallway and quiet atmosphere failed to instill its intended emotion, tranquility.

After shutting the door to their elegant room, Freddy raced to the window and looked through the thick curtains. Sadi followed him with some hesitation, as if some kind of predator lurked in the space behind the curtains. The only illumination came from the window.

"Helen is on the fifth floor, in one of the rooms," Freddy said after closing the curtains again. "I need you to stay here while I go get her. It may take more than an hour, so please try to be patient, although I know that will be difficult. I am sorry."

"What is she doing here?" asked Sadi, hope in her voice and fear in her eyes. She brushed her hair from hiding her eyes and tucked it behind her ears.

"I do not know," Freddy lied. He could not tell Sadi the horrible truth. "But I am getting her back."

Freddy paused after placing his hand on the door handle.

"Do not be concerned when the hotel loses power."

94

Sadi

After Freddy left Sadi alone in the hotel room, she walked several times from the window to the door and back again. Every time she reached the door, she put her ear to the wood and listened, but heard no sound in the hallway beyond. At least, she expected to hear some noise coming from the rooms above or below her, but nothing came from them either. The silence in the apartment felt like another lead blanket of depression weighing down on her.

While waiting, the street lights from outside slowly became the only light illuminating the room. An irrational fear warned her to keep the lights off. Light could attract unwanted attention. Even though no one in the hallway would know of her presence with the lights illuminated, she decided to take no chances. Nothing about the situation made any sense so why should she try to think rationally?

Freddy's command to wait helped Sadi fight the temptation to run up the stairs to the fifth floor and kick in every door. If she had a gun, probably nothing would have stopped her from running hysterically into the hallway. To help pass the time, Sadi opened her purse and withdrew the knife. For a long time she just sat on the bed and watched the blade reflect the low light from the windows. Disturbing images of using the knife consumed her thoughts.

"Breathe, just breathe," she whispered and the sound of her voice helped expel the demons haunting the room. "You can't help her if you lose control. Freddy knows what he's doing."

She had to trust Freddy. He claimed to know Helen's location, the pivotal piece of information required to rescue her and seemed willing to risk his life for them. Now he just had to retrieve Helen.

He had the ability to know what people were going to do. Evidence confirmed the claim. He answered her unspoken questions on several occasions. At the time, his actions made her feel uncomfortable, but now the memory gave her hope. She also refused to entertain the idea of Freddy being wrong, traveling to the wrong hotel in the wrong city.

She still refused to conform to social conditioning and call the police. They would ruin any chance of finding Helen. She could not call them anyway. They would not believe her, the story about Freddy and the crystal. Even without telling them the specifics, what could they do, break into every room? No, the police could only knock on a hotel room door, ask a few questions and then move on to the next doors. Then they would take Sadi in for questioning.

After fifteen minutes of scanning the parking lot and the traffic in the street, Sadi laid down on the bed and closed her eyes. While she lacked the urge to sleep, she hoped the bed would help her focus on listening for any noise from the fifth floor. When she closed her eyes, however, she felt a strong desire to sleep forever, a one-way ticket to oblivion.

No matter how much she wished for an end to her suffering, she could not abandon her daughter. Without Sadi, Helen would be forgotten. That thought scared her more than anything else. Jen lacked the resources to continue the search and her brother lacked the intelligence. Sadi could never quit.

A few minutes later, Sadi noticed a subtle change in her surroundings. The low humming of the air conditioner had stopped, leaving the room in an eerie quiet. All of a sudden, she heard the very faint sounds of people moving in the rooms above her. She listened for a few moments then sat up in her bed and opened her eyes. The light in the room had become significantly darker so she ran to the door in the hallway and slid her hand over the wall until she felt the light switch. When she flipped the switch, nothing happened.

She slowly opened the door and found the hallway darker than her room. After turning to face the room again, she noticed the light from the window had become significantly lower. The sound of a door opening in the hallway to the left, returned her attention to the hallway. Low light from a different room spilled into the dark hallway.

"Power's out," said a voice from an older woman.

"I bet it comes back within five minutes," an older, male voice replied. "They won't let it stay out that long."

Sadi felt an immediate surge of hope after realizing the root cause of the power outage and then amazement at Freddy's accomplishment. The feeling became a strong temptation to run out the door and ascend the stairs to the fifth floor. Before making any rash decisions, however, she shut the door and walked towards the window, stopping when she heard the first knock on the apartment door. A second knock followed the first, then a third and then a fourth, each knock louder than the last.

With her heart pounding she attempted to look through the peep-hole, but saw only darkness. Sadi took a deep breath and slowly opened the door. Freddy quickly entered and let the door shut behind him. She almost expected to find Helen with him, but he came alone.

After the door shut, they exchanged a brief eye contact. Sadi thought his eyes looked focused and cold. No words needed to be spoken. He knew her thoughts. She almost saw her emotions reflected in his eyes. He put his hand on her shoulder and gently pushed her away from the door. She felt confidence and strength from his touch, like a father steadying a child about to fall.

"I need to find your purse, the knife," he said.

"I left it on the bed," she replied and followed him to the bed.

The blade shimmered in the dark room from the faint light outside, almost becoming a light of its own. Sadi stared at the knife for a moment before taking it from the bed. Holding the knife provided a feeling of empowerment. Sadi had to force herself to relinquish the weapon.

With the knife out of her possession, a million questions appeared in her mind. How did he cut the power to the hotel? What would he do next? How much time did they have?

"We are going to find Helen," he said before she could ask the first question and then pulled her a few steps towards the door. "She is on the fifth floor. When we get up there, I am going to find a hiding spot for you and you need to stay there until I come get you. Do you understand?"

His voice provided no option for any kind of answer, not even a spoken affirmation so she nodded. She never experienced Freddy so confident, so decisive, not even at the barn. His confidence seemed to flow inside her as well, raising her levels of hope. For the first time since losing Helen, Sadi could imagine finding her daughter alive.

Without waiting another moment, they walked into the dark hallway where they could see nothing but the wall opposite their open door. All the other occupants on the fourth floor had shut their doors and waited patiently for the hotel staff to restore the power. Freddy held her hand while they walked to the stairwell. During their short walk through the hallway, her eyes adjusted to the low light, but once they entered the stairwell, her eyes failed to penetrate the darkness.

Sadi squeezed his hand hard as they ascended the stairs. His hand became her only connection to reality. The experience reminded her of the vision at the barn when she walked through the dark tunnel with Helen. If she released his hand, she might become lost.

When they reached the top step, Sadi noticed light spilling under the door to the fifth-floor hallway. Freddy released her hand, quietly stepped to the door then placed his hand on the handle and stopped. He turned, looking past Sadi to the last flight of stairs which ended in an impenetrable shadow.

"You need to go up those stairs and wait. When it is safe, I will come back to get you."

"Why can't I go with you?"

Sadi looked behind her to the last flight of stairs and shuddered at the thought of entering the darkness alone. Freddy returned his attention to the door. On the other side, Sadi heard muffled speech, but failed to distinguish any words.

"There are a lot of bad people out there," he said quietly. "These people have security and I cannot protect us both beyond this door. Please just go to the top of the stairs and wait for me. These stairs lead to the roof which is locked. No one will be going up there."

"If you don't come back, what should I do?"

"Call Craig," he said then paused. "Actually, I do not know, but probably. Using your phone can be used later to find you."

"I don't give a damn about that. I'm not leaving without Helen."

"You cannot help her if you are dead," he said pleadingly. "Please just wait for me up there."

He pushed her gently in the direction of the stairs, but she failed to move. At that moment, all the previous despair she felt came crashing down on her head again. Her confidence in Freddy faltered for a moment.

"Why are you so confident that you can handle this? This is my daughter we're talking about. Why should I put my faith in you?"

"I told you," he said, returning his attention to the door. "I know what these people are feeling. I know where they are and can anticipate what they are going to do. I will get Helen back."

Sadi wiped the tears from her eyes and placed her hand on his shoulder. From the tone of his voice she could hear his intention. Her emotional outburst failed to alter his plan.

"Sorry. I didn't mean to doubt you," she said and let go of his shoulder. She started backing towards the last flight of stairs. "Please be careful!"

Sadi slowly ascended five steps and disappeared in the shadows, watching Freddy continue with the plan. He stood for a few moments and listened at the door. The scene reminded Sadi of an actor in a play, listening for the cue to go on stage. Without a look back at her, Freddy opened the door and disappeared into the light.

VII: ANXIETY

When stuck in another head
You can't turn the channel
When all turns red

95

Freddy

Sadi's hand on Freddy's shoulder shocked his whole system. Holding her hand as they ascended the stairs sent pulsating electrical currents through his body. The energy helped pump his heart, helped draw in breath and helped him forget for a moment, the swirling rage filling his mind.

After leaving Sadi in their room, Freddy cut the power to the hotel in three different places. The hotel staff and maybe even technicians from the local power company would experience difficulty restoring the power before midnight. He knew the hotel staff needed to call the power company, but they would also call the police, an unfortunate consequence he preferred to avoid. He hoped to be done before the police came and stopped guests from leaving.

Freddy maneuvered stealthily through the hotel with ease. He knew the location of each hotel staff member. He also knew what they would do if they encountered him and when or if they would be changing their location. Emotions became the key to understanding people. Logic and rational thinking had less influence on humans than their feelings.

In the twenty minutes required to cut the power, he also managed to destroy the computer which stored the surveillance video. Before rejoining Sadi, he took the disc holding the video footage. In a different situation, without the disgusting emotions of kidnappers and pedophiles, he might have even enjoyed the experience.

After Sadi disappeared into the shadows, Freddy stepped to the door and waited a moment for his heart rate to return to normal. He needed a moment to recover from the effect of physical contact with Sadi. He turned his attention to the emotions of those on the fifth floor and especially to those just beyond the door in the hallway. He felt the emotions of impatience and annoyance from the people in the hotel, those who waited for the electricity to be restored, those who knew nothing of the activities at the far end of the hall where dark emotions bubbled like a hot tar pit.

The flood of dark emotions shocked him like Sadi's touch. Against his will, Freddy felt a lack of concern for the welfare of others, especially defenseless children. He experienced the disturbing enjoyment at their suffering. He felt a lust for money stronger than his respect for humanity. He felt like an empty shell.

Before entering the hallway, Freddy realized the reality of his mental situation. He stood before a chasm, just beyond the door. An emotional tsunami had already crashed over him and if he failed to grab something solid, he would be swept away by the immense wall of water. When he put his hand on the door handle, the cool metal on his skin felt like an electrical ground to neutral Earth.

He spent the next few moments assessing the situation.

Normal tenants filled most of the occupied rooms on the fifth floor, but the illegal sexual services took place in the last rooms at the far end of the hallway. No one would be passing those rooms unless they had specific business to conduct. Most of the children were transported into the hotel in luggage, but the compliant ones entered the hotel as the children of their handlers.

The last three rooms on the floor had secret connections where the children could be transferred from one room to the other. For a higher price, the one at the very end of the hall had video equipment for special pornography sessions. Many clients liked to have a video copy of their experience for later enjoyment.

Most of the hotel employees simply thought of the rooms as reserved for VIP guests who desired anonymity, people like wealthy foreign visitors, businessmen, law enforcement officials, celebrities, and the occasional well-known politician or philanthropist. The general public would fail to recognize many of the guests, the ones never spotlighted by the media. The hotel restricted access to the rooms and strictly enforced their scheduled maintenance and cleaning, but they rarely needed cleaning. The child sexual service cleaned the rooms after every use.

Two wealthy customers occupied the rooms that evening, a man from somewhere in South America and a prominent local business leader, the one who purchased Helen, or the evening with her, whatever lasted the longest. His order for a blond girl around Helen's age had gone unfulfilled for several months until the Becerras became the lucky ones to fill the order.

Three older children accompanied Helen that evening, two boys and a girl. They had been abused long enough to forget any other kind of life and were accustomed to the treatment. The staff of the service helped assure a smooth operation and comfortable experience for the clients. They used guns, other weapons and their status as adults to instill fear and intimidation in the children, to control them.

A final doubt made Freddy pause. What if he failed and they lost Helen? What would it mean? Freddy felt almost invincible with his new abilities, as if the alien gave them to him for just that evening. What if he made the wrong assumptions? What if his anger obscured his judgment? The situation had become too serious to change course. He'd already jumped in the strong river current and could not swim back to the shore. Helen's unique emotional signature he felt from just down the hallway urged him onward like the target scent for a bloodhound.

After a final, deep breath, Freddy opened the door and saw the light coming from the far end of the hall. He started walking toward a man who stood in front of a door. The man held a flashlight pointed at the ground, but when he heard the door open, he shined the beam in Freddy's face and the light momentarily blinded him. As Freddy continued walking toward the light, he extended his hand as a shield.

"Thanks for the light, but can you get it out of my face?" Freddy asked, acting only slightly annoyed.

96

Freddy

When the man saw Freddy, he lost concern and felt foolish for shining the light in the face of a stranger. With the hotel's power situation, the man felt more wary than normal. In his memory, the hotel had never lost power, but then again, the service never had any trouble either so he felt no reason to be concerned by a stranger appearing in the hallway.

"Sorry," the guard said and then aimed the flashlight back to the ground. "Hey, do you know what's going on? When's the light coming back on?"

"As far as I know," Freddy answered while casually walking closer. Only fifteen doors separated them. He thought of a lie to help the man feel more relaxed. "The lights should return at any moment."

"Great thanks," he said then returned to face the wall again. He soon lost interest in Freddy.

As Freddy continued walking slowly down the hallway, he turned his attention to the emotions emanating from the rooms in front of him and found only a few rooms unoccupied, the ones closest to Helen which the hotel kept vacant. Normal hotel occupants waited with impatience for the power to be restored so they could go back to watching television.

Fear from the rooms with the children became too palpable and Freddy felt a wave of dizziness, but the man guarding the door at the end of the hallway remained silently uninterested. Freddy breathed deep and forced himself to unclench his teeth to maintain a relaxed appearance.

His short walk felt like an eternity. Freddy stopped finally at the door of the last safe empty room, the nearest one to the man which would fail to raise suspicion, just five doors from where the man stood. With the man on his left, Freddy turned towards the door then he placed his left hand in his pocket and retrieved his door key card. With his right hand, he pulled the knife from the back of his pants, careful not to cut his skin, leaving the gun strapped between his stomach and belt buckle. He liked the feel of the gun pressed firmly against his skin.

Freddy slid his key card several times in the door lock with exaggerated impatience.

"Damn it," he said loud enough for the man to hear. "I forgot about the lock on the doors. The power is out."

The flashlight shined in his direction again. The man said nothing and just grunted in acknowledgment.

"Excuse me," Freddy said innocently, to get the man's attention.

"Yeah," the man said in a feeble attempt to satisfy social propriety.

Freddy sensed the man's annoyance. He felt no interest in helping Freddy or anybody. He just wanted the lights to be restored so he could continue with his normal routine. Freddy felt relief for the negative reaction. The man lacked the instinct to offer assistance for someone in need. His lack of common courtesy helped justify what Freddy planned for him.

"Could you give me some light?" Freddy asked. "I might be inserting this the wrong way."

"It's not gonna work," replied the man, feeling glad for the excuse to refuse assistance.

Freddy turned to the man and started walking in his direction, the knife held to his side, out of sight. He spoke while walking.

"I thought maybe the doors were battery operated. I'll just wait out here for a bit. The lights should be back on in a few minutes."

As Freddy slowly closed the distance between them, he tried to instigate a more involved conversation. For the first time in his memory, Freddy felt no interest in his proximity causing someone else discomfort or anxiety. The man pretended to appear disinterested, but his anxiety levels rose slightly, not from fear, but from the need to choose a course of action.

"Are you locked out of your room too?" Freddy asked, attempting to appear interested in wasting time rather than gathering information.

The man hesitated before responding.

"No, my friend can let me in," he said, offering no other information.

The man had a gun in a holster under his jacket, a stun gun in one pocket and a knife in his belt. He weighed about fifty pounds heavier than Freddy and stood two inches taller so he felt no concern that Freddy would pose any kind of threat.

Freddy stopped five feet from the man and leaned against the wall in a manner consistent with continuing the conversation. Many people like to talk, even when their audience showed no signs of interest. For the first time, Freddy became one of those people. He gripped the knife hard in his right hand, pressed firmly to his leg.

"I never heard of the power going off in a hotel before. Have you?"

The man's feeling of annoyance transformed into alertness. He unconsciously tensed his muscles and shifted his stance to prepare for movement so Freddy decided to delay his move.

"I am glad to have some company in the dark. Carrying a flashlight is not a normal habit for me. I should probably get one."

"Listen," said the man, exhaling in barely-contained anger. "I'm not in a mood for conversation, so just go wait by your door please, or wait in the lobby and come back later."

"Sorry," said Freddy and cleared his throat to hide the dark anger beginning to pump through his veins. The anger stopped the shaking of his hands and prepared him for action. "It is just creepy in the dark stairwells. I do not want to go back down there."

The man felt tempted to insult Freddy for not bringing his own flashlight, but he kept his mouth shut and attempted to appear as if unconcerned about Freddy's desire to spend the time in idle conversation. He hoped the silent treatment would expedite Freddy's departure.

Freddy took a deep breath before starting to walk down the hall toward the man, holding the knife against his leg. Helen's extreme distress and the hopeless condition of the other kids on the other side of the walls helped energize every muscle in his body. He squeezed the handle on the knife and felt the sweat between his fingers and the plastic. The next moment seemed to freeze in time for everyone but him.

The man stood, just staring at the opposite wall when Freddy jumped at him like a grasshopper. Although he lacked any experience as a fighter, Freddy let anger and urgency guide his aim. The darkness beyond the flashlight beam on the floor provided the perfect cover.

The knife dove directly through the man's neck, slipping through his skin and stopping on his spinal column. Ignoring the instant disgust he felt, Freddy quickly withdrew the knife while keeping pressure to the right, cutting through the internal and external jugular veins. He moved too swiftly for the man to do anything other than attempt to grab Freddy's forearm. By the time his fingers made contact, his muscles lost all their strength.

Freddy kept pressure on the man's neck, holding him against the wall while his body slid slowly to the floor. He stared into the man's eyes until the life completely left them. The flashlight rolled from the man's hand, stopping on the floor with the beam of light shining on the opposite wall. Warm blood splattered from the wound onto his hand and felt sticky between his fingers.

In the dim light, Freddy felt paralyzed, looking with shock and disgust at the horrible scene in front of him. He stared at the body until the flow of blood became a trickle then backed away from the motionless corpse to avoid the sweet smell which induced a small gagging sensation. He wiped the blood from the knife and his hands onto the man's clothes.

Freddy needed to quickly remove the body from the hallway, so he grabbed the flashlight and found an open lobby area across from the door to the stairs. Without any other options, he decided to drag the body there.

He set the flashlight on the floor, facing the direction of the lounge and then dragged the two hundred pound corpse with both hands down the hall. The trail of blood would look menacing in the normal lights, but in the low light, the trail appeared as a shadow. He needed to avoid stepping into any of the blood so that police investigators would not easily determine his weight or height.

After placing the body in the corner of the small lounge, Freddy returned to the door of the man's death. While cutting the hotel power, he wore a pair of nitrile gloves from his lab supplies and then returned them to his pockets. The gloves would have saved Freddy from having to feel the blood, but the man would have become suspicious if Freddy had worn them in the hallway. He slipped the gloves over his hands again, put the flashlight in his jacket pocket and prepared for the next phase of the rescue attempt.

With his new senses, Freddy ignored the shock and disgust of his violent actions and focused on the feelings of the occupants in the room. Only one of the original three children remained with two adults, a boy. After Freddy cut the power, they decided to postpone the video with the children. While Freddy killed the guard and drug him down the hallway, they had moved Helen and the other children to the next room through a secret passage, and then moved Helen again through another secret passage to the third room, to join the man who purchased her.

The remaining younger boy felt temporary relief at the loss of power, but he knew when the power returned, the adults wanted to film the video with him and the other children. The child's terror at disappointing the two adults became Freddy's terror which ultimately added to his anger. Each wave of anger transformed into energy. Freddy felt strong enough to break down the door with one hand.

In the adjacent room, the other boy and girl feared to displease the client, a single adult man from Colombia. The man felt frustrated at having to wait for the lights, but he emanated no violent emotions. The children knew that if he gave a bad report of the experience, their handlers would severely punish them.

Before raising his hand to knock on the door, Freddy removed the gun from under his belt and attached the silencer to the muzzle. The quiet squeaking of the metal threads as they joined together broke the silence.

With the gun in one hand and flashlight in the other, he took one final moment to focus on Helen and experience her palpable fear for the older man with her. The old man acted nice, but she did not trust him. She spent all her energy concentrating on rejoining the older girl, her friend. She consciously avoided thoughts of her mother. Fortunately, nothing horrible had happened to her yet. Freddy needed to hurry.

With so many emotions inside his chest, he experienced difficulty keeping them sorted into the appropriate categories, his versus theirs. If he spent no effort keeping them separated, they all became his own and he experienced a severe identity crisis. He concurrently became a criminal, abductor, terrified victim and vicious killer. The horrible memory of seeing the knife sinking into the man's neck replayed over in his mind, clinging and stinking like cigarette smoke.

The anger had grown inside him his entire life, starting when his father left them and then escalated when his mother decided to focus all her remaining attention on his sister. It festered after his mother placed him into the Oregon foster program with one family after another, their psychological diseases finding an outlet in him. During the years with Mr. Smith, Freddy pushed the anger away with ease, like a shirt at the bottom of a clothes drawer, never to be worn again. Away, but not forgotten.

Freddy already decided what to do after locating Helen. If he wanted to get out of there alive with Helen and Sadi, he needed to eliminate all opposition and that meant killing people. The first had been easy, but could he kill another? His imagination made killing easy, but to actually commit the act required Freddy to ignore his instincts. Would his pacifistic instincts return to stop him?

Suddenly, the image of a white ghost ascended from his unconscious mind and entered his conscious thoughts, the image of a little boy, Freddy as a child. He saw the boy's innocence and purity flicker like a candle and then become extinguished. Freddy's eyes filled with tears. His own emotions filled him again. He felt the anguish of when they stripped his youth away from him, and then when they stole Sadi's daughter, and how they would ruin the lives of countless other children.

97

Freddy

He knocked lightly three times in quick succession and wiped his eyes while waiting for the response. He mentally prepared for several different scenarios. If they had a secret knock and he knocked incorrectly, he would feel their suspicion and then pretend to be from the hotel. If they refused to open the door, he planned to shoot the locking mechanism. That would just make his job more difficult, but might expedite the process. Whatever happened, he would enter the room. He had the element of surprise.

To his relief, however, the man on the other side of the door felt no concern. Another adult in the room, the videographer waited in a bedroom with the remaining boy. He had command of the operation and currently played on his smartphone, entirely distracted and slightly annoyed.

The guard inside opened the door slightly. He spoke while waiting for Freddy to push the door the rest of the way.

"Hey Jim," he said. "Figure out when the power's coming back on?"

Freddy responded with silence and then slammed the door into the man, momentarily pinning him to the wall of the short entryway. During his sudden burst of energy, Freddy assessed the man's mass. The man behind the door weighed much heavier than the guard he killed. Before the man had time to respond, Freddy quickly jumped past him into the living room and let him slam the door shut.

After the door locking mechanism clicked, the man turned to find a gun pointed at his face. Freddy allowed the man enough time to recognize the gun before aiming the bright flashlight into his eyes, momentarily blinding him.

"What the hell," said the man while using his hand to shield the light.

"Down the hall," Freddy said with as much confidence as he could generate. He stepped backwards to increase the distance between him and the larger man, then motioned with the flashlight beam to move. "In with your boss."

"Take it easy with that thing kid," the man said after seeing that a younger, much smaller man stood before him. He spoke with mock concern for Freddy's safety. "Neither one of us wants to get hurt."

"Just move," Freddy said, and then realized the man needed more motivation. "I have no problem shooting you right here. I already killed your friend outside, but if I can help it, I do not want to kill anyone else."

The man's eyes narrowed as he tried to determine the truth of Freddy's statement. When he finally recognized the truth, he started moving forward. The man turned away, took a few steps in the direction indicated and prepared to spin around and knock the gun away, but Freddy shoved him with the flashlight and knocked him off-balance. He stumbled forward and became angry at himself for not acting sooner.

"Nice try, now keep moving," Freddy said.

If the man decided to attack, Freddy planned to shoot him. He felt tempted to shoot the man in the back of the head anyway and move with ease through the apartment, but he just squeezed the gun instead, keeping pressure on the trigger.

The man led Freddy to a side bedroom. A soft light seeped from beneath the door onto the plush carpet. After he opened the door, Freddy immediately noticed a movie camera atop a tall tripod which faced a large king bed with its light shining on a smaller man and boy there. The smaller man had male-pattern baldness, with a mixture of dark brown and gray hair on the sides of his head. He casually looked up from his smartphone after the guard and Freddy walked inside the room. When he saw the gun, his eyes burst open wider.

He started to stand from the bed, but stopped himself midway. A boy lay on the bed behind him, partially covered by a blanket with his bare chest showing. Even though only the blanket covered him, he did not feel too concerned about being exposed.

The bald man stared at the guard with contempt in his eyes, angry at the guard for letting Freddy inside the room, much less afraid than Freddy expected or hoped. In the low light, his eyes looked dark, almost black.

"What is this?" the bald man asked after returning his complete weight to the bed.

He set the smartphone on his lap with one hand covering it like a favored pet. The boy sat up after recognizing the angry tone of the man, supporting his weight on his elbows. His gaze shifted between the two men and Freddy. The boy felt confused and prepared for something horrible to happen.

"He says he killed Jim," the guard said in explanation.

"Shut up!" said Freddy through clenched teeth.

He held the gun firmly in his right hand. The guard stopped at the bed and turned around to face Freddy. He looked at the gun in the brighter light, focusing on the silencer attached to the end. He watched for signs of weakness, an opportunity to leap at Freddy and the smaller man wondered why the guard failed to do it already.

"Who are you?" asked the bald man.

Freddy ignored the bald man and kept his eyes on the guard still standing.

"Sit down big guy and stop thinking you can find a way to jump me. I am not afraid to use this."

As the man slowly lowered himself to the bed, Freddy stepped to the side of the room where a sofa lay against the wall. He took a small pillow from the sofa and placed it in front of the gun. Freddy feared that his small suppressor would fail to muffle the sound of the exploding gas sufficiently. Maybe the pillow would help contain the noise.

"I asked you a question!" the man said, and gulped when he saw Freddy aim the pillow at his head. He forgot how losing control of a situation felt. People usually treated him with fearful respect. His burst of fear transformed into anger. "Who are you? We don't keep any money here, you fucking idiot."

"I am not here for money," said Freddy, feeling an unexpected satisfaction at the man's reaction.

He felt a strong urge to just shoot them, but stopped himself. He had no interest in striking a conversation with the men, but maybe he would feel better about executing their final judgment if they helped incriminate themselves.

"What did you do to Jim?" asked the guard finally, gaining courage from the gun aiming at someone other than himself.

"I did just what you want to do to me," Freddy said with the pleasure of being the one in control of the situation.

The bald man wanted to use a knife on Freddy and feel the warm blood on his hands like what Freddy experienced. Freddy never wanted to plunge a knife in someone's body again, but he did want to pull the trigger and watch the bullet penetrate their skulls.

In the silence following his statement, Freddy realized something. After killing the guard, his emotional load decreased. The negative emotions he felt from others changed by an infinitesimal but noticeable amount. Killing the two men in front of him would relieve him of even more foulness. Before delivering their final sentence, however, Freddy wondered if he could reveal to them their worthless state.

"Now it is my turn to ask questions. What are you doing in this hotel?"

The guard looked at the smaller man next to him, waiting for him to answer. He acted as if he felt too much fear to speak, but Freddy knew the truth. He hoped to cause a delay until someone came to their rescue.

The man had just made a phone call, informing his employers about the power loss in the hotel, and now he cursed himself for not requesting backup. Fortunately for Freddy, the hotel staff disliked contact with the men and usually avoided visiting the fifth floor. If that situation changed, he hoped to anticipate any visit. Freddy had full faith that his new ability would not fail him. If the alien wanted to lead Freddy into a trap, he would know very soon.

"If you're hoping for me to incriminate myself, you're even stupider than you look."

The man threw insults often. They came naturally to him and he hoped to make Freddy angry enough to make a mistake in judgment.

"Even if you get something incriminating on whatever recording device you've got, it won't hold up in any court. My associates will make sure any evidence you acquire, will end up as worthless garbage, like you."

Freddy felt his lips stretch into a sincere smile and the man recognized the look. The men were going to give him more than enough motivation to do what he so desperately wanted. Before proceeding, however, Freddy wanted to hear them admit to going against their consciences, if they had them.

"Then you will not object to telling me why you think it is OK to hurt children?"

The man laughed this time with relief and sincere humor. His plan to stall until help could arrive might be successful. He turned to his right, directing his voice to the boy behind him.

"Hey Kristoff, are we hurting you?"

"You're not hurting me," said the boy in immediate response.

Freddy could feel the boy's anxiety, his fear of making the man angry. Having another armed man in the room, scared the boy much less than the bald man sitting in front of him. Adults with guns always accompanied the bald man.

Freddy just happened to be a new adult to consider. Only two options came to the boy's mind. They would all be killed or this new player would be his new handler. The boy's feeling of hopelessness amplified Freddy's desire to squeeze the trigger.

Behind the pillow, Freddy moved the trigger a few hundred micrometers closer to shooting. The only obstacle to the man's death was the insignificant resistance of the trigger.

"See," he said. "We're not hurting anyone. We're paying the little shit, for Christ's sake."

"What about the other boy and the two little girls? At least, they are getting minimum wage, I hope?"

"You seem to know a lot about us," said the man with sincere curiosity.

"I know too much."

The bald man hoped to change the conversation from their criminal activities to a topic of his choosing, and regain control of the conversation. He desperately wanted to discover Freddy's identity.

"Let me give you some advice, little man with a gun," he continued. "It's dark in here and we won't be able to positively identify you. That's fortunate for you. Your only chance of escape is to get the hell out of here and run back to your goddamned church group or whatever hole you crawled out of. If you were smart that's what you would be doing."

"My questions first," Freddy said, intending to inspire the man with the hope of survival. "Are the girls getting minimum wage for their services?"

"Alright," said the man with feigned disappointment. "So you want to go down that road?"

Bullies often gave Freddy the same kind of condescension at school. The man reminded Freddy of one small but popular boy who always called Freddy a retard. He remembered just looking at the ground in shame. Now, Freddy looked the man straight in the eyes. He could see the fake smile on his face.

"Yes, I want to go down that road."

98

Freddy

"Let me teach you something about life," said the man, adjusting himself on the bed and preparing for a long answer.

Freddy felt impatience, an urgent need to hurry, but he wanted to hear what the man had to say.

"With enough money," the man continued, "people can get whatever they want. That's it. I'm just a businessman providing a service. If I don't provide it, someone else will. These are just business decisions. You can keep your naive and childish view on life, but it won't change reality."

"What does your older client want with the blond girl?"

Freddy felt his hand start to shake with anger, behind the pillow. Before he eliminated the men before him, he wanted them to understand the consequences of their actions. They needed to understand why they had to die.

The man shook his head, considering his words carefully, feeling more uncomfortable and planning to lie. While Freddy waited for the man's answer, he saw the truth and it sickened him even more.

"When he's done with her, she'll be fine," he said finally.

"You lie," Freddy whispered.

Freddy changed his aim to the guard, but kept his eyes on the bald man. He wanted to see the man's reaction when he pulled the trigger. When the hole appeared between the guard's eyes and he fell silently on the bed, the bald man winced. The guard's blood splattered the back of the bed and wall, and the bullet cracked the thick headboard.

For the first time in his life, Freddy felt a gun's recoil, but his perfect aim failed to give Freddy as much satisfaction as seeing the fear on the bald man's face and feeling the fear in his chest. In panic, the boy silently scrambled farther to the other side of the bed, pulling the cover up to his neck, as if to separate him from the dead body. He stared at the corpse, almost expecting to see movement.

"You are so fucking dead," the man hissed in the hopes of intimidating Freddy. He scooted away from his fallen employee in order to avoid getting blood on him. "You'll never make it out of here alive. We've got people all over this hotel. In fact, people are on their way up right now. If you run now, you might..."

"No one is coming to help you," said Freddy with mock sorrow and wished the first guard had been as clean of a kill as the second one.

Freddy looked into the bald man's eyes and felt the man's fresh terror and anger. He felt a momentary pleasure, but then all of a sudden, he thought of all the kids who passed through his business, how no one had been there to help them. The man no longer held any interest for Freddy. Only eliminating the bald man mattered. Killing him would give Freddy no pleasure.

The man's eyes filled with shock and for a moment, his mind went blank. Afterwards, he knew that Freddy saw inside him.

"What are you going to do?" he asked then decided to not wait for the answer. If he could just get Freddy to keep talking, he might have a chance. "Listen I'm just a middle-man. I can give you names. I can tell you whatever you want. Just name it."

"I do not need any more information from you," Freddy said with finality.

The bald man did not have the time to say any more. Freddy put a hole in his head, in the same spot as the guard. Contrasting with the violence of his death, the man's body peacefully fell back on the bed. After a short pause, Freddy removed the pillow from the muzzle of the gun then waited for his heartbeat to stabilize. With the two additional men dead, Freddy recognized a significant decrease in his emotional load.

Should he have killed them? Maybe he should have forced the man to help retrieve Helen? After just a moment of reflection, however, he realized the truth. He would have done the same thing again. The world improved with less of these psychopaths. If he failed to rescue Helen, at least he helped clean up some trash before his exit from the world.

Freddy turned his attention to the boy on the bed who anticipated a similar fate, like a deer in a headlight. The boy almost welcomed such a clean and painless death. Freddy thought he looked twelve or thirteen years old. He had blond hair and seemed to be small for his age. In as non-threatening of a manner as possible, Freddy held up the gun in a sign of peace. He had little time for the boy, but he could not just leave him.

"I will not hurt you," Freddy said.

He put his gun under his belt then slowly reached inside his jacket and removed a thick bundle of cash. At first, the boy winced and expected a knife or other weapon. When he saw the cash, however, he relaxed and his emotions transformed into hesitant curiosity. Freddy slowly extracted several fifty-dollar and hundred-dollar bills, stepping slowly toward the boy and extending his hand with the money. The boy stared at the money as if Freddy planned to trick him. He wanted to take it, but fear kept him motionless. He just saw Freddy kill two adults and still felt shock at the disturbing memory.

Freddy placed the money on the bed then put the rest of the cash back in his jacket. He had several thousand more dollars remaining.

"You do not want to be here when the police arrive, understand?"

"Yes," the boy said then snatched the money from the bed in front of him.

"Good," said Freddy without a smile. "Take the money and when we're done here, get far away from these people. Will you do that?"

"OK," he responded as if in a trance and then slowly gathered the blanket around his naked body. He stood from the bed and backed away from the dead bodies.

"This room is connected to the one next door?" Freddy asked. While waiting for the response, Freddy felt relief from the boy and the intention to lead Freddy to the back of the apartment. "Will you take me there?"

"It's in the back of a closet, to the right out of the bedroom."

The boy felt more relaxed with the money. He still doubted Freddy's sincerity, but his level of anxiety became significantly lower. The boy slowly began moving towards the door, keeping himself as far away from Freddy as possible. Freddy followed with the flashlight through the dark apartment. Both of them felt better after leaving the room with the two corpses.

"I have a friend over there," the boy said with pleading. He led Freddy to another room, opened the door and waited for Freddy to enter. "Please don't hurt him."

"What about the girl?" Freddy asked after stopping in the doorway and shining the flashlight into the new room.

"I don't know her very much, but they made us do a video together once."

Freddy looked at the boy in the eyes, who gulped. Freddy's gaze reminded the boy of the deaths he just witnessed. While watching Freddy dispose of his oppressors, he began to think of Freddy as invincible, maybe omniscient, someone to obey or face horrible consequences. The memory of all the blood on the bed flooded his mind. He feared to offend Freddy or give him any cause for concern.

The boy attempted to close the gate of unpleasant thoughts by imagining a successful escape with his friend into the darkness. Freddy understood the coping mechanism. As a child, Freddy escaped into his mind whenever a situation became too difficult to bear. He felt guilty for inspiring such fear in the boy, but for the moment, that fear would keep him from running away.

"If I enter the other apartment, will you stay here and wait? I will bring your friend back and then you can leave."

"I will wait."

"Show me how," Freddy whispered.

"There's a sliding door at the back of the closet," the boy answered in a whisper.

The boy led Freddy to a closet in the back of the dark room. After stopping at the door, he placed his hand on the handle and prepared to open it, but Freddy stopped him. Before the boy could respond, Freddy placed his index finger over his mouth as a signal for silence.

"Wait. Someone is listening."

Freddy could feel the occupants in the other apartment, a man probably in his late forties, another boy and a young girl who unfortunately did not feel like Helen. The man thought he heard something that sounded like a gunshot from the other apartment, but he doubted his senses.

The man stood with a knife by the adjacent closet door, separated from Freddy by a wall several few feet away. The man prepared mentally to stab at anyone who exited the closet on his side. He waited in fear of making any noise, feeling much more fear than Freddy.

Freddy wondered what to do. Could he go through the secret door and put a decoy into the other room, like his hat? If the man struck at the decoy, Freddy would break his wrist and stab him in the neck with his knife. The other option felt more reliable, wait in silence for the man to leave the closet. Unfortunately, that option required too much time. To help steady his hand, Freddy gripped the knife handle tightly in his fist. Even through the nitrile glove, he could still feel the sticky blood of the first guard on the knife.

Could he be quick enough? Could he kill another man with a knife? Yes, he could. He would do whatever necessary to help rescue Helen and Sadi from a sad future.

"Open the door," Freddy said quietly and calmly.

The boy opened the door of the closet and it swung open without squeaking, then he separated some heavy coats on hooks to make room for Freddy to enter. Before stepping into the closet, Freddy handed the flashlight to the boy.

"Keep this pointed to the ground, but not directly into the closet. When I am ready to open the back door, you shut this one. Nod if you understand."

The boy nodded obediently, standing motionless behind Freddy in the apartment. He looked like a statue, with one hand on the closet door handle and the other hand pointing the flashlight to the ground. His feelings morphed into a mixture of relief, curiosity and excitement. As his new potential tormentor prepared to leave him alone for a while, the boy began to enjoy the memory of seeing his former captors peacefully falling dead on the bed. Freddy felt assured of the boy's compliance.

Before entering the closet, Freddy put the pillow under his arm and removed his hat. With his knife in one hand and his hat in the other, Freddy slid between the parted coats. At the back wall he found a simple sliding door. He placed his hand on the door, turned to face the boy and nodded. The boy quietly shut the door, leaving Freddy alone in a dark closet, with just enough light from under the door to see.

Freddy took a deep breath and began to slowly slide the door open. To his surprise, the door slid open completely without sound, allowing him to enter the other closet in complete silence. After pushing through more hanging coats he finally reached the door knob to the new apartment.

Without pausing, Freddy slowly turned the knob and waited for the man's reaction from the other side. The man on the other side heard the quiet click, or he thought he heard it, but in the low light he failed to see the knob move. He became confused and waited in vain for other sounds. Freddy waited too.

After only a few moments of silent confusion, the man chose the most desirable conclusion for himself. He only imagined the noises and could return to the living room where his little companions waited. He felt foolish for being paranoid. His thoughts returned to the two children and what he wanted them to do. Too bad he had to wait for the hotel power to return. Light from his phone and the complementary candles would fail to provide sufficient illumination.

When Freddy felt satisfied with the man's absence from the other room and the distraction of his disgusting imagination, he opened the closet door. To his horror, the door creaked loudly and the man's anxiety returned in full force.

99

Freddy

While the man waited for another noise, Freddy returned the hat to his head and took a moment to familiarize himself with his new surroundings. His eyes slowly adjusted to the darkness again. The room looked similar to the other room in the first apartment. He instantly recognized the mirror-image layout and where he needed to go. The low light from the partially open door shone like a lighthouse in the dark of night.

Judging from the flickering light spilling through the open door, the source most likely originated from a candle. Freddy stood for a brief moment just watching the animated light and then without conscious effort, he began to creep towards the open door, drawn to the light like a mindless insect.

His appearance before the occupants in the living room came as a complete shock to all of them, including Freddy. He focused on the man and his ice-cold eyes with a feeling of disgust. The man almost withered under his gaze like hair in a flame.

The man stood in front of a couch with a little girl on his right and a young boy slightly behind her. The girl wore a pretty white dress and the boy wore a white bathrobe. They looked about the same age, maybe a year younger than the one Freddy left in the first apartment. The sight of the captive children next to a man with such disgusting thoughts made Freddy's stomach lurch with anger again. He wished the alien would have given his eyes the ability to fry the skin off someone, instead of the ability to feel their horrible emotions.

"Who are you?" asked the man in a heavy, Colombian accent.

He held a very large hunting knife, pointed like a sword at Freddy. The low light concealed his shaking hand, but Freddy felt the man's fear and the more dangerous emotion, desperation. The Colombian slowly extended his hand to the girl, resting on her neck and preparing to throw her into Freddy if he attacked. The girl made no protest or struggle. She just stared at Freddy with a strange mixture of fear and relief.

"Who I am does not matter," Freddy said and wondered why they all wanted to know his identity. He did not want to know theirs. "Why are you in this apartment with defenseless children and a knife?"

Immediately after asking the question, Freddy realized his mistake. He showed interest in the children. The man suddenly realized his leverage in the situation.

Freddy took two small steps towards the man, forcing him to reveal his next move. In some deep part of his mind, Freddy wanted the man to threaten the girl. The cowardly act would make Freddy's job of killing him so much easier.

In response, the man stepped closer to the couch, then pulled the girl in front of him. His rough handling immediately erased all her emotions, and she moved like an inanimate doll, her lifeless eyes fixed on the floor. The absence of emotion in the girl caused Freddy to shiver. The Colombian moved the knife to her neck, like a hunter ready to skin an animal.

"You answer my question and I'll answer yours," the man said and touched the knife to her throat. "Who are you? Come any closer and I will hurt her!"

In the first room, the two men never even considered using the boy as leverage so Freddy failed to consider that possibility in the second room. He should have shot the man as soon as he entered, but the thought of killing him in front of the little girl caused some anxiety. The children had obviously been traumatized enough in their lives. Freddy did not want to cause more trauma, especially to a young girl.

"I just want the girl," said Freddy casually.

He slowly put the knife in his belt, under his jacket and removed the gun. When the Colombian saw the gun, he pulled the girl closer to him and his eyes stretched wide.

The man watched in fear as Freddy put the pillow between him and the gun. Freddy could think of no alternative to shooting the man in front of the children. He would be unable to overpower the man and prevent him from alerting others in the hotel, including the man with Helen. His heart began pounding noticeably in his chest right before squeezing the trigger. Before shooting, however, Freddy paused. If the girl heard a gunshot she would scream.

Freddy's mind spun like a tornado, fast and furious. He needed to prevent the girl from screaming or at least stop her. If he acted fast enough, he could shoot the man then rush forward and put his hand over her mouth. While considering the situation, Freddy became aware of the boy.

The younger kid with Freddy felt more courage than the older boy waiting in the first apartment. While watching the situation in the shadows behind the man, he waited for an opportunity to rush at Freddy and knock the gun from his hand. If he failed to offer any resistance, his handlers might punish him.

"If you want the girl," the man said in a tone of feigned anger. "I will give her to you in the hallway."

If Freddy followed the demand, the man planned to close the door on Freddy without the girl. Despite his fear, the Colombian hated to occupy the losing side of a confrontation. To make the situation worse, Freddy made him feel small and saw him with the children and knew his dark secret. Once in the hallway, the man felt certain that the guards would kill him. He failed to consider the possibility of what really happened and assumed that Freddy had slipped past them unseen somehow.

In the next moment, Freddy decided to move forward with his plan before the boy gathered enough courage to rush at him. He hoped the boy would be too shocked to act. Without another word, he fired the gun and the bullet hit the man right between the eyes, his third perfect shot of the evening. Just like the men in the other apartment, the man instantly crumpled to the floor. A splattering of blood appeared on the wall behind him with a dark hole in the center where the bullet hit.

Before the corpse came to a complete rest on the floor, Freddy dropped the pillow and rushed forward, putting his hand over the girl's mouth. Fortunately, he reached the girl just before the scream could escape her mouth. She struggled against his hand, but he managed to keep her quiet.

Unfortunately, Freddy failed to anticipate the boy's quick response. Seeing a man shot in front of him had less effect than Freddy hoped. Nothing could shock the boy anymore. He grabbed the gun from Freddy and backed several feet away, out of reach. The boy held the gun with both shaking hands, aimed directly at Freddy's head. Freddy gulped and watched as the boy's chest rose and fell with heavy breathing.

"Let her go," the boy said, his voice shaking as much as his hands.

100

Freddy

"I am letting her go," Freddy said then looked down at the girl's head. "Please do not scream."

When Freddy heard the girl draw a deep breath, he knew she would remain quiet. Slowly, he removed his hands from the frightened child and she ran to join the boy, positioning herself behind him. She looked back at Freddy like an animal in a cage.

"You stay away from us," the boy said while taking a step backward.

He wanted to shoot, but feared missing. Freddy acted just like all the other adults he knew, manipulative and violent. The boy had an intense anger inside him, like a sleeping alligator waiting to be awoken. Freddy understood how he felt. Freddy slowly extended both hands above his head.

"I am not here to hurt you, just them."

"You said you came for the girl," said the boy. "Were you lying?"

"Yes, I was lying to that man, but not you."

Freddy laughed silently at how stupid that statement sounded.

"How are we supposed to believe you?"

With the gun still held tightly in his hands, the boy began to relax and his desire to shoot Freddy diminished. He desperately wanted to believe Freddy, to believe something positive. Could the man who killed the Colombian really not want to hurt or use them? Shooting Freddy might hurt their chances of escape. He liked the girl with him and felt a responsibility to help her. For the first time in his life, he held all the leverage in a situation. Maybe he could devise a plan.

"Please keep your voice down," Freddy requested politely. "We cannot let the man next door hear us. He must not know what happened here."

"What are you talking about?" the boy asked in a quieter voice.

"I will tell you the truth," he said slowly, hoping the children would hear the sincerity in his voice. "I came here for a girl named Helen. Her mother is in the hallway, waiting for me to get her. She is in the next apartment."

The boy instantly doubted the claim, but the girl stepped out from behind him. For a brief moment, the boy made eye contact with her then returned his attention to Freddy, eyes squinting hard.

"You came for Helen?" the girl asked. A new emotion materialized in her mind then, but not hope as Freddy had expected. He recognized sadness and panic. "Her mother?"

"I don't believe it," said the boy. In his experience, parents would not come to a child's aid. He gripped the gun with more force. He did not plan to relinquish his leverage. "It's more lies to make me give this back to him."

Freddy felt his precious time slipping away. The power company might restore the power before he entered the last apartment. People would come and see all the blood in the hall, but Freddy had a worse problem. Even if he managed to convince the girl, the boy would require significantly more time. He might have to change his plans. He might need to let the boy keep the gun.

Should he ask the kid to get his friend Kristoff and then return with the gun? Could Kristoff convince his friend to return with it? Did Freddy have the time to wait? No, he did not. With every passing second, he felt the growing impatience from the man in the next apartment. He might not delay his horrible activities with Helen much longer.

Freddy would have to enter the next apartment without the gun and just his knife. Even with his new extrasensory abilities, he lacked faith in his hand to hand combat skills. The last man on his hit list felt more formidable than the first guard. At least, with the first kill of his life, Freddy had the element of surprise with no child to be used as a hostage.

"OK, keep the gun," Freddy said finally. "Go to the other apartment and find your friend and he can tell you that I am not going to hurt you. The men who held him captive are all dead. They cannot hurt you anymore, but please I need to get the girl to her mother before the power is restored."

"You're the one to stop the electricity?" asked the boy incredulously with a little respect.

"It was a diversion."

The girl stepped in front of the boy, placing herself between them both. She glanced at the ground, at the dead body and became momentarily paralyzed. She imagined the body rising as a zombie.

"I'm going with you, to see Helen," she said finally.

"It is too dangerous," said Freddy. "You cannot come."

"You won't take her away from me," said the girl with a rising voice. "I won't let you."

Freddy finally understood the girl's emotions. Helen had become her new friend, her only friend. In their short time together, Helen became an appendage to the girl, one that could only be removed by inflicting damage. Freddy crouched down to look at her.

"I know how you feel," he said quietly, attempting to mask his impatience. "You want Helen safe. I want that too."

"Yes," she said. "I want her safe."

"Let me tell you what I will do," Freddy said. "I will find you when this is all done and you can see Helen again. That is the best I can do right now."

"You'll come and find me?"

"Yes, like I found Helen," he said putting his hand over his heart. "I promise, but please, I need you two to stay here where it is safe."

"Daryn," said the boy in panic. "Keep away from him."

The boy imagined Freddy grabbing the girl and slitting her throat.

"You can't trust him. He just killed a guy, and maybe more."

Daryn took a step backwards. She wanted to go with Freddy, but thought her companion might be right. She trusted the boy more than Freddy.

"Do you think he'll hurt Helen?" she asked.

"I don't know," the boy responded. "We've got a chance to get away and we've got to take it. Daryn, come with me. Let's go get Kristoff and get out of here."

The boy shook the gun at Freddy and spoke in a whisper.

"Don't follow us or I'll shoot you."

The boy put one hand on the girl's shoulder and started pulling her backward. She resisted, but not enough to stand still. Together, they backed away from Freddy, the boy holding the gun steadily at Freddy's head. Before they disappeared in the next room, Freddy called out to them.

"Where is the secret passage into the other apartment?"

The boy stopped and turned around.

"It's over there."

He waved the gun towards a dark corridor on the opposite side of the room. Freddy peered into the direction indicated and noticed a closet door. After turning to face the kids again, he saw only an empty doorway. They would soon join the first boy who waited anxiously by the closet joining the apartments.

When Freddy looked down at the body on the floor, he noticed the pillow lying next to it. He stared at the new bullet hole as if it meant something and then an idea materialized in his mind. Maybe he could use the pillow to fool the next man into thinking he still had a gun. Freddy retrieved the pillow from the floor and then grabbed the candle from the small lamp stand. Ten seconds later, he entered the final secret door.

The man with Helen waited impatiently for the restoration of the hotel power, but without suspicion of any unusual activity in the other apartments. After Freddy entered the next room, the flickering candlelight caused him to feel as if he entered a dark cave. He felt fortunate to have made a silent journey through the secret passage, his last piece of luck that evening.

101

Freddy

Helen sat in the apartment with the older man and worried about what would happen after the restoration of the hotel electricity. For the first time in her life, the dark had come to her rescue. She preferred the darkness to the stranger who kept telling her how much he liked her dress, her face, her arms, and her legs. When he called her his little darling, she felt a cold chill enter her little heart. He filled her with more anxiety than Mr. Becerra and his wife combined.

She tried concentrating on seeing Daryn again, but that fleeting comfort reminded her of the pathetic little room, the dirty toys, and how her mother would not be there. Still, she preferred to be anywhere other than her present location. To keep herself from crying, she breathed deeply like her mother taught her to do when she became upset. The man might dislike the sound of her crying.

The sadness and anxiety Freddy felt from Helen caused tears to well in his eyes, but his anger vaporized them before they could fall. He extinguished the candle flame with a quick puff of breath and carefully opened the door to the short hallway. As he approached the room containing Helen and the old man, they failed to notice his quiet footsteps. When Freddy got close enough, he could hear the old man whispering so he stopped at the edge of the door into the room and just listened.

When he heard Helen's voice for the first time, his excitement and heart almost exploded with energy. The mental image of Sadi embracing her daughter again gave Freddy a strong urge to run into the room. His memory of losing his gun, however, deflated his momentary euphoria. Without the gun, he had a much more difficult task.

"Come on my little darling," said the older man. He had a deep voice, one that would have been respectable, had Freddy met him in another circumstance. His age probably exceeded fifty years, maybe even sixty. "There's no need to be afraid of the dark. The power will be restored in a few minutes, I'm sure."

"OK," Helen answered.

"Just sit here with me my darling. I'll keep you safe."

Freddy instantly recognized the manipulation tactic. He gave Helen an alternative cause for her fear, attempting to divert her fear from him to the dark. He would be the one to comfort her.

"Am I going back with my friend?" Helen asked tentatively.

"Of course, of course," said the man with amusement in his voice at her silly question. "Like I said, we're just going to play some fun games then you can go back to your little friend. Just relax with me. Yes, like that."

A steady light shone from the room into the hallway. The light looked different than the candlelight from the other apartment, probably from the street lights outside. Freddy stared at the partially open bedroom door from the dark hallway and considered his limited options.

A beautiful plan suddenly appeared. He could creep to the front door and knock. The man would leave Helen in the room and come to answer the door, assuming the service wanted to talk to him. Freddy would attack from the dark and put the knife in his heart and then deliver Helen to her mother. The execution of the plan flowed beautifully in his imagination, but it seemed too easy. Easy felt extremely wrong. Did the service have a secret knock? If Freddy knocked incorrectly, would the man leave Helen? Would he take too much time?

While standing in the dark hallway, Freddy felt his precious time diminishing. He needed to decide quickly. If he delayed action too long, his anxiety level would push his body forward with or without his conscious permission. Freddy made a quick decision, take advantage of his only asset, surprise. He would rush into the room and attempt to stab the man.

Before moving forward, however, he recognized something different about the last man, different from the other men he killed. Not only did he fill Freddy with more disgust, the man also scared him, the first time that evening Freddy felt true fear. His enhanced senses and the gun had helped cover his fears and insecurities. Without the gun, he felt extremely susceptible to failure. What if the alien eliminated his extra sense? A gift freely given could be freely removed. If the alien planned to trap him, Freddy would discover it soon. Freddy longed to hold the gun in his hands again, to feel the kick from the escaping bullet.

The man in the next room seemed composed of pure malice. Greed had motivated the men he already killed. A disregard for the welfare of their victims had enabled those men. The last man got pleasure from inflicting pain on others, a true sadistic psychopath. Sexual pleasure satisfied only half of his needs. Violence satisfied the rest.

In the next instant, he changed tactics again. A surprise attack might put Helen in danger. Since Freddy could not see their position, he doubted the success of rushing into the room and stabbing the man. As soon as the new plan materialized, he executed it.

"Hey mister," Freddy said in the softest voice he could generate.

The man in the next room felt immediate confusion and stopped breathing so he could focus on listening. For a moment, the silence became a tangible object between them and felt as if the air had solidified. Without thought, his lips quietly formed the next words.

"Why don't you let go of the little girl and be a man for once in your life?"

The silence continued for almost ten seconds, the longest ten seconds of his life. Freddy hoped the man would stand and investigate, but he never did or would. As quietly and slowly as he could, Freddy withdrew the knife from his belt. Unfortunately, the blade slid across his belt buckle and made a scraping sound that pierced the silence like a sword.

He quickly placed the knife behind the pillow and stepped into the doorway, holding the pillow in a way that showed the holes from the bullets. Hopefully, the room had enough light for the man to see the obliterated fabric.

When Freddy made his appearance, the man sat erect on the bed and his blue eyes narrowed to slits. He had gray hair and a large waist covered by a white shirt which hung over black slacks. He looked as if he just returned home from a long day's work in an office.

In a flash, the man produced a large knife from beside him. He held the blade in his right hand while his left hand rested on Helen's leg. The blade length surpassed the one in Freddy's hand by at least two inches and the white hilt appeared to be made of ivory.

When Freddy saw how fast the man moved, he took an inconspicuous gulp. Freddy's final opponent had a lot of experience using a knife and would enjoy using one on Freddy.

Helen sat in the man's lap and wore a pink dress with lace. He moved the knife to the side of her head and she failed to notice the blade stopping so close to her delicate skin. The light pouring into the room from the open window reflected off the sharp metal.

She held her hand to the top of her dress just under her neck as if she feared her clothes would fall off. The man had probably unzipped her dress in the back. When Freddy saw her predicament, his anger increased and helped displace his fear just a little. Freddy imagined inserting the knife in the man's neck and slicing it like a peach.

"Who the hell are you?" the man asked with the tone of someone accustomed to being obeyed.

He turned slightly to face Helen and Freddy felt his anger suddenly evaporate. With the hand holding the knife, he brushed her blond hair away from her ear, but she still failed to see the knife. He pulled her head closer to his lips.

"Do you know this man my darling?"

Helen looked at Freddy closely for a moment. After feeling her sudden recognition, he waited with dread for her verbal admission. If he could communicate telepathically, he would instruct Helen to deny knowing him. Before answering, she felt a sudden hesitation, but her fear of the man prevailed.

"He's my mom's friend," Helen said finally with some confusion. Her fear mixed with the relief of seeing a familiar face.

"Your Mom's friend?" he asked and he turned to Freddy. "Come all this way just for me?"

"Just for you," Freddy said with sarcasm.

The man paused and considered the situation. He possessed confidence and the kind of courage difficult to intimidate. He glanced at the pillow then suppressed a smile at how silly he thought Freddy looked with the object. Pillows with bullet holes failed to inspire fear in the man. The older man considered throwing the girl from his lap and attacking Freddy, but the pillow with the bullet holes did cause him to pause. His desired action carried too much risk. He would use the girl to shield himself until he assessed Freddy's true offensive capabilities.

The man lifted Helen higher on his lap and crouched a bit so her head shielded the lower half of his face then he moved the knife to her throat. When she looked down and saw the knife finally, she stopped breathing. His charade of pretending to care for the girl had come to an end.

"After I kill the girl," he said through gritted teeth, his feeling of anger suddenly exploding. "After I kill this girl, I'm going to find her mother and kill her."

102

Freddy

The man pulled Helen's hair so that her head pressed against his lips. She squealed in terror. Muffled sobs exited her mouth in short bursts. While keeping his eyes on Freddy, he spoke in her ear.

"You wouldn't want me to do something to your mother my dear, would you? If this man leaves us alone and goes away, I will let you and your mother live."

"Mommy?" Helen said through her tears, not comprehending the man's words.

"Do not listen to him Helen," said Freddy. "If he tries to hurt you, I will kill him and he knows it."

"There's something not right about that pillow you're holding," the man said, releasing her hair and looking directly in Freddy's eyes. His curiosity returned, but he would only believe in the gun's existence if he saw it. "I see what looks like bullet holes in the pillow. You probably used it on the others, otherwise you wouldn't have made it into this apartment, but something happened didn't it? Your hand looks too close to the back of the pillow."

"You want me to show my gun?" Freddy asked with a shaking voice and an attempted smirk. "Tonight I am not here to give you what you want. If you move the girl's head just a little farther down, I can show you what I have."

"Are we at an impasse?" the man asked sarcastically and with a mocking imitation of the same smirk that Freddy gave him. "Let us just wait until the police come. I already dialed nine-one-one. The power will be restored soon. You do not have much time."

Freddy recognized the facade with some satisfaction. The man only pretended to appear unconcerned, but he started to believe in the existence of a gun. Somehow, he forced the smile to remain on his face. He had to play the man's game, at least until he could find a resolution to the stalemate.

"So when they come, your knife will be at the child's throat? How will you explain that?"

The man looked at Freddy with a mixture of respect, anger, and annoyance.

"You really are a stupid asshole, aren't you? The police will see you and me, and notice the blood all over you. I can see it splattered on your clothes. I was protecting the child."

Freddy looked down briefly at his jacket and pants. Until that moment, he did not notice the blood, but that never mattered. He snickered menacingly and enjoyed the effect on the man, a new twinge of fear.

"You did not call the police," Freddy said blandly while shaking his head.

The old man answered with a cold stare. He believed the sincerity in

Freddy's voice.

"This your last chance," Freddy said, taking a step closer. "Give me the girl or I shoot you. I can hit the top of your head, no problem."

Since he could see no other option, the man decided to accept the challenge. He loved to gamble, loved the rush of taking on a high risk. Betting his life on pure instinct felt good.

"Go ahead. Shoot me," he said fiercely and leaning forward. Helen jumped from shock. "If you miss, you're dead!"

"Willing to take that chance?" Freddy asked in a desperate last attempt. His smile melted and the man noticed. "Is your life that worthless, to bet it on a hunch?"

The man slowly stood on his feet, setting Helen on the ground in between them. He pushed the knife to her throat so hard the blade penetrated through two millimeters of her delicate skin. A dark trickle of blood wound a dark trail down her neck. She squealed and closed her eyes.

"I knew it," the man said in triumph and some disappointment. "I just have to press a little bit harder and this girl dies. How do you like that?"

Never in Freddy's life had he felt so many conflicting and overpowering emotions. They wrapped around his chest like a boa constrictor. Frustration at his helpless situation kept him from lunging at the man in an attempt to stab him directly in the heart. Hatred for the man almost expanded to infinity. Helen's eyes pleaded for him to help her. When their eyes made contact, he felt like exploding with frustration.

Freddy dropped the pillow and extended the knife in front of him. The man had a larger knife, but the dried blood on Freddy's knife made his weapon more menacing. Somehow, he found the strength to remain under control.

"Let the girl go and we can settle this like men. I would rather use the knife anyway."

"Is this what you want?" the man spat and his voice rising like a madman. "Do you want this girl dead? Do you? Do you, you shithead. She will be, once I get done with you."

Freddy felt the man's excitement at the new development. He threw Helen violently to the ground and faked a lunge at Freddy, with a wide smile. Before he moved, however, Freddy anticipated the action and took a few steps backward.

After the fake lunge, the man stopped and took two slow steps towards him. Freddy backed away at the same pace and cringed at the feeling of dark euphoria emanating from the man. The attack reminded him of school and his foster brothers and the joy they seemed to receive from hurting him. This man felt just the same, just older and wearing an expensive suit.

"Let me tell you what's going to happen," the man said while licking his lips in anticipation. "First, I'm going to take that goddamned kitchen knife out of your hands and…ahhh!"

He stopped in mid-sentence, groaning in sudden pain and taking a quick step backward, successfully preventing himself from falling on the bed behind him.

In his panic, Freddy failed to recognize the creature waiting in the shadows or notice when it jumped from the darkness of the hallway and darted into the room. The shadow carried a heavy object and hit the man behind the leg. With overwhelming stealth and courage, Daryn entered the apartment through the secret passage, coming to the aid of her only friend.

103

Freddy

Daryn jumped away from the man and ran to Helen who had scooted across the floor to the wall, positioning herself protectively in front of her friend. Without consciously planning his next move, Freddy's body acted spontaneously by jumping forward and attempting to grab the knife from the man's hand. Instead of taking hold of the knife, however, Freddy grabbed his wrist.

"You little shit," said the old man to the little girl while Freddy's grip tightened on his wrist. The man's expensive cologne tasted sickeningly sweet on Freddy's tongue.

Both girls sat on the floor and watched while Freddy struggled with the older and more massive human. Each opponent held a knife in his right hand and attempted to plunge the blade into the flesh of the other.

After a few moments of grappling, the old man managed to pin Freddy to the ground. To his horror, the man forced Freddy to accept his superior strength and fighting ability. He outweighed Freddy by a good sixty pounds of fat and muscle. While struggling to keep the knife away from his chest, Freddy realized the only fortunate aspect of his present position. Helen could escape to her mother. Freddy followed the only plan his mind could produce.

"Get out of here," he yelled to Helen. "Your mother is in the stairwell. Tell her she has to take you away from here."

The old man pinned Freddy's left hand to the ground then slammed it against the soft carpet several times until the knife flew away from his grasp to land somewhere near the bed. With his massive weight, the older man effectively pinned his opponent's whole body to the ground. After a moment, Freddy pulled his hand free and grabbed the man's other hand which held the knife.

"You're gonna pay for this," the man said with an angry smile. He stopped putting downward pressure on the knife and seemed to prepare for a final push. "Do you know how much money that little girl cost me? But don't worry, I can still get my money's worth out of her and now I get to kill you too."

Freddy turned his head to look at the two girls. They stood like stone statues in a garden.

"Get out of here. Helen run, please!"

Daryn responded quickly and pulled Helen through the entrance and out of sight, heading towards the front of the apartment. With relief, Freddy heard the door to the hallway open and then the quiet click of it closing. Not even his imminent death could destroy the satisfaction of hearing the sound of Helen's escape.

Would he get to experience the reunion of mother and daughter, how Sadi would feel? Hopefully, he could delay his death long enough to feel that. The request seemed reasonable.

With Freddy's attention distracted, the old man released his right hand from Freddy's grasp and hit him on the left side of his head. The sudden blow to his temple brought his fixation on the emotions of the girls to an abrupt end. He required several moments for his eyes to focus again.

"They're gone," Freddy said before his vision returned to normal. "Out of your reach!"

The older man growled like an animal, slammed his hand against the side of Freddy's head again and then spit in his eyes, effectively ending his ability to see clearly. He quickly returned both hands to his knife and resumed the downward pressure. His growl transformed into maniacal laughter as Freddy's resistance began to disappear. The horrible laughter scared Freddy more than his feeling of satisfaction. Would he be killed by a human or a monster?

As the man closed the distance between the knife and Freddy's chest, a strange relief washed over him as he felt the beautiful reunion of mother and daughter in the dark stairwell. The pleasant experience ended, however, when the knife began penetrating his flesh, just over his heart.

The old man expertly twisted the knife until he found a space between two of Freddy's ribs. After reapplying pressure, Freddy knew the knife would soon enter his heart. He did not want to die, especially at the hands of such a monster, but if he did die, his final act had been worthwhile. He saved some children from a band of monsters and rid the world of at least four sadistic psychopaths.

When Freddy felt his own warm blood start to soak into his clothes, he knew the end had come. The knife would pierce his heart, his muscles would soon lose all their energy and his arms would go limp. Instead of delivering oxygen to his brain, his blood would deliver the precious chemical to the floor beneath him. For the final time, he stared into the eyes of his murderer, a final pathetic view of the world. Freddy closed his eyes and tried imagining Sadi, Helen and Mr. Smith, safe.

"She is safe from you now," said Freddy with the last of his breath.

At that moment, the strength in his arms extinguished and his arms dropped, but instead of feeling the knife enter his heart, the blade tip slid violently across his chest, leaving a trail of pain and blood like the wake behind a boat.

"Get the fuck off him," growled an angry female, followed by the sound of the old man falling to the floor.

The man began groaning and then rocking back and forth on the floor next to Freddy, holding the bloody side of his head where the woman kicked him. Freddy opened his eyes and turned to see the blurry vision of Sadi standing over him.

He used his left hand to wipe the spit from his eyes and his right hand to help return himself to a sitting position. As he sat erect, the man's knife slid down his chest. He caught the weapon, dripping with his blood, before it landed on the floor. With relief, he saw none of his blood on the floor around him. Police investigators could use his blood to identify him.

"I thought I was dead," he said, laughing with relief. Real tears fell from his eyes which helped remove the remaining saliva. "I really thought it was the end. Thank you, Sadi."

"Don't mention it," she said, but kept her gaze on the old man, checking for signs of his former vitality returning. When she spoke again, she seemed to be addressing herself. "When I saw Helen again, I just wanted to run away and never look back, but I couldn't leave without you."

Sadi watched the old man for five long seconds, fighting the temptation to crack his skull with another kick, to stop him from moving completely. She felt a strange mixture of anger and panic. Freddy especially felt her immense satisfaction at incapacitating the man. The intense rush of her emotions felt like a deep breath of fresh air.

In a small way, her emotions helped chase the dark thoughts and memories from his mind. He enjoyed the feelings of relief, joy, and hatred. When she felt convinced of their temporary safety, Sadi knelt at his side and parted his clothes to feel the wounds on his chest. As she gently brushed some hair from his wet forehead, her touch felt like fire on his skin.

"I think you'll be all right," she said. "The cut's not deep. Can you stand? We need to get out of here."

"Yes," he answered and felt dizzy as he attempted to stand. "Just give me a second. He hit me pretty hard on my head. Do you think he can hear us?"

Freddy felt nothing but pain from the man on the floor.

"I kicked him really hard," she said and smiled. "Probably gave him brain damage, but he definitely has a pretty bad concussion."

The boy with Freddy's gun stood behind Sadi along with Helen and her friend. Freddy noticed them when Helen began pulling on her mother's jacket. Fear had replaced the relief she felt from the reunion with her mother. She feared being taken away again.

"Mom, can we go home? I don't like it here."

"Of course," she answered, grasping Freddy's shoulder to help steady him. "Freddy's been hurt so we have to help him."

"You really did come to save her, didn't you?" the boy asked from behind Sadi, but with his gaze fixed at the man on the ground.

Everyone turned to stare at the boy, even the girls. The boy feared the man might stand and attack them all. He stepped around Sadi and extended his hand with the gun, pointed at the man's head. The boy bent down until the gun reached just a couple of inches from his skull. He held the gun like a natural extension of his arm.

"Yes, I did come to help them," Freddy answered softly and gently. He spoke as if attempting to prevent a man from committing suicide. "Will you please return my gun now?"

The boy looked to Freddy with confusion and then back to the old man, squinting his eyes in deep thought. He wanted to shoot the man. He wanted to transform the man into a pool of blood, torn flesh, and broken bones. When he began talking quietly to himself, Freddy failed to distinguish any words, but he felt the boy's conflicting emotions. The man represented everything the boy hated in the world. Only his conditioning of obedience and fear kept him from pulling the trigger.

"Come on Freddy, we need to leave," Sadi pleaded.

She cared most about escaping safely with her daughter, but she also wanted the boy to shoot the man. Helen clung to her mother's jacket and Daryn stood behind them both as if hiding.

"We cannot leave without the gun," Freddy said, speaking to the boy. "It will point the police to us. I cannot let you keep it."

"This is a bad one," the boy said in a whisper, tears falling down his cheeks. "Can't let him live. He doesn't deserve to live."

"I will take care of him," Freddy said and extended his hand. "After you leave the room. I do not want the girls to be here when I do it."

"Can't let him live," the boy said to himself. "The police will believe whatever he says, no matter what."

He turned slowly and locked eyes with Freddy, but failed to recognize his presence. He thought only about the gun in his hand and his complete control over the destiny of his enemy.

The boy pulled the trigger a moment later and a chunk of the man's head exploded under him, leaving a bloody mess of bone, brain, and hair on the floor. The following silence became shattered by the scream of a woman in the apartment below them when the bullet passed through the floor. All of Freddy's other gunshots stopped in the outer wall of the building.

For the next moment, everyone stood in shock. Helen buried her face in Sadi's hip, but Daryn and the boy just stared at the body. The gun fell from his hand, hitting the carpet with a soft thud. Freddy stepped forward, careful to avoid stepping into the bloody mess on the floor and retrieved the gun then put the weapon under his belt.

With every movement, the cut on his chest stung like twenty wasp stings. He slowly withdrew half of the remaining cash from his pocket and extended the money to the boy. The boy turned from the corpse and stared at the money in Freddy's hand.

"I gave your friend some money too," Freddy said and suddenly felt the impatience of the other boy waiting for them in the hallway. "This is enough for you to go anywhere you want. Do you have anywhere you can go, safe from here?"

The boy nodded his head. Freddy placed his hand on the boy's shoulder and pushed him away from the horrible scene. The boy's attention shifted from the body to the money in his hand.

"Kristoff has a brother we haven't seen in a long time," the boy said softly. "I think he remembers where he lives."

"Does his brother know about this?" Freddy asked, motioning with his hand to indicate the apartment and the activities that happened there.

"I think so," said the boy.

The thought of letting the other children go somewhere on their own felt like a really stupid idea, but he had not considered how to fit them into his escape plan. Too bad he could not have thought about this complication beforehand. He would need to get them into an area where no one would find them, where they could hopefully start a new life. That thought helped produce an idea. He knew where they might take the three other children.

"No," Freddy said. "That will not work. You can come with us, but we have to hurry."

The emotions of the people in the apartment below them raised his anxiety levels. One person just dialed nine-one-one in panic and were probably explaining to the operator what they heard. Another person felt worried and prepared to call the hotel staff. For the moment, everyone feared to leave their rooms, but people would soon be entering their floor to investigate.

"Freddy, we need to go," said Sadi with desperation in her voice.

Suddenly, Freddy sensed members of the hotel staff heading to the stairs from the ground floor, the stairwell leading to the apartments of death. In just a few minutes, they would pass the dead guard or see his blood on the floor. Freddy quickly led them out of the apartment and into the hallway, the beam of his flashlight lighting the way. They traveled through the hallway to the stairwell on the other side.

104

Freddy

Freddy led the traumatized band of humans down the stairs to a back exit of the hotel. The door opened to the parking lot where a few of the other tenants could be seen heading to their cars. They made eye contact with no one and soon found themselves on the street.

The two boys found their clothing and looked normal while the two girls wore pretty dresses. The people driving on the road who noticed the group just thought of them as a young couple walking with their four children. Freddy knew the police were on their way and somehow knew the direction they would travel, so he took the group in the opposite direction.

No one spoke as they walked, but the boys began to doubt Freddy's good intentions. On several occasions the older one considered running off into the night and taking his friend with him. He instinctively wanted to escape the new adults who controlled them, but hesitated to tell his friend or Daryn in fear of alerting the adults. Freddy felt tempted to let them go, but he put faith in his plan as being the best course of action.

Daryn on the other hand, thought of their journey as an exciting new adventure with a new set of friends. She had become accustomed to think only of the present, not the future. She only cared about escaping the bad men who wanted to abuse her and how much she liked her new friends.

"You are free to go," Freddy said after they reached the car. "But I will be taking you somewhere safe, where I hope no one will find you. If you choose to leave now, please get far away."

He held the door open and waited for them to make their decision. Both boys required only a few moments to arrive at the same conclusion. They believed him. He spoke kindly and they failed to hear any threat of violence in his tone, unlike any other adult they ever knew. No one ever gave them the option of leaving before.

Daryn sat behind Freddy near the window with Helen in the middle and Sadi next to the other window. Both boys sat in the front seats next to him. Instead of taking the same route, they drove back to Portland on interstate five.

When they left the lights of the city behind them and entered the country darkness, Sadi began breathing more calmly and stopped looking behind them, fearful of seeing the police. Her relief also helped calm Freddy's nerves. Maybe he would forget, as she desperately tried to do, about the whole affair. Just another hour and they might be able to do just that.

Freddy drove directly to their next destination, the home of his old case worker, a woman from Hungary named Malika. By some miracle, he remembered where she used to live and by another miracle, she still lived there. He knocked on her door just past midnight. He knew the boys would be safe with her, at least temporarily.

Before Malika answered the door, he knew her state of mind. She felt slightly annoyed about being wakened just after falling asleep, but more worried that someone needed her help. She opened the door as much as the chain lock would allow, then looked to him and then to the car idling in the driveway. When she returned her gaze into his eyes, he failed to see any sign of recognition. She would remember him later.

"Hello Malika," he said. "I am so sorry to bother you this late, but I need your help."

"Do I know you?" she asked.

She had the unmistakable features of an Eastern European woman with short dark blond hair, sharp eyes and a full figure. Old age began to encroach on her once beautiful face. She looked tired, physically and emotionally.

"I used to be one of your foster case kids," he said, the words tasting bitter on his tongue.

Before continuing, he waited. What should he tell her? How much of the story should she know? He had everyone's safety to consider. Knowledge could put her in danger. She squinted her eyes in an attempt to recognize his face then opened the door and stepped into the cool night air.

"How can I help you?" she asked with her face turned to the car.

"I know this is a major inconvenience and will sound unbelievable," he began. "But we have two boys and a girl who need protection. We rescued them from a child pornography ring and they need to be taken someplace safe."

The woman put her hand to her mouth when he mentioned the rescue, then she looked at his chest and noticed the blood on his clothes. His zipped jacket failed to hide all the blood stains. Instead of fearing the sight of the blood, however, she suspected a violent effort to rescue the kids.

"Oh my god," she said in shock and concern. "Are they hurt? Bring them inside and tell me what happened."

On his short walk to the car, he felt her eyes on his back and her sincere desire to help. She suspected no deceit and only cared for the children. Freddy opened the driver's door then crouched down to the boy's eye level.

"You are going to stay with this nice lady," he said while wincing at the sting in his chest. "She will keep you away from the bad men. She is my friend who helped me."

While waiting for their response, Freddy focused on the feelings of any prying eyes from the neighborhood homes and failed to detect anyone's notice. The two boys looked at him for a moment then to the lady standing in the doorway. The woman looked less threatening than Freddy and they instantly liked her. Both boys shrugged their shoulders.

"OK," said Kristoff.

"She will not let anyone abuse you again," Freddy said.

As both boys began to exit the vehicle, Freddy turned to Daryn in the back seat. She pressed her head back against the seat, holding onto Helen's arm.

He would have to spend extra effort convincing her to leave her new friend. Her sorrow caused Freddy to pause and remind himself that Malika would take good care of her. He opened her door and put his hand on her small shoulder.

"This woman will take care of you now," he said slowly. "Helen can come visit you. Will that be OK?"

"Come on Daryn, let's go." the older boy said while standing next to Freddy.

The boy extended his hand to Daryn, but she looked away from him and turned to Helen. She grabbed her new friend with both hands, a look of terror in her eyes. Tears fell from Helen's eyes too.

"We can't leave Daryn," Helen said, turning to her mother.

Freddy looked to Sadi who turned to him with a blank look on her face. He waited for her to speak, but she remained silent. During their drive home, Sadi let the horrible events of the evening consume her thoughts, the killings and how close her daughter had come to a horrible death. She could only think about getting home and locking the doors.

"Helen," Freddy said, turning to point at the lady standing in the doorway. "This lady and the boys will take good care of Daryn."

"She can't go back," said Helen, not understanding. "They'll keep hurting her. They'll keep her in her room and never let her out again. We can't leave her."

Sadi opened her mouth to protest, but the pleading in her daughter's voice silenced her. Then her own tears started falling. In the next instant, she smiled for the first time since leaving the hotel.

"She can definitely come with us."

105

Freddy

After leaving the boys at the social worker's house, the girls remained in the backseat and Freddy drove the rest of the way home as the chauffeur. Images and emotions from the evening played in a continual loop inside his head, his killings then his near demise and finally the moment when Sadi saved his life. The silence of so many negative emotions became his greatest respite, accompanied by the silence in the car.

Freddy felt the occasional glance of his passengers at the other cars which shared the highway with them. Occupants in the other cars felt like aliens from another planet, living their comfortable and secure lives, completely disconnected from the trauma of their fellow travelers. Freddy envied them.

As they took the westbound exit to highway twenty-six toward Hillsboro, a new sensation ripped Freddy out of his musings, a feeling of excitement from Helen. She recognized her surroundings and her heartbeat instantly began to accelerate.

"Daryn," she said, sitting forward. "We're almost to your new home. You're going to love it."

"Really?"

"Just a few more minutes," Sadi said and put her hand on Daryn's knee, the first time she touched the little girl.

Sadi's touch caused the girl's tension to become elevated, but she showed no outward sign. Only Freddy felt her reaction and it produced an additional anger inside him, anger at how her treatment had caused emotional damage. The show of compassion should have helped calm her anxiety instead of increasing it.

Freddy stopped the car's engine in Sadi's driveway at one fifteen in the morning, then paused before opening the door. His passengers seemed to feel his elevated alertness and waited for his signal to move. He felt exposed, like a deer about to enter a clearing.

Would one of Sadi's neighbors notice their arrival? A witness might remember the event and tell a future investigator. If the events of the evening ever became known, he doubted the truth would be made public. The story involved high-profile people and an organization protected by corrupt government officials. If the police revealed anything to the press, it would be false information. The press usually only regurgitated the story presented by government officials. They would handle any investigation discreetly, or else the local police would be excluded and a higher level government agency would take command. His private investigator would need to keep informed of the investigation's progress.

Sadi waited for him to give some signal to exit the car.

“No one is taking notice of us,” he said, looking directly at Daryn. "We can go inside. Helen and Sadi will go first, then you and I will follow them."

“It’s OK,” Sadi said.

Sadi opened the door and led Helen by the hand into the night. As mother and daughter walked to the front door Freddy felt his lips unconsciously stretch into a wide smile. Before Sadi grasped the door knob, the front door burst open and Jen appeared, tears streaming down her cheeks. Helen exploded into tears also then disappeared into Jen’s outstretched arms. While watching them hug, Freddy wiped tears from his own eyes.

“It is your turn Daryn."

Freddy held her hand while they walked to the front door. She grasped his hand tightly, afraid of being released. On their short walk together, he felt a new emotional connection begin to form with the girl, like two pieces of metal welded together. He attempted to discover where the new emotion originated, but failed to distinguish the source, from him or Daryn. After a short moment of reflection, however, he chose not to care.

Sadi held the door open for them, glancing quickly at the houses on the street. She guided Freddy gently into the house with her hand on his back, then crouched down to Daryn's eye level and placed both hands on her shoulders.

"It's alright," Sadi said gently as everyone turned their attention to Daryn. "This is your new home now. No one will hurt you here."

The girl stood in the entryway, staring with surprise at the clean interior of the home. She suddenly felt frightened of all the adults and the new environment. After a long moment of silence, Helen came forward and extended her hand. The frightened girl looked up at Freddy and he released her hand, but with some reluctance.

"Welcome to your new home," Helen said with a smile.

After Sadi closed the door, Freddy felt all the attention switch from Daryn and Helen to him. More people waited for their return than he had anticipated. Before entering the house, he felt the presence of several other people inside, but neglected to concentrate sufficiently on identifying them.

Mr. Smith sat on the couch in the living room with a concerned look in his eyes and one hand on his cane, as if preparing to stand. He waited impatiently for his turn to intrude on the happy reunion and felt an overwhelming sense of relief. Brian Jacobsen stood with one hand on his sister's shoulder, his lips stretched into a wide smile.

Gerald Fuger silently watched the scene from a few feet away. He felt concerned about the unfamiliar little girl who just walked into the house and waited for an opportunity to ask about her. Gerald and Mr. Smith became the first ones to notice the blood all over Freddy’s clothes.

While Jen, Sadi and Brian spoke with the two girls, Freddy approached Mr. Smith on the couch. The old man slowly rose to his feet with the help of his cane then peered into Freddy’s eyes as if looking for something lost. Instead of answering his employer's unspoken question, Freddy followed human protocol and waited for the question first.

“Are you OK?” he asked finally and then placed his old hand on Freddy’s shoulder. Mr. Smith feared to learn the answer, but he asked the question anyway. “Is that your blood?”

“It is mostly mine,” Freddy answered, looking briefly at his chest. “I can tell you all about it on the ride home. I would rather not talk about it here.”

“That’s probably a good idea.”

During the brief exchange, Gerald left his silent observation point between the two groups and approached the two men. He had dark shadows under his eyes and his hair looked like he ran his hands through it a hundred times. When he spoke, he used a low voice so the others would fail to notice.

“I know you probably just want to go home, but before you leave, could I talk to you both outside.”

Freddy suddenly felt very tired, more exhaustion than he ever remembered feeling. He needed his boss to take control of the situation. Mr. Smith recognized the look in Freddy's eyes and nodded then turned to the women.

“Sadi," he said politely and she immediately turned her attention to him. "I need to get Freddy home. I'm sure you understand. I know you'll want to get these two girls to sleep.”

Before allowing them to leave, Sadi embraced Freddy with both arms and held him close. She squeezed tightly as if afraid he would attempt to escape. Her breasts put pressure against his stinging chest, but the exhilaration of contact with the woman completely buried the pain. Freddy had fantasized for much of his life about holding Sadi. The real version felt far superior to his imagination. He wished the contact could continue forever.

“We will never forget what you did for us.”

When she finally released him, he had to wait a moment for the euphoria to end.

“I owe you too,” he said quietly. “You saved my life, so we are even. We did it together, remember?”

Sadi smiled and nodded, but remained silent. Disturbing memories of the evening began to replace her relief. She needed to sleep, then maybe her unconscious mind could begin the healing process.

Before getting in their cars and leaving, Gerald spoke to Freddy and Mr. Smith on the porch. Freddy quickly glanced around the neighborhood and felt no awareness of the three men from any of Sadi's neighbors. The only other people in his sensory range were unconscious.

“Sadi said that the people who had the kids are all dead?” Gerald asked quietly, but did not wait for the answer. “Will anyone be looking for them? Does anyone know where they live? Are they going to be safe tonight?”

Mr. Smith and Gerald turned to Freddy. He looked at the ground to avoid eye contact and to avoid giving too many details. Mr. Smith might form a negative impression of him.

“I did my best not to leave any fingerprints or blood,” Freddy said as confidently as possible, attempting to convince them and himself. He would not mention the two boys they left at his case worker's house. He just wanted to go home. “All the witnesses are dead. No one followed us or know anything about us, for now.”

“Craig should know what to do,” mentioned Mr. Smith. “He can learn what they are up to. Tomorrow, we’ll need to discuss the situation with him, but tonight, you need sleep and I'll need to check your injuries. You're holding your chest like it hurts."

"It does hurt," Freddy admitted. "But, I should not need stitches."

"What do your friends think about any of this?" Mr. Smith asked, turning to Gerald.

Freddy felt a mixture of confusion and a small amount of guilt from Gerald. The man considered lying, but changed his mind almost immediately. After just a short hesitation, he felt like admitting the truth.

"I'm still trying to figure out how and what to tell them. I need to figure it out first."

"Well," Mr. Smith said, almost accusingly and barely containing a sudden burst of anger. Freddy felt like cringing. "You need to discuss these things with this group of yours. Everything started happening when you came into our lives."

"I will tell them," Gerald said, failing to notice the anger. He considered asking Freddy about the alien and his new abilities, but changed his mind. His desire to return to the house and see Sadi overpowered his curiosity. "When I do discuss this with my friends, I'll let you know our conclusions, but we can all talk about that later. I know you need to get home and rest. I'd better go back to see Sadi."

After Gerald left them alone on the porch, a new emotion suddenly overshadowed all others, jealousy. Freddy had already accepted the eventuality of never having an intimate relationship with Sadi, but seeing a possible relationship with Gerald caused a sting more painful than his chest wound.

When Sadi returned into his life again, all the buried feelings resurfaced. Freddy wished that he could stop thinking about her. Her image played in his mind like an addictive tune, repeating over and over and over. Only after entering his car and driving away from her home could he push the feeling of jealousy from his mind.

VIII: CONFRONTATION

Do you really want to be
The author of your destiny?

106

Freddy

On the way home, Freddy explained the events of the evening to his boss and during the explanation, his emotional dam broke. With so many lives depending on him, he'd had to maintain a high level of control, exerting more emotional energy than his strength would allow for long. The story flowed from his mouth without any filter. He decided to keep nothing from his boss or pause to think about the consequences.

When finished, Mr. Smith sat in silence and let the overload of information sink into his consciousness. For a short moment, Freddy feared his boss would become angry at how he handled the situation, but the old man only felt shock and amazement. While waiting for a response, Freddy unzipped his jacket then winced at every gentle touch to his chest. He anticipated a hot shower with pleasure even though he knew how much pain it would produce. He disliked the idea of soaking in a bath of soap and blood.

"I feel somehow that I should not have killed those men," Freddy said to break the silence. "Although, I know they deserved it."

"You did what you had to do," Mr. Smith said. "Try to keep your emotions from influencing your reasoning. Children were in danger and you brought them out of the situation. I would have done the same thing, if I could have."

"Thank you, sir," Freddy said.

Would he ever feel regret for killing those humans? Were they just a product of their environment, and did that justify their termination? Did Freddy, in essence, value their lives less than the lives of his friends? Yes, he did and he accepted that. After a short moment, he came to a conclusion which put his mind at ease, namely that the men had accepted the risk when they chose that line of work.

When they finally arrived in the darkness of their garage Freddy turned off the car and they both just sat there. Freddy waited for the final question his boss wanted to ask.

"So the alien," he began, "or whatever it is, gave you the ability to know what others are feeling? Is that going to be part of you, from now on?"

"I feel what those around me are feeling. It has gradually become stronger since the barn incident. I think it is permanent."

"I feel old," Mr. Smith said after a sigh and then laughed. "So I guess you feel old too, huh?"

"I do not feel physical sensations from others, only emotions."

Freddy put his hand on the door handle then paused when he understood the old man's sense of humor. He had failed to recognize the sarcastic tone in his voice. Would his new ability help him be more normal?

"Oh, I get it."

Although he did not feel like laughing, he made a feeble attempt at a quick chuckle. Mr. Smith patted him on the shoulders and they went inside the house.

During his shower, Freddy fell into a short trance as he watched the bloody water disappear into the drain. The shower process stung almost as much as when the old man slashed him, but he felt clean, as if the shower also helped to remove the painful memories.

Mr. Smith tried convincing Freddy of letting his personal doctor come and stitch his wounds, but Freddy said he had some medical tape which might work. In the morning, they could reevaluate his condition, and if he still needed it, he would not object to calling the doctor. For that night, however, he just wanted sleep. When Mr. Smith's suggested sleeping pills, Freddy declined, fearing that unnatural chemicals would interfere with the healing process.

Before getting into bed, he removed the crystal from his drawer and placed the object on top of the table under the lamp. He almost looked into the eyes of the spider, but then lost his nerve. Did he really want to experience the alien again? The creature or entity had only brought stress into his life. He almost wished everything would just go back to normal.

He turned onto his side to face the crystal with the irrational thought that if he kept the object in his sight, nothing would happen. For a long while, he laid on his bed with his eyes open and concentrated on breathing to help his body relax. He preferred the darkness of his room, over the images of death in his mind. After a while, he experienced difficulty keeping his eyes open.

Almost immediately after closing his eyes, sleep overtook him and then the blue and orange lights started to flow from the eyes of the spider. Like rays of the sun at the dawn, the long and thin tendrils of light slowly wove their way to Freddy. They wrapped his whole body in a spider's web of light, placing him in a peaceful and deep sleep.

107

Freddy

When Freddy opened his eyes, he expected to see the darkness of his room, but instead, he found himself in the middle of an infinite plane with every direction extending to eternity. For an infinite length of time, he stood motionless, at peace. He felt no surprise at being there. All care vanished, his fear for Helen, for Sadi, for himself. His mind became as empty as the plane where he stood. If dying led to his current state of existence, he would never fear death again.

The sound of wind woke Freddy from his state of nirvana. At first, he failed to recognize the faint sound. Eventually, he remembered the sound of wind and for the next eternity, he allowed the cool pressure on his face remind him of the world he once knew.

As awareness of his surroundings increased, he started feeling concern. Would something change and disrupt his peaceful existence? His imagination failed to provide any possibilities and so his concern failed to grow. Freddy simply waited.

The next change appeared as lights in the sky above him. Orange and blue lights intensified slowly, like the wind and reminded him of something, but he failed to remember what. They soon filled the space above the plane, gradually growing brighter like the diffuse glow of a fog. After a while, the lights began to fade and he remembered the concept of time. Maybe the cycle would continue forever, the light growing then dying. His fear of change disappeared and he welcomed each cycle of light and dark.

The light dimmed completely a few cycles later and failed to return, bathing him in complete darkness again. He remembered being a small boy fearing the dark, fearing what his eyes failed to see, but what vividly appeared in his imagination. That life seemed so far away, like a distant memory of another time and another world, another Freddy. He no longer feared the dark.

When a new source of light appeared in the space above the plane, the light originated from the direction he faced. Illuminated points of light appeared far away on the horizon, hovering above the plane like stars. And then, for the first time in his existence on the plane, he noticed movement when a black dot appeared with the points of light. The dot stretched vertically and after a longer time, he recognized the beginning of a familiar shape, a woman, full-figured, slender legs, long dark hair. She stood close enough to recognize her form, but too far away to recognize her identity.

When the figure finished developing into a human adult female, she started walking slowly towards him. He watched her walk for what seemed an eternity. Eventually, he recognized her attire. She wore a tight, dark gray dress with flat, black shoes. He especially noticed her legs, exposed just above the knees. When she came close enough, he noticed the black pearls embedded in the silky material of her dress. They wound around her body in a spiral, ending just below her right shoulder. The oily blackness of the pearls seemed to reflect a light of their own, brighter than the stars behind her.

When he could see her dark blue eyes clearly, they seemed to look beyond him as if she failed to recognize his presence. When she came within three feet he wondered if she would crash into him, but she changed direction at the last possible moment. He imagined an asteroid approaching a large celestial body, reacting to its gravitational field. The woman completed one complete revolution around him, then stopped inches from his face, blocking the lights on the horizon.

"Hello again, Freddy," she said with a smile on the left corner of her mouth.

Her proximity stirred deep memories. Although Freddy forgot her name, he remembered loving her once. He remembered her image consuming his thoughts. She stared at him with an intensity that almost caused his eyes to burn, a sensation broken only by looking away from her face. He looked to the ground at her black shoes then back to her red lips. He avoided her eyes.

"I know you," he said. Speaking helped him feel like a human again, but failed to restore his memory. "I am sorry, but I forgot your name."

"You'll remember soon enough," she replied and her voice overpowered the soft sound of the wind. The smile still lurked in the corner of her mouth, taunting him. "Why don't you tell me how you feel. Talking about your emotions might be therapeutic."

Freddy tore his gaze away from her red lips and looked to the beautiful ground of black marble. He closed his eyes, attempting to assess his emotional state.

"I feel, like I *should* be tired, but I feel nothing."

"You won't be tired here."

"Why?" he asked after opening his eyes. He made eye contact with the woman, but her eyes failed to cause anxiety. "Is this a dream? It feels real."

"I am supplying the sensory information," she said and her smile transformed into a look of concern. "What do you think of it?"

"I feel relaxed," he said after a moment of internal reflection.

"I want you to be relaxed," she said and placed her hand on his shoulder, as if to reassure him.

The warmth of her hand through his shirt became the first time he felt a temperature differential on the plane. The sensation stirred an obscure memory of a similar event in a dark stairwell.

"I can show you whatever you want to see," she continued and released his shoulder. At that moment, he realized that she knew his thoughts. Her smile returned. "I can give you any kind of sensation you want. I will do whatever you want."

For the first time, he looked to her neck and then to her breasts and found no strength to look away. His sexual attraction felt like a magnetic, living thing. If he extended his hand to touch her, she would let him. If he asked to remove her clothes, she would have let him. She offered herself to him, like a waitress offered to fill a glass with water.

For a long time, he considered the offer. She waited patiently, staring at him with those two beautiful eyes. The thought of having a sexual experience with her frightened him, so he attempted to consider other options. He had no memory of his interests so he experienced difficulty thinking.

“Why don’t I choose something for you?” she asked with a hint of disappointment. “At first, your imagination will be limited.”

“OK,” he said then instantly felt something at his feet.

108

Freddy

Freddy looked down to see rising black water. The water filled the plane completely and he soon stood in a shallow ocean, the points of light glistening on the water's surface. The dark ocean continued to rise and quickly reached his chin, but he had no time to panic. The water soon passed over his mouth and nose, and finally his head. Before he could gasp for breath, he felt something at his lips, trying to enter his mouth, a tube with oxygen and nitrogen. He opened his mouth and allowed the gas to enter his lungs. The surrounding water felt ice-cold, but it had no effect on him.

He looked from the ground to find the woman still standing next to him. She had no such tube in her mouth and did not appear bothered by the surrounding water. When she opened her mouth to speak, her words entered his consciousness through a different route than his ears.

"On this side, you really don't need to breathe," she explained. "If you remove the tube, you'll be fine. I just didn't want you to panic."

The lights remained behind the woman, but they looked fuzzy and shimmered with the invisible movement of the water. Freddy looked upward, but could see only darkness. When he looked back to the woman, however, she had disappeared and the ground had transformed into a muddy sea floor. He began to feel the pressure from miles of seawater pushing down on him. The sensation caused no pain and felt comforting almost, like being wrapped in heavy blankets.

He watched as sea creatures lived their lives around him, as they swam, as they hunted, as they died. Many had lights of their own. He saw anglerfish with large fangs. He saw sharks, eels with sharp noses, starfish, crabs. He enjoyed watching the glowing jellyfish swim around his face.

Most of the creatures swam close for an inspection, curious about him. When he extended his hand to touch them, they allowed him the pleasure of feeling their cold, slimy skin. He enjoyed the experience so much that he almost forgot about the woman. He hoped the time there would never end.

"Your world is full of beauty," the woman said suddenly from beside him.

The voice had a rich tone, a deep feminine quality. When he turned to see her standing next to him, a giant anglerfish swerved to avoid hitting her. Freddy took several moments to appreciate her beauty, like he did for all the other beautiful creatures around him.

"It is," he agreed.

The water drained away almost instantly, leaving him on the flat plane again. After surveying the bareness of his surroundings, Freddy felt a loss. He missed the comfort of the water pressure, the company of other living creatures, the feeling of being in an inaccessible place. He remembered her saying that she could show him anything so he began thinking of several other experiences he wanted. A thousand ideas entered his mind and he felt difficulty deciding on what to experience first.

"What's next?" she asked then patiently waited for his answer.

"I would like to remember," he said and the words surprised him. He suddenly felt the void in his memories, a loss of identity. Did he really want to remember?

"Remember what exactly?" she asked.

"Before being here," he said slowly. "I was somewhere else. Can you help me remember?"

"Let's not do that just yet," she said as if she already seriously considered the request. "I've got something better first."

Before he could respond, however, the ground caught his attention. He looked down and noticed a shadow on the plain, stretching from his feet to the horizon. The shadow slowly grew darker with the surrounding ground growing brighter. Then he noticed the top of his shadow racing to meet him. When the shadow disappeared under his feet, he turned to look at the sky and had to shield his eyes from the intense lights above him.

Shortly after looking up, however, his eyes grew accustomed to the intense light and he recognized a beautiful spiral galaxy with two arms spiraling around each other. While looking at the several hundred billion stars in the galaxy, he realized something exciting. He could focus on any one of the stars, and see the objects orbiting them. The galactic light became more intense towards the center, but he could still see each star distinctly.

Freddy briefly looked away from the galaxy and saw countless smaller objects in the black sky above him. When he returned his attention to the galaxy, it seemed slightly larger. He required only a moment to determine the meaning. The massive conglomerate of celestial objects raced towards him at a fantastic speed. To grow at such a rate meant that it traveled faster than light.

He suddenly felt a pair of eyes focus on him, like a parent appreciating the curiosity of a child. He tore his gaze away from the sky to meet the eyes of the woman.

"What is the reason that you are keeping my memory from me?"

"You require a respite," she said while returning her gaze to the sky. "Another occupation for your mind. Experiencing this with you also gives me pleasure."

He fought the urge to return his attention to the sky. Only her alluring form provided the necessary counter-temptation.

"What happened to me?"

"I can show you anything," she said, keeping her gaze skyward. "We can explore molecules, the atom or even smaller energies. Those have immense beauty."

The offer almost overpowered his attraction to her, but fragments of his memory floated just out of reach, like a fading dream. He desperately wanted to catch the memories before they completely disappeared.

"I appreciate what you are showing me," he said, fearing to disappoint her. "But I want to remember."

Instead of receiving a look of disappointment, the woman turned to him, her smile growing wider. She walked slowly around him and stopped just behind his back. After placing her warm hand on his shoulder, she pointed to the horizon with her other hand.

"Watch," she whispered and then all the light vanished, leaving them both in complete darkness.

109

Freddy

Freddy felt her cool breath on his right ear and he smelled the familiar scent of cinnamon and for a small moment at least, the two sensations replaced the light.

He saw nothing at first, but a small point of light soon materialized just above the horizon. The new light looked like a star, but differed from the previous stars in the galaxy which appeared in three dimensions. No other objects orbited the new star and the light only existed in one dimension, a single point. The next moment, the single star exploded into a cluster of other stars and then one of the stars separated from the rest, rising high in the sky.

Freddy jumped in surprise when the lone point suddenly expanded into two dimensions. The transition required his vision to readjust to the new shape, causing a momentary sensation of dizziness. Then the new object of light began flying towards him, transforming into the shape of a human, the glowing ghost of a human. The female apparition flew directly towards Freddy and he soon recognized her, his mother, slightly overweight with greasy brown hair and tight-fitting clothes. When she crashed into him, the impact instantly restored several unpleasant memories. He remembered when she rejected him, then sent him to live with his first foster family. The next point of light transformed into the ghost of his sister. When she crashed into him, he remembered the humiliation of being caught shoplifting. Then the foster family members crashed into him. Freddy cringed with every impact.

Ghost after ghost crashed into him, restoring memories of painful experiences. Then the young woman Sadi and her brother Brian crashed into him. They restored his first pleasant experiences, feelings of fun and belonging. After the ghost of Sadi and Brian, he turned to see the woman standing next to him and felt the thrill of recognition. She resembled Sadi in every way imaginable.

Next, the ghosts of several college professors and Mr. Smith restored more pleasant memories. He remembered the first time in his life when he felt needed, useful and appreciated. He remembered his love of learning, the wonder from contemplating life and the universe. Several other acquaintances joined with him. Freddy remembered valuable and unique experiences from each.

After the ghosts of his college classmates and professors and internet friends, he had a short reprieve and tried to let these final memories push away the others, but then a demon rushed towards him like a rocket, the first man he killed. The man had a large gash in his neck with spurting blood and eyes nearly exploding with pain. His other victims from that nightmare followed the first. One by one they all crashed into him. Freddy threw up his hands in a failed attempt to shield the impacts.

The last point of light stayed on the horizon. After attempting to focus, the point expanded into a rectangle and kept expanding until he could see the crystal, the one with the embedded two-dimensional spider. The eyes of the spider glowed with blue and orange lights of their own and Freddy remembered how they could make him lose his sense of time and memory.

After all his memories had been restored, he almost wished to live without them again, become one with the plane. Why had he wanted to get them back so fast?

"Curiosity killed the cat," he whispered while staring at the crystal in the sky.

Freddy suddenly felt a strong desire to focus on the eyes of the spider. For the moment, however, he simply stared at the object as a whole. Beautiful orange and blue lights shimmered from the surface and the experience reminded Freddy of watching the sun at dawn. He watched the scene for a long while until the experiences in the hotel began to creep back into his mind. The memories felt almost too painful to bear. How would the horrors of those two days affect Sadi's and Helen's lives? Would they cause permanent damage?

When the woman spoke again, her voice sounded like the wind from a distance.

"To forget," she said, "just look into the eyes of the spider."

Without turning from the horizon, he considered the option of forgetting. The suggestion tempted him, but did he want to endure another restoration of his memories? Also, if the crystal erased his memory, his state would be more pleasant, but did Helen and Sadi have that option? Despite all his conflicting emotions, abandoning painful memories seemed wrong, no matter how horrible. They had become a part of him.

In the next moment, the crystal disappeared and another light returned to the sky. When he looked up, he noticed the galaxy again. The beautiful sight instantly consumed all of his attention, temporarily relieving Freddy from the burden of his memories. He spent a long time watching the swirling mass of stars and other celestial objects.

"Helen was not kidnapped by chance," he said to himself.

"Nothing is by chance," the woman whispered in his ear.

The sound of her voice woke him gently from the dark abyss. He tore his gaze away from the galaxy to stare at her. Although she resembled Sadi in every way imaginable, the figure beside him felt like an alien creature, something inexplicable.

"You set this up," he accused and he felt an anger begin to grow inside his chest. The emotion reminded him of the hotel. "What was the purpose, to make me into some sort of hero?"

"There's no reason to speak rudely," she said in a tone of slight amusement. "You are my guest here and you're not returning the hospitality. Have I not been hospitable?"

"Yes," he answered without attempting to hide the hostile tone. "This is my imagination. How can I possibly be a guest in my own imagination?"

Her eyebrows rose in feigned shock, but she remained silent.

“It is an impossible coincidence,” he said. “You come in contact with me, then Helen is abducted? It was wrong of you to put her in that position and permanently scar her.”

After a moment of silence, she took one step closer to him.

“You saved her, did you not?" she said, her eyes opening wide. "Damage averted and justice served.”

After she failed to deny his accusation, Freddy felt justified in his anger.

“How did damaging that poor little girl serve justice? To serve justice, you would be punished for what you did. Those who put people in dangerous situations are just as liable, and sometimes more than those who do the actual damage. Not only will Helen be scarred for life, but who knows what will happen to Sadi because of it. When those men connect her to what happened, her life will be over.”

Freddy extended his right hand towards the creature who resembled the woman he loved and squeezed his fist in anger. He wanted to crush her beautiful throat, but restrained himself. He did not, however, lower the volume of his voice.

“I killed people,” he yelled at her. “I killed them! I did not want to kill anyone.”

The woman’s smile remained unperturbed, his physical threat having no effect. He wanted her to feel his anger, to cower before him. While keeping her eyes fixed on his face, she turned her head from side to side as if in inspection. The action reminded him of a lizard.

“What child would you prefer they stole?” she asked as if sincerely interested in his response.

“No other child,” said Freddy instantly. “Of course no other child.”

“That human who took Helen would have chosen another child.”

Freddy felt like the woman had poured a large bucket of ice water over his head, extinguishing the flames of his anger with a sizzle and transforming it into hot steam. He felt drained, then filled with a new emotion, sadness for what could have been.

"What are you?" Freddy asked finally.

"Who do you think I am?"

"Will every answer be another question?"

"What do you think?"

"Why did you do it?" Freddy asked, deciding to change the subject. "Why me? Why Helen?"

Before answering, the woman who resembled Sadi shrugged and raised her eyebrows, as if she acted on a whim.

"So you could practice."

"Practice?"

His next thought never completely formed. The atmosphere shook with a terrible thunder and a tornado appeared in the sky. The swirling cloud collapsed the galaxy, combining all the stars together into a singularity of blinding brilliance. When he turned away and faced the woman, her blue eyes opened wide and swallowed him whole.

End of Book 1

About the Author

Hyrum lives in Washington State with his wife and four children, and works as an engineer for a semiconductor manufacturer. He grew up in the desert of Utah to a very large family. After graduating from the University of Utah with a B.S. in chemistry, he acquired an advanced degree in chemical engineering at Oregon State University where he fell in love with the Northwest and has stayed ever since. He spends as much time as possible with his kids and enjoys showing them the world, especially the wilderness. When he's not working or with his family, Hyrum enjoys hiking, a good book or movie, or just grabbing a coffee with friends at a cafe.

32273520R00219

Made in the USA
San Bernardino, CA
01 April 2016